Troutfishing on the Tees - Me and Tony Blair

Graham Dransfield and Patrick Dransfield

Published by GRAHAM DRANSFIELD, 2025.

This is a work of fiction. Similarities to real people, places, or events are entirely coincidental.

TROUTFISHING ON THE TEES - ME AND TONY BLAIR

First edition. June 28, 2025.

ISBN: 978-1068251900

Written by Graham Dransfield and Patrick Dransfield.

Table of Contents

Dedication

Dedication

This book is dedicated to the memory of David Lewis (1941 -2022) Chairman in perpetuity of the Doghouse Cricket Club.

To Peter and Louise

Happy reading -

Enjoy the book.

[illegible]

Acknowledgements

I really enjoyed writing this book. Many thanks to my brother Patrick for the original idea and all his contributions and encouragement.

Thanks also to Noel de Guzman for the brilliant cover design.

I would like to thank Kirsty, Michelle and Tim from The Book Dragon, Stockton-on-Tees for their sterling work in getting this book published. I would also like to thank Martin Ouvry for helping me to 'reverse engineer' a sitcom script into something resembling a book.

I would like to thank friends and former colleagues for their help and encouragement, almost too numerous to mention, but in particular: Sharon Hancock, Rose Hague, John Wintle, the late Paul Birkett, Joe Irvin, Nathan McAdam Freud, Nisha Burman Taylor, Dee Miller, Carol David Daniel, Caz Sipos, Drusilla Gabbott and Ola Kabia for helping me to believe in this book. Special thanks go to Jake Milner, whose Ph.D. research on industrial decline in the North East is reflected in the book.

Thanks to the Dransfield/Drake clan for all your support, in particular my cousin Lynda Relph-Knight, and brother Jon, second of the 'latter-day Bronte sisters', and the first to show us the way forward by publishing a book

Thanks also to the 26 Club, particularly Max, for the very helpful Author's Interview that has helped to promote this book.

Thanks to my wonderful children: Rachel and Will for their unflagging support and invaluable advice, which I foolishly ignored. Also, to their lovely partners Dan and Sadie.

Thanks to Annie for your love, wisdom, and support. Thanks for keeping me grounded, Annie!

One final, big thank-you must go to the once mighty ICI PLC, without whose implosion in the noughties this book would not have been possible.

Troutfishing on the Tees - Me and Tony Blair

Dateline June 8th 2000: 'Blair bombs at WI'.

That day's headlines marked a turning point for the New Labour project.

Meanwhile, Northern chemist, enthusiastic cricketer and would-be libertine Dr Steve Hemmings wakes up alone in 'Tony's' Sedgefield, County Durham constituency following a painful marriage break up.

Tough on Brexit, tough on the causes of Brexit! 'Troutfishing' comically charts Steve's hapless decline from aspirational Mondeo Man to washed-up Baby Boomer, his 'career' mirroring the decline of British industry at the hands of callous, southern-based politicians of all stripes.

"A reprise of 'The Likely Lads', but with a sliver of ice for its spine,

Graham Dransfield's 'Troutfishing' is authentic, very funny and poignant." Dr John Bagshaw.

Graham Dransfield has conjured up an engaging and quirky Northern tale with dashes of humour. About a man facing up to the daily grind with its occasional setbacks. Who is quietly determined to seek out some of life's better moments.'

Colin Babb Author, Journalist and Broadcaster.

Troutfishing on the Tees - Me and Tony Blair

This is a work of fiction. While it may reference real public figures and historical events, the narrative, dialogue, and characterizations are the product of the Author's imagination. Any resemblance to actual persons, living or dead, beyond intentional fictionalization of public figures, is entirely coincidental.

The inclusion of real individuals, such as Tony Blair is intended for satirical purposes and should not be interpreted as factual representation. The author makes no claim to portray the views, intentions, or actions of these individuals accurately beyond the realm of fiction.

-

-

-

-

-

-

-

-

-

-

Trigger Warning

The book contains themes some readers may find distressing, including:

· Psychological trauma and mental health struggles

· Death and loss

· Strong and derogatory language

· Adult themes

Reader discretion is advised.

Chapter 1: 'Grievous Angel'

DATE: THURSDAY JUNE 8TH 2000, A Cottage, Rokeby Village, County Durham.

In an untidy living room, a forty-something white man was having his breakfast. This consisted of a piece of toast with marmite and a cup of strong Yorkshire tea. Dr Steve Hemmings sat blinking in the early morning sunshine as his hangover continued to haunt him. Outside, by the unwashed window, sat a 1995 blue Ford Mondeo.

The man made a somewhat dishevelled figure. His grubby kimono-style dressing gown revealed more flesh than any visitor – male or female – might have wished to see. His cat Dalmy looked on, unimpressed.

His hands were, however, scrupulously clean, having been washed and dried exactly seven times. A smaller number would have run the risk of his contaminating the house, the neighbourhood, maybe the whole world. A larger number would have brought catastrophic bad luck, especially the King Unlucky Number 13.

The left hand reached for a biro, one amongst ten other objects that he was carrying, namely:

1. The keys to the Mondeo parked outside.
2. A BT Roamer 300 pay-as-you-go mobile phone.
3. A wallet full of unsuccessful betting slips interspersed with photos of his two children (no money). *
4. Tissue paper.
5. Anti-psoriasis pills.
6. Business cards – his own, plus a couple from people he had met on his travels.
7. A red (credit size) card with The British Chemicals Company (BCG) 7 Business Principles inscribed on it.
8. A half empty packet of 10 cigarettes, plus box of matches.
9. Gold Spot breath freshener spray.
10. A BCG Site Entry Badge with his photo on it.

*The reader may be surprised to learn that the owner saw nothing whatsoever strange in this juxtaposition.

Normally, he would have written in his journal, a legacy of one of the many management-training courses that he had attended. Today, however, he had decided to write to his local MP: none other than the Right Honourable Anthony Charles Lynton Blair, Prime Minister and First Lord of the Treasury.

Steve scribbled away, oblivious to the advancing time and despite the competing attempts for attention from Dalmy, so called by Steve's children because of his colouring – white with black markings.

The cat was feeling rather neglected. Steve kept him fed okay, but Dalmy was getting irritated by his increasingly frequent nocturnal forays. The cat reasoned that hunting at night should have been his province! Of course, during the day he was missing too. Off to that beloved job of his – so full of hope when he set off in the morning, and usually so grumpy when he got back at night.

The cat liked it when his children came to stay. They gave him the attention he deserved. That was only every other weekend though. Other times, Steve was off on his prowls. Dalmy wished he'd keep the house tidier as well. And when was he going to get around to giving him a cat flap, like all his friends in the village? He was losing respect! Dalmy kept reminding him of this by leaving the odd present, but to no avail; he simply cleaned it up and told him off. His owner's mind seemed to be on other things.

Steve scribbled on even as the cat walked all over his writing paper.

Dear Tony

I wish to share my concerns regarding the importance of signed one-way access at petrol stations following a 'near miss' yesterday.

Steve paused to remember the upsetting incident.

Firstly, the squealing of brakes, as he stopped within 1 cm of an oncoming red Vauxhall Corsa. The Corsa driver, a short, muscly man with multiple tattoos, had got out to confront him as he'd emerged from his Mondeo into the driving rain, in his beige double-breasted gabardine coat.

'There's no sign to say I can't come his way,' Steve protested. 'Not that I think you'd be able to read it!' he added, somewhat unhelpfully.

'You look like a pervert to me,' the Corsa driver commented, observing the flasher's mac. 'I bet you're one of them paedos!'

It was time for some humour to calm the situation.

'Yeah, that's right,' Steve agreed, before putting on his best Elvis karaoke voice.

'I am a paedo, I am a paedo. Uh. Uh.
I've got 5 miles on my speedo...'

he sang mockingly, whilst opening his coat.

The little man exploded. 'That's shockin'. Absolutely shockin'.'

He aimed a massive haymaker, which Steve narrowly evaded then returned to the refuge of his Mondeo.

Meanwhile, the Corsa driver's dumpy wife pointed Steve out to the cashier in the pay kiosk, as he frantically reversed away from the forecourt.

Steve returned to his letter.

Things could, however, have been much worse. Had we collided, due to the lack of signage – the consequences can only be imagined.

On the subject of road traffic safety, I must bring your attention to the Angel of the North, or "Angel of Death", as I now call it.

My friend Geoff believes that it is a complete waste of taxpayers' money and should be melted down.

How many kidney machines would that buy? he wondered.

My personal concern is that this monstrosity is perched on a hill overlooking a busy stretch of motorway. Already, numerous accidents have been caused by its distracting presence. Perhaps it could be remoulded, re-sculpted and placed outside the Redcar steelworks – "the true heart of the industrial North-East".

Or please allow me to suggest a third way, if I may...

Why not transplant it to a quieter spot in our wonderful Sedgefield constituency, as a monument to a truly great PM?

Best regards

Steve

DR STEPHEN HEMMINGS

Perhaps a little explanation is required here. The Angel of the North is now unanimously considered to be a cultural icon, epitomising the indomitable spirit of the North-East. It was not ever thus. The project was very nearly stopped by fierce local opposition on the grounds of cost, aesthetics, interruption to TV transmissions, road safety and even possible Nazi overtones. The Gateshead Councillor, who pronounced it to be 'beautiful' on its unveiling, was met with widespread scorn. It was a good job that social media was not around at the time, or the iconic statue could easily have been vandalised – or worse – and the Councillor's life would have been made a misery. Criticism back then was fortunately restricted to his being challenged in local pubs.

The late Brian Sewell cited the kidney machine as the standard unit of philistinism to counter opponents of arts expenditure, who would question why such money was not being spent on the NHS. Ironically, Sewell himself hated the Angel, calling it the most vulgar of Anthony Gormley's works. But, there again, he always did hate all things Northern.

Steve did have a point about road safety though. The Angel of the North has consistently made the Top Ten of most dangerous heritage sites to drive past in the UK, reportedly causing over 50 accidents between 2013 and 2018.

Steve finally remembered to check his watch.

'Shit the bed! Late for work again!!' he said to himself, then worse:

'I promised to give the Chairman a lift to Eston. Bollocks!'

The man in question lived in an adjoining village with his widowed mother. His name was Geoff Huckstead, a salesman in his late fifties. A confirmed bachelor, he had nonetheless had numerous relationships, none of which had been strong enough to prise him away from his parents, despite the odd 'accidental' pregnancy.

Ironically, Geoff was ahead of his time, valuing friendship over romantic love. 'Mates are mates' was his eternal motto. He certainly beat the Spice Girls' 'friendship never ends' on that one. He was a 'Rules Boy' long before 'The Rules' were invented.

His true love was cricket and the Outcasts Sunday Team, which he ruled with an iron rod. It was this love that had brought Steve and the Chairman together. Today, as his car was 'in dock', he had summoned the Steve to ferry him to his early meeting.

Steve finally jumped into his Mondeo, which matched his house in its internal state of entropy (his children would fight for the right to tidy it out and collect the many coins that had been spilled on the floor of this Aladdin's Cave on wheels). It was now five years old and becoming progressively more expensive to maintain. Despite his nominally high salary, Steve's finances were already stretched by maintenance payments to his ex on top of the rent and upkeep of his cottage plus the spiralling cost of his 'social life'. MOT anniversaries inevitably brought about a cash flow crisis as the garage reported more and more repairs required to keep the car legal. Most poignantly, it was not the company car he had always aspired to. Steve comforted himself with the thought that it was symbolic of 'Mondeo Man', the template voter that his hero had targeted in the 1997 election. He could, at least, pride himself on being a trendsetter.

Chapter 2: 'The Chairman'

Steve arrived at the Chairman's residence at 8.45am. The man himself was waiting impatiently, resplendent in his blue blazer and stripy tie, not to mention his shiny, unnaturally-coloured, orange-tinged black hair. Steve had been irritated by this intrusion on his daily routine, but felt honour-bound to answer the call.

After all, it was Geoff who had really rallied to his support during his painful marriage break-up while others had distanced themselves from him. A lot of Steve's friends and colleagues (work and cricketing) had made snide comments, mainly behind his back. 'Lost to the cock, lost to the cock' (he had a habit of repeating phrases for dramatic effect) was all Geoff would enigmatically say. He had been there for him during the dark early days of the separation. Steve owed him a huge debt and felt he had to put up with his manipulative behaviour, even though he sometimes suspected that Geoff had sniffed an early opportunity to find a new wingman. It was Geoff who had got him on his feet again, going out 'tashing'. It was Geoff who knew all the best pubs and clubs for picking up single women of a certain age. It was Geoff who had also introduced him to the Outcasts cricket club, where he was given regular opportunities to bat and to bowl, but more of all that later...

The car pulled up on the front drive and the passenger door opened. The Chairman, a tall, heavily built man, eased himself into the vacant seat and pushed it back, before pulling his seat belt across but refraining from securing it.

'You're late, Old Son' was his opening remark as the car reversed out of the drive.

Silence reigned as the car continued its journey south over the A19 Tees Flyover.

Geoff it was who broke the silence. 'Are you sure you don't mind giving me a lift, Old Son?' he said, sensing the hostile atmosphere.

'Not at all,' replied Steve, pulling a face.

'I wouldn't have asked, but I've got a meeting with my accountant first thing,' he ventured, before adding, 'I'm not making you late, am I?'

'No, it's absolutely fine. I'm on flexi-time,' Steve said a little too grumpily.

'But that boss of yours doesn't like you arriving after 9 o'clock...' Geoff interjected.

'You could say that!' Steve agreed with feeling.

'Well, it's not out of your way, is it? Eston is on the way to the BCG, isn't it?' Geoff reasoned.

'Not going via your house, it wasn't,' Steve muttered under his breath, before answering audibly, 'No, not at all, Geoff.'

Steve switched on the radio to try to get some respite from Geoff's stream of consciousness.

'Now with our thought for the day is the Reverend Griselda Pitmarch, parish priest for the church of Saint Aloysius in Shoreditch, London...'

'Today is the Saint's Day of Saint Merardus, an avid 5th Century follower of Saint Augustine. It prompted me to think about how are we, as Christians, to reconcile our attitudes to sexuality?

'Here's what St Augustine, himself, had to say, in the 4th Century:

'"If it was good company and conversation that Adam needed, it would have been better arranged to have two men together as friends, not a man and a woman."

'Those words may sound very controversial, even shocking, as we embark upon the 21st Century...'

Geoff was genuinely surprised. 'What's wrong with that? Sounds spot on to me!' he said as the speaker continued to drone on.

Steve rolled his eyes once more. 'Really?'

'What's not to like? I've said before that we should all have our bollocks removed!' Geoff continued.

'That sounds painful!'

'Humanely, of course!'

'And totally unnecessary...'

'No, it makes perfect sense. We could all concentrate on cricket, football, horseracing, and the art of conversation without unwanted distractions!'

Steve was aghast. 'Oh, come on, Geoff!'

Geoff was not for stopping. 'And we'd probably be able to run faster too...'

He paused to ask Steve a question. 'Did you know that 99% of male National Hunt racehorses are geldings?'

Steve shook his head. 'What's that got to do with anything?'

'Well, you'd never win the Grand National, flying with those full tanks!' Geoff leant over to give Steve's crotch a tweak to reinforce his point.

Steve's eyes watered momentarily as the car careered from one side of the road to another.

'Sometimes I can't believe you!'

'Please yourself!' Geoff replied grumpily, before leaning forward to retune Steve's car radio to TFM, the local commercial station.

'Hey! I didn't get to hear the end of that. It was just getting interesting...' Steve said irately.

The Reverend Pitmarch was replaced by Sonique's *It Feels So Good*. The DJ announced that this was this week's Teesside Chart Topper (it also happened to be the national number 1) before handing over to the News.

'Good morning. This is TFM. Here is the News at 9am...' the newscaster intoned before moving on to the main news of the day.

'Prime Minister and local MP Tony Blair took an unexpected battering from members of the Women's Institute when he addressed their annual conference yesterday. There was booing and heckling as he attempted to speak... '

Geoff could not resist having a dig. 'Your man certainly got a bit of a caning yesterday.'

Steve rose to the bait like a salmon to a hook. 'What do you mean "my man"?'

Geoff pulled out a copy of Steve's letter to Tony Blair from the door compartment. 'So what's this, then?'

'Nothing.'

'What are you writing to that twat about this time?'

'Nothing,' Steve repeated sullenly.

'Come on. Out with it...' Geoff was insistent.

'The importance of signed one-way access at petrol stations.' Steve sighed.

'You're kidding me!'

'Well, he is my constituency MP.'

'I know the man is a pillock, wasting millions on eyesores like the Millennium Dome and the Angel of the North and all, but even I don't wish that on him... Signed one-way access?' Geoff shook his head.

Steve was swift to point out the fatal flaw in his argument. 'You could hardly blame him for the Angel of the North. That was started before he came to power. I do feel, though, that he should get something done about the number of road accidents it causes. Actually, I've added that to my letter. Anyway, I thought he was your man, too!' Steve concluded.

'Don't know what you mean!' Geoff was incredulous.

'You said that you'd voted for him.' Steve smirked triumphantly.

'Only because the other lot were so useless,' Geoff admitted reluctantly. 'I wouldn't do it again. Anyway, as you say, he's <u>your</u> constituency's MP.'

'So he is, but that doesn't necessarily make him my man!'

Geoff decided to change the subject. 'And you can give me a lift to Coffin Dodgers tonight?'

A flabbergasted Steve turned round towards Geoff, causing the car to nearly hit a male pedestrian, who promptly flicked a 'V'-sign at the departing car.

'Steady on, Old Son!'

'But I thought it was <u>your</u> turn!' Steve felt a sense of cruel injustice.

'Oh. No. No. Remember, my car's at the garage. It might not be ready.'

'Really?' Steve was sceptical.

'Cheer up. You had a good night at the Grave Diggers last night.' Geoff was upbeat.

'No, not really,' Steve insisted.

'I thought you were getting on pretty well with the one-legged Fran,' Geoff reminisced.

'Nah. She kept arm-wrestling me to stop me getting close. Anyway, I couldn't get a stiffy,' Steve concluded.

'Oh dear. The path of true love never did run smooth with you, did it?' Geoff was disappointed.

'No, Geoff,' Steve said as he finally pulled over by a concrete precinct of shops.

Geoff opened the door. 'Thanks for the lift. Good luck with that boss of yours!'

'Pleasure!' replied Steve ironically.

Steve watched as Geoff walked into a betting shop signed 'Eddie Edwards, Turf Accountants.'

'Shit the bed!' Steve concluded.

As he drove away moodily, Steve reflected on his careering career.

It had started so well at Trivalent. He had established their world leadership in titanium-based composites. These were all the rage at the time, so his star had shone brightly for a while. Unfortunately, internal politics, the early 90's recession and the fact that there was bugger-all market for titanium-based composites had conspired against him. The business had closed down suddenly and Steve had been headed for the dole queue. Then had come the deus ex machina.

An unsolicited and glowing testimonial from an admiring DTI Project Monitor to a Trivalent company director had meant that he had not only survived but thrived. He'd been promoted two whole grades. Indeed, he'd found himself leading a team of twelve people all of a sudden. This had proved tough, but his technical plan had worked, hadn't it? He had seen off a mutiny, a severe dislocation to the business, caused by a change of ownership. He'd triumphed. The new products that he had masterminded were now selling in their millions. He had been able to replace the ne'er-do-wells with better people. He now worked for the mighty BCG, just like his father before him.

All in all, it had been a great triumph over adversity. But, but, but, what reward had he got? They'd imposed Stuart Appleby, Stuart-bloody-Appleby of all people, to be his boss. What had he done to deserve that? Stuart Appleby, the Pariah of the Trivalent Managers club, notorious for his instant opinions and put-downs. Stuart Appleby, who would be sitting in his office lying in wait for him. Stuart Appleby, who had cultivated a cult of personality amongst Steve's staff at his expense. Stuart Appleby, who had subverted Steve's last appraisal into a show trial.

And still no fucking company car!

Chapter 3 'Toxic Release'

Steve finally arrived at the Blackring Chemicals Group (BCG) Elton Centre, Redcar around 9.30am. It took him another 5 minutes to find a parking place. Around him was a heroic landscape of chemical plants, emitting a multitude of varicoloured vapours.

The centre was a large 1970's complex of labs and offices. As usual, he struggled to negotiate the turnstile entrance into the main building.

An alarm was now going off. A female Tannoy voice announced, 'Warning. Code 2 Toxic Release. Danger. Code 2 Toxic release. Take Shelter. Take shelter. Warning. Code 2 Toxic Release. Take shelter.'

The men and women in lab coats that Steve passed by were carrying on their normal business, unperturbed. Steve hurried up towards his block. The over-filled briefcase did not help. He looked again at the watch – 9.43am – as he finally got to the lift.

He removed the Homer Simpson tie that had been protruding from his briefcase and hastily tied it round his neck. That would take a bit of weight off, especially with all the random food deposited on it. Now he faced a dilemma: take the lift or shin up the stairs? Steve's claustrophobia got the better of him, and he mounted the stairs.

Steve almost ran along the 4th floor corridor, passing an office marked 'Mr Stuart Appleton: Business Technical Manager'.

The door was ajar, in compliance with company 'open door' policy.

'Phew. Made it!' said Steve as he neared the end of the corridor.

Suddenly the door opened fully, as if in a horror movie.

A short, smartly dressed man in a waistcoat stepped out.

'Good afternoon, Dr Hemmings. We've been waiting for you.'

'Good morning, Stuart. Sorry. I had to give a friend a lift in.'

'It's up to you to manage yourself' was the sanctimonious response. 'Hope you haven't forgotten that we have a communications meeting at 10am.'

Steve had forgotten. 'OK. I'll be there.'

'And remember, we've got Debbie Gould coming today, so tidy yourself up.'

'OK, Stuart.'

Steve walked out of Stuart's sight, adjusting his clothing, including tightening the crumpled Homer Simpson tie.

'And don't wear that Simpsons tie!'

'Umm.'

'And one more thing...'

'What's that?'

'No falling asleep!'

'It's a medical condition...' Steve protested.

'So far undiagnosed!' Stuart countered. 'I'll be watching you!' His words rang down the corridor.

Steve finally got to his office. He was about to put his suitcase down when Dr Paula O'Donnell arrived at the door.

'Morning, Steve. You said you wanted to meet me about my new product launch.' 'Oh, sorry, Paula. Yeah. I'm afraid that'll have to wait. Communications meeting, remember?

'Oh. Feck. I forgot.'

'I'll see you later.' Steve waved Paula off before reaching for an energy drink. Steve was glugging down the sickly coloured potion when Margaret, the garrulous office cleaner, arrived, blocking the door.

'Good morning, Dr Hemmings. How are you?' asked Margaret cheerfully.

'Fine, thanks, Margaret,' Steve grunted as he tried to push past Margaret's imposing figure.

'Glad to hear that someone is. My sciatica's really playing me up.' Margaret remained lodged within the doorway.

'I'm sorry to hear that,' Steve replied insincerely.

'And I've got to go to the school on behalf of our Darren. The headmaster says he's been misbehavin'.'

Steve looked at his watch. 'I'm sure he wasn't...'

'I'm going to complain to the governors, I am. He's being bullied, that's what it is.'

'I'm sure you will.' Steve tried again to escape.

'Shockin' it is. Mind you, it's that Tony Blair's fault.'

'How do you work that out?'

'People like him, they just don't care for people like us,' Margaret opined.

'Seems OK to me. Wrote me a nice letter when I was having problems over my kids' education.' Steve felt he had to take a moment to defend his hero.

'Yeah, but he did he get anything done?' Margaret remained sceptical about politicians, even New Labour ones.

'Well, no. That's not the point, anyway.' Steve looked at his watch again.

'Politicians. They're all the same, you know.' Margaret paused. 'Apart from that nice Mrs Mowlem, maybe...'

That nice Mrs Mowlem, Dear Reader, happened to be Dr Margaret (Mo) Mowlem, who was at that time one of five members of the cabinet who represented a North-East constituency. She had been spectacularly successful as Northern Ireland Secretary and rewarded with a 'non-job' by Tony Blair in his latest cabinet reshuffle. (She replaced a similarly fated colleague, who believed that his sacking had been due to his own insistence on living in the North-East and 'missing out on the London cocktail circuit'.). Any connection with Tony Blair feeling in any way threatened by Mo's success is entirely coincidental.

'Your MP! Well, if she can sort out Northern Ireland... perhaps you should write to her!' Steve suggested

'Hmm. Maybe I will.' Margaret finally stepped to one side as Steve set off for the meeting.

Chapter 4: 'Project Mallard'

It was 9.57am. Steve still had several hundred yards of long corridors to negotiate. Maybe he could get there in 5 minutes. Maybe they would still be settling into their seats when he arrived. Maybe they might wait for him. He was the third most important person in the room, after all...

At the bottom of a set of stairs, disaster struck...

'Whoa! Stop right there now,' commanded a podgy, clipboard-carrying woman in a hi-vis jacket.

'Oh, Adele. What now?' Steve protested.

'Firstly, no running in the corridors or down the stairs.'

'And secondly?' asked Steve.

'Your non-use of the handrail is in direct contravention of our Safety, Health and Environmental Policies.'

'Ah. SHE who must be obeyed?' Steve joked, trying to push past her.

'It's no laughing matter. Do you know what the number one cause of lost-time accidents is?' Adele asked rhetorically.

'Slips, trips and falls,' Steve answered with tired irony.

'And for every four thousand of these so-called minor incidents, there is a potential Bhopal or Chernobyl!'

'Well, I'll certainly bear that in mind.' Steve looked at his watch again. 2 minutes late and counting.

'You certainly shall,' Adele proclaimed.

'Well, I'll be on my way,' Steve said hopefully.

'No. You won't. I want you to go back up and down those stairs at an appropriate pace, holding the handrail!'

'What?' Steve was incredulous.

'Go on. Do it!' Adele commanded Steve.

'I am in a hurry to get to a meeting,' Steve tried to explain.

'Never mind your meeting. Do it or I will report you to the Site Safety Committee – and you wouldn't want that, I can assure you!' Adele was adamant.

'That's blackmail,' Steve complained.

'It's for your own good,' Adele assured him.

Steve reluctantly walked up and down the stairs in the correct manner.

'OK. I'll let you go now. A man in your position should know better. Chairman of the Site Health Committee indeed! You should practise what you preach!!'

'Laters' was Steve's nonchalant parting shot.

When he finally got to the meeting room, Steve found a well-ensconced Paula sitting next to Stuart, smiling angelically. There were 15 more people crowded round the table. Everyone had to shuffle around to make room for him. Stuart stared daggers at Steve, especially at his crumpled Homer Simpson tie.

'What are we going to do with Stephen?' thought Stuart to himself as Steve pushed his way into the meeting. Stuart couldn't believe that Steve had got as far as he'd got, never mind going any further, which he seemed to want to do. When Stuart had become Steve's boss, he had taken soundings of his staff. Their views had not been complimentary. Sure, there had been success over the past four years with new products and maintaining business continuity, but the consensus was that all of these things were achieved despite him, rather than because of him. Sure, these people used to work for Stuart himself and maybe they just wanted to boost his ego, but everything had been in place when Steve took over. He'd just had to press the buttons. He'd never showed leadership, he'd never taken a stand with anyone, never confronted anybody. Basically, Steve was crap.

Stuart shuffled the papers in front of him and cleared his throat. 'Were there any more questions regarding the latest business bulletin? For those who were here to listen to them, that is...' he added caustically.

Stuart looked round the room over his pince-nez glasses. There was no response.

'Very well, then... It's a great privilege to have Debbie Gould here today. She is going to give us a talk about the latest prospects for BCG and will answer any of your questions. Please feel free to ask her any question you like. This is a 'caps off' meeting, which means that we are all equals here.'

Stuart sensed a slight murmuring among the troops. 'Although that should go without saying, of course...' he added hastily. 'Take it away, Debbie!' he concluded.

A bespectacled, rather plain auburn-haired woman in her mid-40s rose to her feet and headed to the overhead projector at the end of the room.

'Yes, as Stuart said. Ask me any question you like,' she said, forcing a smile. Steve could not help noticing that she seemed a little nervous, not her usual ebullient self. Her hand trembled as she placed a scruffy, smudged and misspelt transparency on the overhead projector. In the corner of the transparency, there was a bright green leaf resembling deadly nightshade.

Debbie commenced her address to the troops. 'Right then guys, here we go. As you all know, there was a merger last year between BCG and Belladonna Industries. What exciting times these are!'

Debbie placed the next transparency onto the OHP with trembling fingers.

'We've picked the low hanging fruit. We now need to go the hard yards!'

Steve noticed a couple of the younger members of the team suppressing giggles as they marked a small piece of cardboard conspiratorially. Really, he shouldn't have given out 'Bullshit Bingo' cards for last year's Secret Santa, should he?

'Our costs are too low and our margins are too high – hang on – our costs are too high and our margins too low,' Debbie said as she struggled to stop the corners of the transparency from curling up.

'So I'm here today to announce the set-up of a task force to execute Operation Mallard,' Debbie continued as she continued to struggle with the recalcitrant transparency. All of a sudden, the atmosphere became a little more tense.

'Why Mallard, you may ask? Well, it was a very fast streamlined locomotive, and I think it broke some sort of speed record.'

Steve couldn't resist the temptation to help Debbie out. 'Mallard, LNER Class A4, managed an average of 126 mph south of Grantham[1] on the East Coast Main Line[2] in 1938...' he interjected helpfully.

Debbie continued: 'Thank you, Steve, for that clarification.' She tried to suppress the irony in her voice before proceeding. 'And we need to be like that at BCG!'

---

1. http://en.wikipedia.org/wiki/Grantham
2. http://en.wikipedia.org/wiki/East_Coast_Main_Line

Steve started to feel the effects of his previous late night as he stared at the beige walls and tried to concentrate. The room was too crowded for him to go and grab a coffee from one of the silver flasks that sat on the small table opposite. It was disgusting anyway. Slowly but surely, he drifted off into a reverie as Debbie carried on with her peroration.

* * *

Steve is dressed as Elvis on a stage with Paula, who is dressed like a conjuror's assistant, in gold lamé. She stands next to a flip chart. There is a band behind Steve and the bass drum bears the legend 'The Mallards'.

The audience is made up of Steve's BCG colleagues, with management at the front row. They are booing and slow handclapping.

An unabashed Steve takes the mic.

'Well. Uh. Uh. Let me tell you about mah latest achievements. Sorry, mah team's latest achievements.'

The booing continues. Steve launches into *Blue Suede Shoes*.

On the 'one', Paula points to the flipchart. 'Spending £100K below budget.'

Steve continues to sing. On the second line, Paula turns over the flipchart.

'BCG nominated for Tees Valley Innovation Award for nano-sunscreens'.

The booing continues even louder.

Steve gyrates in his jump suit. On the third line, Paula reveals the next page.

'1 new product launched in 2000. 2 more in the pipeline.'

Steve approaches the front of the stage. 'And don't you...'

This proves to be a very bad idea.

Steve is shouted down by Stuart: 'Get off. You're crap! You're crap! You're crap!'

Steve stops singing *Blue Suede Shoes*, but continues with the Elvis impersonation. 'Well alrighty. I'll finish with a little number by a little old band called the – uh, uh – Smiths.' Steve launches into *What Difference Does It Make?*

'Huh. Huh. I'm the eclectic Elvis,' Steve explains after a couple of lines, picking up on the looks of sheer consternation from the audience.

The audience pelt Steve with belladonna fruit, also known as deadly nightshade. Steve counters by throwing flowers back at them a la Morrissey. This does not stop the deluge of black berries.

'Uh. Uh. Looks like I'll have to leave the building...' Steve concludes. He runs out hand in hand with Paula.

* * *

Slowly, but surely, Steve's consciousness returned to the office meeting. Debbie was still speaking.

'So...just as Black and Decker sell holes and not drills, we at BCG no longer sell chemicals, we sell effects!' Debbie concluded with these triumphant words and looked around the room. Steve's prolonged outage had not escaped Stuart's attention.

'Do you have any questions for Debbie?' he enquired, staring straight at Steve.

Steve picked up the rhetorical gauntlet that had just landed at his feet.

'Uh. Uh.' (He hadn't quite got out of Elvis mode.) 'By selling effects not chemicals, does that mean that you are merely trying to charge customers higher prices for the same old products?' he asked.

Debbie was equal to the challenge. 'Oh, no. we are looking to partner with our customers to push the innovation envelope...'

Steve noticed his younger colleagues eagerly crossing off yet another word on their cards. Steve could not resist the temptation to press Debbie further.

'Well. How come my team is the only one to develop new products around here?'

There were approving nods from some of the members of his team.

Debbie frowned. Stuart decided to come to her rescue.

'Oh, so Debbie – the future is bright?'

A stage whisper could be heard from somewhere around the table.

'No, it's fuckin' orange!'

Steve could not resist an inner chuckle at the mordant Teesside wit.

Laser beams sprang forth from Stuart's eyes as he glared around the room.

Debbie continued unabashed. 'Thank you, Stuart, and yes, of course it is, once we have achieved the necessary synergies.'

Steve knew a corporate euphemism when he heard it.

'Synergies? Is that code for redundancies?' he asked.

Debbie was quick to quash this impertinent enquiry. 'No. No. No. Frankly, Steve, I'm surprised at this level of cynicism.'

She paused for a moment before continuing. 'Some people will have to undergo transition. According to our 7 Business Principles, of course. I trust you've all got our little red card safely about your persons?'

Steve took out the aforesaid red card-like object from his wallet. 'Oh yeah, I abide by them at all times, Debbie.' Steve's ironic tone brought about a wave of nervous laughter from around the table.

At this point, Paula decided to intervene with a more amenable question.

'And what are you doing to promote women in science – in particular those returning from a prolonged career break? Will there be opportunities for us... sorry, rather, them,' Paula corrected herself hastily, 'to step into positions that may become vacated?'

Debbie was relieved at the softer line of questioning. 'Yes, we at "New BCG" have a cornerstone policy on equality, also enshrined in our Business Principles'.

At this point, Paul, a nervous senior technician, decided to ask for a clarification.

'What do you mean by "transition"?' he asked, running his fingers through his white hair.

Debbie decided to give a reasonably honest reply. 'Well, it means that you will have to be redeployed.'

'Redeployed... within the company?' Paul asked pointedly.

Debbie squirmed 'Well, erm... not necessarily. It will depend on your personal circumstances and individual skill set.'

'You mean there will be redundancies!' Paul countered.

'In the fullness of time, possibly.' Debbie was starting to founder.

Stuart decided that enough was enough. 'Well, I think that's all we have time for,' he announced, whilst looking at his watch. 'Let's all thank Debbie for giving up her time, in the usual way,' he said as applause ensued from around the table.

Stuart had one last announcement to make. 'OK, we'll be back again in the autumn, when Professor Roddy Bartholomew will give a talk on the collaboration opportunities that the Central Research Group have to offer all of us at BCG.'

Steve knew this to be a lie, so one could imagine his shock when Debbie simpered, 'Oh, that should be so exciting for you all.'

Unfortunately, this was not before he had blurted out 'That conman!'

There was knowing laughter around the table as Stuart and Debbie glared at him with even greater intensity. As Stuart finally brought the meeting to a close, Steve realized that he needed to make a quick getaway. He got up and pushed his way through the inadequately sized room and was the first to make it to the door.

Without looking back, he walked as fast as he could down the long corridor – to no avail. There was no escape.

Stuart's voice boomed down the corridor.

'A word, please, in my office – NOW!'

Chapter 5: 'Follow The Yellow Brick Road'

Let's take a moment to step back and look at the big picture. The cold winds were blowing over BCG, or 'New BCG' as they now liked to call themselves. Once considered the Bellwether of British Industry, whatever one of those is, BCG had sadly declined over the years like many of its manufacturing contemporaries. Despite a 1980s resurgence under a dynamic and charismatic Chairman, the underlying story had been one of retreat after retreat. By the late 1990s, the company had belatedly come to the conclusion that diversification was the way forward, conveniently forgetting that they had already disposed of their pharmaceuticals and specialty chemicals interests in the early 1990s to fend off a hostile takeover by a predatory baron of enterprise. Under the tutelage of a new CEO (please note, not Chairman anymore), they had acquired a new empire of diverse and exotic products, like, erm, candle wax and starch. Dubbed 'Mr Drippy ' by BCG diehards who were (rightly) sceptical of him, the new man had unusually come from a non-BCG, non-Chemicals background.

Talk about selling your inheritance for a mess of pottage! His stewardship had led to mounting debts, a plummeting share price and the fire sale of their remaining crown jewels. Ironic, really, as the whole object of the exercise had been to please the City of London, close to where 'Mr Drippy' now spent his retirement in a £10 million town house. Like a certain other contemporary figure close to Our Hero's heart, he would spend the rest of his days insisting he was right.

For the troops on the ground, life had gone on, but it was a far cry from the Job for Life that whole families in the North of England had come to expect. Working for the 'old' BCG had been rather like being a civil servant, but on significantly better pay. As BCG declined, like the ploughman in Breughel's 'Fall of Icarus', BCG employees had continued to till away while the odd colleague would come crashing out of the sky at increasingly regular intervals.

Professor Roddy Bartholomew's Central Research Group were a case in point. With apologies to the Holy Roman Empire, they were neither Central (tucked away in the basement of the Elton Centre) nor Research (they did very little of that), and they were a Group in name only. Although Roddy was (by far) the highest paid of them, he was not officially in charge. A BCG senior manager had been assigned to this task, mainly to keep the mercurial Professor Bartholomew (and his merrie men) in some sort of check.

Avoiding the use of their overpriced facilities had become a bit of a game for Steve and his fellow Technical Managers. Sure, they had some brand spanking new shiny, state-of-the-art equipment – you could look at individual atoms, for instance – but it was far too expensive to use. This was because some bean counter at Corporate HQ had decreed that there should be an 'internal market', whereby individual businesses would have to pay for their services – more than external organisations had to pay.

The CRG was a throwback to the days when BCG had been a true scientific pathfinder. A central group at the disposal of all divisions of BCG to help conduct long-term research. What was not to like? Plenty, as it happened – mainly the Directorate's insistence that the group should somehow balance its books. Managers like Steve were routinely strongarmed into blowing any surplus budget they had on irrelevant vanity projects. Money that could have been used on useful things like training staff.

Then there were the people... Misfits! Neither fit to work in the private or university sectors, but all supposedly world experts in their fields, burning up company money on besuited travelling to international conferences to publish their latest papers. As for Roddy, Steve had had a recent narrow escape from his clutches. A fully costed-out proposal to use the latest cutting-edge drying techniques to dry 1kg of powder for £100,000 had made his much-derided ultra-filtration efforts look like value for money. Come to think about it, that had been CRG's idea too! Steve much preferred to work with genuine universities, who offered much better value. That was before the inception of the dreaded Full Economic Costing model, but that's for another day.

The Elton Centre was a 1970s creation, set on the edge of what had been a massive chemicals complex. One could compare the site at night, with its flames and twinkling lights, to Blade Runner, but one would be wrong. It was the other way round. The brothers Scott had been brought up in the North-East and the site had been the inspiration when designing their sets.

The architecture of the Centre was vintage brutalist – an ugly, sprawling four-storey red building with darkened windows. Presumably, the small lake outside had been an attempt to offset this. For many years, the lake had been colonised by an ever-burgeoning colony of aggressive Canada Geese. A surreal touch at the Centre entrance was a bronze statue of Elton John. Steve had been told many versions of how it had come to be there.

The most plausible one went something like this... The Centre was named after a nearby village, which was now abandoned – hardly surprising, given the petrochemical behemoth next door. When it had come to the official opening ceremony for the Centre, the organising committee had soon discovered that no self-respecting Senior Royal wanted to touch such a gig with a bargepole. Princess Margaret was said to have objected that 'it would bring on my asthma, darling' as she'd puffed on yet another cigarette. Being ingenious Teesside folk, the committee had thought to itself, 'If it's the Elton Centre, why not Elton John?' It had so happened that the Great Man's beloved Watford were playing at the Boro' on a convenient weekend, so to their surprise, he'd agreed.

The bronze statue, complete with monster spectacles, was commissioned to a less-than-talented local artist as a mark of gratitude from the good Burghers of Teesside. Leading up to it, someone had thoughtfully decided to put a narrow pathway of yellow bricks. Some cynics remarked that this yellow streak was rather evocative of the local management. Sadly, like BCG, the corroded statue was now a sorry sight, although much beloved by the geese, who targeted it like a World War II U-Boat pen, especially the glasses. But, like its subject, it was still standing.

Steve and BCG went back a long way. He had been born in Stockton-on-Tees and then brought up in Runcorn. The link between these two distant industrial towns was that his dad worked for BCG. Steve had always looked up to BCG. His dad had earned a comfortable salary as a Senior Middle Manager, which afforded the family a detached house with no less than three sheds in Runcorn's leafy suburbs. Steve grew up there with his younger brother David and much younger sister Rowena. Towards the end of his career, his dad had become eligible for a company car. Sure, it was only a Mini Clubman estate, but it was a status symbol, nonetheless.

Steve fondly remembered the coach outings to Chester Zoo, the outdoor fetes and the children's parties. As a teenager, he had liked to go to the local BCG Recreation Clubs at weekends to see bands of surprising stature, such as Nazareth and Thin Lizzy, and try to get off with local girls. It had been at 'the Rec' that Steve would occasionally encounter Gill, his future ex-wife. Sadly, he'd never had the courage to ask her up for a dance. It might have saved him a lot of future heartache if he had.

Indeed, BCG was arguably the reason that Steve had gone to Oxford. His father, a bluff Yorkshireman of humble origins, felt that his own career had been unfairly impeded by toffee-nosed Oxbridge types with plummy accents. None of that sort of class prejudice was going to stop his son! Steve had been pushed towards a career at BCG that would surpass that of his dad. Never mind the fact that it had entailed going to boarding school, which he hated; Steve was going to Oxford to read chemistry! When he'd reached the dreaming Spires, Steve had soon discovered that after many years of declining milk round recruitment, a career with BCG was now reserved for the crème de la crème – not Steve, then! Lesser chemistry graduates went to companies like Trivalent (a specialized inorganic oxides supplier, dismissed as a one-product company by the highflyers) or were shunted into marketing shirts and shampoos. As a last resort, there was always the dreaded chartered accountancy option.

When Steve had joined Trivalent, his dad had bemoaned the fact that it was only half-owned by BCG. Steve had spent some of his most productive years (when he looked back on it) at Trivalent.

Then the day dawned, late in 1990, that BCG took over the rest of Trivalent. The part owner, a materials company, had over-stretched themselves buying up rubbish companies and had had to sell their 50% stake to BCG for a song when the early 90s recession kicked in. Ironic, really; perhaps someone at BCG should have taken note.

Oh, joyous news for Steve! 'This is the happiest day of my life! My parents will be so proud,' a grinning Steve had exclaimed to a disbelieving Trivalent Director when staff had been gathered to hear the news. He had blithely ignored the wise words of an ex-colleague who had upgraded to BCG. 'If you find Trivalent restricting, you will find it a paradise of freedom and creativity compared to BCG!' As the warning had been issued over a pint or six of beer, perhaps he had forgotten.

Initially staff were reassured that there would be no changes. Then, Christmas came and went for staff to discover, via company noticeboards, that the Trivalent Managing Director had been replaced by an unknown BCG sub-Director. End of message.

Five stifling years followed. Trivalent were 100% owned by BCG, but were not a full member of the family. It had felt like a country under occupation. Promotions dried up, salary increases, and bonus payments were denied. Worst of all, BCG developed a habit of sending their most problematic managers to Trivalent, like an old aristocratic family despatching their idiot sons to the colonies.

Then had come Steve's lucky break. He had recently been appointed Technical Manager of the Sunscreens Group when his small part of Trivalent was admitted into the BCG mothership. BCG were now into specialty chemicals, having dismissed them as 'frilly bits' just a few years previously. Steve was now a fully-fledged BCG employee. Never mind the resentment of his erstwhile Trivalent colleagues, who felt he had collaborated with the Enemy, onwards and upwards – now for the company car!

Unfortunately, Steve had soon discovered that BCG managers looked down on their new Trivalent colleagues. But Steve had an Oxford degree, didn't he? Not good enough; his Ph.D. had been from a red brick university. Steve had soon discovered that the BCG Elton Centre was not the Emerald City that he had been seeking.

Chapter 6 'The Future's Bright...'

Steve sat facing Stuart. Photos of Stuart's ugly wife and children stared out at him.

Stuart came straight to the point. 'You fucking showed me up in front of Debbie!'

'How come?' asked Steve innocently.

'Well, firstly, there was Alec and Samantha tittering over those business bullshit cards!'

'Oh, 'the Lovebirds'! That wasn't me!'

'But we all know who bought them, don't we?' Stuart leaned forward menacingly.

'May have done... it was a Secret Santa!' Steve insisted.

'I was at that Christmas party too you know! And unlike you, I can remember what happened!'

'I didn't mean them to get them out in a BCG Meeting.'

'Did you not?' Stuart was unconvinced. 'Never mind! I'll deal with them separately. I'd like to talk to them about all the canoodling and carrying on they're doing – in works time. It's upsetting other members of staff. And they're both in relationships outside BCG.' (Back in 2000, this was still considered to be a subject of legitimate concern for management.)

'I thought I was their line manager...'

'Yes. But you're useless at discipline!'

'Let me use this chance to disprove that myth, then.'

'No. I'll do it. I shall look forward to that!' Stuart said with a sinister smile.

I bet you will. You're just jealous! Steve thought. *Just because you're not getting any, doesn't mean you should take it out on those who are!* Steve then reflected that he was currently in the same boat as Stuart. But there was always Coffin Dodgers that evening. Maybe he would get lucky there. Certainly, he was in with a shout, if the Chairman was to be believed. At least he had prospects. His thoughts were interrupted by Stuart's next assault.

'Anyway, it's your behaviour we're here to discuss!'

'I didn't do anything wrong.' Steve sat up straight in the uncomfortable straight-back chair, which contrasted sharply with Stuart's deluxe swivel model opposite.

'Well first there was that blurted-out comment about Roddy Bartholomew.'

'Sorry, I couldn't help myself.'

'OK. I'll let that one go. I wouldn't pay him or the CRG in bent washers, if it was up to me! I was under pressure from Debbie to invite him,' Stuart added by way of explanation for his feigned enthusiasm at the meeting.

'Well, I'm glad we see things the same way about that one.'

'Yes. Don't forget that it was me that rescued you from that disastrous powder-drying exercise.'

Steve squirmed in his seat. 'I never thought it was a good idea...'

'As I remember, you brought me a purchase requisition to sign, which I vetoed!'

'Well, I did have a handsome budget surplus that year.'

Stuart raised his hand to prevent further argument. 'Much more serious were those smartass questions you kept asking her. When you were awake, that it is!'

Steve was defiant. 'Well firstly, I have a medical condition...'

'Where's your doctor's note then?'

'I can't get the medical profession to see things as I do, but believe me it's an affliction.'

Stuart raised an eyebrow.

'And we were encouraged to ask questions. And one of the Business Principles is to speak openly and candidly amongst your colleagues.'

Stuart was unimpressed. 'Not when it shows me up, it doesn't!'

Steve pulled out his little red card. 'Well it says here – Business Principle Number 2, I think. You should trust your colleagues at all times and assume that their intentions are good ones. '

Stuart shook his head. 'Don't make me laugh. I don't believe that any more than you do. I'm assuming that you're not a complete fool?' he said, peering over his pince-nez glasses. 'Anyway, I don't trust her,' Stuart continued.

'Debbie?' Steve was taken aback.

'Yes, Debbie. She's a political animal. Hasn't got an innovative bone in her body. She presides over a bunch of superannuated Oxbridge-educated deadheads – present company excepted, naturally...'

'Naturally...' Steve replied uncertainly.

'Who think she's the bees' knees,' Stuart continued his diatribe.

'Wow. I didn't know.' Steve was blissfully unaware of the tensions above his head.

'Anyway, back to you. I also noted that you fell fast asleep within 5 minutes of Debbie starting to talk.'

'Sorry Stuart. I tried...'

'And you were late!'

Steve had the perfect excuse. 'I was held up – by Margaret.'

Even Stuart understood that one. 'Oh. Understandable, I suppose – but you showed yourself to be utterly unprofessional in that meeting.'

'Am I not allowed to ask searching questions?'

'Listen, Stephen. I'll give you a bit of career advice, shall I?' Stuart leant back in his unfeasibly large chair.

Steve sat up in his much smaller chair. He was all ears.

'When you're stuck down a deep hole... stop digging!'

'But what about my Tees Valley Innovation Award nomination?' Steve protested. 'What about the new products?'

'They count for nothing round here. You heard! What counts is holes, not drills! Now get out of my fucking office!!' Stuart's voice reached a crescendo.

Steve shambled out of Stuart's office to see Paul coming down the corridor to greet him.

Paul held out his hand. 'I'd like to thank you, Steve.'

'Thank you, Paul. For what?' said Steve, still shaking Paul's hand.

'For saying what everyone was thinking.'

'Really? It was nothing.'

'No, it took guts to do that.'

'I didn't realise...'

Paul gave Steve the benefit of his long experience working for BCG.

'First of all, everyone knows that 'Professor' (Paul spat out the last word with particular disdain) Roddy Bartholomew is a complete fucking charlatan!

'Then there's the "restructuring programme".' Again Paul could not hide his contempt. 'I've heard it all before. It's all bollocks. Operation Mallard – Operation Mallet more like! There's redundancies on the way. You mark my words!'

Chapter 7: 'The Road To Hell'

The long-awaited evening finally came. Steve's car sped through the village of Port Clarence, formerly known as Samphire Batts. This name was about the only exotic thing about the place, apart from the dancers in the local pubs and clubs. Just on cue, the car passed a seedy hostelry with a sign outside: 'Stripper's (sic) every Friday lunch time'.

Geoff sat impassively in the passenger seat, seemingly oblivious to Steve's irritation at this lengthy detour.

Steve could not bear it any longer.

'What the fuck are we going this way for? This road leads nowhere. This truly is the road to hell!'

'Patience, Grasshopper,' was all Geoff could muster by way of reply.

'Look we're going to Coffin Dodgers in Acklam, West Middlesbrough, right? Why not go the whole way and have me drive via bloody Hartlepool and get us hanged as monkeys?'

'Ah! You forget about our very own Transporter Bridge. You'll see!'

The car turned a sharp corner and joined the short queue to be shuttled across the River Tees. The world-renowned Tees Transporter Bridge had opened in 1911. It had survived Zeppelin raids in World War 1 and aircraft raids in World War 2 and various subsequent attempts to close it on economic grounds. Painted blue, since 1961 it had stood as a proud symbol of Teesside's industrial heritage. It also connected Port Clarence to Saint Hilda's, the area north of Middlesbrough railway station, known locally as 'over the border'.

Finally, the Mondeo drove off the transporter platform and into a grim post-industrial area. Working girls thronged the streets, including one dressed as a Red Indian squaw and another as a French maid. Cars moved slowly past them, including a silver Renault Scénic that looked suspiciously like Stuart's company car. If only Steve could remember the number plate details!

Steve's jaw dropped. 'Bloody hell!'

'See? Well worth a look.' Geoff was triumphant. 'I hear 'Robocop' wanted to clean it up. Why bugger up an important local industry, I ask you?'

'Well I don't think the esteemed former Detective Superintendent will be coming back from his enforced career break in a hurry,' Steve said knowingly as he scanned the assorted delights. 'Anyway, how did you know about all this?'

'Local tourist attraction, as I said. Our esteemed club Vice President, Peter Kennedy, likes to come for little drives around here. He took me along with him. Just the once, mind,' Geoff added all too hastily.

'Well, I suppose it beats a trip out to Roseberry Topping for interest,' Steve commented drily.

Geoff continued his tale. 'He got a letter from the Cleveland Police recently, warning him about his future conduct. What would his dad say? Magistrate and general pillock of the community, he is! Young Peter would love to follow in his footsteps, but his fondness of houses of ill repute keeps letting him down. Went to four massage parlours in a day once. Out of control!' Geoff rolled his eyes for effect. 'He's out of control!!'

'Oh, that explains why he's nicknamed Ray, as in Parlour.' A lightbulb went off in Steve's head.

'Yes, the Romford Pelé himself,' Geoff confirmed. 'Indeed. Also why he's now the proud owner of a Skoda Felicia,' Geoff added.

'Oh yeah. Not really your typical estate agent's car. I wondered what happened to that nice Audi that he used to have...' Steve mused.

Geoff gave Steve a knowing look. 'Expensive hobby, I'm afraid. But aren't all women?'

'By the way, why are we going to Coffin Dodgers tonight? I'm still knackered from going to Gravediggers last night. I would have preferred a quiet night on the sniff in Yarm,' Steve complained.

'There's more "tash" at this place, and what we want is snatch isn't it?' Geoff asked rhetorically.

'I suppose so, but a night off to recharge the batteries wouldn't do any harm.'

'I thought you were made of sterner stuff. Anyway, you can always sleep it off tomorrow morning. That charming boss of yours won't mind, will he?'

'Yer jerking aren't yer!?' Steve affected a broad Teesside accent.

'How was your day, by the way?' Geoff leaned over solicitously.

'Alright, I suppose... in the end... no thanks to you!' Steve said sulkily.

'I'd be careful what you say, if I were you! Don't forget that potty you've got stowed in the boot.' Geoff's face became menacing.

'Suffice to say that my tardy arrival this morning didn't go unnoticed.'

'You don't have to worry though, do you? You work for THE BCG. Job for life, man, job for life!

'Not anymore, it's not.' Steve shook his head. 'DEFINITELY not. Fortunately, I have higher aspirations,' Steve added mysteriously.

'What do you mean, higher aspirations?' Geoff was suitably intrigued.

'As you will remember, I got passed up on my last *well-deserved* promotion.'

'No worries on that score. We never heard the last of that one.'

'Yeah. Left me just short of the company car grade. So... I'm still driving this ageing pile of junk.' Steve banged the steering wheel in frustration. 'Which reminds me, the MOT's due next week! Shit the bed! Like my beloved Leeds United, I'm condemned to eternally coming second. '

'Well that latter quality will stand you in very good stead with the ladies you'll be meeting tonight.' Geoff smiled. 'It's like shooting fish in a barrel here. In fact, I've a feeling in my water that you might be tickling some trout, yourself, by the end of this evening!'

The Anvil Pub finally hove into view.

'Ah. Here we are! Next turn right!' Geoff commanded.

This had better be good, Steve thought to himself. If his career had had its ups and downs, those did not even begin to compare with his personal life. He had come late on to the romantic scene. Having spent his formative years at boarding school and then a cloistered Oxford college, which had been mixed in name only (there had still been a 6 to 1 ratio of male to female students back in the 70's), had seen to that.

Then, miracle of miracles, Gillian – a girl he had been sweet on back in his primary school days – had arrived in the northeast as a civil servant, as a result of a half-hearted government initiative to bring more jobs to the area. He had run into her, by chance, at an arts event in Stockton. They had wasted little time in starting a relationship, which had led to two children – Robyn and Kris – and marriage, but not necessarily in that order... Steve had been happy. He had despaired of finding the right woman, let alone being a father. All had seemed set fair until the relationship had started to cool.

There had been rows over money, over housework, over the children. Their sex life had faded to nothing. Steve had started to remind himself of the lost years in his late teens and early twenties, when he should have been shagging anything that moved. He had had the odd temptation towards the end but had managed to keep it from Gill. Not that she had seemed to be all that bothered. Then the first bombshell... Gill had announced that it was over. At first, she'd been reluctant to reveal why. Then there had come the second bombshell: she'd told him that she had found someone else. Then the third bombshell: that someone else was another woman!

The woman concerned was Gloria, a mutual acquaintance, with whom Gill had caught up at a Girl Guide troop 25-year reunion in Runcorn some five years previously. And oh, the duplicity, the deception! Gill had taken to visiting Runcorn ever more frequently. Ostensibly, it had been to show off the grandchildren to her parents, but really, she had been dropping off the kids before driving further south for passionate weekends of nonstop muff-munching (as Steve imagined it) with Gloria in Solihull.

When it all came out, he had been devastated, not least by the rejection for another woman. His brother and sister (both younger) had been supportive. David had maybe been a little over-enthusiastic about pointing out the normality of this development, but then again, he did live in Islington. Rowena, now with a young family in British Columbia, was around ten years younger than Steve, so was similarly unfazed by the circumstances, whilst agreeing that betrayal was betrayal whomsoever it was with. His septuagenarian parents, in retirement in North Wales, had also rallied round, although he had had to put up with the odd remark from his dad along the lines of, 'at least, you could have chosen someone heterosexual!'

Since the big split, Steve had been left with a toxic combination of an urge to catch up for last time and a burning desire to prove himself. There had been two or three brief relationships, the longest-lasting having been Steve's six months with Sarah. Sure, she'd had a pleasant personality and had proved to be the epitome of the naughty nurse in bed. The problem was Steve hadn't really fancied her. Sure, she'd had a nice body and long blonde hair, but Steve couldn't get past the craggy facial features. No amount of doggy position sex could get around that problem. In any case, Steve had read in GQ Magazine that the average British man could expect to have sexual relationships with ten women during their lives. He had some catching up to do. Time to move on!

The Mondeo finally pulled up in the car park of The Anvil Pub.

It was time for Coffin Dodgers!

Chapter 8: 'Common People'

The two ageing likely lads got out of the car. As if on cue, lightning flashed across the sky, followed by a roll of summer thunder. Geoff and Steve rushed across the car park to reach the door before the ensuing deluge.

Over the door hung a banner with the legend, 'Welcome to Middlesbrough and District Singles Club'.

On it was a group photo of the committee. At the forefront were a plain woman in her 50s and a male Dracula lookalike of similar vintage. They were flanked by an unprepossessing collection of perms and comb-overs. Ominously, one or two of the background figures had been expunged with a black felt tip pen.

Geoff and Steve entered the inner sanctum. A sign on the wall proclaimed, 'Welcome To Middlesbrough And District Single Friends Club'. The two hastily put on ties. Steve remained faithful to his Homer Simpson number, while Geoff sported a red and black diagonal striped kipper of 1970s vintage. They stepped out into a veritable Aladdin's Cave of opportunity. A large, darkened room opened up in front of them. The disco lights flashed and then morphed into something that suspiciously resembled a swastika. Music blared out over a nearly empty dance floor. A couple of unattractive 50-something women danced half-heartedly to the strains of Shania Twain's *Feel Like A Woman*.

Dracula stepped out from nowhere to bar Geoff and Steve's further progress. 'Can Ah see your membership cards please, gentlemen?'

Geoff tried to explain that it was Steve's first visit as he showed his card.

Dracula was unimpressed. 'Well it's £1.50 for you and £3 for him. You're 2 minutes behind the last entry time, but Ah'm prepared to make an exception this time.'

He then turned to Steve. 'You are single, aren't you, son?'

'Erm, yes,' was all Steve could muster by way of a reply.

'We'll need a divorce certificate or a letter from your local Vicar or some other responsible person to prove that you're not married.'

Steve was taken aback. 'Right now?'

Brenda, the plain woman from the poster, came to the rescue. 'Let him past, Ray. Poor lad's come all this way. You will bring some certification next time, won't you? Anyway, welcome to Middlesbrough and District Single Friends. MAD singles for short. We're all mad here.' Brenda laughed uproariously at her own joke. 'It's nice to have a bit of new talent,' she added, giggling.

Brenda leered at Steve and pinched his bottom. Steve hastily walked away to a conveniently situated table, while Geoff went off to the bar to observe the time-honoured tradition of 'He whose turn it is, will be bought the first drink'.

As Geoff plonked the drinks on the table, Steve noticed some younger women at a nearby table. Before he could make proper eye contact, he was rudely interrupted.

'Excuse me, gentlemen, but this is a "committee only" table. You can't sit here.' Dracula pronounced as he flitted back into view.

Geoff was unimpressed. 'So you're telling us to move?'

'Ah am indeed.'

The following exchange ensued.

Geoff: 'Well, nobody told us we couldn't sit here.'

Dracula: 'Look in front of yers. There's a clear notice saying "Committee only".'

Geoff: 'Well why isn't there anyone sitting there now?'

Dracula: 'They're working behind the scenes for the benefits of the members.'

Geoff: 'Tossing themselves off in the toilets, more like. Supposing we don't want to move?'

Steve intervened to head off the brewing confrontation. 'Geoff, look – there's some interested parties at that table. Let's go over there.'

Following a cursory glance at the four women sitting at the nearby table, the dysfunctional duo picked up their pints and walked over to the table next to the women.

'Don't fancy yours much. Seems keen on you though,' Geoff observed wryly.

'A bit of an "8 pinter" though, but. Not sure I could manage that.' Steve was not to be drawn.

Meanwhile, the group of ladies were drawing their own conclusions about the newcomers.

'Why look at them? I divn't know which is the seediah! And ah mean Ah've seen dyed hair before, but that's ridiculous. What a pair of Scoundrels!' their most extrovert member, Ros, declared.

The women were a motley bunch. Ros and Julie, with their bosoms threatening to spill out of their ridiculously low-cut dresses, made a passable impersonation of the 'Fat Slags' of Viz fame. On the other hand, Karen was tastefully dressed in a matching blue top and skirt. Also quietly dressed, Di, the perennial designated driver, made up the foursome.

Geoff nodded over to them and clapped them with a winning smile. The girls all laughed.

'I don't know, the younger guy looks quite cute,' Karen observed.

'Cute? That usually means you think he's kind of nice... but you don't want to shag him.' Ros laughed uproariously at her own joke, joined by Julie.

Di was solicitous. 'Now then, Karen. Don't be getting your hopes up. You said that you'd given up on men after Gareth.'

'Well why am I here, then, if I've given up on fellahs? This place is such a cattle market though!'

The evening wore on.

One thing the regulars of MAD appreciated was routine.

Around half past nine, it was time to mix things up a bit.

The DJ made his announcement right on cue.

'Now then, ladies and lads... it is time for our first 'slowey'. Now you know the rules – pass on to your next partner after each verse so we can all get to know each other. '

Some couples got together on the floor. Brenda came and grabbed Steve. Geoff stayed in his chair.

'Can you waltz?'

'No.'

'Well, now's the time to learn.'

Brenda dragged Steve on to the dance floor as the DJ announced: 'First up, we have a number by the delectable Miss Patti Page...'

'She must be 70 years old, if she's a day,' Steve muttered under his breath, observing that by no means would the thrice-married Miss Page have been the oldest woman, nor the least glamorous, in the joint. He continued to waltz awkwardly with Brenda. She smiled and passed him on to a much more attractive lady – Karen.

'Hi. Do you come here often?' Steve could not have been accused of originality.

'No. It's my first time. What a dreadful place.'

'Isn't it? But how come you're here, then?'

'My friends insisted I come.'

'Same here.' Steve looked over at Geoff, sitting impassively at their table. 'Glad they did. What's your name?'

'Karen. I'm from Nunthorpe.'

'I'm Steve. I live in Rokeby. See you later,' was all that Steve was able to get in before they passed on to their respective next partners.

Shortly after, the interval came to interrupt all the fun. Brenda tapped the mic onstage as Steve and Geoff continued to talk amongst themselves.

'Testing. Testing. Shh. Shh. Shh. I'd like to make a few announcements. Firstly, there's a wedding coming up for 2 of our members. Stand up Terry and Jean!'

A 60-something couple stood up to rapturous applause. The man had a heroic combover, with hair going off in three directions.

Brenda continued her address to the troops. 'There's a walk to the Cook Monument on Sunday... '

Geoff and Steve continued to talk despite shushes from all around.

Geoff had been watching Steve's moves on the dancefloor with some interest. 'Looks like you're well in there. What's she called?'

'Karen. She lives in Nunthorpe.'

Geoff rolled his eyes theatrically. 'A lady from the East. Beware of ladies from the East! They're all mad! As my old friend Jack used to say, "All women are mad, only some are madder than others".' Geoff paused to give his considered judgement. 'Anyway, bit of a helmet raiser, eh?'

Steve tried to be nonchalant. 'Yeah, not bad... I'd say about 2 pints.'

'What's that mean?' Geoff was curious.

'It was devised at work by me and my office mate at Trivalent.'

'I thought he was a "toe toucher".'

'No, that was Jeremy. This was Lee, his predecessor, the "Laboratories Lothario". Anyway, it was basically a handicapping system, like with the horses.'

'Go on...' Geoff was all ears.

'Well, it was how many pints would you need before you could shag them. Zero was perfection. Four was OK. Then it went up to 8 for really ugly.' Steve thought for a moment. 'Well actually it went up to 10, then there was SP...'

'SP? As in Starting price?' Geoff was puzzled.

'No. Are you in the habit of paying for sexual services, Geoff?'

'No, no, no. Course not. They should be paying me!' Geoff blushed suspiciously.

'No. It means stomach pump!' was Steve's triumphant and all-too-loud conclusion.

Brenda was not impressed 'You two shush. There's people wanting to know if they've won the raffle!' Brenda continued on her merry way. 'And the winner of our first prize – a bottle of Malibu – is pink 327.'

'That's mine!' Steve exclaimed, and got up on his hind legs to go and saunter to the stage to collect the much-coveted award.

The fact that this was Steve's debut at Coffin Dodgers had not gone unnoticed by the ageing clientele. To be honest, his win was about as popular as a tarantula in a lucky dip with the good denizens of MAD. His win was met by booing and snake-like hissing.

At the ladies' table, it was time for Julie to make a pronouncement. 'Men! They're only good for one thing, and they're no good at that!' She curled up her little finger to emphasize her point to uproarious laughter.

Ros took a swig from the vodka miniature hidden in her handbag. 'Ah'll drink to that. Once they get to a certain age, they start to smell too.'

'What do you mean about getting to a certain age?' Julie countered. 'Take my Bob... By lad, he hummed when he was still eighteen. Ah cannot recall what I ever saw in him.'

'Or smelled!'

Julie lit up a cigarette. 'And oh, those skiddies on his boxahs. Ugh!'

Ros wanted a smoke too. 'Ah give us a tab, Julie man. I'm gasping.'

Julie reopened her pack of ten. 'Not the only thing that you're gasping for!'

To the background of more uproarious laughter, Dracula came over.

'Excuse me ladies, but Ah noticed that one of you was consuming alcohol that was bought off the premises. You should know that's strictly forbidden. And may Ah remind you there's no smoking allowed at tables adjoining the dance floor.'

Ros took a luxuriant drag from her Embassy Regal. 'Ah, Haddaway and shite man. No-one'll notice.'

Dracula was unmoved. 'We have strict orders from the management to stamp out this sort of thing. Please desist or Ah'll have to escort you off the premises.'

'Ah piss off man!' Julie got up and beckoned Ros. 'We'll go outside.' The two trudged off with Karen and Di in tow. A smug smile crossed Dracula's features.

Turning round defiantly, Ros shouted back after him, 'We'll be back!'

'That went down well,' Geoff suggested ironically as Steve put his prize down on the table. 'By the way, it looks like the lovely lady from the East has departed these shores.'

'Shit the bed!' was all Steve could say, before continuing, 'In that case, why don't we go on to Yarm?'

'Yes, why not? We might pick up one or two stragglers,' Geoff concurred.

They both rose up and started to make for the door. This prompted further jeers from the hardened veterans.

'Leaving so soon?' one man shouted out.

'Why it's an absolute disgrace! Stays long enough to win the raffle prize, then buggers off home,' exclaimed the woman sitting next to him, before crying out 'Fix!'

Steve and Geoff continued to run the gauntlet, finally passing the desk in the entry hall under the watchful eye of Dracula.

'Do yous too gentlemen want a pass out to come back in?' he shouted after them.

'Nah. We're leaving,' replied Steve as they made for the door.

And there it might have ended. Those readers who have watched the film 'Sliding Doors' will know how chance circumstances can change peoples' lives. This was certainly the case for Steve and Karen. But let's fast forward to the following day, when Steve would arrive at work, still wearing his 'Coffin Dodging' clothes from the previous night.

Chapter 9: 'She Blinded Me With Science'

A dishevelled Steve finally arrived at his office to find Paula lying in wait for him.

She sat cross-legged across from the small table that Steve employed for one-to-one conversations, in direct contrast to Stuart's more confrontational approach.

Steve would have frankly preferred a little downtime to reflect on the events of the previous evening. Still, there was nothing else on the morning's agenda, and this was a good chance to tell Paula some home truths about the rate of progress on her project.

'Top of the morning to yer, Doctor Hemmings!' Paula exclaimed.

'Morning, Paula,' Steve said wearily.

'So, Steve... do you still want to talk about my new product launch?' Paula sensed his reluctance.

'Do you mind if I just go across to my computer to check on my emails?' Steve was playing for time to gather his wits. 'Why don't you make us both a cup of tea in the kitchen next door?' he continued.

Paula fixed him with a laser-like glare.

'OK. Let's not bother,' Steve said as he walked over to his desk chair and fired up his PC. 'Yes! Yes! Yes!' Steve shouted, punching the air, as he read a particular email.

'What's that? A commendation from the BCG Chairman?' Paula asked sardonically.

'Even better! I got a reply from Tony Blair,' Steve said excitedly.

'Oh, that eejit. Can't say I'm impressed.'

Steve started to scroll down on his screen.

'Well, read it out to me, then.' Paula couldn't stop her curiosity getting the better of her.

'I thought you weren't interested.' Steve smirked over his shoulder across the office.

'I'm not going to sit here in silence while you read it to yourself, so I'm not.'

'OK. I'll read it out loud.' Steve beamed. A quick word of explanation may be necessary, before Steve reads out the email, Dear Reader. It was not an actual email from Tony Blair, Himself, but as a sentient, intelligent being, I guess you already knew that. LOL.

Dear Dr Hemmings

Regarding your letter dated June 8th: I have read it and noted its contents.

I can say that I certainly share your concerns regarding the importance of signed one-way access at petrol stations and will give the issue my fullest attention in the coming months.

I hear what you say about traffic safety aspects around the Angel of the North. I appreciate your unease, although I find your reference to it as the 'Angel of Death' a tad emotive. Allow me to deal with your proposals point by point:

I believe that your friend Geoff's suggestion that it should be demolished and sold for scrap to save HM Treasury some money may invoke damaging accusations of philistinism for the New Labour Project. In any case, I am sure that Mr Brown won't need the money after he has completed his masterly gold bullion sell-off.

Your suggestion that it should be melted down, re-sculpted and placed outside the Redcar steelworks – 'the true heart of the industrial northeast' – is interesting. I fear, however, that it would provoke internecine tensions within our region. In any case, it's in Mrs Mowlem's constituency, and she already gets enough publicity as things stand.

I find your other suggestion that it should be dismantled and transplanted to a quieter spot in the Sedgefield constituency, in honour of my premiership, very flattering. I fear, however, that my friends and colleagues on Gateshead Council have grown rather fond of it and would object rather strongly.

With kind regards

Tony

The Right Hon Anthony Blair MP

'Good, eh?' exclaimed Steve enthusiastically.

'He just thinks you're a local loony who needs humouring' was Paula's withering conclusion.

'Thanks, Paula,' Steve said ironically before re-joining her at the small table. He couldn't help noticing what nice legs she had, but suppressed this intrusive thought. He needed to deliver a management bollocking.

'Oh yeah. Tell me how, on God's earth, you're going to achieve a product launch in 18 months' time?' Steve was not pulling punches.

'I thought I'd explained all this at our product launch meeting on Monday.' Paula was affronted.

'You didn't explain it to me,' Steve said flatly.

'You could have asked questions at the end,' Paula said reasonably.

'What? At the end of a meeting that had already overrun by an hour?' Steve raised his eyebrows.

'I had to let everyone have their say,' Paula said huffily.

'No, you didn't. You were just trying to look good in front of senior management.'

'They told me to be more inclusive on my latest training course,' Paula insisted.

'So you forgot all about your previous time management course then?' Steve countered sarcastically. 'Furthermore, did I tell you about the time I went on a £10k Course at a top management college?'

'Many times.' Paula feigned a yawn.

'And for the first two days, the sum total of our Syndicate's Mentor's contribution to our discussions was to walk out when our meeting was due to end.'

'I think you have mentioned it,' Paula added ironically. 'And that he was a best-selling author who got a mention on University Challenge.'

'OK. OK. Friend of the famous, me.'

'So... your point being?'

'There was method in his madness. I certainly paid more attention to timekeeping, thereafter.'

'Pity that doesn't extend to getting into work on time,' Paula said ironically.

'How many times have you taken away one useful learning point from one of the many courses that I've sent you on?' It was Steve's turn to be sarcastic.

'I know my Myers-Briggs personality type!' Paula smiled sweetly.

'Yeah. As I recall, it's the same as mine. What does that tell us? Try again!'

Paula remained silent. Steve decided it was time to come back to the point.

'So what's the current technical priority?' he asked.

'Well first, we need to stop the product from foaming...' Paula started to explain.

Steve interrupted her. 'Let me stop you there. How many compounds are you screening to do this?'

'Just six,' was Paula's reply.

Steve was not impressed. 'Six? Just six!' he said ironically.

'Well, scientifically, it's a very interesting problem and it'll keep the technicians busy,' Paula continued blithely.

'You what!?' Steve was incandescent.

'Well Dan's doing a Ph.D. part-time, and I need to feed him with rewarding project work for his thesis.'

'This is a commercial product, not a fucking Ph.D. project!'

'I beg your pardon? I could report you for that sort of language, you know.'

'Sorry Paula, but have you never heard of a Gantt chart?'

'What?'

'Never mind. It seems that's another course that I need to send you on.' Steve shook his head and then took a deep breath. 'Look. You're spending 6 months on something that should take 2 weeks. It's always the unscientific balls-aching stuff that takes the time up – like filtration, formulation, getting samples out to customers...'

'But I am a SCIENTIST. All that stuff's feckin' shite.'

'I say fuck, you say feck!' Steve smiled magnanimously. 'OK. Please explain the science to me, then.'

'Well, there's a hydrophilic ethoxy anchor group and a long-chain hydrophobic group...'

Steve hated organic chemistry. It was his personal kryptonite and had nearly cost him a decent degree at Oxford. (Too bad that he now found himself working for a specialty organic chemicals company.) In order to ward off its evil spirit, he promptly drifted off into a reverie.

* * *

In his mind's eye, Steve can see bronzed beauties the length of Redcar beach. They are pouring BCG sunscreen onto strategic parts of their anatomy. They beckon to Steve suggestively. Chief among them is Paula.

* * *

Back in the Office, Paula was continuing to talk technical:

'And then there's an ethoxylate group...'

'Uh. Huh. Oh yes. The ethoxylate group...'

'Are you alright, Steve? Not keeping you up or anything?' Paula was being ironically solicitous.

'Sorry. Just been burning the candle at both ends recently.'

'I was going to ask. How's your love life?' Paula leaned over the small table attentively.

'Complicated. I finished with Sarah a couple of months ago...'

'Oh dear. You seemed so happy together at that leaving do!'

'History now. Time to move on.'

'So you've got a successor lined up?'

'Maybe. I was having a bit of a dry spell, until I went to Coffin Dodgers last night.'

'I take it that's some sort of pickup joint for people who should be old enough to know better.' Paula sighed. 'Shall I go back to the chemistry, before you tell me all the sordid details?'

'Nah, don't bother. I'm sure you've got it taped. Just remember to count back from the launch date to see how much time you can spend on the science. And the science is just a means to an end. Right?'

'Yes. If you say so.' Paula sulkily accepted Steve's words of wisdom.

'OK. Will I see you at the Health Promotion event on site – next week?' Steve attempted to change the subject.

'I wouldn't miss it for the world. Have you forgotten? I'm manning the safe sex stand!' Paula said pointedly.

'Try saying that after a few pints.' Steve grinned conspiratorially.

'It's very serious. AIDS is a scourge – and it's incurable.' Paula frowned and looked Steve in the eye. 'You are practising safe sex with all these ladies, aren't you?'

'Erm... what do you mean, all these ladies?'

'You seem to be getting through them at a hell of a rate.'

'Chance would be a fine thing!' Steve said sincerely.

Paula paused to think for a moment.

'So how many sexual relationships have you had in the last twelve months?'

Steve looked down at his fingers and started to count. 'About six,' he concluded before pausing. 'The same number as your anti-foaming agents,' he said, grinning.

'Feck! Feck! Feck! I can't believe that I just heard that! '

'I didn't mean it like that,' Steve added hastily.

'That sounds pretty promiscuous to me!' Paula fixed Steve with another stare.

'Well, it doesn't feel like that,' Steve said defensively. 'I once had six months of enforced celibacy, you know.'

'My heart bleeds. What about that night when you "saw"' – Paula made an ironic inverted commas gesture – 'two different ladies?'

'It wasn't at the same time!' Steve said defensively before adding, 'I just got lucky.'

'I don't suppose that they did,' Paula countered.

'You see, that's the way of it. It's like buses; they all come at once!' Steve explained.

'Holy Mother of Shite! I've heard it all now. You are taking the objectification of women to new extremes, Doctor Hemmings!'

'You know, I didn't mean it like that!' Steve protested.

'Well, what did you mean?'

'I meant, erm, opportunities!'

'Steve! When yer in a fecking hole, stop digging.' Not the first time that Steve had received this advice in the last 24 hours... 'Let me return to my original question.' Paula leant across the small table. 'Were yer practising safe sex with them?'

'Well, erm,' was all Steve could muster.

'Yer mean yer not!'

'Well, you're hardly one to talk. You've got five kids!' Steve retorted.

'But I'm in a monogamous relationship. You're not.' Paula paused. 'I don't suppose you think about the dangers of unwanted pregnancy either, do you? Never thought about your responsibilities on that score, then?'

Steve tried to make a joke to deflect the torrent of criticism. 'Well, it's difficult. Try putting a blob on after a few pints!'

Paula winced at the thought. 'I wouldn't know. I'm a good Catholic!

She then smiled and slapped Steve's wrist playfully. 'You're a very naughty boy, so you are!! You'd better be there at the safe sex stand,' was her parting shot.

'I wouldn't miss it for the world,' Steve muttered as Paula flounced out of his office.

As Steve returned to his emails, the thought of an unwanted pregnancy set alarm bells running in his brain far louder than any fears of AIDS.

Chapter 10: 'Night Moves.'

So, back to the night before...

Steve and Geoff had nearly reached the waiting Mondeo when the sound of giggling could be heard.

It was Karen and friends.

'I thought you'd gone,' Steve said.

'Ah nah,' Julie replied. 'We've just gone out for a tab in peace and quiet and Karen and Di followed us.'

'You mean you're going back in there?' Steve could not hide his enthusiasm.

'Easy cowboy! Yer after Karen, aren't you?' Ros rejoined.

Despite the lateness of the hour, Steve's blush could be seen clearly in the midsummer evening light.

'Well, erm,' he started to mutter.

The Chairman put an arm round him. 'Looks like we're going back in, Old Son.'

When the boys re-entered the pub, they were immediately intercepted by Dracula.

'Sorry, ah cannot let yous two back in without a pass out,' he declared.

'Why not?' Geoff asked.

'It's the rules,' Dracula explained.

'Oh come on!' said an exasperated Geoff. 'This lad wants to have his balls tapped!'

Steve blushed even brighter as the girls returned from their ciggie sojourn, holding up their inked wrists for inspection.

'Ah cannot make any concessions. You two said you were leaving. I can't let you back in without a pass out,' he concluded with a certain sadistic satisfaction, noticing the looks Steve was exchanging with Karen.

'But that was before...' Steve's voice tailed off as he blushed yet again.

'Before what?' Julie asked knowingly.

'Before he knew he was on a fuckin' promise!' Ros shouted.

'Ladies. No swearing, please! I've warned you already!' Dracula was unmoved. Both Steve and Karen blushed this time.

'Oh, let's see what we can find in Yarm. We know where we're not welcome!' The Chairman started to usher a reluctant Steve towards the exit. The girls continued on their way back into the inner sanctum.

Like the sliding doors opening, Brenda came to the rescue in the nick of time. 'Ah Ray, let 'em past. We know they've paid their subs.' She gave Steve a wink. 'Looks like this lad has clicked!'

Steve's blush would have been visible from the moon if he had not been indoors.

Ray reluctantly gave way.

'It's what we're here for,' Brenda concluded before pinching Steve's bum again. 'Remember, you owe me an even bigger one now,' she stage-whispered to a rapidly departing Steve.

When the ageing likely lads got back to their table, the sound of laughter could be heard from the adjoining table.

Ros was quizzing Julie about her favourite subject, her ex-husband's failings.

'So Jules, tell me more about Bob's B.O.?'

'It wasn't just B.O., you know. He never wiped his arse properly, and as for the smell of his cock...' They laughed uproariously. 'Good job I like a bit of cheese!' Julie concluded.

'Just like ripe fucking Camembert?' Ros suggested.

Geoff and Steve were aware of the sounds of laughter coming from the ladies' table but were unable to make out what was being said.

'What is it with women when they get together?' Geoff observed irritably. 'What are they finding so funny?'

'Whatever it is, it's rude,' observed Steve wryly.

'What do we see in them?' Geoff concluded.

Back at Karen's table, Ros was waxing ever more lyrical about the now-departed Billy. 'I remember the time our Billy bowked all over me when he got back from the pub. Still wanted to have sex with me!

'Did you let him?' a horrified Di butted in.

'Did I hellers like! Kicked him out in the morning. That was the end for Billy. ARSEHOLE!' Her voice reached a crescendo. This time Steve and Geoff could clearly discern what was being said.

They were not alone; Dracula came running across to intervene.

'Ladies. Ladies. Please. Please. This is a respectable establishment. Please moderate your language. You're upsettin' the regulars.'

Ros was unmoved. 'What, those sad bastards? There's a reason why they're regulars here. Totally fucking repulsive to the opposite sex.'

'Or their own, for that matter, ' Julie added helpfully.

Dracula was at the end of his tether. 'Now listen, ladies. This is your last warning. I've never had to evict a lady out of here, but there's always a first time...'

The evening wore on. Steve still had not made a decisive move for Karen as the DJ made an announcement.

'Before we get to our end-of-evening slow numbers, I have a special request. We don't normally play Britpop here, but the lady concerned was most insistent. Before we get to our end-of-evening slow numbers, I have a special request...

'So here it is, Pulp with Common People And I hope that Ros will honour her offer,' he voiced over the opening line, before adding 'Only jokin', mind!' much to the relief of the hardcore Coffin Dodgers.

Steve saw Karen getting up to dance, counter current to the mini stampede going the other way. It was now or never...

Steve caught up with Karen in the nick of time, just before a Brylcreemed man with horn rim glasses could beat him to it.

A breathless Steve led Karen on to a nearly empty dancefloor.

'Ooh. I really like this song,' Karen opined.

'One of my favourites too,' Steve agreed.

'I really like the line about wanting to sleep with common people.' Steve grinned.

'I hope you don't think I'm common! I've been to university, you know,' was Karen's immediate riposte.

Steve blushed once again. 'Not at all,' was all he could blurt out.

'But do you want to sleep with me?'

Steve was fumbling for an answer as Ros lurched onto the dance floor, swigging from her illicit vodka bottle and smoking. Spotting one of the pillars at the edge of the dancefloor, she started pole dancing, giggling and out of control as Jarvis Cocker's vocals increased in agitation.

'Yer all fuckin' tossers!' Ros cried out as she swung the half bottle of vodka around. She continued to gyrate wildly and was about to unstrap her bra when Dracula came running on with a couple of committee members. They stood in front of Ros just in time.

'Now then! Now then! That's quite enough. Quite enough. Ah'm going to have to escort you off these premises.' The committee men formed a small circle around Ros as Di came running onto the dancefloor.

'Please. Please. She's upset. She just broke up with her boyfriend. Her husband's not paying her any maintenance,' Di entreated.

'Yeah. Yeah. Fuck the CSA! All men are shite!!'

That was the last straw. Dracula and his goons escorted a loudly protesting Ros away. Di picked up Ros's discarded clothes as Julie got her stuff together back at the table.

'Looks like your friend is about to get kicked out.' Steve thought it would be gentlemanly to warn Karen.

'She's no friend of mine. Bloody ignorant Mackem,' was the surprise response.

'They're all about to scarper.'

'Ay. Never mind. Di's the only one I really like. Can't stand the other two. **You** couldn't take me home, could you?'

Karen waved as her friends departed.

'Yeah. OK. There's just one thing...' Steve tried in vain to look behind himself in Geoff's direction.

'What's that?'

'My friend Geoff. I'm supposed to be giving him a lift home tonight.'

'Oh, he looks well looked after.' Karen could see that The Chairman was in deep conversation with an attractive blonde lady.

We were now into the close-up and personal part of the evening. Ageing couples poured onto the dance floor to smooch to 'Flying without Wings'.

Karen and Steve moved closer to each other before Steve gingerly put his hands behind her back. This was swiftly reciprocated. Out of the corner of his eye, he could see Geoff dancing closely with the blonde lady.

Steve's thoughts began to wander.

Oh good. Geoff's got fixed up. Looks like I am on a promise here, after all. He can take her home in a taxi. Oh, dear, I'm getting a stalk on. I really would like to ask a woman about 'erection section' etiquette some time. Is it OK to have a stiffy? Is it OK not to have one? It certainly seems to drive them away if you don't have one. I still blame the failure of my abortive dalliance with Jeanette on my lack of obvious ardour during the bum clutchers.

His fears proved to be unfounded. Karen moved up ever more closely to him as they smooched away. This was the last dance of the evening. Next stop, Nunthorpe!

A happy Steve walked hand in hand with Karen out into the pub car park.

Unfortunately, Geoff was there, waiting for him by the car.

'You are taking me home, aren't you?' he asked menacingly.

'But Karen lives in the opposite direction,' Steve protested, before going over to whisper in Geoff's ear. 'I thought we agreed that if the driver pulled then the passenger got a taxi? Anyway, what happened with that bird you were with?'

Geoff rolled his eyes. 'Oh, her. Mad as a box of frogs. I mean, completely mad. She's got six kids and now she says that's she's got religion and doesn't believe in sex outside marriage!'

'Well. I'm sorry mate, but a shag's a shag.' Steve wondered what would have happened if the boot had been on the other foot.

'Yes, and mates are mates,' Geoff reminded him even more menacingly, before conceding, 'but, I suppose that a standing cock has no conscience. You go ahead and give her a good snaking.'

Steve fervently hoped that Karen had not been able to hear their conversation.

Fortunately, she had been distracted by the sight of her friends finally being bundled into Di's car by Dracula and his goons.

'We're not going. Fuck off, ya bastards!' Ros shouted defiantly.

Di had finally lost patience: 'Well yers can both walk back to Peterlee then. It's a good twenty miles out of my way, you know!'

'Alright. Alright.' Ros staggered into the car reluctantly.

'You're all banned from here sine die,' Dracula announced.

'See if we care. This place (pronounced play-uss) is tha pits,' Julie concluded.

The girls drove off, Ros and Julie flicking V signs through the back window.

'Get stuffed you Middlesbrough snobs!' Ros shouted from the departing car.

'Ah... good riddance to bad rubbish,' was Dracula's parting shot.

'See you next week, then...' Julie laughed scornfully.

Dracula put his arm around Brenda, who had hurried out to investigate. 'Ah'm sorry if all that upset you. Ah've never had to evict ladies before. Don't know what the world's coming to,' he said sadly.

'I blame that Shirley Williams. Educational standards have slipped. They used to give us the cane in my day,' was Brenda's take on the situation.

'Girls too?' Dracula was nonplussed.

'Ay, girls too. Didn't do us any harm!'

Dracula and Brenda walked back towards the Anvil arm in arm.

Before we find out what happened to Steve in naughty Nunthorpe, let us pause to see what happened on the Chairman's ride home.

A distinctly grumpy Geoff waited in the Anvil car park for what seemed an aeon. He'd already had disputes with regular denizens of Coffin Dodgers when he'd tried to butt in and steal their rides. Finally, a battered black Nissan diesel saloon arrived.

'Taxi for Huckstead?' asked the driver politely.

'About time, too!' the Chairman commented sourly. 'Did you come here via Karachi?'

'No, I came from Khan's,' the taciturn driver replied drily as Geoff climbed into the passenger seat.

Silence reigned as the two headed north over the A19 flyover. As they passed the fertilizer plant tower to the right, Geoff became intrigued at the two photos on the driver's dashboard. One of them was Saddam Hussein, the other a strangely familiar cricketing figure.

'OK mate,' the driver said. 'Where was it you said that you were going?'

"Half a mile beyond the end of Junction Road, Norton, turn right after the roundabout. By the way, why do you have that picture of Saddam Hussein?

'Oh. He is a great man. A truly great man,' the driver answered.

'I thought he was a bit of a bad bugger, myself.' The Chairman was intrigued.

'Oh no. No. No. He is truly misunderstood. He wouldn't let a bunch of women slow-handclap him.'

'Not like Tony Blair, you mean? I thought you'd approve of him.' Geoff was one of those people who assumed all ethnic minorities would automatically vote Labour.

'No, can't be having him, mate. Not this Tony. He is not a straight man. Not like Sir Brian. Not like Sir Brian at all. No straight bat, this one...'

As the car sped on past the high security jail on the left, Geoff had a question.

'So that really is Brian Close on your dashboard?'

'Oh yes. He is a great man. A truly great man.'

'How do you know Closey?' Geoff had to ask.

'He ran a Yorkshire Cricket Club "ethnic minorities outreach" practice session in Bradford in the 1980s. I was truly inspired by him.'

'Really?'

'Told us all about the time he headed the ball to second slip. He couldn't believe his teammate dropped the ball. Gave him a right bollocking, he did.'

'Yeah, I remember that one. Did you get his autograph, then?'

'No, he told me to fuck off, but what a great man. Unbeaten as England captain. Rejected by the establishment, but without him there would be no Sir Ian Botham and no Sir Viv Richards...'

'Quite right. To be told to fuck off by Closey is a great honour indeed! You're a man after my own heart, erm...?' The Chairman enquired.

'Pervez. Pervez Rehman, mate.'

'Well, Pervez, I'm Geoff.'

'Oh. Geoff, as in Sir Geoffrey Boycott?'

'Yes, the very same. You wouldn't fancy a game of cricket on Sunday? Our team's a bit short thanks to our useless captain.'

Pervez paused for a moment before asking. 'Where at?'

'Great Naughton. 2pm.'

Geoff had only just time to spit this out, when the car arrived outside a small detached house – Geoff's home, where he lived with his mother. Geoff opened the passenger door.

'OK. See you mate and that'll be £9 please, mate,' Pervez reminded Geoff of the need to pay for his ride.

Pervez then wrote his mobile number on the back of the taxi business card. Geoff handed over £10, after some rummaging inside his wallet, then pocketed the change and Pervez's card.

'Good. Night. See you Sunday.' Geoff made his way up the drive and into the house.

Chapter 11: 'The Septics'

Apologies, Dear Reader, but you will have to wait still longer before you get to find out what happened in Naughty Nunthorpe on the Night of the Coffin Dodgers. First, let me introduce you to the Septics, whom Steve encountered at lunch time after his conversation with Paula.

If you work for a large and dysfunctional organisation like BCG, you soon learn that you are judged by the company that you keep. At least, most people on their way up the management ladder recognise this.

Steve was not one of them. He was drawn to the dissidents and the misfits like a veritable moth to a flame. Prominent amongst these groups were the self-proclaimed Septics, a set of superannuated middle managers who had seen better days. They would hold court every lunchtime in the BCG Elton Centre canteen, officially dubbed the Lakeside Restaurant. Steve had been warned by Stuart, among others, that these were not the sort of people that you should be associating with if you valued your career. Steve was inclined to ignore the advice, partly out of curiosity, and partly out of his antipathy towards Stuart.

Frank from Procurement was the unofficial leader of the Septics, although Les had been the more senior manager in his time (long past). Les had been the site manager at a BCG site once upon a time. He was now in charge of 'legacy issues'. This mostly entailed settling compensation claims (as quietly as possible) with residents living near former BCG facilities whose soil or water had been left permanently blighted by decades of polluting activity. The other two regulars were Don, a senior scientist who was in the happy position of no longer having any managerial responsibilities, and Toni. The latter was the exception; firstly, in that she was a woman, secondly, in that she had a career path in front of her.

Steve shuffled into the Lakeside Restaurant and bought his customary pie and chips with extra gravy. He spotted the table with the Septics around it and spotted an empty chair opposite Frank.

'Mind if I join you gentlemen?' Steve said as he plonked his tray down on the empty space in front of him. 'Whoops, sorry – gentlemen and Lady,' Steve corrected himself as he spotted Toni sitting at the end.

Frank, a rotund, jolly man sitting opposite, was the first to speak: 'I'm not sure about that. You might get infected.'

'What do you mean?'

'You do know that we're called the Septics, don't you?'

'Septics?'

'Well it used to be sceptics, as in Eurosceptics, but now it's Septics. We infect everyone with our cynicism.'

The other four nodded their heads in agreement.

Les, a smartly dressed grey-haired man, proclaimed: 'Abandon hope of promotion, all ye who enter here.'

'Well, I don't think it's likely...' Steve volunteered with a degree of false modesty.

Toni, a rather earnest thin woman with a Roman nose, butted in. 'You can say that again! Especially considering how you've upset Debbie.' Toni was slightly younger than Steve, but senior in the scientific ranks. Crucially, she was part of the mainstream BCG Research and Development 'Mother Ship', while Steve remained a relative outsider, working for his bolt-on Cosmetics Business Unit.

Steve was shocked. 'Upset Debbie? What do you mean?'

'At your team's meeting yesterday,' Toni explained.

'What did I do wrong there?' Steve was incredulous.

'Asked her awkward questions. That's what you did. When you weren't sleeping soundly at the back.'

'What sort of awkward questions?' Steve was genuinely puzzled.

'About Project Mallard!' Toni continued.

'Mustn't mention the war, Fawlty,' Frank butted in ironically.

Toni leant across to Frank. 'You know what? He even mentioned the "R" word!'

Don feigned astonishment. 'The 'R' word! We can't have that at BCG!'

Toni became agitated. 'Spitting feathers, Debbie was. We had to restrain her from paying a special visit on your boss to make a formal complaint!'

Frank spoke calmingly. 'Now, don't wear yourself out there, Toni. You won't have any energy left to invent all those new products.'

Toni caught Frank's sarcastic drift. 'Thanks for your concern, Frank.'

Frank was not to be outtrumped on the irony front. 'Well it's a never-ending stream of innovation here. Thomas Alva Edison would be proud.'

'Piss off, Frank.' There was venom in Toni's voice.

Steve couldn't let the conversation end without protesting his innocence. 'I didn't mean it that way with Debbie.'

Don arched his eyebrows. 'What, you didn't mean that you thought there would be redundancies – and not all voluntary ones?'

'Well is saying what others are thinking so bad?' Steve enquired innocently.

The other four 'old lags' all shook their heads.

Finally, Les intervened. 'You'll learn. You'll learn. There is a code, you know?'

'At Trivalent, we were encouraged to be open and honest.'

Frank chuckled. 'Yeah, and look where that got you? Taken over by us – that's what.'

Les folded his arms. 'The problem with you, my naïve friend, is that you believe in things. Mark my words! This is no place for believers.'

Steve attempted to continue to eat, but was stopped short by Frank, who was scrutinising his lunchtime fayre.

'You're the Chairman of the so-called Health Committee, aren't you?'

'The Health Awareness Committee. Yes!'

'I hope you practise what you preach,' Frank continued.

'Of course,' Steve said a little hesitantly, remembering Paula's recent admonishments.

'Since when did pie, chips and gravy constitute healthy eating, then?' Frank smirked triumphantly.

'Isn't all eating healthy eating, when one considers the alternative?' Steve retorted.

'Spoken like a true Septic!' Les mock applauded Steve.

Steve went on: 'OK. I try to eat healthily most of the time. It's just that the healthy alternatives in this canteen...'

'Restaurant, please,' Toni butted in.

'OK, restaurant. Anyway, the "healthy alternatives"' – Steve made an inverted commas sign – 'are basically inedible.'

'Most things are, actually, since they put it out to franchise,' Les commented, before asking, 'Don't you think, even so, that it's still a bit much for you to be eating that stuff, as Chair of the Health Awareness Committee?' The last three words were drawn out for maximum sardonic effect.

Steve had to agree, albeit reluctantly. Although the healthy eating, sexual health, exercise and other promotion activities of the Health Awareness Committee were all fine, as far as they went, they were not Steve's main motivation for chairing it. Neither was the fact that it was about the only one of Steve's activities that Stuart and Debbie seemed to approve of (maybe this was the secret route to the coveted company car!). Nor, Dear Reader, was the presence on the committee of five attractive women.

His main passion (as they liked to say at BCG) was mental health, or stress as it was known back then. He had suffered his own share of it, mainly a tendency to OCD, for which he blamed 'Old BCG'. (He and a primary schoolfriend had discovered a cache of mercury during the holidays and had blithely played with it, oblivious to the risks.) He seemed to be the only person on site who seemed to realise that the New BCG was driving everyone mad. Whether it was the prevailing ultra-cautious culture or the ever-present threat of redundancy, Steve was determined to do something about it.

Chapter 12: 'Sex On The Beach'

Steve's Ford Mondeo finally pulled up outside a two-up two-down semi-detached ex-council house. Steve walked from his car into Karen's home, one arm around her and the bottle of Malibu in the other.

Let's fast forward to the morning after, shall we?

Steve found himself waking up naked, entwined with Karen in a spoons configuration. They were both hungover.

'And don't you go sticking that thing up my bum' was all Karen could say.

'Oh, sorry, erm, Karen.' He remembered her name just in time. 'It's just a morning thing.'

'You mean you don't really fancy me? You'd have that smile on your face, whether I was here next to you or not?'

'No. No. No, sorry. I didn't mean it that way. Remind me where the toilet is?'

Steve shuffled out of Karen's boudoir, wearing her ill-fitting dressing gown. On the landing, he encountered a lady in her early 60's with her hair in rollers and a distinct glint in her eye.

'Apologies. I'm not very suitably dressed, am I?' Steve stuttered.

'Hello. I'm Isa, Karen's mam. Pleased to meet you.' Isa held out her hand.

Steve hastily wiped his hand on Karen's cotton dressing gown and gripped on tight to the parting with the other, then shook hands with Isa.

'Er, pleased to meet you. I'm Steve.'

'I heard you and our Karen coming in last night, but I didn't want to interrupt you.' She smirked at Steve. 'I could hear that you were getting friendly.'

'Oh. OK. Thanks. I must dash.' Steve blushed brightly.

'OK. See you soon, my love.' Isa carried on her way.

Steve returned to bed and resumed sidling up to Karen.

Karen was playing *Things Can Only Get Better* on a CD machine to drown out any 'visitor noises'.

'Bloody Amen to that!' was all Steve could say, before he was jumped on by a devil child.

'Meet my little angel daughter, Charlotte.' Karen said laconically.

Charlotte fixed Steve with an evil stare. Her eyes went amber like at the end of 'Angel Heart'.

'Bag of shite! Bag of shite! What is this bag of shite doing in our bed, Mummy?' the devil child enquired.

'This is Uncle Stephen,' Karen tried to mollify the child. This did not stop Charlotte from using Steve as a human trampoline.

'Get off him at once, Charlotte!' Karen shouted.

'Shan't!' Charlotte cried out.

Happily, Isa popped her head round the door. This had an immediate calming effect on the child. 'Are yers goin' to get dressed for your nana now, petal?'

The child stopped bouncing on Steve.

'Nana's got a new Kellogg's variety pack!' Isa added.

'I want the Coco Pops before anyone else gets them!' the child cried out. 'None of that shite Muesli that you try to feed me, mummy!' she added, before running out of the door.

'I do try.' sighed Karen.

Steve cuddled up to her closer. His early morning tumescence was still all too apparent.

'Oh! Alright then, but be quick! We've both got work to go to.' Karen hissed.

The next thing that Steve could remember was Karen's alarm going off at 8.15. Horror of horrors! He had fallen asleep on the job.

'Oh. Oh. Sorry, Karen. Too many late nights,' Steve explained. 'What time is it?'

'A quarter past eight. I need to get ready for work, so don't be getting any ideas about finishing what you started,' Karen said sternly.

A dejected Steve was forced to disengage. 'Shit the bed! I've got to get up for work too. I'll just about get there in time.'

'Oh. You couldn't give me lift to work, could you?'

Steve groaned inwardly. 'Where's that?'

'Marske-by-the-sea. I work for Clough, Day, Hardwick and Mannion solicitors. I thought I'd told you all this last night.'

'Oh, so you did.' *Only a nine-mile detour, I suppose,* Steve thought to himself before announcing, 'Alright then. Better get on.'

A still-naked Steve was just getting out of the bed when the door opened.

An unabashed Isa entered the room, carrying a metal tray.

'I thought I'd bring yous two a nice cup of tea.'

'Oh. Thanks very much, Isa,' Steve said as he retreated hastily back under the duvet.

'Thanks, mam,' Karen said nonchalantly.

'I thought you two would like it good and strong, so that's how I've made it,' said Isa as she put the tray down on the rickety bedside table before departing.

'So you met my mam, already?'

'Yes, on the landing, when I went to the bathroom.'

'Ho. Ho. That was good timing!'

'Yes. Suspiciously so.'

'Ay. She likes to check out the talent, she does. No secrets between me and my mam, you know.'

The bedside phone rang.

Steve heard Karen saying. 'Oh. Right, Di. Really? Well, no, it can't be helped, and I hope you're alright.'

Steve could overhear murmured conversation on the other end of the line.

'It's perfectly OK. I'll make sure that Tracy gets to school. You just concentrate on getting yourself better.'

There was further murmured conversation on the other end of the line.

'OK then, bye. We'll be round in 20 minutes,' Karen promised.

Steve could hear a murmured bye on the other end, before Karen turned to him.

'That was Di. She took bad in the night. Been on the toilet ever since she got back from running the others back to Peterlee.'

'Oh, dear.' Steve tried to sound concerned.

'You don't mind giving Charlotte and her friend Tracy a lift to school, do you?'

Steve was in a quandary. He really needed to get a shower, get dressed and get to work. Still, he felt he had to atone for the failure to finish what he'd started half an hour previously.

'Oh, alright then.' He sighed.

'You don't have to, you know.' Karen sensed his reticence.

'OK. OK. Not a problem,' he said (ever the gent).

Steve was interrupted by the sight and sound of Charlotte coming running in, crying.

'Mummy. Mummy. Mummy.'

'There, there, petal!'

'I see that the bag of shite is still here!'

'Now then, you know his name is Steve, and he's going to help me and Nana get you to school.'

Charlotte shrieked, 'What, me, get in his car?!! He could be a nonce!! I want him checked out first!'

'Now then, my sweet, we don't have time to do that. Anyway, I'll be there with you – and we're picking up Tracy.'

Charlotte was not to be appeased. 'He could be a nutter. Drive us off Hunt Cliff. We could all die, mummy!'

'I'm sure he won't. Will you, Steve?' Karen tried to reassure Charlotte.

Steve shook his head and smiled wanly.

Charlotte remained implacable. 'This is child abuse. I'm going to report you. Have you never heard of stranger danger, you ignorant bitch?'

'Charlotte Summers, you are getting in that car. So go and get dressed. That's final!' Karen demanded in vain.

'Shan't. Shan't. Shan't.'

'You'll do as you're told!' Karen was becoming increasingly desperate.

'I'm going to ring my dad! Get him to take me away from here and my strumpet of a mother!' Charlotte threatened.

Isa walked in and cuddled the child.

'There. There now. Are you going to be a good girl for your Nana?

A now calming-down Charlotte eventually nodded her head.

'I'll do it this once, but I want a full police check before I get in a car with that horrid, smelly man again,' Charlotte reluctantly agreed, before adding, 'I bet he's got a small cock and all!'

'Oh. No, he hasn't!' Karen and Isa cried out inadvertently in unison.

Steve couldn't help smiling at this much-needed boost to his ego as Isa led Charlotte off to get changed.

'That's the nicest thing anybody's ever said about me,' Steve whispered into Karen's ear. 'Are you a fan of Sex in the City?'

Karen nodded enthusiastically.

'Just call me "Big" then, eh?' Steve smiled slyly.

'Well, I'm glad you're happy about that. Sorry about all the kerfuffle just now. I don't know what's come over our Charlotte. She's not normally like this.'

'Yeah, right,' muttered an unconvinced Steve as he made for the shower.

It was nearly nine o'clock when Steve's car finally dropped Charlotte and Tracy off at their junior school.

Charlotte turned round and flicked a departing V Sign at Steve as he and Karen drove off.

Steve was looking anxiously at his watch as his car fought its way through the early morning traffic when Karen's mobile rang.

Karen could hear Ros and Julie on a conference phone from their Call Centre in Peterlee.

'Oh hello, to what do I owe the pleasure?' Karen said, not without irony.

Julie got straight to the point. 'We want all the gory details from last night, don't we, pet?'

'But I'm in the car with him. Can't talk right now,' Karen protested.

'Yer have to! We're on a 10-minute break. Julie persuaded the boss to let us use the conference room, so it's now or never,' Ros insisted.

'Ay. Got a soft spot for me, he has,' Julie interjected.

'Not so soft from what I hear!' Ros cackled loudly.

'You shouldn't talk about Colin like that,' Julie protested before returning to the interrogation. 'Come on, Karen, spill the beans. Did yer...?'

'Oh, alright, then. Yes.'

Steve squirmed in his seat as he propelled the Mondeo towards Marske.

'How many times, then?' Ros needed to know.

'Two and a half,' was Karen's cryptic reply.

Steve looked decidedly puzzled.

'What do you mean, two and a half?' Julie was equally mystified.

'Ah nah (I know).' Ros got the drift. 'Fell asleep on the job, man, didn't he?'

'I couldn't possibly...' Karen tried to maintain a modicum of decorum as Steve blushed ever brighter.

'Ee. Fellahs. What are they like?' Julie concluded.

'I bet he's a right dorty hoond though, but,' Ros suggested.

'He's Oxford-educated, you know,' Karen protested.

'That's even worse. Even dortier imaginations. That's what an education does for yer,' Julie countered.

Ros reminisced. 'Ay. I slept with a Cambridge man once.'

'Bet he had a dark blue vein, though but.' Julie sniggered.

'Porterhouse blue, no less!' Ros sniggered back.

'Was that the one that gave you chlamydia?' Julie enquired.

Steve tried to keep his eyes fixed on the road ahead as the Mondeo neared the salubrious seaside town of Marske.

'Ay, it was. On a Conference in Durham, he was,' Ros agreed.

Karen was tiring of the conversation, which was increasingly bypassing her. 'I'm going to have to go in a minute.'

Julie continued to interrogate Ros about her scholarly encounter. 'Was that the night you went commando?'

'Ay, I gave him a bit of a Sharon Stone flash. The rest is history, like.'

'Couldn't wait to get into your non-existent knickers, could he?

Karen made another attempt to end the conversation as the car passed the Ship Inn. 'I'll really have to go now.'

'Are you alright, then?' Julie suddenly became solicitous.

'Yes. He's driving me to work.'

'That's good. We were concerned about you, weren't we, Julie?' It was Ros's turn to play the caring friend.

'Yes. I'm fine, just fine,' Karen said.

This caused some alarm bells to go off in Steve's head. In his experience, women, starting with his mother, only used that expression when they were anything but fine. Well, he had fallen asleep on the job, hadn't he? A lot of women would have found that pretty insulting, never mind unromantic.

He pulled the car up outside Karen's workplace.

'I'm going to have to ring off now. Bye.'

'Bye, Karen!' Ros and Julie said in unison.

'And don't let him drop off next time,' Ros added.

Karen rang off and leaned over to kiss Steve goodbye.

'Er, so it's alright about me falling asleep on the job?' he blurted out.

Karen simply put her finger to his lips and kissed him again, before getting out of the car. Inside the office, metaphorical curtains twitched.

Steve drove away feeling that a weight had been lifted from his shoulders (well, maybe not precisely that part of his anatomy). Never mind that he was running late for work. He would man up and take the lift this time. One hundred and twenty-nine days of sexual frustration had finally come to an end!

The afternoon at work proved to be happily unexceptional. Steve managed to avoid Stuart all day and left promptly at 4pm, as was his wont on a Friday.

He had, however, found time to compose an email to his hero. There was a matter that had been burning in his mind that he felt he needed to bring up, now that they were mutual correspondents. Such was its urgency that he switched to email mode so that the recipient would get to see it all the quicker.

Dear Tony

Thank you for your kind reply to my last letter. I'm glad to hear of your shared concern about health and safety matters. As you should know, it is of paramount importance in what is still our largest local employer – the chemical industry.

I have to say, however, that I was disappointed to see you bounding up the middle of a flight of stairs at a recent European Summit meeting. Not only were you almost running, but you were also not holding the handrail. Maybe it did look energetic and dynamic on telly, but you should know that slips, trips and falls are the biggest single cause of accidents in the chemical industry, and furthermore, that for every 4000 lost time accidents, there is a potential Bhopal or a Chernobyl.

As a role model to the nation, I think you should set an example to the rest of us. Maybe you could mention it and apologise next time you are on Question Time? By so doing, you may save countless lives...

Steve

Chapter 13 – 'Quiz Night'

It was Friday night. A freshened-up Steve found himself in his village pub, as was his wont on a normal weeknight. Normally, he sought out the fleshpots of Teesside on a weekend, but the Chairman had summoned him for reasons that remained undisclosed.

Although officially called the Dog and Gun, the pub was better known to locals as simply 'The Dog'. The place had seen better days, as had most of the clientele. There were tablecloths and menus on the tables, in an effort to convince punters that this was some sort of upmarket gastro pub, but the fading green curtains and the grease stains on the ceiling told another story. A new landlady, Mary, had recently taken the place over, ably assisted by her twin sister Alex. Although the advent of two attractive redheaded young women on the scene had caused a temporary upsurge in custom, the inescapable problem remained that the place needed a lot of money spending to restore it to its former glory. Mary and Alex were broke.

'Good evening, Steve. How are you keeping?' Mary asked, as her sister hovered in the background.

'Ah, good evening, Alex. How are you?' Steve replied.

'I'm Mary, remember?'

'Sorry, Mary. I always get you two mixed up,' Steve said as he turned towards Alex, before hastily adding, 'Hi Alex.'

'Hi Steve!' Steve was not the most observant of men, but he couldn't help noticing a meaningful glance coming his way from Alex.

'Anyway, what'll you be having? Your usual?' Mary interrupted Steve's reverie.

'Yes, a pint of Strongarm please.' The words had hardly parted from Steve's lips when Geoff walked in.

'Good evening, Colonel. Timed that well, didn't I?'

'And a pint of lager for him.' Steve said resignedly.

Steve paid for the drinks. They walked from the bar and sat down at a small table.

'So, you wanted to see me...' Steve said uncertainly.

'First of all, tell me about last night, then...' Geoff rubbed his hands with glee.

'Well, I shagged her, I did. Gave her a right good seeing to, despite being pissed as a fart,' Steve said with a little too much bravado.

'But you were driving...' Geoff chided him.

'We finished off that bottle of Malibu, then I spent the night.'

'Oh, well done. I'll put the flag out for you.'

'There's just one thing...' Steve looked anxious.

'Ye-es?' Geoff drew closer.

'I didn't bother with a blob. I was a bit too pissed for all that sort of stuff.'

'Well, boys will be boys. What's the problem?' Geoff was genuinely perplexed.

'I could have got her up the stick, for all I know,' Steve conjectured.

'Well, you do get into some scrapes,' Geoff observed, before commenting, 'You will insist on shagging the young ones. Mind you, I don't blame you. They get crusty flanges as they get older, you know.

'What do you mean?' Steve pulled a face.

'Well, the minge goes all yellow. You don't really want to be going down for the gravy, when it comes to that. Avoid old boilers. Take it from me...'

'Thanks for the tip.' Steve was genuinely horrified. He tried to change the subject.

'You wanted to talk to me about something. Top secret, you said on the phone.'

'Oh. Yes. That!' Geoff leaned forward conspiratorially, fixing Steve in the eye. 'Well, you know we're struggling to get teams out at the moment.'

'Oh. Yeah. Competing league fixtures, weekends away, christenings, the dreaded barbeque...'

'Yes, all of those things, but you've left one major factor out!' The Chairman grabbed hold of Steve's knee to emphasise his point.

'What's that?' Steve asked.

'Our useless...'

It was at this point that Geoff's stream of consciousness was interrupted by Ron, the Outcasts' captain, walking in with his golden retriever dog Jason.

'Good evening, gents,' Ron said breezily. 'I'm not interrupting anything?' he added as Geoff recoiled away from Steve's knee.

Ron was a world-weary character in his fifties, always smartly dressed, still retaining a south London accent despite three decades up north. He had been a part-time footballer, then football manager, whilst retaining a salesman's role. He had progressed from bricks to patio doors. Recently, his world had been torn apart by his wife of twenty-five years setting up home with a local bookie. Recent disappointments had not caused him to lose his sardonic sense of humour, however.

Steve sighed and looked over at Geoff, who was still guarding a nearly full pint. He finally got up on his feet. 'What can I get you, Ron?' he uttered reluctantly.

'The usual. Pint of lager, please, Stephen,' Ron replied with a smile.

As Steve slowly got to his feet, he stopped, unable to help himself asking, 'What or who was useless, by the way, Geoff?'

A swift kick in the shins was delivered by way of reply.

Steve let out a gasp of pain.

Jason responded with an admonitory bark. 'Are you sure that I wasn't interrupting anything, gents?'

'No. I was just making sure he got your pint in, before you died of thirst,' Geoff commented drily.

Once Steve had hobbled his way to the bar, he found that Alex was waiting to serve him.

'A pint of lager for Ron please, Mary – sorry, er, Alex.'

Alex winked at Steve. 'One day you'll get it right. I hope you don't mix up names with all those girlfriends of yours!'

'Oh. No. No. Not yet, anyway.'

'So you've got a new one then, I hear.'

'How did you know that? I've only just met her.'

'You should talk more quietly. I overheard what you were saying.'

'Not all of it, I hope.' Steve looked concerned.

'Your secret's safe with me. Bit of a one, aren't you?'

'Dunno. Until the age of forty, I'd only been with two women.'

At this point Geoff called over, 'And one of them was his mother!'

Alex smiled. 'And now you're playing catch-up, are you?'

'No. No, it's quality, not quantity that counts,' Steve protested.

'I'll believe you. Thousands wouldn't.' Alex paused for a moment. 'So how many women have you had since your fortieth birthday?' Alex asked slyly.

Steve paused to think and started to count on his fingers, hesitating at times and retracting the relevant finger.

Finally, the answer came. 'Only about six.'

'Only about six!' Alex pulled a face. 'You're such a tart!'

'Well, it's like buses. They all come at once.' Steve blushed brightly as he realised his repeated faux pas. 'Pardon the pun.'

Alex giggled.

'People forget the long dry spells – up to six months, a year even,' Steve continued.

'My heart bleeds for you.' Alex laughed mockingly.

At this point Ron shouted over, 'Mind you don't get blue balls, young man! Come on, where's my pint?'

'Oh, sorry, Ron. Here it is.'

Steve walked back to the table hurriedly.

'That'll be £1.80, please,' Alex called after him. 'By the way, what's her name?' she enquired when Steve returned to the bar.

'Oh, it's...' Steve had to think for a moment. 'Karen!'

'Well, make sure you bring her here, then. Mary and I want to check her out,' Alex concluded.

'Yes, we certainly do.' Mary had sidled up to Alex behind the bar.

'Oh, alright then. But it's a bit early doors...' Steve said hesitantly, before returning to his chair.

'You might need to get to know her rather quickly, from what we've been hearing.' Alex giggled.

Steve blushed bright red and hurried back to his table, where an impatient Geoff was waiting.

'What was all that about? You were ages.' Geoff was unimpressed.

'Just getting the third degree from Alex and Mary,' Steve explained.

'Why? What have you been up to, son?' Ron couldn't help asking.

'Geoff will tell you.' Steve smiled.

'You know what, Ron?' Geoff asked theatrically before pausing. 'He deserted me for the pleasures of the flesh!'

'Truly shocking behaviour!' Ron commented ironically, knowing what would have happened if roles had been reversed. 'Coffin Dodgers, was it?'

'Yes. Deserted me, he did. Disappeared off to a house of ill repute in Nunthorpe.'

'Well, there's plenty of them there,' Ron had to agree before turning to Steve. 'Steve, son. What have I told you about Ladies from the East?'

'She's nice,' Steve retorted, before a hesitant 'I think...'

Ron continued his questioning. 'And you left your mate to fend for himself?' he added, already sensing that there would political consequences later that weekend.

'Yes. Serious matter, that. There could be repercussions...'

'Yes indeed. Chairman. About time young Stephen got The Potty Award.' Ron, who was not a great fielder, was getting his retaliation in first.

'What, again???' Steve was dismayed. 'But I thought it was for bad fielding.'

Ron and Geoff shook their heads in unison.

'One day, you'll learn, son,' Ron commented sadly.

This was the cue for Geoff to put some pressure on Ron. 'Have you got a team out for Sunday, by the way?'

'I'm working on it, Geoff. One or two lads still to check on.'

'You mean that you haven't got a team...' Geoff snarled.

'Don't worry, it'll all be sorted by Sunday.' Ron was unconcerned.

'Well, I may have a player for you,' Geoff volunteered.

'Oh, do us a favour, Geoff! I remember the last time you helped out!' Ron was unimpressed.

'I gave you my book of contacts!' Geoff sounded surprised.

'Yeah, these so-called contacts had moved, retired or, for the most part, fallen out with you!' Ron paused for breath. 'Then there was the one who'd facking died!' he concluded.

'Who was that?' Geoff interjected.

'Can't facking remember. Didn't half upset his widow, though.' Ron sniffed.

'What did?'

'Me calling, asking if he wanted to play cricket on Sunday. Distraught, she was. Hardly surprising, really. Would have been his 80th birthday, she said.'

Geoff folded his arms. 'Well, you can't win 'em all,' he concluded. 'Anyway, this one's keen. And useful, I suspect...'

'What's his bleedin' name, then?'

Geoff lapsed into his habit of uttering malapropisms. 'Perverse Raymond.'

'And how did you meet him?'

'He's a taxi driver...'

'Taxi diver? You don't half pick 'em!' Ron rolled his eyes 'That's no good. They might change his shift at the last moment. I'm not holding my facking breath on that one. Anyway, how did you meet him?'

'He was the fellow who took me home after young Steve here left me to my fate in the Coffin Dodgers car park.'

'I don't think...' Steve protested, before he was interrupted by a friend of Geoff's walking in.

Geoff looked up. 'Now then, Stan, what are you doing here?'

Stan was a local TV celebrity, around Geoff's age – a corpulent, yet charismatic man wearing a blazer and sporting a bushy, black moustache. Much like Geoff, actually, apart from the moustache. As he was instantly recognisable to the majority of inhabitants of Teesside, his entry had caused something of a stir in the pub, which had filled up rapidly.

'Alright, you old bugger. I'm doing the quiz; it's for charity. Thought I'd find you miscreants here.' Stan shook hands with all three of the Outcasts contingent. This did not go unnoticed by the occupants of the other tables.

Stan pointed to a banner. 'Didn't you see that over the bar?'

Sure enough, there was a sign saying 'Charity Quiz Night. Quiz Master: Stan Beardsmore, star of local TV and radio. Cash prizes. Meat draw. Raffle.'

'Oh yeah... I remember now. Must have had my mind on other things,' Steve mused.

'And we know what that is!' Geoff volunteered. 'The whiskers! Can't keep his mind off it, can't Steve. Tash happy, he is Stan, tash happy!!

'You're only jealous,' Ron muttered cynically.

Stan shook Steve's hand again. 'Good to see you, Steve,' Stan said, before adding with a wink, 'Mind you don't go blind!'

'I wouldn't do that. You don't know where it's been!' Geoff could not help himself from commenting.

Stan laughed and went off to the bar.

Ron was not planning on staying. 'I was just planning on having a pint, then scarpering.'

'Go on, stay with us, man. What have you got to go back to, since your missus buggered off with your best mate?' Geoff was insistent.

'You don't have a personal computer, do you?' Ron enquired, by way of changing the subject.

'What's that got to do with it?' Geoff was incredulous.

'I'm in correspondence with a very lovely lady in Sweden.'

'She can wait. Make yourself unavailable, that's what I always say.'

The conversation was interrupted by Stan's voice coming over the PA.

'Hello and welcome to our special charity quiz night. All entrance fees will go to charity. We'll have a special raffle, but there will still be a prize for the winning team. Tonight, we are having a special prize of £100 – yes, £100, ladies and gentlemen.'

'Uh. Uh. That's why The Ayatollah's here.' Steve had spotted something.

'The Ayatollah? Who's that?' Geoff and Ron enquired in unison.

'See that dark haired gentleman over there, with his anorak mate?'

Geoff and Ron both nodded.

'He's a notorious quiz "pro". Goes round all the local pubs. Focuses on catchment areas of sink comprehensives. An unhappy by-product of Shirley Williams, you might say. They say he's been on "Brain of Britain".'

'Why not "Who wants to be a millionaire?"' Ron asked.

'No, he's far too much of a loser to make any real money,' Steve concluded. 'Sips a half of Coca-Cola all night. He's just here for the cash.'

'Yes; looks like a bit of a crook.' Geoff peered over his half-moon reading glasses.

'Got banned from the Star, he did.'

'Why's that?'

'They give beer tokens as prizes.' Steve explained. 'No good to him, of course, so he tried selling them outside the pub. Miserable git!'

Geoff was not to be outdone. 'Well, if it's skulduggery you're after, you need to watch the team over there and all.' He pointed to a group of five: mum and dad, plus grandmother, plus daughter, plus friend.

'Why, what do they do?' Ron was intrigued.

'Highly competitive, they are. The old woman volunteers to collect glasses towards the end of the quiz, even though she doesn't work here.'

'What's wrong with that? Sounds very public-spirited,' Ron protested.

'She does it to spy on everyone's answers,' Geoff explained.

'Really?' Steve managed to take his eyes away from the attractive daughter.

'Yes. Whatever you do. I'll make sure I cover up our answer sheet, when she comes round... Nasty buggers!' Geoff advised, as he peered once again over his reading glasses.

Half an hour later, the quiz was in full motion. Geoff had assumed the role of team scribe and was scribbling down the answer to the previous question, which had caused some intense debate, as Stan asked the next one.

After a mediocre picture round, it soon became obvious that the Outcasts were getting more than a little help from the chair. Questions about horse racing, Millwall football club and little-known cricketers helped to propel the boys to a promising position at half-time.

Stan announced that he would come around and collect the answer sheets within five minutes. In the meantime, there would be a break for the raffle and the all-important meat draw.

Mary and Alex came round with raffle and meat draw tickets.

'Fancy some meat, lads? I bet you like some more red meat, eh, Steve?' Alex winked.

Geoff smiled and answered on behalf of the beetroot-faced Steve. 'Oh, very much so. A bit of pork sword never did anyone any harm, did it?'

Steve, Geoff and Ron proceeded to buy various coloured tickets as Doreen of *Ask the Family* sidled up behind them.

'Glasses please, gents,' she chirped, as Geoff hastily covered up the team answer sheet. Jason growled in sympathy.

'I haven't come to check on your answer sheet, you know.' Doreen was indignant.

'Best to be safe. Best to be safe.' Geoff smiled sardonically before turning to Steve. 'Something this young man should be mindful of.'

'We don't cheat,' Doreen said pointedly.

Ron rose to the bait. 'What do you mean by that?'

'That quizmaster, he's a fellow cricketer, isn't he?'

'Yeah. What about it?' Ron was unimpressed.

'He's fed you the questions. Sussex cricketer indeed! It all seemed very suited to your team.' Doreen then stalked off to the bar to return the empty glasses which she had so altruistically collected.

'OK. Could you swap your answer sheets now please. Then hand them in, when you've finished marking them, and I'll give the answers.'

After he had collected the quiz sheets and his young female assistant had scored them, Stan's baritone voice came booming over the PA system.

Stan continued: 'So, the leading three teams with 1 round to go are, in ascending order...

'In third place, ALPHA KAPPA PSI with twenty-eight points...'

'That's the quiz anoraks,' Steve whispered, as Stan paused.

'In second place is ASK THE FAMILY with twenty-nine points...'

They needed no introduction. Stan paused even longer.

'And in first place is the OUTCASTS with thirty points.'

Geoff gave the thumbs-up to the other two, blithely ignoring the booing sounds coming from the other tables.

Stan then announced the last round.

'And finally... the last round tonight is on fillums.'

Steve was disappointed. 'Not so good on films.'

Stan proceeded to bat on for the Outcasts, asking questions about films that he suspected they knew about. He even got a question in about Steve's beloved Creedence Clearwater Revival ('What was the Dude's favourite band in the Big Lebowski?', if you must know).

Finally, in the name of fairness, Stan relented and asked a question that was not designed to suit the Outcasts. Nonetheless, he expected one of them to know the answer: 'And tonight's final question is... What was Jennifer Gray's character's name in the 1987 film "Dirty Dancing"?'

The other teams started writing down their answers immediately. Ron and Geoff look bewildered.

Steve scratched his head. 'Shit. It's on the tip of my tongue...' It was at that moment that Steve's mobile phone started to ring loudly.

He answered, forgetting that this was a gross breach of quiz etiquette.

'Oh, hi,' Steve replied, then leant over to the members of his team. 'Excuse me a minute.'

Geoff shook his head as Steve walked outside. 'Whiskers mad, he's whiskers mad.'

Once outside, Steve was given the treatment by Karen. 'Why haven't you phoned me tonight, then?'

'Oh, sorry. I lost track of time,' was all he could say in his defence.

'Why's that?'

'There's a quiz on in the Dog tonight. I'd forgotten about it.' If Steve thought that this was a satisfactory reply, he had another think coming.

'Why didn't you invite me to it!?' Karen hissed.

'That's because I'd forgotten about it.' Steve remained logical.

Karen sighed. 'Oh, well. I couldn't have come anyway.'

'Why not?'

'It's mam's bingo night, so she can't babysit.'

'OK. Can I phone you back in a few minutes?' Steve started to feel the time pressure vibes emanating from inside the 'Dog'.

'Why?'

'We're into the last round of the quiz, and I must return to my team.'

'Who's in it, then?' Karen was suspicious.

'Oh, just Geoff and Ron.'

'Who's Ron?'

'Our cricket captain,' Steve explained.

'Oh. Alright then. But you will phone me back, won't you?' Karen conceded.

'Yeah. Just hang on tight, baby.' A lightbulb flashed off in Steve's mind. 'Got it! You're a genius!'

'What are you on about?'

'The answer.'

'What answer?'

'Never mind. Talk to you later...' Steve rang off and dashed back to rejoin his teammates.

'Got it! Got it!' Steve beamed.

'There's a lot of things that you've got,' Geoff said impatiently. 'What do you mean?'

'The answer to the last question.'

'It's too late, mate. We just handed in.' Ron shook his head.

'That's what comes with being distracted. Remember what I said about flying on full tanks yesterday!' Geoff wagged his figure at a retreating Steve, who chased after Alex as she collected the scoresheets.

'Alex, Alex. Can I just have our answer sheet for just one moment?'

'Anything for you, Steve.' Alex smiled.

Steve hastily scribbled 'Baby' for the last question. This did not go unnoticed by the family team, or other interested parties, who looked daggers at him.

'Thanks, Alex,' Steve panted.

'Any time, Steve. Any time.'

Steve returned to the table.

'Who was that on the phone then? TNM by any chance?' Geoff asked.

'What's TNM mean?' Steve never could get Geoff's revolting acronyms first time round.

'The New Minge!' The Chairman did not disappoint. 'Yes. To make things simple, I think I'll refer to her henceforward as Tina.'

'I should have known it would be something rude.' Steve sighed.

'Last of the true romantics is our Geoff.' Ron smirked.

Steve returned to the original question. 'OK. Yes, it was Karen. She was wondering why I hadn't invited her here.'

Geoff was incredulous. 'You weren't seriously contemplating that, were you? On a lads' night out?

'Yeah. Why not?' It was Steve's turn to be surprised.

'You need to set the ground rules from the start. Two nights a week, MAXIMUM! That's all you should give 'em. The rest of the time you should be out enjoying yourself with your mates,' Geoff explained.

'Don't listen to him, son,' Ron counselled.

Geoff carried on regardless. 'Or perusing other opportunities.' Geoff also had a talent for malapropisms.

Steve was smug. 'Ha. I don't need to do that now.'

'Listen to me. You always need at least one on the subs' bench. Remember the six months you went without a dip. Howling at the moon you were by the end of it! Out of control! Out of control!' Geoff rolled his eyes theatrically to reinforce his favourite saying.

'I wasn't that bad,' Steve protested.

'Oh, yes you were!' Ron and Geoff were in unison.

'As I remember, that all ended when you had the one night stand with the fish fryer from Billingham. Gave a new meaning to the term "vinegar strokes," that did.'

'Alright. Alright.' Steve winced at the memory.

'Oh dear. Conduct rather unbecoming an officer and a gentleman.' Ron sniggered.

'Yes, indeed! What would the BCG think of this behaviour?' Geoff added

'Hmm. Not sure if they'd be too shocked, from some of the stories I've heard.' Steve was unable to explain further before they were interrupted by the quizmaster.

'OK. Ladies and gentlemen, we have a winner!

A frisson of anticipation went round the pub.

'Firstly, I'll read out the answers to the last round.'

Stan made his way through the answers until he got to the last question.

'And finally the answer to the last question is... I think nearly all of you got this. BABY.'

Stan paused for a few seconds. 'OK. I'll read out the top three teams.'

'Well, actually, we don't have a third place... in joint second place with thirty-eight points are Alpha Kappa Psi and Ask The Family.'

The announcement was met with polite applause.

'So, the winners of the £100 cash prize are The Outcasts with thirty-nine points!'

Steve punched the air. Ron and Geoff took turns to shake his hand.

'Could I have a representative of the winning team come up to the front, please?' Stan's voice boomed out.

Ron pushed Steve forward. 'Go on, son. You were the star!'

Steve eagerly got up to collect the money. To his surprise, there was widespread booing round the pub, including shouts of 'Cheat! Cheat!' from the family table. Steve shook hands with Stan as the booing rose to a crescendo.

As Steve made his way back to his table, Doreen almost barged him out of the way in her rush to remonstrate with Stan.

'Did you see that? What sour grapes!' Steve gasped as he finally made it back to the Outcasts' table.

'Never mind that. Hand out the cash.' Geoff held out his hand.

'OK. Thirty for you and thirty for Ron and thirty for me. What to do with the rest of it?' Steve doled out the cash.

'Get another round in, son. Mine's a double.' Ron made the appropriate gesture.

'Go on. And me.' Geoff entered into the spirit of things.

'Congratulations. What'll you be having, then?' Mary asked once Steve got to the bar.

'Three double whiskies and whatever you and Alex would like.'

'Thanks. We like brandy. That'll be £10 please.'

'Oh, that worked out nicely...' Steve smiled.

'Like your questions tonight,' Mary commented wryly, observing the looks of opprobrium around the pub.

Steve blithely took the drinks back to the table. 'There you are, gents.' He placed the drinks on the table.

Steve finally sat down and raised his glass. 'To victory!' The Outcasts clinked glasses as Jason barked out his approval.

They were interrupted by Stan's voice.

'I'm sorry, ladies and gentlemen, but there have been some serious allegations of cheating by our winning team...'

'What???' Steve was incredulous.

'Yes. May I remind everyone that use of mobiles during the quiz is strictly forbidden and results in instant disqualification.'

'But it was my girlfriend...' Steve shouted across.

Stan shook his head. 'I'm afraid I'm going to have to ask you to hand back your winnings to me, and then we'll have a tie break between the two teams finishing second.'

'Never!' Steve shouted, looking across at the other team members for support.

Ron demurred. 'Better go and give it back son.'

Ron and Geoff handed Steve their winnings before sending him up to the Quizmaster's table to boos and slow-handclapping from all around the pub.

Steve handed over £90.

'I'm afraid you're £10 short.' Stan shook his head after counting out the money. 'Soon burnt a hole in your pocket, didn't it?'

Steve had to dig deep into his wallet. Fortunately, there was still £5 left over from the previous evening's 'Coffin Dodgers Float'. Unfortunately, that was all he could find in the wallet. He had to go through his jacket and trouser pockets for what seemed an eternity until he found the required amount.

'Bloody cheats. Ed Giddins indeed!' Doreen shouted out as he headed back to the table.

'It was my girlfriend on the phone, you know,' Steve retorted.

'What's that got to do with the price of fish!? How do we know she wasn't feeding you answers?'

Steve could stand it no more. 'Because I'm clever and you're not!' he said very indignantly, with his hands on his hips.

'I'll have you know I was a teacher!' It was Doreen's turn to be indignant.

'So what?!' Steve had never regarded teachers as being particularly clever.

Stan's voice boomed out. 'Calm down, please. We'll have the tie-break question in just a minute.'

Steve finally sat down with his friends.

'I hope you've learned your lesson. What did I tell you about ignoring their calls when you're not tashing them?' Geoff advised.

Ron had another angle on things. 'She must have given you the answer, the way you came running in.'

'No, but it did come to me when I was talking to her.' Steve admitted.

'How?' Ron probed further.

'I said "talk to you later baby" when I rang off.'

'So you wouldn't have got that answer if you hadn't taken her call?' Geoff said thoughtfully.

'Not necessarily. It was on the tip of my tongue,' Steve confessed.

'Not the only thing that's been on the tip of your tongue recently, I'll be bound.' Geoff smirked.

'In other words, they got you bang to rights, son,' Ron concluded.

'Not necessarily. I am innocent!' Steve sulked.

The conversation was interrupted by Stan announcing the tie break question.

'Here is our tie break question. In what year was test cricketer Mark Ramprakash born?'

This was met by groans from the Outcasts and outrage from Ask the Family.

Geoff shook his head. 'Good old Stan, trying to help us till the end.'

'Bloody hell. We would have won anyway.' Steve could not believe his bad luck.

'Let's go before we get lynched,' Ron concluded as he gathered up Jason's lead and led them out of the pub.

Chapter 14 – 'Funky Weekend'

Steve disobeyed the Chairman's instructions and spent Saturday with Karen. Worse than that, he turned down the opportunity to attend a cricketers' speakers night in Guisborough, leaving Geoff unimpressed. What could have made him turn down the counter attraction of an evening of anecdotes from ex-Yorkshire cricketer Doug Winston?

Mercifully, Isa took care of Charlotte while Karen and Steve got down to some serious shagging. *How come you remember so few details?* Steve mused afterwards, despite the intensity of the experience at the time. The sights, the sounds, the feelings – not to mention the smells. What Steve could remember was that Karen was into doggies but didn't go too far off the beaten track otherwise. Anything around her rather lovely bottom was strictly verboten, apart from the doggies, of course. As for the action scenes, it was more Nine and a Half Minutes than *Nine and a Half Weeks*. Not that Steve minded too much, after such a drought. But had he made her come? This became a new anxiety for Steve. There had been much moaning and groaning, but...

Steve never had the heart to ask her about that, nor did he broach the vexed question of contraception or unplanned pregnancy.

By six o'clock on Saturday night, they both needed to slow down a bit, so the evening was spent in Tony's Chinese restaurant. So far, so good. Unfortunately, duty called on the following day.

As Steve lay entwined with Karen in her bed, his mobile phone rang.

'Oh, hello, Geoff. How are you this fine Sunday morning?' Steve said cheerfully.

'Thought I'd interrupt you from polishing your rocket.'

'Oh, no need for that at the moment.' Steve grinned over at Karen, as she lay in the bed.

'So you've got company. I hope you're not ignoring my good advice about making yourself unavailable.' Geoff's voice was far too audible.

'Yes. Yes.' Steve would have stepped outside the room, if he hadn't been naked.

'So you're still worried about getting her up the stick, are you?' Geoff asked.

Steve looked over nervously at Karen. 'Anyway, to more important matters: have you got the kit for this afternoon?' Geoff continued.

'Yes, I've got the kit,' Steve said wearily.

'And the potty...?

'Yes, the kit – and the potty.' Steve yawned.

'Not that you should worry about that. You've been fielding very well lately. I think maybe it's Neil's turn today.'

'Yes, good idea. He's always good value for money.' Steve put on a Corporal Jones voice. 'Doesn't like it up him, Captain Mainwaring.'

'Yes, indeed. Except for one thing! He answered the call. I managed to get him to come with me to the cricketers' evening.'

'I'm glad you found someone,' Steve answered a little patronisingly.

'That's what mates are for!' Geoff declared ominously. 'And you missed a couple of really good Sir Geoffrey Boycott stories!'

'All the speakers do them, I think you'll find.' Steve was now digging a large hole for himself.

'Well, I can see where your loyalties lie. These things will all be remembered when the potty committee meets.'

'But you just said that I wasn't in any danger!' Steve protested, before noticing some impatient looks coming from the other side of the boudoir. 'Anyway, I'd better get on, then. Bye.'

'Get back on the nest again, you mean? I'll leave you to it. Don't do anything I wouldn't do!'

Steve turned round to see Karen was frowning.

'You must excuse Geoff, he is somewhat... erm... focussed,' Steve explained.

'Well, I was hoping you could condescend to make a whole weekend of it. What are you doing today?'

'Playing cricket, of course. Didn't I tell you?' Steve couldn't believe that something so important had slipped Karen's memory. 'At Great Naughton, remember?' Steve looked across at Karen. Her boobs seemed to jut out towards him in an aggressive manner, all of a sudden.

It was then that Steve made his fatal mistake. 'You don't fancy watching, do you? You can always go and get one of Suggett's ice creams if it gets boring...' After a long pause, he compounded his error. 'You can bring Charlotte along, if you like...'

Chapter 15: 'PMT – Pre-Match Tension'

To be honest, the Outcasts XI for that day was not the strongest team that they had ever put out. Little wonder, when one looked at the abilities of the senior members of the side, AKA 'The Committee'. The duties of this august body were somewhat mysterious, apart from the weekly duty of determining who received the dreaded potty award. More of that later...

The Committee

1. Ron Crabtree (Capt.)

Although Ron had been a professional footballer, his cricketing ability had never nearly matched that. In the autumn of his career, he was content to captain the Outcasts. This meant that when he did bat, he never lasted long, and commanded operations from first slip – ideal for someone with a hip replacement, but not for bowlers at his command.

1. Geoff Huckstead (Chairman)

A fiery fast bowler in his youth, Geoff was now an adhesive opening batsman. Very classical in his approach, his technique had been honed by long hours practising in his back garden. Unfortunately, he was increasingly prone to outstaying his welcome in the middle, leaving the lower order to play catch up. His dark and somewhat intimidating presence had caused him to be nicknamed 'The Hooded Crow' by some club members, but never to his face.

1. Neil 'Pifco' Patterson (wicket keeper)

Was a top wicket keeper in his day, but that day had long gone. A natural worrier, which may have explained his premature baldness and his distinct lisp. Liable to stand on his dignity. He had been the Outcasts CC's long-suffering fixtures secretary until a recent fall-out with Ron. Slavishly loyal to the Chairman, who repaid him with endless scorn. Susceptible to admitting the most embarrassing personal details to the Chairman in confidence (the latest bombshell being that he had 'hemowwoids'). These confidences were invariably broadcast to as wide an audience as possible. Watch out, Neil!

1. Dr Amir El-Nile (Ophthalmologist, President, Generous Donor)

Very posh spin bowler in his fifties, injury-prone and very short-sighted for an eye surgeon. Like Neil, slavishly devoted to the Chairman. Great upholder of English traditions, such as the Outcasts' potty award, but not keen in upholding them personally. Very good at bribing himself out of trouble when his fielding let him down, as it often did.

In fact, the majority of the team were over forty, with the Committee all being over fifty. There was even a sexagenarian – Trevor Coey, an Ulsterman in his late sixties, known as 'Private Godfrey', but still more sprightly than many of his younger teammates.

Hopes were therefore pinned on the younger members of the squad, not least the unknown quantity of Pervez. Nonetheless, they considered themselves to be good enough to see off the opposition. The Old Eldonians were after all a bunch of posh southern softies whose main asset was their umpire. The latter being a Yorkshire man, with no connections to the school, but a sufferer from an unjustified admiration for Toffs: an enduring weakness of the lumpen proletariat, as we have found in recent years.

It had not proved to be a very pleasant journey to the Great Naughton ground for Steve and Karen, though little did Steve know that the match would cause relations to take a turn for the worse – much the worse.

Firstly, for Steve, it was match day. It is difficult to describe the gut-churning anxiety that many players, including Steve, feel on the morning of a cricket match.

This was particularly true of specialist batsmen, for whom one ball could effectively end their afternoon – especially if you hated fielding, as Stephen did. It didn't get better with age, either. Happily, Steve had added his donkey drop bowling to his repertoire. The Outcasts gave him an outlet to express this skill, particularly useful when it was necessary to concede quick runs to the opposition. It would, however, have been unfair to brand Steve as a 'declaration bowler', despite the perennial unhelpful shouts of 'Pull out the pin!' from his fielders. He was more than that, as his average of 25 with the ball attested. He was capable of the odd 'Shane Warne' ball that left far superior cricketers dumbfounded. With career best figures of 8-53, he felt that his true talents had been wasted.

But then, there's the yips, which are particularly cruel for left arm slow bowlers. Even the best of them – ask Phil Tufnell or Monty Panesar. The problem is that you are making a circuitous run up to bowl, between the stumps and the umpire, at someone who is not your mirror image, a problem right-handed bowlers habitually have with left-handed batsmen (Ha! Ha!). Steve had had the yips early in his career, and his bowling had been viewed with suspicion by captains ever since. This may have had something to do with the odd ball that was released in the general direction of extra cover. On the subject of cover, there was the leg-side long hop, which had everyone diving for it.

Playing for the Outcasts brought the added jeopardy of the Potty – an instrument of terror, sometimes referred to as Pol Pot. It had been introduced by the Chairman ostensibly to improve the side's fielding. In reality, it was there to humiliate anyone whom Geoff felt to be deserving of it. After the match, all Outcast players would be required to stay behind while the Committee deliberated in a back room (usually at great length) to decide who would be the unworthy winner. (N.B., Dear Reader, that Steve's vice captaincy did not qualify him for a place on said Committee.) Anyone who defied orders by leaving straight after the match would not be asked to play again (a sanction that was becoming increasingly threadbare as recruitment figures dwindled).

Once the imaginary white smoke had billowed from the Committee Room, the Chairman would go to the bar and have a plastic piss pot (signed by a host of cricketing dignitaries, including one legendary all-rounder contemporary of Ian Botham) filled up with at least one pint of beer in full view of the players. Ice cubes would be added, along with a plastic turd acquired on a tour of Blackpool. The Chairman would then give a long speech, laced with inappropriate humour, noting all fielding (and other) misdemeanours, before proudly announcing the winner at the end. This was usually prefaced by a Columboesque 'Oh, I almost forgot' as the intended prey started to breathe more easily. The victim would then have to drink the whole contents of the dreaded vessel in one go, taking as little time as possible, whilst being jeered by both Outcast and Opposition players and hangers-on.

Reactions to the award amongst the players was mixed. Some, such as Nathan Storr, the opener, saw it as simply a free pint. Others would be mildly annoyed, but would succumb with good grace. The largest group would be visibly annoyed and not succumb with good grace. Steve and wicket-keeper Neil belonged to this category. (Guess which group the Chairman favoured?) Those with deep pockets would attempt to bribe themselves out of it (this was allowable – nay, actively encouraged – by the Committee). Most notable of these was Dr Amir El-Nile, whose appalling fielding each week must have cost him very dear. Others simply refused this ritual humiliation and never darkened the Outcasts' doors again.

Steve was therefore not in the most tolerant mood as he drove towards the Hambleton Hills. Charlotte had played up all the way. The offer of a Suggett's ice cream had fallen on deaf ears. Cricket was boring. The countryside was boring. Cows were boring and smelly. Sheep were boring and stupid. Vanilla ice cream was boring. Why couldn't she go for a Big Mac? Why indeed couldn't she just stay at home and play on her PlayStation?

Steve tried hard to suppress his impatience, bristling at her mother's passiveness in the face of the continual verbal onslaughts, punctuated with a vocabulary worthy of a celebrity chef. He couldn't help feeling that he'd made a mistake in inviting them both along. (You were certainly right there, Stephen. LOL!)

Finally, they arrived at the cricket ground. The Chairman was already there, having cadged a lift off Neil.

'So, where's Mrs Patterson this afternoon? She normally likes to come and see you play,' Geoff enquired.

'Oh, Mawianne? She'll be along soon. Amir picked her up,' Neil replied with his trademark lisp.

Geoff's eyebrows arched. 'Oh, really? How's that?'

Steve could not help but pick up a certain insinuation in the Chairman's interrogation.

'She doesn't finish teaching her Sunday school class until 12.30. It's near where Amir lives.'

'Hmm. I see...' Geoff's eyebrows arched again.

It was now clear to Steve that Geoff was hinting at something, although poor old Neil seemed oblivious to this.

They were interrupted by the arrival of the aforementioned Amir with Mrs Patterson.

Amir bounded out of the car. 'Mr Chairman. What a pleasure and a privilege it is to see you. And you, honourable vice-captain.' Amir paused to size up Karen. 'And who is this vision of pulchritude that you have brought along with you?' Amir enquired of Steve, who duly introduced Karen to him. Charlotte stuck her tongue out and told him to fuck off before he could go any further.

'And you, our most diligent fixture secretary.' Amir moved seamlessly on to Neil.

'Ex-fixtures secretary. Won's doing it now, wemember?' Neil bridled.

Geoff changed the subject. 'How was the Sunday school class, then, Marianne?'

> Mrs Patterson, a comely lady with dyed blonde hair and a floral dress, blushed. 'Oh. Very good, thanks, Geoffrey.'

'I hope you taught 'em about the evils of pleasures of the flesh,' he added.

'Oh, no. We don't do that sort of thing anymore.' Marianne shook her head.

'More's the pity. Give them a bit of fire and brimstone. That's what I say.' Geoff was a stern moralist when it came to other people.

'Oh, no. None of that these days.'

'Well, I do hope that you give them the Ten Commandments.'

'Oh. Yes, we still do that.'

'Especially Commandment Seven!?'

'Which one's that?' Neil asked.

'Oh. It's that rather inconvenient one about not committing adultery,' Amir added helpfully. 'Not applicable to me, of course.' Amir smiled, before adding hastily, 'of course, my religion does not approve of it either.'

Mrs Patterson squirmed. 'No. No. We don't go into that sort of detail. They're only about eight years old, you know.'

Geoff was unmoved. 'Learn the little buggers early. That's what I say.'

At this point, the other players started to arrive and headed for the dressing room.

Chapter 16: 'TMI – The Match Itself'

Once most of the players were changed, Ron went out to the wicket and won the toss. As the Outcasts' openers (Peter and Nathan on this day) went out to bat, they were heartily clapped onto the field by a group of players wearing gaily coloured harlequin caps.

Only ten Outcasts players were present. Pervez had not yet arrived. This led to heated discussions on the boundary edge between Ron and Geoff, with Amir attempting vainly to act as mediator, until a clapped-out taxi arrived noisily. Out jumped Pervez, in immaculately pressed whites with the Pakistani test logo, his shirt collar turned up Geoffrey Boycott style, and a green Pakistani team cricket cap.

'Well, if it ain't bloody Imran Khan. Come on, Perverse – get padded up,' Ron barked.

Meanwhile, at the wicket stands was Nathan Storr, star batsman of the team. Happily, when Nathan played for the Outcasts, they tended to win. He was not noted for his personal hygiene, though, prompting the Chairman to reflect, 'I love the smell of Nathan in the morning. It smells of victory!'

Surrounded by harlequin caps, Nathan was struggling to make an impression and was struck on the pad for the umpteenth time. Posh shouts of 'How is that?' rang out. He was duly given out LBW by the Old Eldonians' umpire – a blatantly biased decision. He pointed at his bat as he skulked off the pitch.

This gesture did not go unnoticed by the umpire. 'Are you trying to tell me something, son?'

'Nothing!' Nathan replied, somewhat petulantly.

'Well fuck off back to the pavilion and look in the scorebook, then!'

The Outcasts' innings then progressed slowly to its conclusion of 149-6 off 40 overs. Highlights, if they could be called such, included Geoff being given out stumped by Ron, in a covert attempt to speed up the scoring. This was doomed to failure as he was replaced at the wicket by the even slower scoring Steve, who batted out the rest of the innings in characteristically dogged style. The only true highlight was Pervez's maiden innings for the

Outcasts. Having announced himself with a first ball six, he narrowly failed to make 50, more of that later...

Steve almost redeemed himself during the Old Eldonians' innings with his ultra-slow bowling. After a late introduction by captain Ron (far too late in Steve and Geoff's opinion) he took 3 wickets, including a clean bowled with a 'slower one'.

'Any slower and it wouldn't have fucking got there' was Senior Pro Ritchie's wry observation.

Ultimately, his efforts were thwarted by further (Neil, Ron and Geoff had already dropped catches) poor fielding (a dropped 'dolly' catch by Amir and a missed stumping chance by a tiring Neil), combined with a shocking 'Not Out' LBW decision ('it was keeping too low') by the Eldonians' umpire. The fact that he had scored so slowly during the Outcasts' innings, oh and run his batting partner Pervez out, may also have had something to do with the Outcasts' defeat, Dear Reader.

The players shook hands and walked off the pitch.

Noone bothered to retrieve the ball that had sailed into the distance of Steve's last delivery.

Steve was not the only one to feel frustrated at the end of the game. Sitting on the boundary edge, Karen was beginning to wish that she had not accepted Steve's invitation. She had little interest in cricket, and Charlotte less so. It was already proving to be a long day, and Steve seemed to be preoccupied with his teammates.

Furthermore, she was feeling rather peckish. She had had to defer to the players at the tea interval, only to find that the likes of Nathan and Ritchie had pretty well scoffed the lot by the time it was her turn. Worse, it had proved impossible to persuade Charlotte to come with her to get a 'boring' ice cream. Steve had managed to rescue a pallid-looking sausage roll and a handful of soggy crisps for her (ever the gent!). Happily for her, Charlotte had turned her nose up at these crummy offerings, but that had left both of them feeling very hungry. Perhaps they could make a quick getaway and there would still be time for Steve to take her to a nice country pub for an evening meal. (Think again on that one, Karen!)

Chapter 17: 'PMS – Post Match Shenanigans'

Steve made a beeline for Karen as he walked off the pitch, only to find that she was talking to one of the Enemy.

'Did you enjoy that?' the Eldonians player asked solicitously.

'It was OK. Charlotte got a bit bored, though.'

While she was talking, Charlotte was playing around in a disconnected way.

'Have you met Guy from the Old Eldonians?"

'Only on the pitch. I got him out!' Steve bridled.

A very tall young blond man in immaculate whites, multi-coloured blazer and the trademark harlequin cap held out his hand. 'Guy Downing-Thomas. Pleased to meet you, er...?'

'Steve. *Doctor* Steve Hemmings.' Steve proffered his hand reluctantly.

'I say, you do have a most charming young lady friend!' Guy volunteered.

Steve was unimpressed. 'Why, thank you.'

'And may I apologise for the behaviour of our umpire? Absolutely corrupt, he is.'

'You can say that again.'

'Got no connection to the school. Used to be a plumber (pronounced plammer). Insists on following us round on tour with that awful wife of his.'

'Well, he sure won you that game.'

Karen stared pointedly at an empty glass as Steve waxed lyrical about the shortcomings of the Old Eldonians' umpire.

Guy was quick to spot the opportunity. 'I can see that Steve's neglecting you. Can I get you a drink?'

'Oh, I'll have a dry white wine, please. Oh, and a packet of crisps, please!'

Guy paused, before enquiring, 'And what about your lovely daughter?'

'She'll have a coke. Thanks.'

Steve was not to be left out. 'I'll have a pint, please, Guy,' he said meaningfully, before remembering that the real business of the day – the all-important Potty Meeting – was about to start. He rushed off to bribe Geoff to make sure he didn't get the dreaded award.

'Geoff. It's my round. What can I get you?' Steve panted, after he had got to the bar.

'No thanks. Amir is sorting me out,' was the ominous reply.

A smiling Amir came over. 'Oh, esteemed Chairman. Here is your pint.' Amir handed over the pint of Foster's that had been requested.

'Thanks, Dr El-Nile,' Geoff said with a wink. 'It won't be long before we get that potty meeting started...'

It was annoying that Amir, whose abysmal fielding had almost single-handedly lost the game, had been able to bribe the Chairman before he had, but surely the prize was heading in Neil's direction, following his missed catch and stumping. Had Geoff not indicated this in the morning? Steve's only misdemeanour had been a misfield – different currency from a dropped catch. Nonetheless, Steve felt a frisson of trepidation as he walked back into the lounge. His mood was not helped by the sight of that bloody Guy Downing Thomas blatantly sharking on Karen as she sipped delicately on her dry white wine.

'Where's my pint?' demanded Steve.

'Oh, sorry, old chap, I forgot. I'll get it later. Toodle-oo. Must dash!' Guy suddenly felt the need to be elsewhere.

'Thanks, Guy,' Steve muttered through gritted teeth.

'See you later Karen... and your lovely daughter,' were Guy's parting words.

'What were you doing, letting that posh git go and chat you up like that?' Steve asked Karen angrily.

'Well, you would go shooting off.'

'Sorry, it was important for me to buy the Chairman a pint.'

'Why?'

'You'll see...'

'Anyway, Guy was cute.'

'He's probably off to bend over for the soap with his posh chums in the showers.'

'You're prejudiced, you are. They're just the same as us, you know.'

'You reckon?' Steve hissed sarcastically.

'He just seemed lonely, that's all. Not the only one, as it happens!' she added pointedly, before providing some reassurance. 'Far too young for me anyway, so stop worrying.' Karen put her hand on Steve's knee to reassure him that they were still on good terms (well, sort of) before he disappeared once again to the dressing room to get changed into his civvies.

Once inside the dressing room, Ron had decided to give the team a post-match pep talk to try to overcome the air of disappointment.

'Bad luck, lads. Those twisting public school baggers, eh?'

'Well, we've had to contend with their cheating umpire every year, and we've still managed to beat them,' Geoff volunteered. 'Catches win matches! Catches win matches!' he added menacingly.

'Oh, so true, beloved Chairman. I hope you won't be too harsh on the transgressors,' Amir chipped in, to Steve's all-too-obvious annoyance.

Speak for yourself, Amir. Can't believe this, Steve thought to himself, as he recalled the dropped catch by Amir off his bowling.

'You must have a potty exemption, otherwise you would be odds-on favourite, followed by Neil,' Steve chuntered under his breath all too audibly.

'Did you have something to say, Mr Hemmings?' Geoff enquired.

'Dr Hemmings to you!' Steve retorted to laughter from the other players. Realising the potential import of dissing the Chairman, he added, 'Sorry Chairman, I was just reflecting on the cruelties and sad ironies of this cricketing life.'

'You don't have to drop a catch to get the pot, you know...' Geoff growled ominously.

Ron clapped his hands. 'Anyone unavailable for Ripon next week?'

No hands went up.

'That's a nice change,' Ron declared before turning his eye to Pervez. 'And you, Perverse? You'd like to play for us again?'

Pervez nodded.

'Ha. Ha. We've not announced the potty award yet,' Ron quipped. 'OK. Time for a shower, and I'll see you all in the bar.'

When Steve got back to the bar, he was a little perturbed to find that there was no sign of Karen or Charlotte. Any anxieties he may have had on this score were, however, eclipsed by fear of the ritual humiliation of receiving the potty award in front of his new girlfriend – when she finally rematerialized.

Back in the dingy backroom bar, The Committee finally convened. Seated round a table were (in clockwise order) Ron, Amir, a somewhat fearful Neil and the Chairman. Neil had pushed past Amir to be able to sit in the strategically favourable position next to the Chairman. The piss pot took pride of place on the table alongside a battered copy of Wisden.

'Right, gentlemen. It is now our most solemn and holy duty to bestow the Private Godfrey Fielding Award to the most deserving member of the team. Firstly, I think that Neil and Amir should swap places,' Geoff said, with a sadistic grin.

Neil reluctantly swapped places with Amir.

'Now, Mr Captain, a summary of the match, please.'

Ron was quickly into his stride. 'Well, we didn't get enough runs, but a good debut by Perverse – till he got run out by Hemmers, of course...'

'Ah. Yes, our libidinous vice-captain, sometimes nicknamed "haemorrhoids".' Geoff's lip curled as he observed Neil squirming to his right-hand side.

'Then, it looked like we might nick it, but we let a few go in the field.'

'Including yourself?' Geoff interrupted.

'Ah nah, that one flew past me at slip. No chance.' Ron was the first to get his excuses in.

The committee men then took turns to exonerate themselves from all blame for their various misdemeanours. Excuses included getting sun in their eyes (Amir), being distracted by Charlotte and therefore obviously Steve's fault (Geoff) and the wrong sort of wicket keeping gloves (Neil).

Meanwhile, back in the clubhouse bar, Steve was involved in intense discussions with Pervez and Peter. There was still no sign of Karen or Charlotte.

'No, I don't think you'll get it, Steve. You only made one misfield. Others dropped chances. Especially Amir,' Peter reassured him.

'Yeah, but they're all on the committee. Pervez, you dropped one, didn't you?' Steve was looking for other possibilities.

'Oh, you are a hard school, you are. Yes, I did get hit on the head, if you call that a dropped catch,' Pervez argued.

'What would Closey say?' Steve countered.

'Yes, and they do like to give the award to debutants. I wouldn't be too surprised...' Peter insisted.

Before Pervez could react, an anxious Karen returned to interrupt the learned discussion.

'Now look, I've heard enough. My daughter has gone missing, and all you're bothered about is this silly award. Honestly, you men!'

Her diatribe was interrupted by Ron coming out of the meeting.

'Pervez. Could you come into the Committee meeting? We'd like to ask you some questions.'

'Yeah, fine. Whatever.'

Pervez accompanied Ron to the back bar, leaving Steve and Peter to deal with Karen.

Geoff peered over his half-moon glasses, as Pervez entered the hallowed chamber.

'Now then, Perverse, you do know why you're here, don't you?'

'Something to do with a fielding award?' Pervez asked innocently.

Geoff held the potty up. 'Yes, the Private Godfrey memorial award.'

'But that's your nickname for Trevor, and he's not dead!' Pervez commented.

'Well into his dotage, he is. He may as well be,' the Chairman said.

Ron grew impatient. 'Let's cut to the facking chase. You dropped a catch, didn't you?'

'Well, hardly. Ball hit my head when I was fielding close in.' Pervez was incredulous, despite the heads-up he had already received from Steve and Peter.

'You mean that you didn't have time to react? Was the sun in your eyes, perhaps?'

'No. No. No. I tried, but it flew too fast. Man, it flew too fast. I thought to myself afterwards, what would Sir Brian have done? But no time!'

Geoff sat impassively. 'OK. I think you should pay a 50p fine, then we'll have a vote,' he concluded.

Pervez duly put in his 50p as Ron motioned him out of the room.

'We're normally lenient to debutants...' the Chairman lied, as Pervez left the room looking puzzled. 'OK. Let voting commence...'

Meanwhile, in the clubhouse, Charlotte had been found and was berating her mother in an extremely loud voice. 'What sort of a caring mother are you?' she asked rhetorically. 'I disappear for a fucking hour and you stay here drinking with that new fancy man of yours?'

'But darling, I...'

'You just don't care, do you? Preferring the dubious delights of that man's cock to looking after your poor neglected daughter!' Charlotte continued, to shocked looks from around the clubhouse.

In the back bar, Ron looked fixedly at Geoff. 'My vote's for the Chairman.'

'I think we should stick to the worst offenders,' Geoff said, peering over his glasses once more, before turning to Neil. 'You can vote for yourself, you know.'

Neil did not take the bait. 'My vote's for Steve Hemmings.'

This was followed by a pregnant pause.

'Very good then. Mr President? What about you?

'My vote is also...' Amir began, before he was interrupted by The Chairman.

'I think you should concentrate on those who have actually missed chances.'

'Well, that would include me.' Amir was hesitant.

'As I said to Neil, you can vote for yourself, if that's what you want.' Geoff winked at Amir for effect.

'Then regrettably and although it pains me to death, I must vote for my brother committee member, Mr Neil Patterson.' Amir finally took the hint.

Neil looked crestfallen. Ron smiled wryly. Geoff rubbed his hands with glee.

'OK. We have 1 vote each for 3 deserving and not-so-deserving' – Geoff took a moment to glare at Ron – 'candidates, so I have the casting vote.'

The tension in the room mounted as the Chairman paused.

'Neil, as one of the candidates is you, could you come outside and have a word?' he finally pronounced before all the committee members exited the room.

Back in the bar, the air of expectation mounted as Amir and Ron walked back in.

'What's happening?' Nathan asked. The two committee men, however, remained inscrutable.

The prolonged delay increased Steve's sense of irritation. He really wanted to get away from the place. Maybe he and Karen could dump Charlotte with Isa and enjoy the rest of the evening. The longer this dragged on, the less chance became of that happening, and the greater the chance of more misbehaviour from Charlotte. It was also obvious that Karen was not a cricket fan. He couldn't even buy himself another drink, just in case he had to drink from the dreaded pot and render himself unfit to drive home – never mind doing the business with Karen later on.

Meanwhile, out on the cricket pitch, two figures could be seen against the setting sun.

On reaching the wicket, Geoff pronounced, 'OK. Neil. Let's stop here.'

'Yeth, Chairman,' Neil uttered meekly.

Geoff brandished the potty in one hand and the copy of Wisden's Cricket Almanack in another. 'Get on your knees! Get on your knees!'

'What do you mean, Geoffwey?'

'Get on your knees and promise that you will never keep wicket as badly again.'

'But, Geoffrey. You said that I kept well!'

'Yes, but you cost us the game at the finish.' Geoff repeated his demand. 'On your knees!'

'You are stwipping me of my dignity, Geoffwey. I will not get on my knees,' Neil said stubbornly, no doubt aware that the eyes of everyone back in the bar were upon him.

'Really? You dare to defy an order from your Chairman?' Geoff continued before concluding, 'Then I'm afraid the potty award is yours.'

'But I don't want it,' Neil said pleadingly.

'I'm sorry, but you'll have to have it,' were Geoff's final words before he accompanied the condemned man back to the main bar.

On arriving, Geoff handed the potty to Amir, who had it filled with beer plus ice. He then placed the obligatory plastic turd to float in the middle and stood in front of the assembled players and their partners as Amir handed the feared vessel over to him. Neil looked on in fear.

Geoffrey began cheerfully insulting other members of the team. Trevor was a schoolfriend of Gerry Adams and had traded his batting pads in for incontinence ones; Amir was an illegal immigrant born on the back streets of Baghdad (Geoff's grasp of geography always had been shaky); Pervez was wanted by MI5...

As he droned on, an increasingly tense Steve reflected on how things would be different if he were in charge. It was high time for the Outcasts to be reinvented as the 'New Outcasts', was it not? For starters, instead of this anachronistic booby prize, he would instigate a Man of the Match Award. They were now in a more inclusive, forgiving era, weren't they? What could have been more inclusive than a positive award, maybe some book tokens (anyone for Harry Potter?). It might have attracted the much-needed young blood to the team. (Dream on, Steve!) Ron and Geoff seemed oblivious to the adverse effect the potty was having on recruitment – not to mention retention – of players. Come to think of it, he should have been Man of the Match today, had Pifco not fumbled that stumping opportunity.

Karen, meanwhile, grew ever more impatient. It had already been a very long day, and what was this dreadful man doing speaking about his own team in such an offensive and dog whistle racist way? What was she still doing in this awful place with a man she had only met the previous week?

Unfortunately, Charlotte's thoughts were so unprintable that they cannot be shared with a civilized audience.

Geoff finally cut to the chase.

'Ah, I nearly forgot. There's our vice-captain, with an emphasis on vice: Dr Steve Hemmings. Steve is a renowned chemist, but not so renowned for his athleticism, and he misfielded badly today. He also suffers from cirrhosis!'

Karen was alarmed. 'Cirrhosis? Really?

'He means psoriasis,' Steve reassured her.

'Not to mention chlamydia, cancroids, gonorrhoea and gout...'

'I don't have any of them, either!' Steve said indignantly as laughter broke out all around.

'Neither is he renowned for his love life,' Geoff continued. 'So, I'm very pleased to see he's brought along the second Mrs Hemmings today... with a ready-made family, I see.'

The audience turned to stare at Charlotte, who responded by bursting into tears and running off, flicking V signs. She had disappeared from sight by the time her mother could go looking for her.

'Steve, this award could have been made for you. You are a major candidate,' Geoff concluded, before turning on Neil.

'Finally, we have Mr Neil "Pifco" Patterson. Why "Pifco", you may all ask? You may well think it's an ironic reference to his utter baldness. But no, it's something far more intimate, and I couldn't possibly divulge it.'

Groans ensued from the audience, orchestrated by Amir. Geoff stood pondering his next pronouncement.

'Oh, alright, then. Neil suffers with the old Farmer Giles, and has to dry his arse every day and night with a hair dryer.' Geoff made suitable gestures behind his bottom to maximise the ribald laughter emanating from the audience.

'But Geoffrey, I thought you wouldn't say...' Neil protested.

The Chairman smiled, before continuing unabashed. 'Now, Neil is the worst wicket keeper in the world, and unsurprisingly, he missed a couple of chances late in the game. Old age creeping in, was it, Neil?'

Geoff clasped the Cricketer's Bible to his chest, looked heavenwards and entreated the hapless Neil one more time. 'Brother Pifco, will you kneel down and repent!?'

Neil stood firm. 'No Geoffwey, it was the gloves!'

The Chairman made the sign of the cross, before pronouncing, 'Very well then, and without further ado...' Geoff paused for effect.

The audience held its breath, not least Steve, as Geoff waited to pronounce the unlucky winner.

'I will hand the Private Godfrey award to Neil "Pifco" Patterson!'

Steve, now standing alone, heaved a huge sigh of relief.

Neil was about to step forwards when the Chairman held his hand up to stop him. The audience groaned. The butterflies returned to Steve's stomach.

'Ah, wait a minute... Neil, I'm giving you one more chance to redeem yourself. If you get on your knees in front of these good people and swear on the Cricketer's Bible that you will never, never keep wicket as badly again, I will spare you!'

'No, I couldn't possibly!'

'You know you want to confess.' The Chairman held the pot in front of his nose and whispered in his ear. 'One of Steve's nephews used it last week. It's been washed out, of course...'

Neil finally succumbed. 'Oh, alwight then!'

'I knew you'd see sense in the end.' Geoff ushered Neil away from the bar to create more space.

Neil knelt down in front of the gents' toilet door, holding the Cricketer's Bible, and read out. 'I swear on Sir Geoffrey Boycott, Brian Close and Ian Botham that I will never, never keep wicket as badly again. So help me, Jack Wussell.'

'There! That wasn't so bad, then, was it?' Geoff grinned.

Before Neil could get up, Charlotte came bursting out of the ladies' opposite shouting 'Mummy' and tripped headfirst into Neil's rear quarters, thereby hurting her head somewhat and his piles even more.

Loud cries of anguish rang out around the Great Naughton Cricket Club bar.

In the ensuing melee, Charlotte ran out, followed closely by Karen. Geoff then made a further announcement.

'In view of Pifco's act of contrition, The Private Godfrey Memorial award now goes to Doctor Stephen Hemmings!'

'Shit the bed!' Steve swore audibly. He really thought he'd escaped this time. Much as Geoff had liked to keep people in suspense, he had never before announced a winner, then reversed his decision. Steve was very tempted to refuse, but remembered what happened to people who did.

He reluctantly stepped forward as his teammates slow-handclapped him and started to drink to loud cheering, spilling much of the contents down his front. At least Karen had not been there to witness it. But where was she? Where was Charlotte?

He found her outside, tending to a bawling Charlotte. 'Oh fucking hell, I really got stitched up there. I didn't even drop a catch.' Steve wanted to share his anger.

'Never mind that, I have a badly injured child here.' Karen was unimpressed.

'Nah. Cuts and bruises. What about Pervez? He got a cricket ball right between the eyes.' Steve was equally unimpressed.

'You just don't care, do you? Take us home now!' Karen demanded.

'OK. I'll just say good night to the lads.'

'Well, they are your priority, aren't they?' Karen said sarcastically.

On the way in, Steve passed by the Chairman, who had noticed the strained atmosphere between Karen and Steve and the still-bawling Charlotte.

'Trouble in paradise, eh?' He smirked.

Steve still insisted on popping his head round the clubhouse door, while Karen stared daggers at him.

'Good night, everyone!'

Karen and Charlotte walked with Steve to his car.

If the journey there had been tense for Steve, it was as nothing compared to the journey home.

After a few minutes of awkward silence punctuated only by sobs from Charlotte in the back of the car, Karen opened up. 'And another thing. You reek of beer. Are you sure you're fit to drive?'

'Yes. That potty was only my second pint. We can thank your posh friend Guy for that. Yes, I'm OK,' Steve explained reasonably.

'Do you realise that you're endangering my child's life?' Karen demanded.

'Don't let that drunken devil drive us home, mummy!' Charlotte screamed from the back seat. 'I'm going to ring Childline!' Happily, for Steve, she did not possess her own mobile.

'I had to do it. It was a matter of honour.' Steve sighed.

There was a long pause. Unbeknownst to young Steve, Karen's thoughts were veering from rebellious to mutinous, and would have significant consequences in the days and weeks to come.

'You and your mates. They're more important to you than I am, or my daughter.'

Steve made the mistake of glancing heavenward, albeit momentarily.

'Drive me home, we're finished!' Karen concluded, before silence descended again.

Meanwhile, back at the cricket club, a smiling Chairman was drinking with the rest of the team (well, most of them) in the bar.

'Did I note an element a hint of friction between our two lovebirds?' he observed with maximum self-satisfaction.

Ron nodded his head. 'And I think the bleeder's gone off without the team kit bag.'

'Yes, he did leave in something of a hurry,' Geoff agreed. 'You'd better look into it.'

Ron grabbed a key from the bar and scuttled back to the visitors' changing room to investigate while the Chairman continued to hold court.

'Oh, Dr El-Nile. About that lift to Yarm that you offered me...' Geoff looked around. 'Oh, now, where's he gone?'

Meanwhile, in the dressing room, Amir and Mrs Patterson were naked together in the showers. The turning of a Yale lock was heard. Ron entered to collect the team cricket bag. Amir hastily closed the shower curtain as Ron picked the bag up before making out the silhouettes behind the curtain.

Ron dropped the kit bag and shook his head.

'Bladdy hell. You can knock me down with a feather!'

Knowing that this was information he could use to his advantage, should the need arise, Ron retrieved the bag and headed out of the changing room posthaste, leaving Amir and Mrs Patterson to look at each other aghast.

Chapter 18: 'Alone Again Or...'

The following week proved to be a doubly difficult one for Steve. Lovelorn, he longed to make up the breach with Karen. The Chairman counselled otherwise – repeatedly. The best way to get Karen back was through maintaining strict radio silence! All the more so if Steve was still anxious about having impregnated her. (He was.) She would assuredly make contact in good time. He would only weaken his hand through being the first to blink. On the subject of hands, his right hand grew ever stronger, not to mention his right wrist.

Work offered little solace, punctuated by repeated disagreements with Stuart, still sore about being shown up in front of Debbie. A mini-heatwave made his southwest-facing office nigh on uninhabitable in the afternoons, the large plate glass windows offering an early example of the Greenhouse Effect.

At least, there was the Health Awareness Day to look forward to – and oh, there was one bright spot. He had received confirmation that he (sorry, his team) had, as expected, been shortlisted for a local Innovation prize, and Jim Dickson had kindly agreed to attend the Ceremony.

Now in his late fifties, Jim Dickson MBE was Director of Technology for BCG's Belladonna Division, and now sat on the main company board. A tall, shambling man, nobody quite knew what he did or how he had got there. Apart from his all-round bonhomie and high-flown academic qualifications and visiting professorships at Russell Group Universities, it had to be said that he had presided over a particularly barren spell for BCG technical advances. Perhaps it was his ineffable talent for managing upwards and a canny eye for favourable publicity. Steve had always got on with him on the rare occasions that they had met. A shared passion for cricket was certainly one thing they had in common. Unfortunately, unbeknownst to Steve, both Debbie and Stuart despised him with a vengeance.

Back to the negatives. All week, Steve waited for a reply from his hero, Tony Blair. Answer came there none.

Even cricket did not offer any cheer, despite this being the hottest and driest weekend for many a year. Ron had failed to put together a team to play on the Sunday. The fixture had had to be cancelled, adding to Steve's and the Chairman's frustration.

This had at least given Steve the chance to spend more time with his children, on his designated weekend. A sumptuous roast beef dinner at the Dog had taken the place of a hasty big Mac and fries. Not that his kids seemed to appreciate it. They busied themselves fighting amongst themselves and speculating about his relationship with the bar staff – in the rare times that they were not engrossed with their Game Boys, that is.

Chapter 19: 'One Too Many Mornings'

The following Monday morning, a dejected Steve made his way downstairs, hastily doing up the front of his kimono as he entered the front room. The bay window exaggerated the goldfish bowl effect at the front of his untidy house. Steve had an irrational fear of being reported for flashing, even if it was in his own home. It really was about time that he got some net curtains fitted, but he just couldn't be arsed.

Steve simply had to make an entry in his journal, even though he should have been setting off for work by now.

Number of acts of self-pollution since last week 8*

Number of alcohol units drunk 42 (including that fucking piss pot).

Number of losing bets 25. (Well, it was Royal Ascot week).

Number of fags smoked 23 (3 cadged off Mary and Alex, when I got back from cricket).

Number of shags 0. Not even a sympathy job.

* Well above average. The hot weather must have something to do with it, plus the fact that Karen hasn't been there to share my stiffy.

Anyway, cheer up, it's the Health Committee Meeting today. I know my team have been working hard to prepare for the big day next week. At last, a chance to star. It's time some people realised that there's a health in health and safety.

Actually, I think I feel another message to Tony coming on...

When Steve finally made it to the office, Steve had a pleasant surprise waiting for him. An email from his beloved leader! This would certainly soften the cruel blows he had suffered over the previous week.

Dear Steve

Thank you so much for your latest email. I do apologise for my non-compliance with your company Health and Safety procedures. I hope you understand that I was trying to get to a crucial meeting with my fellow EU Leaders.

> **Please let me reassure you that Health and Safety is never far from my thoughts and that industrial injuries have fallen by 25% in the three years since New Labour came to power.**

Steve tried to suppress the thought that this fall may have coincided with a comparable decrease in UK manufacturing jobs since 1997. His Leader, however, went on to reassure him.

> **I can also assure you that whilst being a staunch supporter of our local chemical industry, I am also a supporter of the growth of new knowledge-based industries that will transform the UK into a high growth 'tiger economy '.**
>
> **I look forward to your next missive.**
>
> **Sincerely**
>
> **Tony**

As he read the reply, he was interrupted by a knock on his office door.

Before Steve could finish re-reading the email for the sixth time, the door opened. Paula entered unbidden.

Steve tried in vain to hide his on-screen letter.

'Top of the morning to you, Dr Hemmings.' Paula liked to exaggerate her Irishness in an ironic way.

'Good morning to you as well, Dr O'Donnell. What can I do you for?' Steve's attempt at classic English humour fell flat as Paula clocked Steve's unkempt appearance and the on-screen letter despite his best efforts to cover it up.

'You have remembered the Health Committee Meeting, haven't you?'

'Of course,' Steve protested, before looking at his watch. 'Oh, my. Is that the time?'

'Yes. We'd better get down to the Meeting Room,' Paula said before observing, 'Aren't those the same clothes you were wearing on Friday?

'Yes. Yes,' Steve mumbled.

'Thought it was a bit whiffy in here.' Paula laughed as Steve recoiled in horror. 'Only joking,' she said as she squeezed his arm.

'Glad to hear it,' Steve said as he got up from his desk.

Paula's eyes narrowed. 'So... I hope all's well with the new romance.'

'Yeah. Yeah. Couldn't be better,' Steve replied, avoiding Paula's gaze.

'You're feckin' lying! It's all over, isn't it?'

Steve mumbled a non-committal reply.

'So, the good ladies of Teesside are in danger once again!'

'The bad ones, too.' Steve's attempt at humour was met with a withering glance.

Steve's blushes were saved by Margaret walking in.

'Good morning, Dr Hemmings, and to you, Mrs O'Donnell.'

Margaret turned on the vacuum cleaner, thus drowning out Paula's protests regarding her wrongful title.

Margaret shouted out over the din of the vacuum cleaner.

'I've written to that Mrs Mowlam.'

'Well done. You should get a reply pretty quickly,' Steve said, smiling at the response that he'd got from his political hero.

Margaret was less sanguine. 'I'll believe it when I see it,' she shouted.

Steve looked at his watch and gestured to Paula that it was time to leave the office.

'Excuse us, Margaret, but we've got a meeting to go to,' he barked as he and Paula departed on to the first long corridor.

'OK, you got away this time. But I'm wanting a full account after the meeting of what's happened. All the gory details!' Paula demanded.

'Not sure I want to tell you too much,' Steve replied sheepishly.

'So, last Thursday, you were blutered again. You pick up some young woman at a singles club. You give her the works over the weekend, then cruelly dump her so that you can endanger other women. What kind of Chairman of the Health Committee are you?'

'It wasn't like that,' Steve protested.

'And what the feck is that message from that eejit Tony Blair about?'

'I don't know what you mean,' Steve mumbled as they walked on.

Whether by accident or design, Steve's self-appointed Health Committee consisted of five women and one man – Steve, the Chairman.

The other four women were already sitting when Paula and Steve walked in.

'Morning all,' Steve said breezily.

'Morning Steve!' the other committee members replied.

Steve immediately walked over to the coffee station and grabbed himself an undrinkable coffee with milk and two sugars, then took his seat. (Everyone else had helped themselves to water from the bottle sitting next to the coffee.) Steve spied the untouched dish with the fancy biscuits that invariably looked better than they tasted and helped himself to a couple.

'OK. Today is a very important meeting,' Steve began portentously as he finally sat down. 'We'll be putting the last touches to our planning for the Site Health Awareness Day, and we'll be discussing the outcomes of the Stress Survey that we undertook earlier this year.'

Steve then turned to the rather demure woman sitting on his right.

'With that in mind, I've co-opted Michelle from the Human Resources Department to join us. First of all, she will discuss the findings of the survey. Welcome, Michelle,' Steve concluded expansively.

'Hello, Michelle,' the other members piped in unison.

'Let's start with the Stress Survey. Michelle, what did you make of it?' Steve asked.

Michelle was an attractive, neatly dressed dark-haired woman in her thirties. Now that she was sitting next to him, Steve couldn't help but notice that her dress was somewhat low-cut and revealed a very ample bust.

'Well, I was surprised by the overall levels of reported stress. I thought people were a lot happier than that,' Michelle began.

'Well, it was a mixture of personal and workplace stress...' Steve volunteered, whilst reflecting, *Pity about the wedding ring!*

Michelle continued, 'And then there were all the rude comments about the company.'

'Yeah. And the management...' Steve smiled.

'Yes. I didn't expect such a strong response to the question on workplace bullying, either.'

'Hmm.' Again, Steve didn't share her surprise.

'But the biggest surprise of all was the collective insecurity about job losses.'

'But, that shouldn't surprise you. Project Mallard and all,' Steve butted in.

'That was only announced the other week, Steve.' Paula was quick to correct her boss.

'Oh. Yes. Sure. I'm a bit surprised too,' Steve admitted.

'Even taking into account Project Mallard – which will only affect 10% of employees, if that – it came as a surprise,' Michelle continued.

'What, that the other 90% of the workforce were worried about their jobs?' Steve asked.

'Yes. We've had our ups and downs over the past few years...' Steve couldn't help noticing the undulations of her bosom as Michelle spoke those words. '...but things have been pretty flat for a while.'

'I wouldn't say that!' Steve couldn't help saying, earning himself a sharp look from Paula. 'Well, how do you plan to act on this?' he added hastily.

'Well, we need to think about that. Remember, not all the workforce answered it.'

'Well, I thought that 70% was pretty good.'

Michelle carried on, 'Also, we could also question the statistical basis for the survey.'

'90% is 90%, surely.' Steve always found that HR people were somewhat allergic to the obvious. 'What about the employee helpline that I've been suggesting?'

'An employee helpline isn't in our budget for this year,' Michelle replied flatly.

Steve decided it was time to move on. 'Oh. OK. Thank you, Michelle. Let's go to the next item on the agenda. The Health Awareness Day. Who'd like to start?'

Paula went first. 'As you know, I'm doing the safe sex awareness stand. I'll be blowing up lots of condoms to illustrate the point,' she added gleefully.

'I hope it doesn't shock anybody. You know what fuddy-duddies they are around here.' Steve smiled.

'Well, let's liven them up a bit!' Paula continued. 'I've also got a nurse from the local NHS Trust to do a demonstration with a banana. You could do with watching that one, Stephen.'

Steve blushed. 'Let's not go there, shall we?'

Claire, a slightly overweight, bespectacled fortyish lady caught Paula's drift.

'Why, has the "babe magnet" struck again? Well, I don't know what they see in him!' She snorted. 'I'm organising the aromatherapy and the reflexology. I've also got a lady to do Reiki. Agnes is going to organise the tai chi, salsa dancing and the Pilates.'

'Sounds good.' Steve nodded his head enthusiastically.

Agnes, a thin, attractive lady in her thirties, confirmed: 'Yes, I've got Patricia to come down from Gateshead to do the Pilates class again. You do remember Patricia from last time, don't you, Steve?'

Steve thought to himself, *Wow, she's gorgeous, seemed to like me too!* before saying aloud, 'Oh yes, of course. Very good.'

Steve had once been advised on a training course that playing poker would not be a suitable profession for him. Paula cast him a knowing glance as he tried to wipe the smile off his face.

Finally, Angie, a matronly lady in her fifties, spoke up. 'And I'm doing the Healthy Eating and the Smoke Awareness. We'll be having a cooking demonstration of a healthy recipe that you can cook for just £1...'

Once the meeting had been going for over ten minutes, the caffeine quickly wore off. Inevitably, Steve drifted off into one of his reveries.

* * *

To the background music of 'La Vida Loca' by Ricky Martin, Steve imagines himself walking through a hospital ward full of BCG managers lying in their beds. The beds have signs on them noting their conditions. These include 'Terminal Impotence', 'Raging Horn' (nil by mouth), 'Premature Ejaculation', 'Delayed Ejaculation', 'Vaginismus' and 'Gerontophile', as well as 'Chancroids, Chlamydia and Gonorrhoea'.

The Health Committee ladies are dressed as nurses/cheer leaders. They have packets of condoms in their hands, which they wave about. They are joined by the Chairman, who enters the ward, somewhat incongruously.

The 'nurses' taunt Steve with the chant, 'Come and have a go if you think you think you're hard enough!'

Steve suddenly notices that he is undressed from the waist down and attempts to cover up.

The 'nurses' taunt him further. 'What's the matter with you? Nothing we've never seen before.'

Enter Patricia, wearing a leopard skin leotard. She is carrying a Pilates ball. She plonks the ball down and proceeds to exercise provocatively on it as Geoff, dressed as Pontius Pilate, also observes, washing his hands dramatically from the potty. The nurses start to make Tai Chi moves as Patricia writhes on the ball. Steve looks down in horror as he notices his state of arousal.

The nurses reach for syringes from the hospital trolley (in synch) and squirt water all over Steve's nether regions. Geoff then tips the contents of the potty on to his supine body, as Steve falls to the floor, clutching his groin.

* * *

When Steve came round, Paula was speaking. 'What we're trying to do is make people wake up to the fact that they're responsible for their own sexual health.' She fixed Steve with yet another meaningful look. 'Isn't that right, Steve?'

'Yes.' Steve cleared his throat. 'Oh. Yes. Most important to encourage people to help themselves.' He paused. 'OK, is there any other business?'

'No, Steve,' the committee replied in unison.

'Well, I really think this is excellent – a credit to you all,' Steve went on. 'Thank you, Steve,' came the concerted reply.

'No. I really do think this is excellent,' Steve enthused. 'In fact, this time, I'll invite Debbie Gould and her management team for a preview early doors.'

'Are you sure that's wise, Steve? I'm not sure they'll be overly impressed.' Paula had a bit more political nous than her boss.

'Well, they should be. The company is encouraging one of us to be passionate about health and safety.' Steve stood up and put his hand on his chest. 'We're not just talking the talk, we are walking the walk!' From his vantage, he couldn't help but cop one more view of Michelle's chest.

'OK. Thanks everyone,' he said as he hastily sat down again.

He was pleased to see that Michelle gave him a nice smile as she walked away. Maybe she hadn't noticed his (involuntary) down blousing – or maybe she had and quite liked it. The other ladies were all smiles as they left, except for one. Paula's sidelong glance made sure that he knew that she, for one, was unimpressed.

The latter part of the morning brought a call from Geoff, who was, as ever, full of helpful advice – the gist of it being that he shouldn't worry; Karen would come back. Above all, for his part, Steve must continue to maintain strictest radio silence if he really wanted her back. In any case, would he really want her back if she was up the stick, Geoff couldn't help reminding Steve.

Lunch time came, and Steve made his way to the Lakeside Restaurant.

Les opened the batting for the Septics. 'I'm intrigued to hear more about the sexual health demonstrations that your health committee is promising us all next week.'

Frank leant forward. 'We'd like to know if you're giving any personal demonstrations.'

Steve blushed bright red. 'Oh. No. No. No. Not at all.'

'Why? What with all those ladies at your command,' Frank insisted.

'It's not like that at all!' Steve was indignant.

'Jings! Why hide your light under a bushel? You're quite a man about the town, so I hear, Dr Hemmings,' Don weighed in.

'Why, what have you heard?'

Frank tapped his nose. 'Remember, we know everything!'

'This all takes me back to the good old days in Heckmondwike,' Les reminisced.

'Oh, not that story again. The Christmas party!' Frank groaned.

'Ay. Scenes from Sodom and Gomorrah they were. Everybody pissed, couples copulating on the photocopier – interesting images those. We put them on the notice board. Folks doing it over the desks. Two pairs on the board room table. One couple in the lift,' Les continued unabashed.

'Do remind us how they avoided getting caught,' Frank asked in a tired voice.

'They jammed it between two floors. Strictly against the rules – even then.'

'Still nothing to what the "grown-ups" got up to,' Don chipped in.

'The grown-ups?'

'He means the bosses, the Executive. Our "elders and betters",' Terri explained.

Steve was intrigued and asked for further information.

'I've been with the company a long time and got to know some well-connected people. Do you know why Bowen split with his wife?' Les asked Steve.

'Oh, the Chairman before Stuart Williams?'

'Yes, him. He gave his missus a dose of clap. A member of the Parish committee, she was, and all!'

Steve looked suitably shocked.

'Yes. They used to have these parties in the company's central London flat. World at their feet back then, of course...'

'Ah. The good old days!' Frank beamed.

'They'd eat the finest foods, quaff the finest champagne, snort the best cocaine – some of them, at least – then they'd bring in the "extra pillows" for the night...'

'What – prostitutes?' Steve asked.

'Escorts, please. From the top agencies. £1000 a go – even back then.'

Terri shook her head. 'All men in those days, of course.'

'Yes, the good old days, indeed!!' Frank confirmed, smiling at Terri's all-too-obvious disdain.

Steve continued his interrogation. 'So, Bowen was part of this scene?'

'Absolutely. Bit of a lad he was, behind that stiff exterior. Well, he was from the valleys.' Les impersonated a Welsh accent. 'Shag anything that moved, that one.'

'So how come his wife got a dose?' Steve asked naively.

'Well, how do you think?'

'But surely they used condoms, didn't they?'

Don acted dumb. 'What, him and his wife? I'd think they were a bit old for that sort of caper.'

'No, the escorts, of course.'

'Nah. They'd paid so much that they thought they were immune. The girls were supposed to be clean, so no need for any of that killjoy stuff,' Les said.

'Perhaps they should have asked for their money back,' Terri suggested sardonically.

'Or maybe they should have all gone to our sexual health demo next week!' Steve said brightly.

'Or maybe not... I have a feeling it will be highly unedifying.' Les pulled a suitably disdainful face.

Frank looked at Steve intently. 'Even if you don't give a personal demonstration, young sir!'

With that, the conversation faded away. Steve continued to plough his way through his 'healthy meal'. He was unsure which way to take the notoriety the Health Awareness Day had already achieved, but he always was a firm believer in the saying 'any publicity is good publicity'. What he did know was that he had a dull afternoon ahead of him, struggling against the effects of the pie, chips and extra gravy to stay awake. Later that afternoon, it was obvious that his best attempts had failed. He was lapsing into deep sleep when his office phone rang.

Steve answered the phone, wiping the dribble away from his chin.

'Oh, hello, Karen!' Steve could not hide the surprise in his voice.

'I thought I'd just ring to see if you were OK.'

'Yes fine. What about you?'

'OK, except it's that time of the month.'

'You mean it's your period?' Steve got ready to celebrate.

'Yes, I'm afraid so.'

'Well, never mind about that.' Steve grinned, before asking hesitantly, 'To what do I owe the pleasure?'

'Well, if you're going to be like that, I'll end this conversation,' Karen answered peremptorily.

'OK. Sorry. Sorry. Sorry. I thought you'd finished with me.'

'That shouldn't stop me caring about you. I was just ringing to see how you were.'

'Oh. Ok.' Steve was really going to need the Chairman's advice on how to interpret this call.

'I'm surprised that you haven't called me, actually,' Karen magnified Steve's need for further guidance.

'Oh sorry, it's been a busy old week or so,' Steve lied.

'Anyway, what I was trying to say was that I still care about you, OK?'

'And I care about you, too.' Steve tried to sound sincere.

'OK. I've got to go now, but I'll be in touch later in the week.'

'I look forward to that.' Steve put on a high-pitched soft voice. 'Bye.'

'Bye darling.' Karen also affected a high-pitched voice.

No sooner had Steve replaced the receiver, when he leapt upwards, punched the air and performed a little jig around the office.

'She's got the painters in!' he exclaimed. Unbeknownst to him, Paula had let herself in.

'Does that mean what I think it means?' she demanded, abruptly ending Steve's impromptu celebration.

'I do wish you'd knock,' he said irritably as he turned round.

'I was afraid I might wake you up,' Paula explained. 'I came round twenty minutes ago, and you were well away with the fairies!'

'Oh, yes. You know I've been under a lot of strain recently.'

'Most of it self-imposed! I presume you were relieved because you've been riding bareback once again!'

'OK, so I was,' Steve said sheepishly.

'It's not only unwanted babies that that behaviour can lead to, and you should know!'

'OK. OK. I thought it was the beginning of a deep, meaningful relationship, if that's any excuse.'

Paula fixed him with a stare. 'So, it was Karen, your latest conquest.'

'Of course. Serial monogamist, me.'

'So, she's not finished with you, after all?'

'She said that was still the case...' Steve said doubtfully.

'Oh, do show some emotional intelligence, man! You should know that women don't always say exactly what they mean!'

'And we poor men are supposed to decipher the signals, eh?'

'Yes, exactly that. It's not too difficult, you know?'

Steve shook his head and changed the subject. 'So, what did you want to see me about?'

'That pre-demonstration to Debbie and her managers on Health Awareness Day... Are you sure it's wise?'

'You're not the first to ask me that today,' Steve muttered.

'Well, as long as you take responsibility...'

The challenge brought out Steve's quixotic streak. 'Of course! Let's shake up those dinosaurs.'

'OK. Let's.' Paula smiled.

Chapter 20: 'Follow The Rules'

Back at the Rokeby ranch, that evening, Steve got a call from the Chairman, wanting to meet him in the Dog as a matter of the utmost urgency.

Steve didn't go to the Dog on a Monday night, as a rule. But Geoff had summoned him, and he was at a loose end, after all.

Of course, he could have tried cleaning his untidy house. Steve knew that many people (mainly women in his experience) would have been quite content to do that. That prospect certainly didn't float his boat. Haddaway and shite! He had a cleaner in every other week to do that. What did he pay her for, after all?

There were also the health considerations. Drinking on a Monday night would surely end up pushing his weekly alcohol consumption well over the recommended twenty-one units! And then there was what Paula had told him about walking the walk. Steve paused. Or was it twenty-eight? They would keep changing the guidelines. One couldn't keep track! All Steve knew was that they kept going down for no particularly good reason. Twenty-eight – that was still doable!

Half an hour later, Steve and Geoff sat across each other in a nearly empty pub, as if in an 'Alas Smith and Jones' sketch.

Steve opened the conversation, once Geoff had brought the pints over for a change. 'So, what was it that you wanted to talk me about?'

'Same subject as I wanted to talk to you about the other Friday,' Geoff replied mysteriously.

'Which was? Don't leave me in suspenders!' Steve joked.

'Plenty of time for that!' Geoff raised his right hand imperiously. 'Let's start with "Tina"... Have you heard from her yet?'

'Funny you should mention that. She phoned this afternoon,' Steve mused.

'I knew she would. What was that I said about maintaining strict radio silence?' Geoff rubbed his hands in glee.

'Well, she didn't say anything about getting back with me...'

'No. No. No. She wouldn't, would she?'

'What do you mean?'

'I mean she's playing you along, man!' Geoff's eyes narrowed as he looked directly at Steve. 'Now then, what about that other little matter...?'

'What other matter?'

'You thought you may have got her in the family way!' Geoff exclaimed all too loudly.

'Oh, no. I've been reassured on that one. Red sails in the sunset, if you see what I mean...' Steve replied, again, all too loudly.

'Very good. Very good. So, you're off the hook.'

'But I was wondering why she made that call?'

'Oh. They're all nuts.'

'I was wondering, should I go and see her this week?'

'No. No. No. Absolutely not. Are you mad as well?' Geoff then added logically. 'Especially as she's indisposed right now. What good is there in going and seeing her if you can't loose off?

'Well. There are other ways...' Steve answered reasonably. Finding himself meeting a look of total incredulity, he went back to asking questions. 'What should I do, generally speaking?'

Geoff leant back in his chair and looked for several seconds, as he thought about this, before finally proclaiming, 'Ah. I've got it!'

'Go on then...' Steve was all ears.

Geoff folded his arms like Chief Sitting Bull. 'Shag her. Shag her as much as you can!' Then, he added, 'While you can!'

'But you said not to go to see her...'

'Of course. As I said, she's indisposed...'

'What about going over and just cuddling up to her?' Steve was a sucker for naïve questions. 'They like that sort of thing, I'm told.'

Geoff rolled his eyes as if Steve were mad. 'No. No. No. That just won't do!'

At this moment, Mary, who had been hovering within earshot, came over to collect Steve's empty glass.

Geoff stopped her from going back behind the bar. 'Hey, Mary. Stop a minute. You can resolve an argument I've got with this young man here...'

'Of course. What do you want to know?'

'I want a woman of the world's perspective on this...'

'And you reckon I'm one of them,' Mary answered somewhat defensively.

‘OK. A woman’s perspective then...’

‘OK. Go on...

‘What would you think of a man who came round to your place for the night and just cuddled up to you?’

Steve blushed.

‘Well... I’d think he was rather sweet...’

Steve blushed redder.

‘But you wouldn’t consider him siring material, would you?’

‘He’s not a horse, you know,’ Mary retorted before adding, ‘Well, I don’t know. I don’t think I’ve ever had anyone do that.’

‘Precisely. Just too confusing all round, that type of behaviour.’ Geoff approved of her reply. ‘Don’t worry, you’re not going to have that happen to you, unless you are exceptionally unlucky!’

Mary looked at both men quizzically. ‘What’s all this about?’

Geoff answered swiftly, ‘I think young Stephen here has gone a bit soft, if you get my drift...’

Mary giggled and walked away.

Geoff leant over the table to an ever-redder Steve and grabbed the sleeve of his jacket.

‘You see, it’s cock that they want! Good, strong cock.’

‘If you say so, Geoff.’ Steve sighed.

‘And as for “Tina”, As I said, shag her as much as you can, while you can.’

‘Who says I’ll get another chance?’ Steve looked at his feet sulkily.

‘Oh, you will. Surely, you will. “Mystic Geoff” here can read the signs.’ Geoff looked heavenwards at the mock Tudor beams.

Steve remained unconvinced. ‘Well, I’m not sure...’

Geoff stared heavenwards again. ‘Look! It’s written in the stars. But it won’t last.’

‘Why do you say that?’ Steve was intrigued, despite himself.

‘Never does with the really pretty ones. Listen. I will tell you a story.’ Geoff commenced, ‘I had a friend, no longer with us, unfortunately – name of Jaguar Jackie. He was a used car salesman...’

‘Yes, go on.’ Steve was all ears.

‘Well, I used to see him around the local racetracks and nearby pubs. He’d often have a really pretty dolly bird on his arm. Then there’d be another and then another.’

‘So?’

‘One night, he was on his own. Out on the pull in Yarm, just like me. And I asked him what had happened.’

‘Why did you ask?’

‘Because the time before he’d been with this gorgeous bird. And you know what he said to me?’

‘What, then?’

‘He said they never last more than two years, you know – a bit like one of his cars, come to think of it. So... you’ve got to make hay while the sun shines. And that’s what I’m telling you!’ Geoff grabbed Steve’s sleeve once again to emphasise his point, then sat back and finished his pint. ‘Now go and get me another. It’s your round,’ he concluded.

‘OK. Same again?’

‘Yeah, same again!’ Geoff frowned. ‘No actually, I’ll try a pint of the guest beer...’

Steve walked to the bar. ‘I’ll have a pint of Strongarm and a pint of Old Knacker.’

‘That for him?’ Mary asked.

‘Yep.’

‘Figures!’ Mary pulled the two pints for Steve before adding, ‘You shouldn’t listen to him, you know.’

‘Who do you mean?’ Steve was ever the asker of naïve questions.

‘“The Old Knacker”, of course... He’s only jealous... and I wouldn’t mind it if a man came and just cuddled me all night. Especially if I was feeling fragile.’ Mary flashed a smile.

‘Hmm. I don’t think you heard his last piece of advice...’

‘I don’t think I’d want to.’

‘Fair enough. I won’t repeat it, then.’

‘No need. I like a man with all round skills, like cooking.’

‘Oh, I can do a bit of that.’

‘Really? What can you do?’

‘Oh, anything with mince, really...’

‘Well, I like a good chili.’

‘Oh, I can do a really good one of them...’

‘Well then, I’ll come round and try it out,’ Mary said, to Steve’s surprise.

‘OK. You’re on!’

‘My next night off is Wednesday. I’ll come round about 7pm, shall I?’

‘Good. I look forward to it.’ Steve grinned from ear to ear.

‘See ya then.’ Mary high fived Steve before he finally returned to the table.

‘You were gone a long time,’ Geoff said testily.

We have already discussed Steve’s unsuitability as a poker player. If he’d known what was best for him, he’d have played his cards closer to his chest.

Instead, he smiled. ‘Yeah, well...’

‘And what’s that muck you’ve bought me?’ Geoff frowned at his handled pint glass.

‘Old Knacker,’ Steve replied matter-of-factly.

‘Looks flat as a fart.’ Geoff harrumphed.

‘Mary figures it suits you, Old Knacker...’ Steve betrayed his naivety yet again.

‘We’ll just have to rename you “Gordon,”’ Geoff grumped.

‘Why Gordon?’ Steve was out to break all world naivety records.

‘As in Gay Gordon! You and all that “sensitivity”!’

This stung Steve into further indiscretion.

‘Well, it works!’

‘What do you mean, it works?’

‘I’m cooking tea for Mary on Wednesday!’ Steve concluded with a triumphant smile.

Geoff was temporarily lost for words, before commenting, ‘I thought we’d agreed that it was Alex who liked you.’

‘So did I, but hey ho. Maybe I’ll get them both!’ he smirked.

Geoff forced an encouraging smile. ‘Oh, well done! I see you’re following my advice about developing an active Subs’ bench.’

‘Yeah. Glad I came in now! What was it you wanted to talk to me about?’ Steve was all smiles.

'Ah. We'll come to that.' Geoff' lowered his voice conspiratorially. 'First of all, remember my advice. No leaving it in to soak!' Geoff raised his voice, so that he could be heard throughout the pub.

At this moment, in walked Ron with Jason. 'He's not getting into mischief again, is he?'

Geoff suddenly looked even more uncomfortable than Steve did. Things did not get any better when Steve tried to change the subject.

'So, Geoff. What was it that you called me over to talk about, then?'

Geoff fixed Steve with a withering look. 'Never mind that. Let me repeat. Don't leave it in to soak!'

The rest of the evening passed by in awkward small talk, punctuated by Ron proffering reasons why he hadn't been able to raise a team the previous day – holidays, weddings, and barbeques featuring strongly in his explanations – to which Geoff retorted that barbeques had not featured in his day and that decent God-fearing folk used to get married on a Saturday.

Steve rather switched himself off from the conversation, preferring to think about the prospect of entertaining Mary. At the end of the evening, he returned under a fullish moon to his untidy house, having consumed about half of his weekly alcohol units allowance. It seemed that he was back in business. At least, he was happy about that.

Chapter 21: 'Sick Company Syndrome'

Date: Monday June 26th, 2000, 7.30am

At last, the day had dawned. Steve sat downstairs in his untidy house. He had an email to write.

To the Rt. Hon. Tony Blair MP

Dear Tony

Continuing the theme of my last note, I'd like to bring your attention to the subject of Health Promotion in the workplace and invite you to our Health and Safety Day at BCG today. I realise that this is short notice, but if you happen to be in the vicinity, you would do well to drop in on the exciting activities that will be taking place.

People talk a lot about Health and Safety, but I feel that they neglect the Health component. As you point out, accidents in the workplace are showing a pronounced downwards trend. Unfortunately, this is not the case with health-related issues, in particular: stress.

I like to think that we have an example of best practice taking place at BCG today. There are activities and displays related to stopping smoking, sensible drinking, healthy eating, safe sex, sun awareness, physical fitness and of course stress awareness.

Best regards

Steve

After showering and putting on his best work clothes, he went out to his car, carrying a blue kit bag, and drove off.

No sooner had he walked into his office and fired up his computer to check out his emails than in walked Paula. Steve had promised to give her a lift to the Site Medical Centre.

'Are yer ready, then?' Paula demanded.

'Just checking my emails. Oh look, there's one here from Debbie!'

'What's it say, then?'

Steve read out the email.

Hi, Steve.

Good luck with the Health Day today. I can't wait to hear how my team get on with it. Roy Elliott and Don Challis in a salsa class, I ask you? What a hoot! Make sure you video it.

Steve's face darkened as he read the next bit.

Unfortunately, I've been called to an urgent meeting in Brussels and cannot attend. Please accept my sincere apologies. I'm sure the day will go swimmingly without me. Good luck!

With very best wishes,

Debbie

'Damn!' Steve cried out in anguish.

'Never mind. The rest of them will be there. We'll show 'em,' Paula reassured him.

'Yeah. I'll just post a quick response, then let's go down there.'

Steve typed a hasty response.

'Hang on, I'll just check it's gone OK.'

As Steve checked his Sent box, Paula spotted the name of the last email recipient.

'Oh, yer haven't been writing to him again?'

'Oh, it's nothing...' Steve hastily closed his outbox.

Paula was not to be denied. 'Come on. Show "nothing" to me, then.'

'OK. It's about today's event,' Steve admitted.

'What about today's event?'

'I've invited him to it.' Steve beamed.

'And yer really expect yer man to turn up here, then?' Paula asked with increasing incredulity

'Why not? He's a local MP. The chemical industry is of vital importance to the local and national economy. We've had members of the Royal Family visit here...'

'Yeah. Very minor ones. I showed them round, remember?' Paula was quick to point out.

Steve grimaced at the memory of his non-invitation on that particular tour. 'Yeah. I think he should be aware of the ground-breaking work that we are doing with health promotion in the workplace.'

'But you can't even get your Head of Department to come.'

Paula's invective was interrupted by the appearance of Margaret.

'What's all this you're doing about safe sex, then?' she demanded.

'We're trying to educate people,' Paula explained.

Margaret crossed herself. 'No good will come of it. You mark my words!'

'Why not?' Steve intervened on Paula's behalf.

'Avoidance of eternal damnation beats education any day. Am I the only good Catholic around here?' Margaret brandished her crucifix necklace to emphasise her point.

'I can see what we're up against. Let's go.' Steve picked up his car keys and made for the door to avoid further confrontation.

The Elton Site was one of the largest chemical industry locations in Europe. It was roughly two miles from the Elton Centre to the Training Centre. On the way, there were numerous chemical plants.

'Wow. Not been around the site for ages. It still looks impressive,' Paula observed.

'Yeah. one or two gaps around the place, though, like missing teeth in an ageing boxer's mouth.' Steve pointed out a pile of rubble to the right.

'What's that one over there?' Paula pointed to some twinkling lights and large tanks to the left.

'That's the 6,6 ethylene diamine plant. BCG sold it to Lefevre in 1998.'

'And that one?' Paula pointed straight ahead.

'Oh. that's the propylene plant. That went to Schmidt...'

'And this one here?' Paula pointed to a bright orange flame emanating from a tall steel stack.

'That's the naphtha processing plant. That's now with Western Industries Inc. I hope they look after it. That bad bugger could blow up half of Teesside!'

'Yer good at this. aren't yer?' Paula was suitably impressed.

'Bit of an anorak at heart, me.'

'There don't seem to be many left that still belong to BCG...'

'Well, there's one just there. That's the propylene oxide plant.' Steve pointed out a relatively small unit. 'But that's under threat...'

'Why's that?'

'Now then,' Steve explained, 'as you will know, propylene is the main feedstock for propylene oxide. When BCG sold the propylene plant to Schmidt, they signed a 3-year supply deal.' Steve stopped the car at a traffic light. 'That's up for renewal. Schmidt want to charge a lot more for the propylene and the European Commission didn't like Schmidt selling the propylene to BCG cut-price anyway...'

'Wouldn't it have been simpler for BCG to have kept the propylene plant in the first place?' Paula asked.

'You tell me! I don't think that the city would have liked us hanging onto it. We're not into commodity chemicals anymore, remember?' Steve paused before concluding, 'And we were broke because of our acquisition strategy.'

'So let me get this right. We sold the plant cheap to a competitor, but we're the main customer for the product, and now they want to charge us more than we can pay because of Brussels – and this makes sense to the financial whizz kids?

'As I said, don't ask me. Ours is not to reason why. Ours is to do or die. Remember?' Steve made a final turn right.

The car finally pulled up at a rather dilapidated post war art deco-ish building with BCG Training Centre emblazoned on it. There was a similarly dilapidated smaller building next door, with green doors and red crosses painted on. This was marked 'Medical Centre'.

Steve and Paula got out of the car and walked into the Training Centre. People were setting up displays, massage tables in side rooms and mats for a Pilates class.

The lovely Patricia clocked Steve immediately. 'Hello there, Steve. How are you? Are you going to have a go at this again?' she asked in her lilting Geordie accent. Steve's tongue was nearly hanging out at the sight of her black leotard, to Paula's manifest disapproval.

'Well, I'm not sure after I pulled my muscle last time.'

'Why ay, but I massaged it better for yer.'

Steve smiled at the memory. 'Oh. Yes. That was nice. OK, I'll be there.' Steve gave her the thumbs up sign as he and Paula walked on.

'There's no hope for you. I thought you had a girlfriend?'

'Ex-girlfriend, remember!'

'I'm not so sure about that. There's unfinished business there. You mark my words,' Paula said presciently.

'Funnily enough, you're in agreement with my friend Geoff, for once.'

'That sleazeball of a so-called mate of yours! What does he say?'

'That I should hang tight until she comes back, then restrict meet-ups to 2 times a week.'

'And that's "The Rules" for men, is it?'

Steve was getting decidedly sulky. 'Suppose so.'

'Well, it's worked so well for you so far, hasn't it?'

Steve and Paula were interrupted by a posse of men in blazers and ties, plus a couple of suits. Stuart was amongst them.

A balding early middle-aged man was the first to speak. This was Roy Elliott, one of Debbie's loyal lieutenants.

'So, this is it, then?'

'Yes. What do you think?' Steve asked enthusiastically.

There was general muttering from the blazers and suits.

Paula intervened. 'Come on, fellers. Let me take you to the sexual health demonstration.'

'Well, that's all very well for the lads on the plant. Eight pints on a Friday night, then rat up a drainpipe. Don't think it appertains to us,' Roy answered sniffily.

'You'd be surprised!' Paula looked pointedly at Steve.

'But we're BCG managers!' Roy protested.

'Exactly!' agreed Paula, looking once again at Steve.

Paula led the deputation through to a small room. There was a stand with various posters. It was bedecked with multi-coloured condoms, blown up as balloons. A nurse, in uniform, was waiting.

'Welcome, gentlemen...'

Paula introduced the nurse. 'This is Nurse Sharon Smith from the Sexual Outreach department of the local NHS Trust...'

'Waste of public money!' exclaimed Roy.

Paula carried on brightly. 'She goes out to local businesses and schools to spread the word of safer sex.'

'Yes, I do.' Sharon smiled.

'Any interesting stories, Sharon?' Paula asked her well-rehearsed question.

'Well, there was the time that we went out "over the border" at Christmas to spread the word to the working girls...'

'How did that go, then?'

'Alright. I think that the girls were already pretty clued up about safer sex. They gratefully accepted the gifts, though.'

'Must have been pretty scary, though.'

'Yeah. A lot of guys in suits and posh cars driving very slowly. A couple of them even propositioned me!'

The atmosphere from the suits and the blazers was turning decidedly hostile.

Paula sensed the antagonism. 'OK. Let's get on with it. Sharon, what are you going to show us?'

'I'm going to show you gentlemen how to put a condom on.'

This was met by general embarrassment.

Sharon continued. 'Here's a banana, which I'm using to represent a penis. I'm now going to get a condom out of a packet.'

'Do we really need to see this?' Roy protested.

'You never know. And if you don't, your kids probably might,' Sharon suggested cheekily.

'I don't think so!' Roy shook his head.

Sharon continued the demo to squirms of embarrassment from the suits and the blazers.

'We then slide the condom, with the teat end pointing outwards of course, onto the penis...'

Sharon then put the condom clad banana into her mouth to ever more incredulity.

'You should also use it as a barrier for oral sex... Mmmm. Taste that fruit!' Sharon concluded blissfully.

Belatedly sensing that this wasn't going well, Steve called a halt. 'OK. Let's move on.'

'We have leaflets on HIV protection, pregnancy – oh, and prostate health, if you want to come back later for a check-up,' Sharon insisted, slowly donning a pair of surgical gloves.

The posse moved on uneasily.

'Well, that was disgusting and uninformative. What have you got next?' Roy asked.

'Let's have a look round. Over there, we have reflexology, over there's aromatherapy, then we have reiki and Thai massage.'

A masseuse poked her head round a curtain and clocked Roy.

'Ah, hello, sir. No happy ending today, then?' she blurted out.

'I don't know what she means,' Roy said.

Roy hastily walked on, looking very flustered.

Steve's Septic friend Don butted in. 'But all this is completely without scientific foundation. You'll be telling us that you've got homeopathy next!'

Steve blushed. 'That's over there,' he said, pointing to the next stand.

'Ye Gods! This used to be a reputable chemical company!' Don looked heavenwards.

Steve proceeded to dig a bigger hole for himself. 'Well, if you want science, there's magnetic food sensitivity testing over there.'

Don was not impressed. 'Kinesiology! Kinesiology! Bloody charlatans!!'

'So you don't like it, then? Well, it worked for me,' Steve replied defensively.

'Obviously a prime case of mindless over matter!' Don noted sarcastically.

'Then we have a stop smoking information desk over there,' Steve said proudly.

'My staff don't smoke,' Roy commented stiffly.

Steve attempted to carry on regardless. 'There's also alcohol awareness and drugs awareness information next door.'

'There's no druggies round here.' Roy remained unimpressed.

'What about Phil Handley?' Steve recalled an apprentice who had died of an overdose.

'Oh, yes, him. Most unfortunate. Bad business, that...' Roy was temporarily silenced.

Gerry, a plant manager then volunteered, 'And one of my lads tested positive after a near miss...'

'I hope you sacked him on the spot,' Don said caustically.

'No. We gave him counselling and time off to sort himself out,' Gerry explained reasonably.

'What?' Don was incredulous.

'It's company policy. Seven business principles, remember?' Gerry smiled.

'You didn't allow him back, did you?' Don grew ever redder.

Steve resisted the temptation to offer him a free blood pressure test.

'Yes. He's OK now. Family man. Got a baby with his partner. He just went off the rails for a while.' Gerry smiled again.

'They ought to be fired on the spot. Company's gone soft. In my day...' Don was about to launch a new tirade when Steve interjected.

'We also have information on stress at work.'

'You mean the "new bad back"?' Don hissed, before adding, 'Bloody shirkers.'

Roy concluded, 'Most unedifying! I've seen enough. I'm forbidding my staff from coming here. If they do, they do so in their own time!'

'Hear! Hear! New Age nonsense. I would do the same if I still had any staff,' Don agreed.

Steve lost his cool. 'You should remember that there's a HEALTH in "Health and Safety"!'

'Right. I'm off!' Roy announced.

'Me too!' Don agreed once more.

Roy and Don strode off, taking most of the posse with them.

Gerry and Stuart remained.

Gerry spoke up. 'Well, I think it's good, what you're doing. I'll certainly be encouraging my lot to come down for this.'

'Yeah. Bloody stuffed shirts. Well done, you!' Stuart added.

'Thanks. I wasn't expecting that.' Steve tried not to look too surprised.

'You're doing something decent for a change. I only wish that you could bring some of the passion that you showed today to your regular day job.' Stuart still couldn't resist having a dig.

Steve and Paula (who had remained silent throughout the previous contretemps) returned to Sharon's sexual health stand.

'I don't remember that oral demonstration being in the script!' Steve felt that Sharon had gone too far.

It could not be said that Sharon was repentant. 'I'm sorry, I couldn't resist. What a bunch of stuck-up pricks! Wish I'd got my hands on them!' She flexed her gloved right hand menacingly.

Paula remained at the sexual health stand. Steve walked on to the stop smoking stand. 'Good morning, Angie. How's it going?'

'Oh. Quite well. I've handed out a lot of leaflets. Also, I've got a few names for the next "stop smoking" workshop.'

'Oh great! Put me down for that!' Steve volunteered, to Angie's surprise.

'But you attended the last one, didn't you?'

'Yes, I did. I managed to stop for 3 months after it.' Steve grinned.

'What made you start again?'

'Oh. My girlfriend at the time smoked like a chimney. There were times when I couldn't resist.'

Angie smiled. 'Let's not go into that, shall we?'

Steve looked around, looking somewhat puzzled. 'Anyway, what happened to that "'smokalyser" we were supposed to be using to show whether somebody was smoking or not?'

'Couldn't use it, I'm afraid.'

'What?'

'Health and safety. It involved people taking a puff from a cigarette. Strictly verboten on the site.'

Steve sighed. 'How's about the healthy eating demonstration?'

'Well, we had our problems over that too, but we managed to get the risk assessment through in the end.'

'So, you could cook healthy food for the attendees?'

'Yes. There were issues over open flames and food hygiene in a non-canteen setting, but we got there in the end.'

'Well done. Thank you for that. What about the blood sugar test?'

Angie shook her head. 'Oh no. Absolute no. No. Involved penetration of the skin. Needles, etcetera. No way could we do that. I did mention it at our committee meeting.'

Unfortunately, that had happened somewhere in the middle of Steve's reverie. 'It's health and safety gone mad,' he muttered. Noticing that he may have been overheard, he added audibly, 'Oh yes, so you did. Well, thanks a lot, Angie; I do appreciate it.'

As Steve walked on, Patricia ran up to him.

'Mind yourself, Trish. Not too fast. Slips, trips and falls, remember,' Steve quipped.

'Sorry. I was just coming to say that our Pilates session is about to start. Do you care to join us?' Patricia smiled her radiant smile.

Steve attempted to reciprocate. 'Oh. Yes. I'll be right there.'

Steve went out to his car to get his kit.

Minutes later, he re-emerged from the changing room in gym shirt and loose shorts with cheap trainers. He was wearing a headband. Steve opened a door and entered the Pilates session.

The room was spartan in décor, with off-white painted walls. The rusting window frames were painted green. There were six other participants waiting – all female. There were mats on the floor with large balls next to them. At the front stood the lovely Patricia. As soon as Steve walked in, she called the group to order and switched on the music on a ghetto blaster portable cassette player. *I'm Spinning Around* by Kylie began to blast out.

'Right. We'll start off with some ball manoeuvres, beginning with "the Cat",' Patricia announced.

Patricia continued to lead the session. Steve struggled to keep up with the exercises and to keep himself under control whilst watching Patricia's movements. The loose-fitting shorts threatened to cause embarrassment.

'Keep down! Keep down!' Steve kept repeating to himself, as inaudibly as he could. Steve looked around to try to distract himself, but all around all he could see were scantily clad hotties who were starting to perspire gently by now. Even worse, in his rush to join the class, he hadn't stopped to notice that Michelle was one of them. There she was, in a fetching black leotard that was one size too small for her ample bosom.

Why did all the attractive women on site decide this was the session to attend? Steve thought desperately.

He certainly was fighting a losing battle with his loose-fitting shorts. Finally, he was soon resorting to the ultimate deterrent. 'Ann Widdecombe. Ann Widdecombe,' he moaned in a last vain attempt to suppress his ardour.

It was all too much. Steve fell off the ball, twisting his ankle and straining his groin in the process.

'Aagh,' he shouted out as he writhed on the concrete floor.

Patricia hastily stopped the session and ran over to the stricken Steve, followed by the other class members.

'Steve! Are you alright? What you done?'

Steve writhed in agony, ensuring he stayed prone to hide his embarrassment.

Undeterred, Patricia felt his thigh. 'Where does it hurt, pet?' she asked in her sing-song Geordie lilt.

As the pain intensified, Steve was finally able to roll over and point to his groin. Patricia started to feel for the injured spot, causing Steve to roll over once again.

Patricia smiled. 'Well, I don't think that you're that badly injured, then,' she concluded.

Michelle was next on the scene. 'The Surgery's right next door. Let's take you through there and get the nurse to see to you.'

'Uh. Uh,' Steve groaned, as he rolled over once again.

'OK. Let's get you up, then.' Patricia took one of Steve's arms.

Patricia and Michelle hauled Steve up and supported him as he limped to the medical centre.

If the Training Centre seemed dilapidated, it had nothing on The Medical Centre. It was an ageing building, packed no doubt with asbestos, at one time. Two red crosses were painted on the windows of the twin doors. Fortunately, BCG retained a residual medical staff, so he was seen to reasonably promptly by a cheerful, matronly nurse, who examined his ankle thoroughly and concluded that it was only a sprain, but that he should get an X-ray at his earliest convenience. She seemed less concerned about his groin. The nurse then spent not a little time strapping up Steve's right ankle before advising him to stick to simple, traditional physical pursuits like running and swimming. And no, she hadn't felt inclined to join his (committee's) health awareness extravaganza.

By the time he arrived back in the Training Centre, the fun was over. The exhibitors were folding up their displays. The healthy cookery display had finished, judging by the number of unwashed plates lying around. Paula had left, as had Patricia. Happily, other members of the Committee had remained to clear up, including Michelle. She readily volunteered to help Steve wash up the dirty dishes. The pain enabled Steve to suppress his carnal thoughts as they stood next to each other at the wash bowl, although he still could not resist the odd peek at the top of her black leotard.

As lunch time approached, Steve finally hobbled back outside to his car, changed and drove back to the Elton Centre.

Once back in the office, Steve wasted no time in composing a furious memo to Debbie cc BCG's CEO, cc Tony Blair. He had one leg supported on a chair as he furiously thumped away on his PC keyboard. Steve was about to correct the Memo, sign it, then despatch it when his door opened. A clipboard appeared, followed by a woman in a high-vis yellow jacket.

Steve groaned at the sight of Adele, who was evidently on the warpath.

'I have grounds to believe that there has been a reportable incident involving yourself.'

'Erm, yes.'

'Can you describe the incident to me, please, in your own words?' Adele got her pen ready to write on the clipboard.

'Well, I was participating in a Pilates class...'

'Pilates class? What authorisation did you have for that?'

'Oh, we did a full risk assessment before the last one.' Steve was relieved that he had not cut that particular corner.

'Well, strictly speaking, you should have renewed it for this occasion, but I'll overlook that.'

'I was following Patricia's instructions when...'

'Patricia? Who's Patricia?' Adele's smelled blood.

'The Pilates class instructor.'

'Does she have a certificate to work here?'

'Well, now.' Steve looked thoughtful. 'She went through the site induction video. Made her late for her class last time, as I remember...'

'Hmmm. I'll have to check on that one. She needs to be an accredited contractor to work on site. What's her name?'

'Patricia Armstrong.'

'Just a minute. Trading as?'

'I dunno. Patricia Armstrong, I suppose. I'll get her card for you. Anyway, I was attempting the 'Cat' manoeuvre when I pulled a muscle in my groin and twisted my ankle.

Adele consulted her clipboard. 'Did this require medical treatment?'

Steve looked heavenwards. 'Yes, you know it did.'

'Now, don't you get curt with me, now. What treatment did you get?'

'The nurse strapped up my ankle and let me go.'

'OK. I think that seems to be in order.' Adele scribbled on her clipboard. 'I'll have to make full report, of course...'

Phew. That could have been worse, Steve was thinking to himself when Adele turned to go.

As she reached the office door, she stopped and turned around, as though she was Lieutenant Columbo. 'And just one more thing...'

'What?' Steve asked wearily. His ankle was beginning to give him serious gip.

'How did you get back here?

'I drove, of course.'

'But were you fit to drive? I'm not sure you were. It's your right leg, isn't it?'

'Ye-e-e-s.'

'Your ability to use the brake pedal could have been compromised.'

'Really?'

'A tanker carrying hazardous materials could have come out in front of you. You could have crashed into him, setting off a major incident.'

'Oh, come on...'

'No. No. No. We have enough explosive chemicals on this site to set off a hundred Hiroshimas. You could have taken out all of Teesside.'

'I only drove two miles. It could have been after a football five a side...' Steve protested.

'That's irrelevant. I'll have to report this as a major near miss.'

'What happens then?'

'You'll be hearing from us, although we have more of a "no blame" culture these days, so I think you should escape disciplinary action.'

'That's reassuring,' Steve said sarcastically.

'I think that's everything. I'll wish you "Good Day".'

Adele marched out of the office, clipboard in hand, and slammed the door behind her.

Steve slumped in his seat before observing, 'And I thought I suffered from OCD!'

Steve returned to his PC monitor to complete his memo.

Enter Paula...

Steve turned away from his PC screen.

'Oh hello, Paula. How did the rest of it go?'

'Alright, except we didn't get the turn-out we'd expected.'

'That figures. What a bunch of arses!'

'Anyway, are you alright?'

'Yeah. Just a slight strain,' Steve wheezed.

'What're yer writing now?'

'Nothing.' Steve immediately tried to hide his screen.

'We're not going through all that again. Out with it!' Paula demanded.

Steve sighed and started to read out his

Memo to Debbie Gould

cc Sir Timothy Whittaker-Sampson (CEO BCG),

Rt Hon Tony Blair MP.

Health Awareness Day (Lack of Support)

Dear ~~Debbie~~ (correction) Dr Gould...

I was very concerned by the lack of support given to ~~my~~ the Health Promotion Day by fellow managers. The Day was supposed to give a new approach to health promotion within the workplace and tackle emerging threats such as stress at work and HIV infection.

I must say that your colleagues were very hostile to what my committee were trying to do. There was an excellent range of educational displays, from sexual health to stopping smoking, with individual relaxation treatments, such as aromatherapy and reiki.

It was a shame that you weren't there to witness it in person. In your absence, your colleagues behaved abominably, with one or two honourable exceptions.

For a team committed to creating innovation, they seemed very reluctant to accept innovative ideas. No wonder BCG struggles to launch new products.

'I was about to add a last paragraph, correct it and send it off,' Steve explained.

'Yer not going to send that to her, are you?' Paula was aghast.

'I certainly am,' Steve declared, before adding, 'Perhaps you could give me a hand with finishing it...'

'Well, yes. Yer not going to associate me with it though, are yer?'

'Oh. No. So the last paragraph starts: *"These Attitudes belong to the Stone Age..."*'

'Well, that's certainly true.' Paula nodded thoughtfully.

'Now, how do I end it? Perhaps I could strike a more conciliatory note...'

'Let me think now...' Paula mused

Steve got there first. 'I've thought of it!'

'Go on...'

In order to survive in an increasingly competitive global environment, BCG must adopt a holistically innovative approach. This does not solely apply to the introduction of new products but must permeate the whole organisation!

Best regards,

Steve.

Paula took a deep breath. 'Yer not serious, are you?'

'I'm deadly serious. One of these days, people will know that I was ahead of my time...' Steve stopped for thought: *Like Tony Benn!*

Paula frowned. 'I didn't notice him being a part of the present government.'

'But he was ahead of his time on gays, women's rights, racism, nuclear disarmament...'

Paula gave Steve a quizzical look.

'Well, maybe not the last one,' Steve continued. 'They all ridiculed him at the time...'

'And still do!'

'OK. Anyway, I'm sending it. Oh, wait a minute!'

Paula genuinely hoped that this meant that Steve was having second thoughts.

No such luck!

'I've forgotten to add Jim Dickson to the circulation list. He's Debbie's line manager, after all.'

Steve hastily made his final alterations to the message, before triumphantly pushing the Send button.

Paula pursed her lips. 'Well, good luck with that. You're gonna need it!

Chapter 22. 'Let There Be Chili Con Carne'

After work, Steve dashed to get himself showered and dressed in his best 'tashing' gear, consisting of freshly ironed dark blue chinos and a purple Ralph Lauren shirt, completed by a pair of brown brogue shoes. It was the night of Mary's visit.

He had contemplated calling off the soirée, due to his injuries, but concluded that they may just endow with him a certain 'wounded soldier' appeal. It always worked in the Mills and Boon novels, didn't it? Perhaps, it might even pave the way to a 'sympathy shag'. But would his injured groin stand up to the strain? Questions! Questions!

He duly donned his apron and hopped around the kitchen to cook his signature dish of chili con carne using an ever-growing number of utensils. He looked at his watch. It would not be long before Mary's arrival. In fact, she should have been there by now. Never mind, they were always late, weren't they? Anyway, he was still cooking. As he cooked, he sipped from a glass of Rioja and hummed cheerfully.

A quarter of an hour later, he looked at his watch again.

'Only 10 minutes now before it's ready. Better start setting the table,' he said to himself.

Steve spread the red and white chequered tablecloth out and put knives and forks out for two on top. He then added wine glasses, nestling on twenty-year-old coasters depicting the bird life of Britain. He filled a wooden breadbasket with Sainsbury's garlic bread, fresh out of the oven. Just as he was lighting a candle in the middle of the table, the phone rang.

It was Mary.

'Steve, I'm sorry, but I'm going to have to cancel.'

'What? But I'm just finishing cooking.'

'I've just had a booking for twelve places for an evening meal. Can't turn that down, I'm afraid.'

'Well, I suppose so. I'll have to put most of it in the freezer.'

He served out his share of the chili and sat down to eat it alone.

He'd hardly had time to utter his trademark 'Shit the bed!' catchphrase when the phone rang again.

It was Geoff.

'Good evening, Geoffrey here. Thought I'd just check on how your preparations for the ginge minge were going?'

'She's stood me up.'

'Stood you up? I always said her sister was more reliable. Why has she done that?'

'Says she has a big last-minute booking at the Dog tonight.'

'Well, a girl has to make a living.' Geoff's voice was full of innuendo. 'At least you know where you stand in her order of priorities, now.'

'Thanks for your words of encouragement,' Steve grunted.

'Anyway, to more important things. It's Coffin Dodgers tomorrow night, in case you'd forgotten.'

'Well, I don't want to go. I've had it up to here with women this week.'

'Ah no. It's like falling off a bike, remember. You need to get back on, as quickly as possible.'

'Why shouldn't I just try and get back with Karen? You said that she was sending out the right signals.'

'Oh. No. No. No. That wouldn't do.' Geoff paused. 'You just have to sit tight and wait for her to come to you!'

'Yes, but Karen's friends might come and sprag me up, preventing any chances of a reconciliation.'

'I thought you said that they'd been banned.'

'Yes, I suppose so.'

'Anyway, it's my turn. We'll overlook the incident last time. I'll call round at nine. OK?'

'OK.'

'And don't forget the Sub's bench' was Geoff's final piece of advice.

Within seconds, the phone rang again. Steve groaned, but got up again nevertheless and hobbled across the sitting room.

'Hi Steve. It's me, Karen.'

'Hi, Karen. What's the craic?'

'I was just wondering if you wanted to come round tomorrow night? Mam's going out, but you can share a bottle of wine with me.'

'Oh, sorry, Karen. I just made another arrangement.' Steve blurted the words before he had had time to think.

'Not that Geoff again!'

Steve hesitated before replying, 'Well, yes.'

'You're not going to that awful singles club together, are you?'

'No. No. No. Just into Yarm. It's his turn to drive.'

Karen turned sarcastic. 'Well, we have to do what the Chairman says, don't we?'

'No. Not necessarily. I've only just said yes to him. It would be rude to refuse now.'

'You're just scared of him. You are. You're turning down the offer of a night tucked up in bed with a real woman to a night ogling women in a pub.'

Steve started to crumble. 'Well, put like that...'

'Well, it's too late now. You've burned your boats. Me and Charlotte will just have to amuse each other. Good night!'

'Good night, Karen,' Steve said as he put the receiver down followed (not for the first time that night) by 'Shit the bed!'

Steve sat down once again to finish his meal. The phone rang yet again. Steve groaned, but got up yet again. Maybe it was Karen...

'Hi Steve, it's Mary.'

'Hello again. What can I do you for?'

'You'll never guess what. They just rang up and cancelled.'

'Oh no. Can you come round, then?'

'Sorry, it's too late. I've not got time to get dressed up – but another time definitely.'

'Definitely, maybe,' Steve muttered to himself before he began to get suspicious. 'By the way, what was the name of the booking party?'

'Let me have a look in the book. Hutton. Yes, Len Hutton, I think it was.'

'What a coincidence!' Steve said. 'You know, that's the name of a well-known cricketer...'

'So...'

'Oh, nothing. Look, I'll see you back here soon.'

After they had said their goodbyes, Steve put the phone down for the final time.

'The twat! The absolute twat!!' Steve muttered to himself.

Steve took his plate into the kitchen to start tackling the mountain of washing-up that he had left.

Chapter 23: 'Unhealthy Consequences'

It was lunchtime the next day. Time for Steve to limp his way to the Lakeside Restaurant.

Steve purchased his customary lunch of pie and chips and proceeded to join the Septics' table. Terri went straight on to the offensive.

'Well, you really did it this time!'

'What do you mean?' Steve said innocently.

'Upset Debbie. I've never seen her so angry!"

Steve was genuinely astonished. 'What did I do?'

'That memo you sent. I was with her this morning. Steam was coming out of her ears!'

'I tried to make it conciliatory.'

'Conciliatory? Conciliatory? Copies to Tony Blair and the CEO of BCG. What planet are you on?'

'Well, I just said what was in my mind.'

Frank weighed in. 'Well, it's hardly a beautiful one! Tony Blair fucking hell!'

Don felt he needed to explain himself. 'By the way Stephen, it was nothing personal yesterday.'

'It didn't seem that way,' Steve said grumpily.

'OK. Roy got a bit sarky, but I'm afraid it was a crock of New Age shit, as far as I was concerned.'

'And I believe you did yourself a mischief,' Les added gleefully.

'Yes, I sprained my ankle and pulled a muscle in my groin in the Pilates class.'

This was met by guffaws all round, except for Terri.

Les laughed. 'Ha. Ha. Was she worth it?'

Frank confirmed. 'Well worth it, according to the lads on the plant. They'd have all given her one.'

'Now, come on!' Steve protested.

'Sounds like a cunning plan on your part for her to get inside your knickers if you ask me. I like the novel role reversal!' Frank could not help but express his admiration.

Steve blushed. 'It wasn't like that at all – and she's much younger than me.'

'So you've thought about it?' Les could see right through him.

'I didn't mean it that way.' Steve was beginning to wish that he had stayed in his office and had a sandwich.

Frank expressed his admiration once more. 'Underneath that veneer of New Age bullshit, you seem to be a man after our own hearts. We'll have to invite you to the "Smoker.'

'Smoker? What's that?'

'It used to be an exclusively male evening.' Frank looked pointedly at Terri. 'Where there'd be skits on the management...'

'Why Smoker?'

'Well, in between the sketches, there'd be...' Frank paused. '"Other" light entertainment.'

'What he's saying is that there used to be strippers,' Les intervened to enlighten Steve.

'Wow. How long ago was that?'

'Not that long ago, come to think of it. All different nowadays. We have to invite women...'

Terri bristled at the last remark.

'Still, we have a good night. Terri plays the piano,' Les tried to placate her.

Frank butted in. 'And Les treads the boards. Did a brilliant impersonation of Our Beloved Leader, Jim Dickson, last year.'

'Thanks, Frank. Not difficult to do. He sends himself up...'

'I've only met him a couple of times, he seemed OK. He's accepted my invitation to come to the Awards night in Yarm...'

This last remark was met by puzzlement all around the table.

'Oh, we're up for an award...' Steve explained.

'Award. Award? Not your fucking useless Health Committee, I hope?' Frank said.

'No, that got nominated last year,' Steve said without irony. 'This time, it's for product innovation.'

'Don't swear! Innovation? Nobody fucking innovates round here!' Frank was even more unimpressed.

Steve continued unabashed. 'Well, it was developed when we were in Sedgefield. It's for our new sun cream.'

'So, what's new about that?' Don said.

'It's nanotechnology in action...' Steve explained.

'Spare us the bullshit!' Frank said.

'Anyway, I entered for the Tees Valley Innovation Award and we're on the short list. I heard a couple of weeks ago,' Steve continued enthusiastically.

'Good. I wish you well. It might just save you from the Wrath of Deborah. You're a marked man now, you know,' Terri said.

'So, when does the ceremony take place?' Les asked.

'End of September.'

'Well, at least you've got three months' grace,' Les observed.

Steve was puzzled by the reply and asked what he had meant.

'Beware the Curse of the Awards,' Les warned.

Steve remained puzzled.

Frank provided a football related analogy. 'It's like the Manager of the Month award. No sooner does a club manager win it, but his side suffers a terminal decline in form – then he gets the sack.'

'But I'm not in line for the push!' Steve protested.

It was Les's turn to put Steve right. 'Now you really are showing naivety. Has no one mentioned Operation Dead Duck to you, my artless young friend?'

'Oh, you mean Project Mallard? Of course. But it only affects 10% of the workforce, surely?'

'Oh, the innocence of the young! That's what they tell you. This of course omits those who "volunteer" for early retirement.' Les explained. 'Oh, they didn't tell you that,' he added on seeing the surprised look on Steve's face.

'You're volunteering, aren't you, Don?' Frank said.

'Bloody right I am.'

'The wheelbarrows full of cash are ready and waiting to roll!' Don got out of his seat and made appropriate pushing motions. 'That's why I'm going. I reckon they'll change the rules next time round. Don't want to be hanging round here when they do.'

Steve was not satisfied. 'But surely, it's a legal contract. They can't change it just like that. Surely?'

Les was pitying. 'You are naïve, aren't you? Next, you'll be saying that because you're under 50 they'll leave you alone, so you can collect your pension in full.'

'That's what used to happen...'

'That was in the good old days,' Frank said. 'Not now. Watch out! They're only letting Don get away with it because he's so bloody knackered, they can't get out of it this time.'

Les folded his arms. 'The problem with you, Stephen, is that you believe in things. Mark my words. This is no place for believers!'

Following his encounter with the Septics, Steve was hoping for a quiet afternoon reflecting on the unfairness of it all. No such luck! As he was walking down the corridor back to his office, he was intercepted by an irate Stuart.

'You absolute Muppet!' was Stuart's opening gambit.

Despite his shock, Steve couldn't help reflecting it was those who used the word 'Muppet' as a term of abuse who were the true Muppets. What was wrong with the word 'Fuckwit', after all?

'What?' was all Steve could muster by way of reply.

'The memo you wrote to Debbie. She's not happy, you know.'

'So I gather.' Steve started to regain his composure.

'She had me in her office for an hour. Was wondering how we could sack you on the spot!'

'But I thought you supported my health day.'

'Not when you send idiotic memos with copies to the CEO. Have you no idea?'

'Well, I wasn't happy with the way her minions treated me.'

'You should learn to button your lip. And what was that about a copy to...' Stuart started speaking very slowly and emphatically. 'T-O-N-Y B-L-A-I-R.'

'Only in his capacity as my local MP.'

'Yeah, right.' Stuart was dismissive. 'Delusions of grandeur, you have. You are going to sit down with me and write a grovelling letter to Debbie.'

Steve sighed. 'Really?'

'Yes, really.' Stuart started to calm down, remembering his initial support for Steve's initiative. 'And while we're at it, we need to sort out the complaint I've had from the Safety Committee about the circumstances surrounding your reportable injury. I think maybe we can get you off on that one. A course on Safe Manual Handling, perhaps?

'OK. Thanks for that, Stuart.'

'Right. My office, first thing tomorrow – and by that, I mean 8.30 – OK?'

'OK, Stuart.' Steve could not help himself flicking a surreptitious v sign as Stuart walked on in front of him.

'I saw that!' Stuart said, as he turned round.

Chapter 24: 'A Not-So-Divine Evening'

That evening Steve found himself sitting down at a table at Coffin Dodgers while 'Dance the Night Away' by the Mavericks played in the background. Although it was still early doors, Geoff was not impressed by what he saw.

'It's like a bloody stag do in here tonight,' he reflected bitterly.

Steve couldn't help showing his frustrations. 'Yeah, we'd have been better off going to Yarm. Oh, and you do realise that I could have been with Karen tonight.'

'As I keep telling you, shag her some other time. We're after fresh meat tonight.'

'Like what we're seeing all around us,' Steve commented sarcastically, before adding, 'What if her friends turn up and I get caught?'

'Will you stop fretting about that?' Geoff insisted. 'As you keep saying, they've been barred out.'

'Yeah. I suppose so.' Steve looked at his watch. 'Anyway, it's too late for them to be let in. Maybe I should stop worrying.'

'There's a good lad! I knew you'd come round to my way of thinking!' Geoff concluded.

Meanwhile, unbeknownst to our seedy heroes, Julie, Ros and Di were driving towards The Anvil.

'I don't know why you're bothering with this. You're banned.' Di, the ever-reluctant driver, spoke as the car neared its target.

'No-one bans us from anywhere and lives to tell the tale!' Julie announced fiercely.

Ros giggled. 'And don't worry, we've got a plan, haven't we Julie?'

'Ay. I reckon that Dracula will fall for it,' Julie concurred.

'You could even say swallow it!' Ros added, cueing raucous laughter from them both.

'Don't you worry Di, we'll see you right,' Julie reassured Di, although they rarely did.

As the car pulled up in front of the Anvil, Ros gave her instructions to Di. 'Now just you wait here. We'll use our feminine powers of persuasion on Dracula!'

Di found it hard to imagine what feminine powers these were, but nonetheless stayed in her seat as the other two walked towards the pub entrance.

Ros and Julie had hardly crossed the threshold when they were challenged by Dracula.

'Wait a minute. Where are yous two ladies going?'

'Oh, sorry we're late, Mistah,' Julie volunteered.

'Never mind that. I banned you two *sine die* on behalf of the committee two weeks ago.'

'Can't you overlook that now, pet?' Julie made big eyes at Dracula.

The Master of the Doorway was unmoved. 'No! Your behaviour was totally unacceptable. We can't be havin' that sort of thing.'

The girls revealed a proposition that might just persuade him to change his mind.

Ros whispered in Dracula's ear, 'How do you fancy a quick gobble outside?'

'Gan on pet. I bet yer gagging for it,' Julie added.

'And I swallow!' Ros licked her lips alluringly.

Dracula reached for his silk handkerchief to wipe his brow. 'I-I-I can't leave my post.'

'Go on, it's after half eight now. Nobody else is going to come – except you of course, if yer were to accompany us outside!' Julie reasoned.

'Do yer like T Rex, Mistah Dracula?' Ros enquired.

'Can't say I do. More of a Frank Sinatra man, me.'

'Ay. I can see a bit of Big Frank about yer. Very dapper!' With that, Ros grabbed Dracula's crotch. 'But did ya know that T Rex had a song banned in South Africa, because of supposed references to...' Ros paused for effect and whispered. '...oral sex!'

Dracula could stand it no more. 'OK. OK. I can't be long, mind.'

Meanwhile, back in the Anvil, Steve was still looking at his watch.

'Can't we go to Yarm now?' he asked as he took the last swig from his pint of beer.

'I've still got nearly a full pint to go,' Geoff replied.

'I've got a bad feeling about this.' Steve could sense that the train doors were about to slide shut.

'Patience! Patience! We'll head on once I've finished my pint.'

Steve realised that, as Geoff was driving, he would want to savour every last drop.

'What are you worrying about?' Geoff went on.

'Have you ever seen *Sliding Doors?* Steve attempted to explain his anxiety.

'What's that when it's at home?'

'It's a film.'

'Oh, there was I thinking that it was something that Ron sells.' Geoff lowered his voice and looked around. 'We need to talk about him very soon, by the way. It's a funny name. What sort of a film is it?'

'It's known as a Rom Com.'

'A what?'

'Romantic comedy.'

'Like *Some Like It Hot*? There was a film and a half!'

'No. More like *Notting Hill,*' Steve tried to explain.

'Isn't that the place down south where they have a riot every August Bank Holiday?'

'Yeah. But also a film starring Hugh Grant and...'

'Oh him! Well, we all know what happened to him!' It had been almost exactly five years since the incident with Divine Brown on a hot summer night in LA, but it certainly remained fresh in the Chairman's memory.

Little did the sleazy pair know that as they spoke, a similar act was being planned in a car park near them.

Ros and Dracula set off together with Julie in tow. 'I've got to make sure that my friend Ros is safe,' she explained to a reluctant Dracula. 'Anyway, I like to watch. Yer don't mind, do yer? I might even join in.' Julie grinned.

Ros gave Dracula's crotch another squeeze to keep him onside.

'Yer do keep yourself clean now?' Ros asked. 'I don't want no cheese or any Bobby Charltons in me teeth.'

'Bobby Charltons? What's them?' Dracula was puzzled.

'Pubes stuck under the hood, like a Bobby Charlton comb-over.'

'Oh no. Absolutely no reason to worry about that. I don't have one.' Ray hesitated before explaining. 'My parents believed in cleanliness.'

'So you're a clean-cut lad, then, are yer Ray?' Ros gave Dracula another squeeze. 'All the better!'

Once they had reached a secluded spot behind a group of parked cars, Ros issued the order. 'Open your flies now. Let the dog see the rabbit.'

Dracula duly opened up as Ros knelt down. 'Come on, let's see it.'

'I've got it out now,' Dracula protested.

'Oh so you have. Where's me magnifying glass? Not very big, is it?' Ros said mockingly.

'Come on, get on with it,' Dracula commanded, not noticing Julie reaching for her handbag.

Ros moved her head aside as Julie took a quick succession of photos with her digital camera. Flash! Flash! Flash! Poor Dracula didn't know what had hit him.

'Smile please. You're on *Candid Camera*,' Julie shouted.

Ros laughed out loud. 'Hee. Hee. No. *You've Been Framed*, more like!'

Dracula hastily re-adjusted his clothing. 'This is outrageous! You can't do that!!'

Julie held the digital images up to his face. Dracula made a vain attempt to grab the camera back off her, but Julie was far too quick.

'We just have. Now you're gonna let us in, aren't you?'

'Over my dead body,' Dracula spluttered.

'I can walk up to your beloved Brenda right now and show her these!' Julie insisted.

'What would the Committee think?' Julie added.

Ray was left with no option but to nod and sigh as they walked back through the car park.

Julie banged on the driver's window. 'Come on, Di. He's letting us in.'

Brenda immediately got up to greet the incoming party as they filtered into the pub. 'Ray. I thought we'd banned these girls.'

'Well, I didn't ban this one.' Ray pointed at Di.

Brenda was unimpressed. 'So....?'

'Well, these two have apologised for their behaviour last time and this young lady has promised to vouch for their future good conduct. Haven't you?'

Di tried not to look surprised. Ros gave her a wink, which was all too visible to Brenda.

'Well, I suppose so...' she stammered.

Brenda arched her eyebrows. 'Well it all seems a bit fishy to me. I'm not convinced. I think I'm going to have to consult the rest of the committee.'

Ray blanched. 'I'm not sure that's necessary,' he said, before reasoning, 'Look Brenda, we're a bit short on the distaff side tonight, if you see what I mean.'

'Well, the gentlemen here would have to be a bit desperate, but OK. I'll allow it.'

If Ray thought that his suffering was at an end, he was sadly mistaken.

Julie turned to him. 'Thanks for your understanding – Sir[c].' She giggled.

Brenda broke the awkward silence that ensued. 'I don't know what's been going on, Ray, but I want a full explanation,' she said, before adding helpfully, 'in your own time, of course.'

It was at this moment that Steve looked up from watching Geoff's slowly diminishing pint of beer. 'Oh, no. Look who's just arrived!'

Geoff turned round and laughed. 'Well, that'll certainly liven things up. How did they get in?'

The girls walked past Geoff and Steve's table.

Geoff patted the seat beside him. 'Hey, girls. Come and sit down here. Tell us how you got in.'

'We couldn't possibly...' Ros smirked as she parked her oversized arse next to Geoff.

'Let's just say that Dracula's a Roundhead rather than a Cavalier!' Julie laughed uproariously at her own joke.

Ros plonked herself next to a frowning Steve. 'Anyway, what are you doing here? Shouldn't you be with Karen?'

'We've split up. Didn't you know?' Steve grumped.

'Ay. But I also happen to know that Karen was wanting you back, if you played your cards right.' Ros pinched Steve's bottom.

Geoff was not to be thrown off the trail. 'Never mind all that. So, let's get back to how you girls got in?'

'Why!? We used our feminine powers of persuasion on Dracula.' Julie shuffled herself closer to Geoff.

'It's a hard man who can resist the offer of a good gobble, Ah've always said,' Ros chipped in.

Geoff and Steve both laughed with the girls. Di did not join in on the merriment.

Steve could not resist making a joke. 'So, it was role reversal on Dracula then?'

Ros was puzzled. 'Don't know what you mean, pet.'

'Sounds like you sucked the vampire?'

'Oh. Ay. Yes, right enough, but in the end, I didn't have to.'

'That's right. The powers of modern technology came to the rescue,' Julie chipped in, waving the digital camera.

At that moment, Dracula himself walked past in animated conversation with Brenda.

'How're you doin' Sir[c]?' Ros called out.

'Don't push me,' Dracula warned, with as much menace as he could muster.

'Have you explained yourself to Brenda yet?' Julie was unfazed.

'I told her that you were on best behaviour...'

'Come on Ray. Don't rise to the bait,' Brenda insisted, before whispering in his ear. 'I don't know why you let them in, in the first place.'

Destiny's Child *Say My Name* started to play.

'Oh, I love this one,' Ros shouted out.

Julie agreed. 'Ay. Enough of this explaining how we got here. Gerrup, you two.'

Ros and Julie proceeded to drag Geoff And Steve onto the dance floor. Geoff danced uncomfortably with Ros.

'They don't often play anything decent here,' Julie shouted at Steve.

'Sorry, I can't hear what you're saying...'

'It's not often you get any decent songs played in here.' Julie put her arms round Steve.

'It depends on what you call decent. Anything after 1995 leaves me cold. I liked Britpop, but since then...'

'Ay. I think you're more suited to Di than me. She likes that old shite. You should ask her for a dance, when you get the chance.'

'I don't know.'

'Not given up on Karen, then?'

'Well maybe not, but I'll ask her...'

Later, Steve had followed Julie's advice and was dancing close up to Di.

As *When You Say Nothing At All* by Ronan Keating came on, Steve was pressing himself ever closer into Di's midriff.

'Ever seen *Notting Hill*?' Di asked.

'Funny you should mention that. I was just saying to Geoff about Hugh Grant...' Steve decided not to pursue that particular line any further.

'You look a bit like Hugh Grant,' Di said.

'Really? Anyway, I can't remember who I was seeing at the time, but I took her to see it.'

'This is one of my favourite songs from one of my favourite films, actually.'

'Yeah, it's OK. Bunch of well-off Londoners pretending to be ordinary people, though.'

'Even the cute Welsh one, who...' Di made a hand gesture. '...did a lot of that...?

'Oh, him. He was just put in a bit of rough, then there was the disabled one – and the sodding dwarf...'

'Now then, don't get carried away. Some people might find that offensive. Anyway, what's the situation with Karen? Are you finished, then?'

Steve hesitated. 'Er. Yeah.'

'I can see that you're not.'

'Well, maybe not.'

'OK. I might be interested in you, but Karen's a good friend. You make sure you've sorted it out with her first.'

'OK. I will...'

'Does Karen know you're here, by the way?'

'No. I said we'd gone to Yarm.'

'You're naughty, you are! Like Hugh Grant in more ways than one.'

Steve smiled.

'Anyway, your secret's safe with me,' Di continued. 'I'll make sure the other girls don't sprag on you...'

'Thanks, Di. I'm only here because of Geoff, you know.'

'Ay. I think you're decent enough, but you should be your own man...'

Di and Steve's conversation was interrupted as an incident flared up off the dance floor.

'Will you stop these innuendos!' Dracula shouted.

'What do you mean, Sir[c]?' Ros retorted.

'Ah mean that Ah don't give in to blackmail. Any more of this and you are banned, and this time you're not coming back.'

'Oh, fuck off and die, man. Spoken like a guy with a very small cock,' Julie enjoined.

Dracula lost patience. 'Right. You're out. I gave you the benefit of the doubt and you've taken advantage of my good nature. I'm getting the committee to escort you off the premises.'

'I can't understand why he let you in, in the first place. Get out!' Brenda added.

Di realised that her evening was about to end. 'Oh, dear. Looks like I'm going to have to drive them home early again,' she whispered in Steve's ear as she led him off the dance floor.

Di paused before she went to rescue the others. 'Now, remember what I said.'

'OK. Yeah. I will,' Steve said.

Di led her protesting companions away, pursued by sundry committee members.

Steve returned to his table.

Geoff had been watching him. 'What a pity. You seemed to be in there.'

'Oh, I don't know...' Steve was unconvinced.

'You're still thinking about Karen?'

'Well, maybe...'

'Look. As I've told you many times, a standing cock has no conscience. You have to make hay while the sun shines!'

'She said I should sort things out with Karen before I could get into her knickers.'

'Women!' Geoff rolled his eyes before looking around. 'There's nothing else here for us. Let's have an early night, shall we?'

As they walked out, it was still light – something that never ceased to impress Steve. 'Wow. It's still broad daylight, almost,' he exclaimed.

Geoff took a much gloomier perspective. 'Yes, but the nights are already getting darker. You may not have noticed it. But, soon you will. Drives me mad, it does...'

With that, they got into Geoff's car and drove off into the near midnight sun.

Chapter 25: 'Booty Call'

Steve was not ready for bed as he re-entered his untidy house, despite the need to rise early for the 8.30 meeting with Stuart. There was still a large pile of washing-up from the previous evening's abortive tryst with Mary to do. Instead, he switched on the Adam and Joe Show on Channel 4. As he slumped on the sofa, he began to doze off.

* * *

Steve is at Le Mans. There's a starting grid with coffins lined up. On the opposite side of the track there are a line of ageing men in racing overalls and crash helmets (including Steve and Geoff) getting set to sprint across the track.

Finally, the long awaited Tannoy announcement comes.

'Now, Coffin Dodgers. It's time to dodge your coffins. Gentlemen, start your engines.'

The men go stumbling after the coffins, who twirl around in dance formation, evading their collective grasps.

The reverie culminates with Steve at the top of the winner's podium, flanked by Geoff and Ron. There's a wreath round his neck. The podium sitters start to spray magnum-sized bottles of Newcastle Brown Ale over each other.

Steve then holds up an urn triumphantly to a crowd of ecstatic headstones.

'Ich bin ein Coffin Dodger!' he exclaims in incorrect German, just as a ringing sound can be heard.

* * *

On the sixth ring, Steve surfaced back into consciousness and grabbed the receiver just in time.

To his surprise, it was Karen on the line.

'Hi, Steve. It's me. I thought you were still out, the time it took for you to answer.'

'Oh, no. Good clean-living boy, me,' Steve fibbed, before chuckling. 'You should know that.'

'So, you're at home now. How was Yarm?' Karen continued suspiciously.

'A bit boring. That's why I'm home.'

'Just as well. I've been trying you on your mobile for the last two hours...'

'Oh. It's a bad signal there,' Steve fibbed again.

'I'll cut to the chase. I need you over here right now.'

'What for?'

'I think you know what for!'

'But I thought it was your...' Steve almost put his foot in it before explaining, 'I can't drive over, I'm afraid. I've had too much. It was Geoff's turn, remember?'

'Well get a taxi, then. If I mean anything to you, get a taxi!' Karen was not to be put off.

The ability to drive was not the only competence that had been affected by the alcohol. 'Well, I'm not really in a fit state...' Steve said limply.

'I don't care. If you think anything of me, get yourself over here. I want a good seeing to,' Karen demanded.

Steve decided to stop looking a gift horse in the mouth. 'Alright, I'll ring a taxi. Ciao for now.' Steve sighed.

Steve put the phone down, before shouting 'Shit the bed!' whilst banging his head against an imaginary wall.

Twenty minutes later, Steve found himself aboard Pervez's taxi.

'Well, what a coincidence. I ring Teesside Taxis, and I get you.' Steve was puzzled.

'No coincidence, mate. I heard the details from the office. I said, "I'll take this one. He's a friend"', Pervez explained.

'Well, thanks.' Steve was suitably impressed.

Steve pointed at the twin portraits of Saddam and Closey.

'So it's right, what Geoff said.'

'Oh yes. They are truly great men in my estimation. Truly great men.'

'Well, I'll agree about Closey,' Steve conceded.

'Anyway, if you don't mind me asking, why do you want to go to Nunthorpe at this time of night?' Pervez enquired.

'I got a summons from Karen.'

'A booty call, right mate?'

'Oh, is that what one of them is?'

'Right mate. I know all about them. Good source of business for me at this time of night.'

'Only trouble is... I've had a skinful of beer tonight at Coffin Dodgers. I'm a bit concerned about my, erm, wou-know-what,' Steve confessed.

'Well, I do know what,' Pervez reassured Steve. 'I have always wondered. Premature ejaculation – premature for who, I ask you?'

'Actually more like Brewer's droop, if you get my drift...' Steve felt a pronounced lack of Chi.

'I think I might have just the thing for you, mate.'

Steve was all ears.

'Blue pills. I call them Victory V's. From the finest laboratories in Lahore,' Pervez explained.

'They're not counterfeit?'

'Oh no. Totally genuine. My grandfather – peace be upon him – passed away five years ago. They would raise his cock up from the dead, I tell you. Rising above Lahore – magnificent!

'Erm. How much are they?'

'For you, Steve, mate's rates. I'll give you ten for £10.'

'OK. Deal. You don't do anything else, do you?' Steve made a smoking a joint gesture.

Pervez was affronted. 'No, that's drugs, mate. I just like to help my friends out.'

'Of course. Not drugs. Herbal remedies, perhaps?' Steve smiled.

'Exactly. You are an educated man,' Pervez concluded as the taxi pulled up outside Karen's house. Steve got out and paid Pervez his fare plus the cost of the pills.

The following morning, Steve woke up, intertwined with Karen, as her bedside alarm rang.

Karen sat up and stretched out, revealing her upper body in a rather pleasing way, before turning to Steve.

'Well, thank you for a fantastic night.'

'Well, thank you, too. The pleasure was all mine,' was Steve's rather oily response.

'You started off a bit slowly, mind,' Karen chided.

'Well, I'd had a few drinks...' Steve started to explain.

'It was only when you went downstairs for that glass of water that things started to happen...'

Steve mustered all his powers of quick thinking. 'It must have had magic properties. Holy water!' he exclaimed, as he kissed her fully on the lips.

Steve snuggled up to Karen, before looking at his watch.

'Shit, is that the time? 8.20? I need to be in work.'

Steve got out of bed hastily.

'You said you don't have to be there until 9.30.'

'Appointment with Stuart. I forgot.' Steve started dressing hurriedly as Karen's mobile started to ring.

'Oh. Hi. Yeah, he's with me now...'

Steve started to look worried as Karen continued to address the mobile.

'He was where? The Singles Club? Well, thanks for letting me know.'

'I can explain!'

'No need. This time we are finished. Get out!'

'But I've not got my car.'

'Well you can get a frigging taxi. The same way that you came. Get out!'

As a dejected Steve was getting into Pervez's car a little later, Charlotte came running into Karen's boudoir.

'That horrid man isn't coming her anymore, is he, mummy?'

'No, darling, he's not. '

'And what's that he's dropped on the floor?'

Karen picked up a blister pack almost full of blue pills.

'It looks like fucking Viagra to me, mummy.'

Meanwhile, in Pervez's car, the events of the night were being dissected.

'So she kicked you out, did she?'

Steve explained that one of Karen's friends had spragged on her.

'For doing what?' Pervez asked.

'I went to the Coffin Dodgers Singles Club last night, if you remember...'

'So what? You were single at the time.'

'So, I was – and I was only following orders from the Chairman.'

'Yeah, you can't diss the Chairman, can you?'

'Illogical women!' Steve concluded.

'Too right,' Pervez agreed. 'I wonder who it was who informed on you.'

'Ah. Cherchez la femme,' Steve agreed. 'I reckon it must have been one of the fat lasses.'

'Are you sure? What about the quiet one?'

'Di. No, she's too nice to do that.'

'But, you told me last night that you reckon she fancies you.'

'Nah. Nah. She wouldn't do that.'

'So, she's got the motivation. Cherchez la femme.' Pervez repeated Steve's words in a broad Teesside accent. 'It's always the quiet ones, you know?'

'Hmm. I hope not,' Steve said, although the seeds of doubt had been sown in his mind.

'Anyway, did you need the pills?'

'Well. Yes.' Steve hesitated. 'Just the one, mind – worked like a dream, it did.' Steve winked.

'Glad to be of assistance.'

'Not sure I'll be needing them again in a hurry.'

'Save the rest up for your future conquests,' Pervez reassured Steve, who lived in constant fear that he had had his last shag on earth. 'Maybe you should give that Di a ring.'

'Haddaway and shite,' Steve retorted, before beginning to search his pockets. 'Shit the bed! They're not there!'

'You mean you left them at Karen's house.'

'Oh no. I think I did. These bloody chinos. The pockets are rubbish.'

'Why not ask for them back?'

'You're jokin', aren't yer?'

'Never mind. Tell her they're for your skin condition.'

'Yeah. She is a bit naïve. Maybe that will work...'

Chapter 26: 'Call Of Duty'

At least Steve had a nice surprise when he finally got to his office: a sympathetic email from his hero.

Hi Steve

So sorry to hear of your travails re spreading the word out about healthy living. I always try to keep myself trim, despite the demands of office. Between you and me, 'five times a night' Cherie wouldn't have it any other way!

Actually, I can truly relate to your problems. One or two of my colleagues could certainly do with losing a few pounds, I can tell you – starting with my deputy John Prescott. Imagine him doing Pilates. No, let's not. Then of course, there's Gordon. A few pounds off those jowls of his and he might start looking like a future PM! Then there's the appalling Mrs Mowlam... In contrast, I can't seem to get Peter Mandelson out of the gym...No, let's not go any further.

Finally, just a thought, but perhaps you could try and find a 3rd way. Emphasise the conventional stuff to the powers that be, like stopping smoking, while slipping in your more radical agenda when nobody's looking. It's certainly worked for me.

Best regards

Tony

This was not before he had had yet another uncomfortable encounter with Stuart. The fact that he had got in approximately one hour late had not helped.

'Did I not say 8.30 sharp?' was Stuart's opening gambit.

'Erm, I had some personal issues,' Steve mumbled.

'Haven't I told you before? You should keep your personal issues to yourself!'

Exactly the management attitude that's stressing everyone out, Steve reflected.

'Anyway, let's not waste any more time,' Stuart said pointedly, reaching for a pen and paper. 'You will write a message to Debbie apologising for your behaviour.'

'Which particular behaviour?' Steve asked.

'We have quite a choice, don't we?' Stuart agreed ironically. 'Shall we go with your splenetic email concerning the Health Awareness Day?'

Steve reluctantly picked up the pen and paper.

'You will then go to your office and convert it into an email,' Stuart commanded.

Steve thought for a moment. 'Same circulation list, as before?'

'I think we can leave out the BCG CEO and Tony Blair.' Stuart poured on the sarcasm. 'But we'll keep her line manager, Jim Dickson, shall we? And I'd like a copy!'

Half an hour later, the apologetic email message had been duly scribbled out.

Dear Debbie

I am so sorry for the embarrassment caused by my email concerning the Health Awareness Day.

As you know, I have a passion for raising awareness of the key health issues of the day – most of all stress reduction. I now realise that the email – and its circulation list – caused you a considerable amount of anxiety. It must also have upset you deeply.

Please accept my sincere apologies for my inconsiderate behaviour.

With Best Wishes

Dr Steve Hemmings

'There, that didn't hurt too much did it?' Stuart asked with a hint too much satisfaction.

Steve gathered up the script and made for the door.

'And don't forget, I am going on holiday after today, so I want to see a copy of it by close of play, OK?'

Steve nodded his agreement and let himself out.

'And no V-signs when you're the other side of the door' was Stuart's parting shot.

Of course, Steve defied this instruction as soon as he had shut the door behind him.

Once back in his office, he started by re-reading the email from his hero. Wasn't he trying to tell him something? Perhaps he shouldn't be sending this grovelling email to Debbie at all. Had he not got the backing of the Prime Minister himself?

His defiance grew as another thought struck him. Stuart was going on holiday after today, wasn't he? He probably wouldn't notice it if he didn't receive a copy of the email with all the clearing of the decks that he had to do by 'close of play' (by the way, as a cricket fan, our hero deeply resented non-fans like Stuart using the phrase).

Then there was Debbie herself... she always disappeared for around three weeks at the end of July up the Amazon or somewhere exotic like that, didn't she? Maybe she would come back with some rare tropical illness or get bitten by a snake or a tarantula or a crocodile even. The insects were nasty, too... Steve happily pondered the multiple misfortunes that may beset her in equatorial climes. In any case, she wouldn't be back until August, when Steve himself would be on holiday. That's it! He would leave the manuscript of the apology in his untidy desk drawer and wait until the end of the holiday season. Surely, it would all be forgotten by then!

Chapter 27: 'Running On Empty'

Steve's journal, written from a Teesside filling station, September 18th 2000.

Call me Mustafa. Mustafa Shag.

It's now approximately 80 days and 7 hours since my last shag. No luck on that fucking holiday. I thought a holiday camp in North Wales would have been like a cattery for pussy.

All those single mums. Gagging for it, I should have thought.

All that Welsh rain seemed to dampen their ardour.

My kids didn't like it much either...

Number of acts of self-pollution since my last shag: about 40.

There would have been more, but for a strict monitor-wrist policy of only 1 act of self-pollution per week for the past 3 weeks. The theory being that strict control of the spunk supply S1 will hasten the day that the siege is broken.

Doesn't seem to work any better than its economic equivalent.

Number of pints drunk last week: around 30 (I'm cutting down!).

Number of losing bets: over 100, but still, I did get Millenary in the Leger, probably breaking even overall.

Number of fags smoked: 210 i.e. 21 packets of ten (Oh dear, this is getting expensive).

And now I'm going back to the grindstone once I've finished with this sodding queue.

List of things to do:

1. Avoid Stuart
2. Get briefing from Paula re new product introduction.
3. Talk to that woman from the Safety Committee about the 'near miss'
4. Send invites out for the Teesside Innovation Awards night – most notably Jim Dickson, our esteemed innovation leader
5. Letter to Tony Blair, beloved nation leader

The last stragglers from the management cadres had returned to BCG from their French gites, Greek islands and English Heritage cottages. Time to go back to work, or maybe not. Steve sat on a garage forecourt somewhere off the trunk road, waiting for the long queue for petrol to move forward. His summer clothes, sandals and all, belied a gloomy disposition, made ever gloomier by the running commentary on the radio news. Steve continued drumming his fingertips on the faithful Ford Mondeo's steering wheel as the toots from the car horns grew ever louder.

Could things get worse? Yes, they could!

Radio Teesside had some further bad news.

'And finally... local industrial chemicals giant BCG has suffered a dramatic slump in its share price on the back of a profits warning, which has just been announced.'

Steve sat bolt upright as the dreaded news issued forth. 'Shares were as low as 59p at one point,' the presenter continued, 'but have since recovered somewhat.'

'What to?' Steve asked out loud.

'The company has struggled with low profits and mounting debts since making a series of acquisitions in the late 1990s.'

'You don't say?' Steve banged his fist on the steering wheel. 'Shit the bed! What about my share options?' Steve had yet to take in the wider ramifications of this development.

'And now for the weather... A band of cloud will cause showers and light drizzle across the region for most of the day, so don't forget to take yer umbrellas with yer...' trilled a female announcer.

The programme then returned to music as Ronan Keating's *Life is a Rollercoaster* started to play.

An apt choice, Steve thought to himself, except with BCG the only way seemed to be down. *Just gotta ride it, like Ronan says.* Steve tried to cheer himself up with that thought.

Steve then drafted a letter to his new best friend, still using the same scrap of paper and bookie pen that he had used for his journal. He resolved to type it up neatly and send it once he finally got to the Elton Centre.

Dear Tony

So sorry to hear about your recent difficulties with the fuel protesters.

What is the world coming to?

It all reminds me of the dark days of the 3-day week back in the 1970s.

No doubt you will sort it out, no thanks to Gordon Brown though. I can't see him standing up and being counted right now. As a gesture of solidarity, I am sending this message by post, as I have full confidence that all essential services will remain as normal, despite rumours to the contrary.

It was also helpful Dear Reader that he could send the letter out free of charge via the company's mail service; it was, after all, a business letter! Back to the letter...

Anyway, more importantly for me, I've just heard that the share price of the once mighty BCG just fell to 59p.

This is a savage indictment of the culture whereby companies pander to the whims of the stock market. 'Live by the sword, die by the sword' is what I say.

Hopefully, New Labour can do something about this sad state of affairs and help return BCG to its former glory.

Yours sincerely,

Steve

He finally reached the front of the queue.

A sign by the pump said, 'Maximum purchase £5 only'.

Steve shook his head at the futility of it all.

'I probably used up more fucking petrol waiting in the queue than I'm putting in,' he said to himself, before putting £5 worth of petrol into his tank and driving off.

The clouds over East Cleveland were darkening as Steve's car finally made it to the still half-empty BCG car park. They opened to the accompaniment of thunder and lightning just as he got half-way to the Elton Centre North Gate.

He received a good old-fashioned drenching, not helped by his choice of late summer attire, including shorts and sandals.

Once inside the building, Steve hurriedly squelched past Stuart's office.

Stuart opened the door.

'Well, look what the cat just dragged in!' Stuart was certainly not one for sympathy. 'A quick word, please, Stephen!'

'What is it this time?' Steve had hoped at least to get to his office to dry himself out.

'Well firstly, I hope you enjoyed your holiday. Where did you go?'

'I went to a holiday camp in North Wales with the kids.'

'Any good?'

'Nah. Not really. Rained a lot, too.'

'I hope you were better prepared for it over there,' the besuited Stuart sneered as he surveyed Steve's bedraggled appearance. 'Time was, guys on your grade and above had to wear a collar and tie.'

Steve suppressed the desire to thump Stuart and walk back to his car. It was, after all, still raining heavily outside.

'Anyway, where were we...?' Stuart continued. 'Oh. Yes. We have some unfinished business from before the holidays.' Stuart paused for dramatic effect. 'You did apologise to Debbie about your behaviour concerning the Health Awareness Day, didn't you?'

Steve shuffled in his uncomfortable seat, while the water formed a growing puddle on the floor.

'Well, er... Ahem. Ahem,' he muttered.

Stuart took note of the growing accumulation of water on his carpeted office floor.

'You mean you didn't! Well, that's a little job for you to start off with.'

'But I didn't do anything wrong. I only stuck up for the business principles – and my own, of course,' Steve protested.

'Stuck up for your own fucking ego, more like. What planet are you on? You will finally apologise to her, won't you?'

'Sounds like I'll have to...'

'OK. Before we go on to the next item... you haven't pissed yourself, have you?' Stuart affected concern as he peered at the wet carpet.

'No, of course not!'

'Then there's the Safety Committee. As you know, I managed to square things up regarding improper supervision of a site contractor, but they're still wanting to declare a major near miss over you driving two miles while unable to control your car properly.'

'So, what happens about that?'

'We'll have to see. I'm trying to persuade them to reclassify it as an Unsafe Act. Just be thankful you didn't go anywhere near any tankers on your drive back.'

'Thanks, Stuart,' Steve replied grudgingly.

Stuart was not finished. 'You're a disgrace to the company, you know.'

Steve blushed crimson. 'How can you say that? Especially with the Innovation Awards coming up this month. I'll show 'em!'

'Shouldn't that be "we'll show 'em"? There's no "I" in team, you know...'

Steve looked heavenwards. 'Yes, Stuart. Anyway, we will win. I can feel it in my water.'

'I wouldn't be going on about water too much if I were you.' Stuart sneered at the drowned rat figure opposite him. 'And how many times must I tell you? The company doesn't care about innovation anymore. It's all "stick to your knitting" and cost cutting. But good luck anyway.'

'Well, look where that's just got us all. You can't even buy a litre of petrol for the value of a BCG share certificate. You could have filled your tank for less, once upon a time.' Steve was getting carried away with his rhetoric.

'If you were the proud owner of a Reliant Robin, maybe.' Stuart brought him back to earth with his reminiscences.

'Can I go now?' He got up, hoping to depart the office with the last shreds of his dignity intact.

'Just make sure you call Building Services to get this mess cleared up once you get back to your office!' Stuart pointed at the puddle on his carpet.

Steve grunted his compliance and made for the door.

'Oh, just one more thing.' Stuart peered at his computer screen. 'Let's book you in for an appraisal. Let's see, sometime this week... Wednesday, perhaps?'

'Should be OK,' Steve muttered.

'No, wait a minute.' Stuart clicked on his mouse. 'Debbie's in Rotterdam.'

'Debbie's going to be at the appraisal?' Steve was incredulous.

'Yes. Part of our new policy of fairness and transparency. She's there to make sure that appraisal scores reflect performance and are appropriately cross-levelled.'

'What about early next week?'

'Nah, I'm on an internal conference on diversity, then I'm on a one-day course on...' Stuart hesitated. '...oh, better not say...'

'Come on Stuart! You can't tell me half a tale now,' Steve implored.

Stuart gave in. 'OK. Strictly between you and me, and I can't say anymore. It's to do with Project Mallard, .'

'That's bollocks.'

'Yes, indeed. Anyway, there was a memo to all Magenta Book staff and above to attend, owing to the exigencies of Project Mallard. I just hope that I don't have to put it into practice.'

'You won't, will you? Our business unit is the most profitable in the company – by a mile. What do Debbie's lot ever come up with? They said only 1 in 10. That shower could lose 1 in 2 and nobody would notice the difference!'

Stuart shook his head. 'You'll never learn, will you? This is deadly serious. Everyone should be worried – and it's the ones that survive that I'll feel sorry for.'

'Why?' Steve clung on to the half-opened door.

'All that stress. All that guilt. "Why wasn't it me?"'

'Like post-traumatic stress disorder?'

'Yes, in a way. Then they discover that they're still not safe.'

'What you mean? I thought this was a once and for all reduction, paving the way for a bright new Tomorrow.'

'Do me a favour! Just like the last one and the one before that? The survivors will wake up soon enough and discover the next wave's about to hit them, which it surely will. Meanwhile, the ones that get let go have the chance to sort themselves out. Move on to pastures new.'

'Bloody hell. Like the ever-stamping boot in *1984*.

'Exactly right, though Steve, do us a favour!'

'What?'

'This is no place for literary quotation. You're not planning a new career as a novelist, are you?'

'Why do you think that?'

'I've seen that little black book you sometimes carry round with you.'

Steve blushed. 'Oh, that's nothing. Nothing,' he muttered.

'What is it, then? You know you really want to tell me.'

'Just my journal. I was told to keep a journal on a self-awareness course.'

'What bollocks! Anyway, young man, we've still got this appraisal to sort out.' Stuart returned to his computer screen.

'Now, Debbie's in management meetings until the end of September... looks like we'll have to go for next month...' Stuart peered at his computer screen. 'No wait! There's a two-hour slot next Friday.'

'Fine by me. That's the day after the Awards night.'

'All the better. You might have some good news for a change.'

'OK. I look forward to that.'

If Steve had not been half-way out of the door, he would have noticed a look of incredulity on Stuart's face.

'Good. Now fuck off out of my office.'

Once Steve finally made it to his own office, he found that Paula was waiting, sitting at the mini-table in the middle of the office. She had thoughtfully made mugs of tea for them both.

'Welcome back, Dear Leader.' Paula beamed.

Steve lifted his hand in ironic recognition and sat down opposite her.

There followed an action replay of the previous conversation in Stuart's office about Steve's North Wales holiday, until Paula asked, 'Any luck with the ladies, then?'

'Nah. They were too busy playing bingo.'

'Thought you'd score there... all those single mums.'

'Well, maybe that was my thinking, but no.'

'What about the kids, then? Did they enjoy it?

'I suppose they did get to see S Club 7 do an impromptu performance on Rhyl promenade.'

At that moment, Margaret waddled in.

'S Club 7? You saw <u>the</u> S Club 7? Me and our Darren, we love S Club 7, we do! Loves that "H" in Steps too, you know.' Margaret, sensing that Steve was not a fellow fan, then added, 'That Rachel Stevens, she's really pretty, isn't she?'

'I'll give you that,' Steve conceded.

'I bet your kids loved it.'

Margaret burst into a rendition of *Reach*, lifting her bingo wings towards the stars of an imagined North Welsh sky.

Steve was underwhelmed. 'How very inapt. I certainly don't think that bit about following your heart's desire applies to BCG at this very moment. Anyway, my daughter would have preferred Eminem.'

'What, at her age? She's ten, isn't she? What about all that foul language? Shockin', that is. Shockin'!' She turned to Paula for support.

'You wouldn't want your kids listening to that filth, would you, Mrs O'Donnell?'

'No, I don't think I would, but you can't stop 'em, you know.'

Margaret was insistent. 'No, I can't stand it. Neither can our Darren. All that stuff he says about fags an' all. Hates smokin' does our Darren.'

Steve rolled his eyes. 'Anyway, Margaret. How is your Darren?

'Well, he's just started at a new school. That nice Mrs Mowlam was ever so helpful.'

Steve was genuinely impressed. 'Oh. I'm so pleased to hear it. How's he doing there?'

'So far, so good. They showed me round before he started. Strict rules on discrimination,' the headmistress said.

'Quite right, too.' Steve nodded.

Paula was also sympathetic. 'That sounds promising. Let me know he gets on, won't you?'

Steve decided that it was time for the small talk to end. Gesturing 'cut' to Paula behind Margaret's back, he then looked at his watch.

'Sorry Margaret, I'd like to chat all day, but Paula and I have a new product to launch...'

'Alright, I'll go. I was going to hoover...' a somewhat affronted Margaret protested.

Steve cut her short. 'I'm sure it can wait until another day. Thanks, Margaret!'

Margaret made her way reluctantly out of the office like a ship of the line, cleaner and all.

Steve was impatient to catch up on lost time and wanted to make sure that Paula knew it.

'What did you want to talk about her Darren for?'

'And there was me thinking you were genuinely concerned about that lad. Getting Margaret to write to Mo Mowlam and all...'

'Look. She talks about that precious son of hers twenty-four seven without any encouragement from outside. And she's got five other kids she could start on about.'

'Alright. Alright. I can see that you're not quite the "People Person" you sometimes make yourself out to be!'

Steve smiled. 'Grumpy old git in the making, me,' he said with a lowered voice.

'Alright. Alright. Now what is it you wanted to discuss?'

'The launch of the water based paste, obviously.'

'Why? It's all going to plan.'

'Is it? Have you sampled a dozen customers yet?'

'Er, no.'

'Why's that?'

'Not enough material. We didn't make enough on the latest trial.'

'Not make enough? We should have had a hundred fucking kilos of the stuff!

'Language, Timothy! Don't you remember we had filtration problems at the previous plant trial?'

'But we would have needed to lose about ninety-nine percent to go short.'

'That's about right,' Paula admitted.

'Ninety-nine percent lost? Ninety-nine percent lost? How did you manage that?'

'We tried ultra-centrifugation instead of ultra-filtration, remember? I think that was your idea for getting round the problems we'd had the time before.'

'No. No. No, it was yours, definitely yours. Innovative way of removing a bottleneck. Technically elegant solution, I think I remember you saying.'

Paula blushed. 'Well, it's done now.'

'Yes, at the cost of another seventy thousand pounds. Another "partial success".' ('Partial success' was Steve's pet phrase for a complete disaster.) 'Those lovely chemical engineers will have my life.'

'Why? It's not in their budget. It's in yours.'

'Try telling them that! They think they run everything. Those sons and daughters of bitches sit on their fat arses, getting paid well over seventy thousand a year for being penny-wise, pound foolish. That plant trial was still value for money compared to those fuckers.'

'Language again! Anyway, we managed to sample the Top 6 customers and we got the sun protection factor data and the UVA star ratings.'

'Oh, I suppose,' Steve conceded. 'I shall report that the trial was a "partial success" (we now know what that really means, Dear Reader) and that we're on schedule to launch in Q4. Next trial, we'll get back to good old-fashioned filtration, even if it takes a day to get the stuff through. No word to our friends the engineers, though.'

'Is there anything else?'

Steve's voice took on a conspiratorial tone. 'Yes. I'd like to show you some sums I was doing before I went away.'

'Sounds intriguing.'

Steve unfurled a pie chart on his office flip chart.

'Now, the green segment represents sales of the first product launch in 1997. The red one represents the silicone dispersion, and the gold one represents the step change product.'

'What about the rest?'

'That's products introduced before I took this job.'

'So, what does it all mean?'

'It means that I'm the only Technical Manager around here to have hit the target for new product introduction. I got 29.8% – well, 30%, near as dammit. 30% was the target that Debbie mentioned when she spoke to us – and I'm the only one who doesn't have a company car!'

'Oh, you missed her last pronouncement, didn't you?'

Steve was worried. 'What, about company cars?'

'No, all that stuff about new products. Old hat, now. They want all managers to cut their budgets by 20% instead.'

'What happened to the "new products are our life blood" shtick, then?'

'It's toast. We've all got to tighten our belts, she said. Furthermore, there's a clamp down on what's deemed to be unnecessary spending.'

'What? On top of Project Mallard?'

'Yes, it's what's called a "bronze-out".

'A "bronze-out"? Sounds quite revolting.'

'For starters, you're not supposed to do any travelling unless it's absolutely necessary for the business or it's for health and safety.'

'Ah, well. It doesn't affect me. Nobody lets me go anywhere.' Steve's face changed as he remembered. 'Shit the bed! There's that Chemical Industry dinner in London early next month I'd been invited to. Black tie job. They can't stop me going to that. BCG are one of the sponsors.'

'Oh, yes they can.'

'But my ticket was paid for by my hosts.'

'Who's that?'

'The company that carried out the plant trial.'

Paula pulled a face. 'You didn't tell me about that!'

'You weren't invited,' Steve replied flatly.

'Oh, the trappings of office! Anyway, talk to Stuart, but it looks like you can't go.'

'Bollocks! I'd better ring the company.'

'Oh, no. You can't do that.'

'Why not?'

'We can't be admitting to it. Might drive our share price even lower,' Paula explained.

Steve was incredulous. 'What? Since when did we become Fight Club PLC?'

'Oh, you mean?'

Steve and Paula shared the joke together.

'The first rule of Fight Club. You don't talk about Fight Club. The second rule of Fight Club. You don't talk about Fight Club!' The rigours of child rearing had meant that Paula had missed out on going to the cinema, but she had managed to catch it on DVD.

Their laughter was cut short as Adele marched in.

'Well, I'm glad you two find something funny, because there's nothing funny about the consequences of your Health Day!'

'Erm. Excuse me...' Paula was taken aback by the brusqueness.

'Adele,' Steve intervened, 'Dr O'Donnell and I are just completing an important discussion about new product introductions.' Steve pointed to the flip chart. 'Now if you don't mind, could you give us a couple of minutes to complete our conversation?'

Adele gave the all too predictable answer. 'You do realise that health and safety comes first – always!' To Steve and Paula's surprise, she then took a more accommodating approach. 'Oh, alright then. Two minutes it is, then. No more.'

With that, Adele walked out. Once she was out of earshot, Paula felt it was safe to express a concern that she had been harbouring over the summer.

'I was going to ask. What was the upshot from the Health Day? I heard you were still in trouble.'

'Ça ne fait rien. I'm hoping they're going to reclassify it from a Near Miss to an Unsafe Act.' Steve crossed his fingers.

'Well, not the first time you've been involved in one of them in recent months!' Paula slapped him playfully on the wrist.

'Alright. Alright. Is there anything else?'

'No. I don't think so.'

'OK. I'd better let la belle Adele back in then.'

'Maybe, try being kind to her. Why not use that fabled charm of yours?' Paula suggested as she departed.

Steve decided that, on reflection, that might be the right approach as Adele re-entered the office.

'Sit down, Adele. Would you like a cup of tea?'

'No thank you, Dr Hemmings.'

Steve's reverted to irony. 'Just as well. You'd probably find me in breach of some health and safety rule, wouldn't you?

'Don't adopt that tone with me, young man! I have good news.'

Steve was taken by surprise.

'Following representations by your management, we – the Safety Committee – have decided to reclassify your near miss as an unsafe act.'

'Oh, thanks. What does that mean?'

'It means, Dr Hemmings, that you are extremely fortunate.'

'How come?'

'It means that you won't be facing disciplinary action.'

'How come?' Steve asked.

'Because of the company's "No blame culture", you will simply be sent on an appropriate training course and advised as to your future conduct.'

'Oh, cool. Actually, I had a question for you.'

'Actually, I will have that cup of tea that you offered.'

'Oh great. All fresh ingredients. You won't regret it.'

Steve went out to the small kitchen to make the tea with his mini teapot. Five minutes later, he returned, mini teapot in hand, then came back in with cup of tea.

'Well, strictly speaking, you shouldn't be allowed your own tea pot in your office.'

'Why's that?' Steve was unsurprised.

'Danger of microorganisms, such as moulds. But I'll let you off.' Adele smiled a very rare smile. 'Anyway, what was your question?'

'I've just heard about the bronze-out. Does that mean that we can't have another Health Awareness Day?'

'Why not? It's a Health and Safety expenditure, after all.'

'I'm not sure that it counted, after the reaction of my colleagues.'

'Oh, don't worry about them. No, it's still Health and Safety, as long as the Safety Committee gets to approve the individual activities.'

'Oh, that's good news. Thanks.'

'My pleasure. Oh, nice cup of tea, by the way.' Adele was opening up. She even attempted a joke. 'But don't forget the biscuits next time!'

As Adele continued to sip her tea, a noise could be heard, increasing in volume and emanating from Steve's pocket. It was *Born on the Bayou*. He hastened to pull the phone out of his pocket. In doing so, he knocked the table, spilling the contents of Adele's cup of tea all over her lap.

Steve was aghast. 'Oh. I'm terribly sorry, er, Adele.'

'It's alright. Accidents happen.' Adele sniffed, before adding hastily, 'I shouldn't really say that, should I?'

While Adele bustled about the office, trying to get tea out of her skirt, Steve rushed out and came back with a cloth and tissues from the adjacent kitchen.

'Here is a cloth. I'm terribly sorry,' he muttered, whilst busying himself ineffectually mopping up the spilt tea on his 'meetings table'.

'It's OK. I suppose it's my fault for drinking tea in a non-designated area.'

Adele sponged herself down, followed by an awkward silence.

Finally, Adele spoke. 'I'll be on my way, then. I may have to put this down as another unsafe act, but you're welcome to put me down as well, since I was a willing participant.'

Adele departed, leaving Steve to carry on wiping his table down.

'Shit the bed!'

Steve then remembered the missed call that had been the cause of the incident. He pulled the phone out of his pocket and noticed, somewhat to his disappointment, that the call had been from the Chairman. He duly called the number.

'Hello. Geoffrey Huckstead speaking.'

'Hi, Geoff. It's me.'

'Ah. Yes. Hello, stranger.' Geoff paused for effect. 'Now, what's this I hear about you not wanting to play for the Outcasts on Sunday?'

'Well, I haven't really enjoyed the last few games. I've had a string of low scores, got tonked all over the field when I've been bowling, and I've had the potty six times in succession now.'

'Well, maybe that's a bit excessive, but you will have to learn to field a bit better, won't you?'

'There's worse fielders in the team than me, you know.'

'Yes, I do know. But shall we say that they have deeper pockets than you have – and are more willing to dig into them, when called upon?'

'Anyway, Ron said I wasn't needed.'

'Fuck what Ron said. Do you want to play?'

'Well, this potty business is getting me down a bit.'

'I understand, but I can say categorically that you won't get it next Sunday.'

'But surely, that's up the Committee. You only have a casting vote.'

'You have my word. You won't get it. Furthermore, you will be opening the batting.'

'Oh. That would be nice. But surely the captain decides that.'

'You're not listening, are you? Fuck the captain!'

'OK. If you say so, but I'm not sure I've got enough petrol to get to the other side of Geordieland and back.'

'Ah. It'll all have blown over by then. Serves those buggers right for making us pay over 80p a litre for petrol though. They say it's to help the environment. Bollocks! They just want to tax the fuck out of us all.'

'OK. With one proviso – I've still got enough petrol by then.'

'Well, I'll drive if needs be.'

Steve was surprised at the Chairman's sudden generosity, and not a little suspicious. 'Really? Why are you so keen for me to play?'

Geoff cleared his throat. 'Ahem. I can't talk about it over the phone right now but put it this way: I'd like to have a little conversation with you after the match.'

'OK. OK. I'll play.'

'Good man. How have the muff purveyors been treating you, by the way?'

'Not so good.'

'No word from "Tina" then.'

'No. Karen hasn't been in touch – and you?'

'I've acquired a friend in the Bedale area. Purely medicinal, though. Hattie, I call her.'

'Why Hattie?'

'As in Hattie Jacques.'

Steve was incredulous. 'Hattie Jacques??'

'Listen, I'll tell you all about it at the weekend. Talk to you later. Bye.'

'OK. Bye. See you Sunday...'

Steve passed the rest of the morning catching up on his emails, but somehow avoiding sending out his long-awaited apology to Debbie. He was a little disappointed to learn that this exercise did not take as long as he had allowed for. It seemed that the world of BCG had got on without him just fine – the disastrous plummet of the share price notwithstanding.

Finally, he looked at his watch. It was one minute past twelve. Time for lunch!

Steve made his way to the Lakeside restaurant. He was quite looking forward to hearing the Septics' take on recent events.

He was surprised to learn that he was the main topic of conversation.

‘Good afternoon gentlemen – and lady,’ he ventured as he plonked his tray down.

Frank, sitting opposite, folded his arms, always an ominous sign. ‘Good afternoon to you, Dr Hemmings. Where have you been this last month?

Terri was quick to hazard a guess. ‘Steering clear of Debbie, I should think.’

Frank unfolded his arms and leaned forward. ‘Have you written that apology to her yet?’

Everyone fell silent. Then, Frank spoke up again.

‘On the subject of elf n’ safety, I hear that you’ve been upsetting Adele again. Spilled tea all over her. You weren’t trying to get into her knickers, were you?’

‘Ah, Adele. I don’t think so. I’d be surprised if anyone has ever gone there – or wanted to!’

Don had an anecdote. ‘Yes, Adele Hitler, as she is not affectionately known around the site. You watch out for her. She caused one of our young scientists to have a nervous breakdown, she did. Four months he waited for this vital piece of equipment. Finally, it arrived from Germany, having been held up in customs for a month. I remember the day it arrived. Made up he was, like a dog with two cocks. Then Adele got hold of it. Guards and trips everywhere. Poor bugger couldn’t use it. Drove him mad, it did.’

Don’s monologue had given Steve time to think. ‘Anyway, how did you know about the spilt tea?’

Frank tapped the side of his nose. ‘We know everything, mate. We know everything.’

Steve tried to change the subject. ‘I thought you’d all be talking about the BCG share price.’

Les waved imperiously. ‘Oh, that... that’s old hat now.’ He then added, ‘Did you hear that Rushton’s resigned?’

‘No, I didn’t. Is it official?’ Steve had not heard.

Les tapped his nose conspiratorially. ‘Not yet, they’re still negotiating the seven-figure ‘Golden Goodbye’, but I have my sources. Closely guarded secret.’

‘That makes a change. These days they’ll tell the City of London before they tell you that you’ve lost your job,’ Frank added.

'Why Rushton, then?' Steve was puzzled. Rushton was the CEO of the smallest of the remaining divisions of BCG.

'Well, someone had to be the scapegoat. Although, in my considered opinion, he is a dickhead,' Frank concluded.

Les agreed. 'Never liked him, myself. I remember when he worked here. Right cockney bullshitter he was. Always up the CEO's arse.'

Steve remained perplexed. 'OK. What did he do?'

'Almighty cock-up in Belgium. They installed a brand new all-singing-and-dancing IT system. Was supposed to take care of purchasing, sales, stock, profit and loss forecast. Everything,' Frank explained.

'Well, that's common practice these days. So what?' Steve was still none the wiser.

Frank went on. 'Unfortunately, they wanted to impress the CEO, so they promised him that they'd install it without a back-up.'

'What was the point of doing that?' Steve exercised his talent for asking naïve questions yet again.

Frank explained further. 'It was going to save the company a couple of million quid. Running two systems in parallel comes expensive, you know. They wanted to maximise their RONA.'

'RONA? What's that?' Steve was baffled once again.

'Well, it's certainly not the bird with big tits in samples despatch,' Frank explained helpfully.

'Return on Net Assets, for the uninitiated.' Les's pitying look left Steve in no doubt as to who the uninitiated might be.

'OK. So, what happened in Belgium?' Steve asked.

'The new system crashed. That's what it did,' Les continued.

'And so? Systems crash all the time.' Steve was still unsure why this should have been the cause of such consternation.

'Chaos. Absolute bloody chaos. Without a back-up, nobody knew what was ordered, what was in stock, what had been purchased.'

Don then weighed in. 'Yes, I was in Belgium at the time. Had people running round the labs scrabbling for every gram they could find. What a shambles! And now our friend Rushton has had to carry the can!'

Frank crossed his arms once more. 'Penny wise, pound foolish. The modern-day bane of British industry. That's what it is. Don't spoil the ship for a ha'p'orth of tar, I've always said.'

'Now. Now. Now. That's a very outdated attitude, Frank,' Don sneered.

Steve remained confused. 'But all this happened a few months ago. Come to think of it, I now remember hearing something about it. Why has it all burst out now?'

'Ah. Ha. Ha. My young friend. Because they tried to spin it,' Les was the first to explain.

'What do you mean, they tried to spin it?'

Don gave a considered view. 'Not the incident itself, but the aftermath. As you can imagine, it pissed off our esteemed customers no end.'

'Sure, but you haven't answered my question.'

Frank took over. 'Let me explain. It took a couple of months to recover from the debacle.' He paused for effect '... but the real damage was done after the customers started to re-order.'

'Surely that was a good thing.' Steve's naïve questions kept on coming.

It was Les's turn. 'Not the way they handled it.'

'What did they do?'

Frank smiled. 'They made an announcement, they did. Everything back to normal. Customers restored. Business as usual. That kind of shite.'

Les finished off the explanation. 'Except it wasn't! They hadn't noticed a significant trend. BCG had become second supplier to our three largest customers.'

'How come they didn't notice?'

Les continued. 'This didn't become apparent in the immediate aftermath of the IT system failure. The customers had to re-stock their inventories, didn't they? Sales were temporarily back up, then "Slumparama east of Java", when the awful truth emerged.'

'So, this morning they had to issue a fucking profits warning. Cue share price collapse,' Frank concluded.

'And Rushton's resignation,' Les added.

Steve was ever the optimist. 'Perhaps I can cast my own little ray of sunshine.'

Frank looked heavenwards. 'You're not going on about that fucking Innovation Award again, are you?'

'Well. Yes. The Awards night is coming up soon.'

Don concluded the conversation. 'Forget it. Even if you win, it'll mean nothing. We're all going to hell in a handcart.'

Chapter 28: 'Who Is Burning?'

Once in his office, Steve logged back into his computer to check his emails. He was disappointed to learn that there had not been any incoming since lunchtime. He decided that it was about time he went to the lab and caught up with his staff. As he was about to get up, a technical journal on his table caught his eye. There was an article on the safety of nanoparticle sunscreens. He really should read that first. He returned to his chair and started to read.

Soon, he was fast asleep in his chair.

* * *

Steve is outside the Elton Centre with the other (female) members the Health Committee dancing around a fire on the grass outside the Elton Centre. They are all stark naked. Some are waving banners with gaudy depictions of the sun. Steve's body and face are painted in sunscreen. He is wearing a wig. Steve can't help noticing Michelle's ample bosoms. At last, he has got to see the whole lot. He is not disappointed. As he looks below, things get even better! Such luxuriance, exceeding even his wildest expectations! Demi Moore, eat your heart out!

By contrast, there is the willowy Paula. It has to be said that despite her small boobs, she comes a close second. Her wispiness downstairs has its own attractions. The hint of red reminds him that he has never been with a true blonde. This in turn reminds him of what might have been with Mary. As his nether regions start to twitch, it is time for a chant.

Steve holds his hands up to the sky.

'We invoke the great Sunscreen God Kalkos to look down upon us today as we make this, our great sacrifice.'

The other Health Committee Members continued to dance and sway.

'All hail Kalkos!

Steve continues. 'BCG's profits have failed these past 5 years because we have ignored her warnings!'

'All hail Kalkos.'

'Through this great sacrifice, we will restore full profitability to BCG!'

'All hail Kalkos.'

'Through this great sacrifice, our share price will wax strong once more! Sacking a board member is not enough, we need the blood of a virgin...'

He is interrupted by Adele running down towards the dancing throng. She is wearing a high vis jacket and a fire helmet.

'Stop! Stop! Stop!' she cries, still at a distance.

Steve replies with a trance-like, 'We cannot stop!'

Adele points to the fire. 'Site rules clearly state no naked flames!'

'These are the fires that will reawaken BCG from its long slumber.'

At last, she notices, to her horror, that they are all starkers.

'And NO NAKED PEOPLE!' she screeches.

Steve makes a sign to his followers. 'Come Officious Woman. We have been expecting you.'

'You're not wearing PPE. I will have to report you all.'

'We are here to save the company.'

Steve then signals again to his disciples, who mob Adele. She is trussed up and pointed towards a large penile effigy with wooden sticks surrounding the base. A ladder leads up to a compartment in the middle.

Adele shakes partly in fear, partly in awe at the size of the phallic symbol.

'Oh my God!'

'Well, you may say that. Ladies, prepare the human offering for the DICKER MAN!'

They rip off her high-vis jacket and fire helmet, along with the rest of her clothes, and replace them with flowing white robes. She is led screaming towards the effigy.

Around the base of the effigy, Septics are on hand, dressed in loin cloths, carrying lit torches. Some ducks are already in one of the bottom compartments (the balls) of the effigy. They quack loudly.

'The ducks are here to symbolize Project Mallard,' Steve announces solemnly.

In the other ball are some pigs. The pigs squeal noisily.

'The pigs are here to symbolize the BCG Board of Directors,' Steve explains.

Adele falls to her knees and begs. 'Isn't that enough?'

'No. The great Gods of the City of London demand more. Our faithful shareholders demand more!'

Adele screams. Steve merely anoints her, using his tea pot.

'Gentlemen. Apply the flames,' he shouts out to the Septics.

They light the straw underneath the balls.

'This is New Age nonsense. The Safety Committee will get you,' Adele shouts out.

'Away with you. The Gods cannot wait any longer.'

The Health Committee ladies push Adele up the wooden ladder and into the main compartment of the phallus.

With flames now licking around her feet, Adele protests, 'You are in clear breach of the Seven Business Principles!'

Adele starts an incantation, as the flames start to lick around her feet.

'Trust your colleagues' motivations. Nothing you do is worth getting hurt for...'

Her cries are drowned out by Steve and the others joining hands and dancing a circle, singing *Reach* by S Club Seven.

As the naked dancers all raise their hands to the sky, Karen appears naked (resembling Britt Ekland). She joins in the dancers. She beckons Steve towards her.

'Come, Lord Stephen.'

'What for, O naked nymph?' Steve struggles to take his attentions away from the gyrations of Michelle and Paula for more than a couple of seconds.

'To collect your reward.'

'Reward?'

'You have single-handedly saved BCG. The Gods dictate that you be rewarded.'

Karen waves Steve's blister pack of Victory Vs in the air. 'See, Lord Stephen! I have the magic love potion!'

She beckons him again. They join hands and head to a nearby toxic shelter.

A plume of smoke ejaculates from the burning phallus. Behind it is the setting sun. As the sun sets, the end of the phallus drops off. Steve looks back to see Elton's statue smiling benignly at him. *Sacrifice* was his first solo No. 1 after all, Dear Reader.

Chapter 29: 'Baby You Can Drive My Car'

Back in the office, Steve is woken by the sounds of *Born on the Bayou* getting louder. Steve answers his phone with one hand whilst scratching his balls with another. Steve continues to scratch his balls throughout the ensuing conversation.

'Oh, hi, Karen. How are you, then? Long time no hear.'

If Steve's reverie had given him hope of an immediate reconciliation, he was brought straight back to earth.

'So, you didn't find anyone on your holidays then?'

'I beg your pardon?'

'I thought you might've found someone else on your recent travels.'

'Nah. Nah. Nah. Why do you ask?' He omits to mention that it had not been for lack of trying.

'I was thinking of giving you a second chance. Or should that be a third one!?'

'Hey, steady on. I was a free agent when I went to Coffin Dodgers, if you remember.' Not sure that was quite the right thing to say, Steve.

Karen decided to offer him an ultimatum, rather than putting the phone down. 'Well, do you want to see me or don't you?'

Steve answered with an enthusiastic affirmative.

'You're not saying that just because you're desperate for sex, are you?'

Steve temporarily crossed the fingers of his ball-scratching hand behind his back.

'No. No, of course not. Whatever made you think that?'

'I know you. Typical man. My friends said I should steer clear, but I must have a soft spot for you somewhere.'

'I think I know wh...' Steve narrowly avoided another faux pas. 'Well, that's nice to hear.'

'So, when shall I see you next?'

'Well this week's a bit difficult...' No time like the present, Steve!

'Not your precious Geoff, is it?'

'No. No. No. I might be pushed with this fuel shortage situation.'

'You certainly know how to make a girl feel important, don't you?'

'OK.OK.OK. Sorry, I wasn't thinking. How's about tonight?'

'I'm busy tonight, but tomorrow would be good.'

'Great. There's a quiz on at the Dog.' How romantic!

'What did I say before?'

'Oh, sorry. I'll take you out for a meal, shall I?' That's more like it!

'That would be nice. But don't be getting your hopes up about afters.'

'Not at all, dear.' Stop scratching your balls!

'You'll have to woo me again after what you did at Coffin Dodgers.'

'But I didn't do anything at Coffin Dodgers.' When you're in a hole, Dear Boy...

'You went there, didn't you!? Isn't that enough?'

'But I thought I was a free agent...' Steve, please stop digging!

'Stephen!'

Steve finally caught the drift. 'Alright then. I'll pick you up at 7.30.'

'Oh, one other thing... What were those blue pills that you left behind in my house?'

'Shit the bed,' Steve mutters to himself again, before saying audibly, 'Oh. They were herbal anti-psoriasis pills.'

'Really? How come they were from Lahore?'

'Oh. I got them from Pervez. He's from round there.'

'I didn't think psoriasis was a particular problem in that locality,' Karen said suspiciously.

'Oh, they were strictly for export.' Good thinking!

'Alright, I'll let you have them back tomorrow night. Oh, and one other thing...'

'What's that?' Steve sighed.

'No need for that tone.'

'OK. I'm all ears.'

'It's Charlotte's birthday a fortnight on Wednesday, which is also the special Teesside gala premiere of *Billy Elliot* in Billingham. Are you free to take us?'

'I guess so...'

'I've got special complimentary tickets from work. Jamie Bell himself will be there.'

'Who's Jamie Bell?'

'You know! He's the 14-year-old from Billingham who plays the title character. It's been on all the radio and TV round here. It's really caught Charlotte's imagination. She can't wait for it.'

'Oh alright. Guess I've been out of circulation. I'll see you tomorrow night.' 'See you then. In the meantime, be good!'

'As always!' He took his free hand away from scratching his balls as he rang off.

It really was time to go and visit the Lab.

That could wait another ten minutes, couldn't it?

Steve reached into his cabinet and pulled out a pile of leaflets depicting company cars.

Steve mused thoughtfully as he started leafing through them. 'Hmm, not bad, but...'

He was disturbed by a knock on the door.

Paula entered before Steve could clear the brochures from his desk.

'What the shite are you looking at those for?'

'None of your business!'

'Ah. Come on, it's company cars you're lookin' at, isn't it?'

Steve blushes beetroot red. 'It might be!'

'What do you want to be looking at them for? Surely your ship sailed a long time ago.'

'Well, thanks for your candour, Paula. You ain't no spring chicken, either.'

Paula laughs. 'I could report you for ageism!'

'Anyway, why not? I'm a late developer, that's all.'

'I think "why?" is more the question. You're not greatly loved by the powers-that-be, you know!' Paula replied archly.

'Not all of them. I think Jim Dickson has a soft spot for me.'

'Waste of space! Nobody ever sees him.' Paula paused. 'So, how are you going to impress him?'

'Haven't I told you? He's coming to the Gazette Awards night. If I – erm, we – win, I think I'm in with a shout.'

'Ah, stop acting the bollocks. You've no chance.'

'You never know. Stranger things have happened. The company needs some good news.'

'And you getting a company car is exactly what's needed to lift morale?'

'No, me – erm, us – winning the Innovation Award. That will cheer people up.'

'So... which one would you pick, then?'

'Well. There's the Ford Mondeo...'

'But you've got one of them already.'

'Yeah, you're right, but they're indestructible – and the new Ghia version is so much more stylish...'

'But it's a Mondeo, the most unsexy car on the planet. Surely, you want something with a bit more pulling power.'

'Paula, I'm shocked, truly shocked! But you're right. How's about the Renault Laguna?'

'Encore, un peux ennuieux. N'est-ce pas?'

'OK. Boring – and French!'

Paula had a suggestion. 'The Citroen Xantia is French, but that certainly isn't boring.'

Steve blushed as he recalled his recent daydream. 'Not sure I like the bit when it self-elevates...' There was a pregnant pause before Steve added 'Very slowly!' Steve thought a bit more. 'Reminds me of some of my nights with Sarah!'

Paula recoiled. 'That's too much information already!' She spotted the next brochure. 'Honda Civic? Surely not?'

'Why not?'

'It's an old people's car,' Paula explained.

'It keeps its value very well.'

'What's the point of that with a company car?'

'Hmm. You've got a point,' Steve agreed.

Paula picked up the remaining brochures. She was horror-struck by the next offering.

'The dreaded Vauxhall Vectra,' she whispered in an awed tone, before shaking her head. 'Surely, surely not. You haven't worked hard all these years to get one of those!'

'What's wrong with it? It's very safety-conscious. You get a free tyre dust cover remover. And it's connected to the atomic clock!'

'I think yer man Jeremy Clarkson summed it up. It's a box on wheels.'

'What about the free hook to hang your jacket on?'

Paula gazed critically at the scruffy state of Steve's attire. 'That's for people with non-crumpled jackets. Not you!'

'OK, it has to be the VW Golf GTI. That's pretty exciting. That'll pull the birds!' Steve corrected himself. 'Sorry, members of the opposite sex.'

'I think you'll find that's not on the company's list of allowed cars. Far too flash for BCG.'

'Oh bugger! How do you know?'

'You're not the only one with dreams of company car ownership'.

'Be careful what you wish for,' Steve admonished Paula.

'Yes, if you want a VW, it has to be a Passat.'

'But, that's so boring. Is there anything else?'

'Yes, what about a Skoda Felicia? My cricketing friend Peter has one of them.'

'I think I'll stick to my Mondeo. By the way, what did you want to see me about?'

'Ah, nothing. Oh yes, I remember. Stuart says that you can't go to that dinner in London, even if your hosts have paid for the ticket. Unless you want to walk there, that is...'

'Shit the bed.'

Chapter 30: 'The Last Match Of The Season'

Steve took one last look at his fuel gauge as his car pulled up into a deserted cricket ground car park. There might have been just enough fuel to get back to Teesside, if he was careful. Geoff gazed at the scene of desolation from the passenger seat.

'What the fuck is going on?' he asked as he got out of the car.

'Nobody's here,' Steve observed.

'First prize for stating the obvious,' Geoff commented sarcastically.

'Our boys may have been held up looking for petrol.'

'No excuse. The roads are deserted. They can't all be looking for petrol.'

'Well, possibly. It could be like the Battle of the Bulge, where all the Tiger Tanks had to go foraging for fuel and Telly Savalas stopped them single-handedly.'

'That doesn't explain where the opposition are. They haven't even got the pitch marked out.'

Next to arrive was Pervez in his taxi. 'Afternoon, Gents. Where is everybody?'

The Chairman answered. 'Well you may ask. Looks like Lord Crabtree's cocked things up again.'

'My boss is going to kill me for using up precious diesel for a cricket match. Now you're telling me the game's off!?'

'I'm sorry, old son, but that's exactly how it's looking.'

Next to arrive was Neil 'Pifco' Patterson.

Geoff greeted him like a long-lost friend. 'Neil. Just the man! You've got the Rimmington CC skipper's number, haven't you?'

'I'm not the fixture secwetary anymore, remember?' Neil protested.

'You've got his number though. On your mobile?'

'I don't have a mobile, Geoffwey.'

Geoff looked heavenwards. 'You must have it somewhere.'

'Not here. It's in my addwess book at home.'

'Well, ring Marianne then and get the number out.'

'Mawianne isn't going to like this. She'll be having her afternoon rest.'

Geoff handed his mobile to Neil. 'Go on. Ring Marianne and be quick about it. This could cost me a fortune.'

Neil walked off to make the necessary calls.

As if to allay Geoff's suspicions about the true nature of Marianne's afternoon siesta, Amir was the next to arrive with West Indian Pro Cornelius Carlisle. They got out of the car and walked over to Geoff. 'Beloved Chairman. What is this scene of bleak devastation?'

'Crabtree. Bloody Crabtree. Where is he?'

After what seemed an eternity later, Ron's car arrived. He exited nonchalantly.

Geoff walked over to him. 'Ron, what's the meaning of this? Lads have come all this way, in the middle of a fuel crisis, and there's no game?'

'Nah. Nah. They agreed to the fixture. I spoke to their captain only on Thursday night.'

'Well, why aren't they bloody well here, then?'

Ron shrugged his shoulders. 'Don't ask me.'

Neil came back, mobile in hand. 'Geoffrey. You haven't got him to do your dirty work for you, have you?' Ron asked sharply.

'Somebody had to find out what was going on. OK, Neil, what's going on?'

'I got their skipper's number from Mawianne. She wasn't best pleased about being awoken from her slumbers by the way...'

'Come on, get on with it. Did you get hold of him?'

'Yeth. He was just about to take his dog out for a walk.'

'Yes, and?'

'He regwets that he rang Cwabbers on Friday night and left a message that because of the fuel cwisis he couldn't get a team out.'

Pervez was not impressed. 'But his team don't have to come very far. What about us? We've come all the way from Teesside!'

Neil explained. 'Some of them live up the Northumbwia coast. It's further than you think. No petwol for miles around. Anyway, he thought we'd have difficulties of our own..."

Geoff folded his arms. 'So, here we are in the middle of bloody nowhere without a game of cricket.

'Not necessawily. Arthur said he'd fix us up with a game come what may. And look – here comes the cavalwy!'

Neil pointed to a large white van as it turned into the car park. Out strode eleven immaculately turned-out under-thirteen-year-old boys, led by a steely eyed red-headed lad, William, tossing a cricket ball menacingly in his left hand.

'What the hell...?' Geoff spoke for the Outcasts.

'Hell indeed, and you are in it. Prepare for a whipping at the hands of the Northumbria Youth,' William exclaimed.

'Well, beggars can't be choosers, I suppose. Let's get on with it and show these impertinent whippersnappers how it is done.'

Later that afternoon...

Geoff threw his cricket gloves into the kit bag in absolute disgust as the Northumberland youth carried William in a triumphal march around the pitch.

The score board told the story: Northumbria Youth 270 for 3, Outcasts 69 all out.

'No-one say a word! Not one bloody word! This has been the most humiliating afternoon of my life, and the worst defeat of the Outcasts in its forty-year history...'

Neil could not help putting Geoff right. 'Are you certain? What about the massacre by the North Stanley Lady Taverners in 1975?'

Geoff brandished his cricket bat towards Neil menacingly.

Chapter 31: 'The Pub That Time Forgot'

Steve and Geoff were driving southwards on the A19. Steve took his eye off the fuel gauge for a few seconds to ask. 'Why didn't I get the potty then? For once I would've deserved it. I dropped two catches and I ran out the Pro.'

Geoff rolled his eyes. 'The Lord giveth and He taketh away.'

'And why not Amir? Three dropped catches! He never gets it!' Steve harrumphed.

'Well, you know why that is, don't you? Very nice pint of Exhibition they had in their clubhouse. Amir is a very generous man.'

'Poor young Adrian. What did he do wrong?'

'Didn't you see his missed, caught and bowled?'

'The one that their 14-year-old opening batsman drove over his head, when he bothered to pitch the ball up?'

'The very same.'

'Surely that was harsh.'

'Still, it's the cardinal sin. Missing a chance off your own bowling.'

'There must have been something else.'

'Well, if you must know, their chairman told me he didn't want to play us again.'

'Why's that?'

'Well, you know all those attempted bouncers he was bowling?'

'Oh, the ones that got swatted to the boundary?'

'It was his son who was batting.'

'So what? He seemed to handle it OK. Can't wrap them in cotton wool, you know...'

'Well, exactly. Very protective his dad was, though. I thought that loss of the fixture had to be taken into consideration, and Amir and "Pifco" agreed.'

'Not Crabbers, then?'

'No, he wanted you to get it, but he was outvoted. Bloody useless twat. Lads paid 80p a litre to come here.' Geoff rolled his eyes again before continuing. '80p a litre - that's what you get for wasting taxpayers' money on the Millennium Dome and the Angel of the North – to play a bunch of juniors! Which leads me to the next topic...'

'What's that, then?'

'Let's wait until we find a nice quiet place to discuss it,' Geoff said mysteriously before changing the subject. 'How's your love life, by the way?'

'Just taken a turn for the better...'

'Oh, tell me more, do.'

'Karen rang earlier in the week. Invited me round.'

'And you took full advantage?'

'Yeah, get in!' Steve's gesticulation almost caused him to swerve off the road.

'Steady on, old Son!' Geoff shouted before lowering his voice to a conspiratorial tone. 'How did you explain away the Victory Vs?'

'I told her they were anti-psoriasis pills.'

Geoff rubbed his hands together gleefully. 'You're learning, boy. You're learning.'

'Anyway, what about you and Hattie Jacques?'

'As I said, medicinal. Purely medicinal.'

'The real Hattie Jacques was quite a one, you know. Gave John Le Mesurier the run-around something rotten, she did.'

'How come?'

'Brought her boyfriend into the family home, she did. Poor old John had to move to the spare room.'

Geoff gave Steve a withering glance. 'Well, I'll remember that the next time I'm gazing at her ample proportions the morning after. Not sure it'll help very much, though.'

'Glad to be of service. When are you seeing her next?'

'I'm taking her for a dirty weekend in Rhyl.'

Channelling Sergeant Wilson, Steve asked, 'Are you sure that's wise, Chairman?'

'Why do you say that?'

'Well, it's not the most romantic of places.'

'It's fifty quid a head on the coach, all in.'

'Well, good luck with that. So, why is it you wanted a private chat?'

'Ah, yes. We need to find a quiet pub on the way home. It'll need to be off the beaten track.'

‘I can’t go too far off the A19. I’ve just about got enough petrol to get us back and for me to get to work tomorrow,’ Steve protested.

‘Let’s turn off here, then...’

Within a couple of miles of turning off the dual carriageway, Steve found himself driving through an old pit village. At the end of a dilapidated row of shops, there was a forbidding looking pub, which had also seen better days.

Steve did not fancy stopping. ‘This doesn’t look very welcoming.’

Geoff disagreed. ‘Looks like it’ll be nice and quiet. That’s exactly what we need for the purposes of our conversation. Let’s stop here.’

Steve dutifully stopped the car outside the pub.

As they walked in, they could see that the pub was festooned with mining memorabilia. In particular, there were several photos from the 1984/5 miners’ strike and Durham Miners’ Galas from around that time. The bar was covered with ‘Coal Not Dole’ towels. On the wall behind the bar was a full-size portrait of Arthur Scargill in heroic pose. The portrait was entitled ‘The President’. The pub was otherwise empty.

Geoff walked to the bar. ‘Come on, it’s my round. What do you want?’

Steve pulled a face, partly at the unexpected generosity of the Chairman, partly at the paucity of drinkable beer options.

‘I’ll have a pint of hand-pulled bitter, if they’ve got any...’

Geoff caught the attention of the landlord, a saturnine man in his sixties. ‘I’ll have a pint of lager and a pint of that real ale.’

The landlord was quick to put him right. ‘It’s all real in here.’ He then turned to Steve. ‘Yer not from round here, are you, son?’

‘Well, actually I’m from Runcorn,’ was Steve’s ill-advised response.

‘That’s doon sooth, isn’t it?’

‘No. No. No. It’s in the North West.’

‘Not to me, it’s not. Carlisle, that’s North West for me. Well, at least yer not from Nottinghamshire. Ah won’t serve scabs in my pub!’

‘I’ve always voted Labour, you know.’

‘Means nothing, that. So did most of the scabs.’

‘As a matter of fact, I live in Tony Blair’s constituency.’

‘Well, I’ll go to the foot of our stairs!’ the landlord scoffed. ‘Ah’m supposed to be impressed by that?! Tory in disguise, he is!’

Steve pointed at the portrait of Arthur Scargill. 'He should have held a secret ballot, you know.'

The landlord turned puce. 'Secret ballot? Secret ballot? Like the police did before they baton charged unarmed pickets? Like the secret services did when they bugged trade unionists' phones and played dirty tricks on them? Like Thatcher did when she torpedoed a compromise deal that the Coal Board made with the NUM six months in...'

Steve had heard all this stuff before from his lefty friends. 'He still should have had a ballot.'

The Landlord now turned purple. 'Why's that, son?'

'It would have been the democratic thing to do.'

The landlord was at screaming point. 'Democratic thing to do???'

Geoff was no socialist, but was aware of the deep scars that the strike had left from his business travels in the county. 'Don't mind my young friend, he does like to express opinions that he should keep to himself. Just can't help it, I'm afraid.'

'Alright. Alright. That's £3.70, please.'

The landlord finally served the pints. Geoff pays. Geoff and Steve find a small table near the bar.

'OK. What have you taken me to this God-forsaken place for?' Steve asked.

'Ah heard that!' The landlord was listening to their conversation.

'Well, I certainly wasn't recruiting you to the Diplomatic corps.'

'Well, what then?'

'This is a matter of the utmost secrecy. You are not to tell a soul.'

The Landlord was still earwigging. 'Ah knew it! Yer from that greasy HQ, aren't you?'

It was Geoff's turn to get irritated. 'Do you mind? We're having a private conversation.'

'Well, watch out, son. The walls have ears and people have long memories around here.'

Geoff turned back to Steve, who was having difficulty drinking the flat pint of vinegary beer that was in front of him. 'The reason I brought you here was to offer you the captaincy of the Outcasts.'

Before Steve could reply, the landlord intervened once again. 'Outcasts? Sounds like Robin Hood and his Merry Men. Bloody Nottinghamshire again!'

Geoff let him have a withering look.

This gave Steve time to think. 'Wow. Thanks. But won't Ron be standing again?'

'Yes. This is why I've brought you to this God-forsaken place. This is the launch of Operation "North Sea Oil".'

The Landlord zoned in once again. 'Yer talking in code again. Are yer sure yer not from Special Branch?'

Steve was now also getting sick of the interruptions. 'No, we're not, and if we were, why would we want to come here?'

'To gather information against the working classes.'

Steve was incredulous. 'Let's get this straight. You're not important anymore. You haven't been these last fifteen years.'

'That's it! Gerroot my pub! Yer certainly don't look like miners, but if yer had been you'd have been scabs. Now gerroot of my pub!!'

The landlord got a baseball bat from behind the bar and waved it at them.

Geoff decided that discretion was the better part of valour. 'I think we'd better go.'

Steve couldn't resist one last dig at the Landlord. 'A baseball bat eh? Have you got Arthur's best Orgreave cap to go with it?'

With that, the two conspirators ran out, hotly pursued by the landlord. Within a few strides, he gave up the chase and satisfied himself with flicking V signs at their rapidly vanishing backsides. 'Scabs! Good riddance!' he shouted after them.

They hurried out to Steve's car.

As they drove away, Geoff spotted two familiar faces heading in the opposite direction.

'Stop the car,' Geoff shouted. The Ford Mondeo screeched to a halt. Had Steve known whom he was stopping for, he would not have done so.

Julie was the first to speak as they emerged from the car. 'What are you two scoundrels doing here? Ah know. Ye've been to see Luscious Lucy, haven't yer?'

'What? Who's she?' Steve asked.

'Local bike. She works in a flat above the shops over there. Near where the colliery used to be,' Ros explained.

'Ay, and there's a pit that isn't closing in a hurry,' Julie added, nudging Steve and Geoff. Both look embarrassed, especially Geoff.

'No, we've been in the pub over there.' Steve pointed behind him.

Julie was incredulous. 'Yer haven't, have yer?

'The Landlord's a right heed the ball. Yer kna. Thinks it's still 1984. Won't serve scabs, even now,' Ros added.

'Yes. We've noticed. He's just kicked us out,' Steve observed.

Julie was not surprised. 'Doesn't like strangers. Thinks yer all from MI5.'

'Yeah. Tell me about it.' Geoff looked heavenwards.

'Ah heard you'd split up with Karen again.' Ros smirked at Steve.

'We've just got back together again,' Steve replied smugly.

'Well, you treat her right this time. No going off to the Anvil, mind!'

Steve glared at them.

Geoff had had something in mind when he had instructed Steve to stop the car. 'Well, actually, ladies, I was wondering if you'd be interested in our cricket club's end of season party...'

It was Geoff's turn to receive a glare from Steve.

'You know us. Always up for a party, we are.' Ros grabbed Steve's arm. 'Where are yer having it?'

'It's going to be in the O'Brien's in Darlington on Thursday, October 5th at 8.30pm. Don't be late.' Geoff continued.

'Will there be any fit young lads there?' Julie enquired.

Geoff had anticipated this question. 'Yeah, plenty,' he said, before adding leeringly, 'and some older ones too.'

Ros was certainly up for it. 'Ha. Ha. We'll be there. Try keeping us away, man.'

'Where are you two going, anyway?' Geoff was curious.

'There's a bandbox tonight in the Dalton.' Ros pointed to the pub which they had so recently escaped.

Steve was nonplussed. 'Bandbox? Wow! I thought they went out with the 1980s.'

'Not around here, they haven't,' Julie explained.

Ros went further: 'They're always good for meeting fellas. Anyway, we'd best be going. See ya.'

'Ay. See ya soon.' Julie and Ros started to walk away towards the pub.

'Not if I see you first,' Steve muttered under his breath.

Geoff heard his comment. 'Why? What's the matter? Don't you like them?'

'They grassed me up to Karen, remember?'

'Oh. Yes, so they did.'

'So, why did you invite them, then?'

'To liven things up a bit. Now then, I take it that you accept the captaincy.'

'But we haven't had the election yet!'

Geoff tapped the side of his nose meaningfully. 'Don't worry, I'll take care of that.'

They got back into the car and managed to get home without further incident.

Chapter 32: 'Awards Night'

Things were certainly looking up for Steve. Four nights later, he found himself dressed in a dinner jacket and black tie in a crowded hotel foyer. Behind him was a sign announcing, 'Tees Valley Business Awards 2000'. He was in an upbeat mood. He'd worked hard to persuade the powers-that-be that the 'bronze-out' did not apply to this event (but only on condition that he finally sent the grovelling email to Debbie).

The Poplars Hotel was a 1960s creation on the outskirts of Yarm. It had been the height of glamour at one time, boasting international footballers (and cricketers), soap stars and chart-topping musicians among its clientele. Even a prime minister (not Tony Blair) had stayed there. The adjoining night club had been the place to be seen right into the 1990s and was a popular 'copping off' spot for locals of all ages. Not just locals – likely lads and lasses from as far away as Newcastle and Leeds would come there to try their luck.

Despite appearances, however, the new decade seemed to be passing by this once premier venue. It was beginning to look dated, and its grand Ionic arch façade was beginning to look more and more clichéd. All the same, Steve was happy to be present at what was still the place to be seen, if you were a Teessider. To emphasise this point, a photographer was circulating to take photos of the guests for an in-house 'Country Life' style society magazine.

Guests were milling around collecting drinks off the waiters. Steve was collecting more than most. He walked up to Paula, who was dressed in a fetching low-cut black dress, bearing two glasses of Prosecco.

'Here you are Paula. Have a glass of the Poplars' finest...'

He stared down Paula's front as he handed over the glass of fizzy white wine.

'Thank you, Steve. Isn't that your sixth?'

Steve was still gazing down at Paula's cleavage. 'Not sure. Who's counting, anyway?'

'And what's down the front of my dress that you so wanted to see?'

Steve pulled away abruptly. 'Sorry, Paula. Was it that obvious?'

Paula smiled. 'Sure, look it,' she said, before joking, 'Nothing to see here, by the way.'

Steve blushed copiously as he recalled his daydream the previous week. Steve's embarrassment was curtailed temporarily by the unexpected arrival of Amir, wearing a white tuxedo.

'Good evening, captain-elect.'

'Oh, hello Amir. What are you here for? And what's this about captain-elect?'

'Oh, don't worry, your secret's safe with me. What the Chairman wants, the Chairman gets. You know I've always said that.'

'So, why are you here?'

'Oh, my team from Tees Hospital Trust are here for the Heart of the Community Award. Please, you haven't introduced me to your ravishing young lady friend.'

'Oh, sorry. This is Dr Paula O'Donnell. Paula, this is Dr Amir El-Nile.'

Amir bowed gracefully and clasped her hand. 'Enchanted to meet you, Dr Paula.'

'And you too, Dr El-Nile.' Paula pointed at Steve. 'And I'm not his girlfriend, by the way.'

'Oh dear. That is indeed a shame. You look so well suited to each other.' Amir was unabashed.

'I'll have you know, I'm happily married with five kids.'

'Oh dear. Well, the captain-elect will have to look elsewhere for a lady to match his talents. I'm not sure he'll meet someone of your calibre, though.'

'That's very flattering...' Paula was unconvinced.

'Anyway, I must re-join my team.' Amir bowed again. 'We're about to be called to our tables. It has been a pleasure and a privilege to have met you.'

Paula and Steve walked towards the BCG table.

'Sorry about that, Paula. Most embarrassing.'

Paula was philosophical. 'Ah, what are friends for, but to drop yer in the shite? I think he meant well.'

They reach the table. There are already four others sitting around it: Jim Dickson, Stuart, Debbie, and Paul the technician. Conversation was polite and restrained. Jim was a tall, stooped figure with a somewhat absent air about him. He was wearing a belt to hold up his dinner jacket trousers.

Attached to the belt was a holster containing his mobile phone. This was popular at the time – with a certain sort of man - that is.

Jim got up to greet him. 'Steve. Good to see you. Come and sit next to me. I hope you're bloody well going to win this award, having dragged me away from the Swainby amateur dramatic group's panto rehearsal.'

Steve was already feeling the effects of the fizzy wine. 'Oh, no, I haven't!' he quipped.

Jim didn't get the joke. 'Sorry, what do you mean by that?' The others round the table squirmed with embarrassment.

'Well, I mean, it's only ninety-six days until Christmas; you've got plenty of time yet.'

'How did you work that out so quickly?'

'Oh, it's a gift.'

Paula mimicked Steve. 'Oh, no, it's bloody well not. It's Asperger's Syndrome, so it is.'

Paula was interrupted by a drum roll as the compere for the evening took the stage. It was none other than Stan, the TV presenter and local celebrity from the Dog Inn quiz night.

'Good evening, Ladies and Gentlemen. So good to see you all in attendance for the renowned Tees Valley Industrial Awards. We have eight awards in all, culminating in the all-important Business of the Year Award.'

Paul was sitting next to Steve on the other side to Jim. He whispered in Steve's ear. 'Do you fancy going out for a fag? It's ages before our award...'

To which Steve whispered back, 'OK. Let's not make it too obvious. Get up and I'll follow you...'

Paul walked off. At that moment, Jim turned to Steve. 'Now, tell me about your family, erm, Steve...'

Steve hesitated for a couple of nanoseconds before making his excuses.

'Sorry Jim, I've just got to pay a call...' This was true; the multiple glasses of fizzy wine were certainly taking their toll.

'OK. We'll resume our conversation when you get back,' Jim said equably.

Steve walked out. Outside the Ionic arch, Paul lit up and handed a cigarette to Steve. 'What do you think our chances of winning this award are, then?'

'Oh, better than the Boro's of staying up this season, I reckon.' Steve could not help having a dig about the local team's poor early season form.

'Now then! Just because your lot are top of the league.'

Steve made a victory fist pump and beat his chest. 'Leeds. Leeds. Leeds.'

'You seemed to be getting on alright with old Davros.'

'Why do you call him Davros?' Steve asked.

'Oh, it goes back to the seventies. When he was still in the lab, he was working on genetically modified viruses. He caused a major incident. Had to evacuate the whole site, they did.'

Steve spotted the opportunity to imitate a Dalek. 'Evacuate!'

Paul shook his head. 'Very funny.'

'But why Davros? He created the Daleks, not a virus!'

'Well, doesn't Davros break a phial full of viruses in a Dr Who episode?'

Steve put Paul right. 'No actually, in "Genesis of the Daleks", Davros tells the Doctor that he would break such a phial, if he had the chance, thus revealing himself to be a dangerous megalomaniac.'

'Like Tony Blair, you mean?' Paul ventured.

'No. No. Tony's alright. I've written to him a few times, actually.'

Paul pulled a face. Steve blushed and changed the subject. 'So... any other reason why Jim's called Davros?

'Nah. The name just stuck.'

'Yeah, I suppose he's a director of R and D, just like Davros was for the Kaleds,' Steve reasoned.

They finished their cigarettes and returned to their seats. Steve took another large gulp out of his glass of wine.

After they had successfully negotiated the jungle of foliage that dominated the foyer of the Poplars and reached their table again, Paula looked at them archly.

'Where have you two been all this time? You've been on the fags, haven't yer?'

'Well, I'm feeling a bit nervous,' Steve admitted.

Paula was unimpressed. 'What shite. And you bein' the Health Committee Chairman an' all!'

Jim looked around the table. 'Oh, it looks like we've run out of wine. I'll order some more.'

Debbie was swift to intervene. 'But the rules of the bronze-out clearly state no liquor on company business...'

Jim winked at Steve. 'Well, we'll have to use a bit of discretion, then, shan't we? We'll order champagne, in anticipation of our magnificent victory,' he said before turning to him again. 'We are going to hit 'em for six, aren't we?'

Steve was confident. 'Oh yes, we'll win alright.'

Stuart was more cautious. 'Well, I wouldn't be so sure. You don't know what the opposition is like.'

Steve was dismissive. 'Oh, no worries on that score.'

'Why not?'

Steve put on a Dalek voice and put his hands out like he was about to exterminate. 'We are the superior beings!!!'

Stuart and Debbie recoiled at this exuberant display. Jim, at least, was suitably impressed. 'Oh. You're a Dr Who fan, are you?'

'Yes, I watched the very first episode. It's a shame about them stopping it.'

'Yes, indeed. You know, I wrote to the BBC in protest.'

'Really?'

'Yes. Never did get a reply...' Jim said wistfully.

Stuart could not resist putting in his two penn'orth. 'Well, I think it had run its course.'

'Never!' retorted Jim and Steve in unison.

Stuart was like a dog with a bone. 'No, it got gradually worse. You had Tom Baker, then Peter Davison, then Colin Baker, then... Sylvester McCoy. Each one worse than the last one. It ended up being a shadow of its former self.'

Steve's reply betrayed his state of inebriation. 'A bit like BCG then!' He laughed heartily at his own joke.

Everyone stared at Steve in embarrassment. Fortunately for him, he was interrupted by an announcement.

'And now for the Heart of the Community Award,' Stan announced.

'Hey up. It's us next.' Paul suddenly became animated.

Stan continued. 'The nominees are Eston Parish Council, Cruickshank Tubing, Tees Hospital Trust, Boro Chemicals, Dormanstown Steelworks and Ragworth Taxis...'

A video played, highlighting the good works done by the various organisations. Meanwhile, the champagne arrived at the BCG table. Steve immediately helped himself to more.

'And the winner is...' Stan opened the envelope. 'Tees Hospital Trust!' Amir bounded on to the stage and shook Stan's hand. They posed with the trophy and smiled while photos were taken.

'Thank you. Thank you, Mr Beardsmore. It is indeed a pleasure and a privilege to receive this award, especially from one as illustrious as your good self. I would like to thank all my team for all their hard work in achieving this award. And you know we need teamwork in this world, so may I say how pleased I am to see the next Outcasts cricket team captain in the audience...'

Everyone looked at Steve, who went bright red.

Amir continued. 'As I was saying, we need teamwork in this world, and who could be a better example and who could be a more at the heart of our community than the Outcasts' beloved Chairman? Although, sadly, he can't be with us tonight, I hereby dedicate this award to Mr. Geoffrey Huckstead!'

There was polite applause. Amir's team did not look best pleased.

Stan drew out another envelope. 'And now for our penultimate award of the evening, the Business Innovation Award. You know, this area has always been renowned for its inventions, right since John Walker invented the safety match in 1829. We have a proud local tradition, and I'm pleased to say, ladies and gentlemen, our nominees tonight are living proof of that tradition being continued.'

Stan paused for applause. 'The nominees are Cleveland University, Eaglescliffe Computers, Vaxholm Metals, Teeslink Mobiles, Terimon Engineering... and BCG.' A video shows the nominees' inventions, including a mobile phone cover that glowed in the dark. Then it was Steve and Paula's turn, in the lab, talking about their nano-sunscreens.

Paul could not resist having a dig at Steve. 'Did you find your way alright, then?'

Steve was puzzled. 'Do you mean to here? Of course!'

'No, to the Lab. Everyone thought you might have needed one of those Sat Navs!'

'I don't know what you mean!' Steve said sulkily.

Paula laughed. Steve gulped down more wine. The videos droned on.

Jim was oblivious to all the byplay around the table. 'We should win this. The rest is crap. Luminescent mobile phone covers, indeed!'

Stan took over from the video. 'And now for the big moment, when we discover who the winner is!' There was a long pause as Stan opened an envelope.

'Well, I'm sure you've all got happy memories of visiting the beach from this summer...' he began.

Paula was already up on her feet. 'We won!' she shouted out loud.

'And I'm sure you're already looking forward to returning next year when we'll all be wearing KALKOS Transparent Factor 50.'

Jim shook Steve by the hand as he got up to claim the award.

'So, the winner is... BCG!'

Applause rang out around the Poplars dining room. Steve lurched as he set off to collect the award. He hesitated for a split second. 'Are you sure you don't want to go up, Jim?'

'No, go on. You deserve it. I'm tired of collecting awards on behalf of BCG. But say something interesting! Tonight's acceptance speeches have been so boring!'

Paula had a word in his shell-like ear. 'Steve, you're a bit squiffy. I'll go if you want me to.'

Steve assumed his full height and launched into a Margaret Thatcher impersonation. 'No. No. No.' He was not going to let his moment slip. 'I'll go. Team effort. I'll just have to take one for the team.' Steve staggered on towards the stage with the applause ringing in his ears. He finally made it to the podium.

Stan shook his hand. 'Well done, young man. '

'Thank you, Stan,' Steve said, continuing to shake his hand for much longer was necessary as the photos were taken.

Stan leant over to Steve. 'Are you ready to say something?'

'Oh, yeah.' Steve righted himself and turned towards the audience. 'Erm, I'm not really sure what to say.'

Nervous laughter emanated from the audience.

'Erm. It's a great honour to be here tonight.' He fumbled in his pocket for speech notes but couldn't find them. There was an embarrassingly long pause while he stood on the podium waving the trophy around. Finally... 'Well, I'd like to thank my magnificent team for all the hard work that they've done in making this award possible.' Steve paused as he spoke, tottering as he did so. Remembering he was merely repeating all the other acceptance speeches, he recalled Jim's voice: *Say something interesting.* 'And I hope that this award will show to the public of Teesside and beyond that BCG is still alive and kicking...'

It was then that Steve decided to impersonate the Black Dalek. 'We may be entombed by our share price, but we live on. This is only the beginning. We will prepare, we will grow stronger. When the time is right, we will emerge and take our rightful place as the Supreme Power of the Universe!' Steve pointed the trophy at the audience, as if it were a ray gun. 'Exterminate!' he proclaimed loudly before holding it aloft triumphantly. 'Thank you, ladies and gentlemen!'

There was mixed applause. Steve walked haltingly back to his seat. Jim applauded rapturously. Debbie and Stuart sat in stony silence.

'Well done that, man! Well done! That certainly wasn't boring. I loved the Doctor Who stuff at the end.'

Stuart turned to Debbie. 'We didn't!' Then, to Steve: 'Don't forget, it's your appraisal first thing tomorrow – and don't be late!' Debbie nodded her approval. Unfortunately, Stuart and Debbie's words of wisdom were lost on Steve. He had fallen fast asleep at the table.

Chapter 33: 'The Poisoned Chalice'

The following day Steve woke up in his bed fully clothed, cuddling up to the trophy; next to him was a letter with a House of Commons heading on it, which had arrived mysteriously overnight.

Hi Steve,

Greetings from Brighton!

I'm pleased to say that the crisis has passed. I can't possibly comment on your remarks about Mr Brown. Re BCG's share price: it's regrettable, but I'm afraid we can't do very much to help. It is not this government's place to intervene in the affairs of private companies. We in New Labour believe in a light touch. Let the markets decide!

We are, however, committed to wealth generation. We believe that through the auspices of our regional development agencies, such as One North East, we can use a fully joined-up approach to regenerate areas like Tees Valley to their former glory. Please watch this space for some exciting developments, which Mr Prescott will be announcing presently.

Yours Ever

Tony

Steve turned over and looked at his radio alarm. It was already 8 o'clock. 'Shit the bed, it's my appraisal this morning...'

Steve finally clambered out of the dinner jacket he'd worn for the previous night's awards ceremony. He staggered downstairs, trophy in hand, to make some tea. While the kettle was on, he started writing in his journal...

'Shit. Shit. Shit. I've got my appraisal this morning and I'm running late. Oh my head. I wish there was something I could do about that – and this stiffy and all. No. No I haven't got time for a ham shank. Karen, where are you when I truly need you?

Still... I showed 'em last night, didn't I? Sorry, we showed 'em. Never mind the share price bollocks, here's 'the Kalkos Pistols', eh? Hey, for once, I'm going into my appraisal in a position of strength. They can't take this away from me!'

Steve kissed the trophy.

'They'd better not make a fuss about me being late neither. After all, I was on company duty until 1am. Right? OK, I'd better just inform my friend Tony about this latest triumph and its significance for the coming resurgence of the UK chemical industry, then I'll finish my tea, then I'll go.'

Steve then scribbled out a letter to Tony Blair.

Hi Tony.

By the time you read this letter, you will no doubt have read in the Evening Gazette of our new 'Kalkos' brand winning the Tees Valley Innovation Award for 2000. I personally believe that this marks a turning point for the fortunes of the chemical industry in this country. Just as you turned round the old dinosaur Labour Party into brand 'New Labour', so shall we progressive thinkers convert old clapped-out BCG into value added 'new BCG'. The old ways must go. Let's leave bulk manufacture to the Chinese and concentrate on the Value Proposition. I will be back in touch soon to offer my thoughts on the way forward for British Industry!

Best regards

Steve

Steve slurped down his tea and went back upstairs to get dressed. He finally arrived at the Elton Centre at 9.14am.

Five minutes later, he found himself knocking at a large, slightly ajar door. It had 'Dr Deborah Gould BCG Personal Care European Innovation Manager' on it. Beneath this, is a slogan: 'My door is always open.' He had the trophy firmly clutched in his hand.

He heard Debbie's voice. 'Come in!'

Steve walked into a very large office, sat down and plonked the trophy down. Debbie and Stuart were sitting on the opposite side of a large desk. Behind it was a large poster of Terry Wogan entitled 'Terry's TOGs'.

Debbie commenced the meeting in jocular style. 'Oh, Steve. Ha. Ha. Ha. I hope you don't mind the poster, do you? I like to put my staff at ease when they come here. I think they appreciate my eccentricities.' Debbie giggled nervously.

'Oh, no. I'm a great a fan of the old Togmeister myself. Always listen to his show.' Steve crossed the fingers of his free hand beneath the desk.

Stuart was in a less jovial mood. 'You're late,' he spat venomously, before pointedly looking at his watch. 'This meeting should have started at 9 o'clock. It's now 9.20am, which means one hour of company time has now been wasted between the three of us.'

Debbie intervened. 'Come now, Stuart. We did manage to keep ourselves occupied talking about Project Mallard while we were waiting.'

'Oh. Can you tell me anything?' Steve was curious.

'Sorry, no I couldn't. Even if I did know, which I don't, it's share price sensitive.' Debbie explained.

'Do you mean to say that you really don't know, Debbie?' Steve was incredulous.

'No. Honestly. I shouldn't tell you this, but it's being managed by three senior executives from other BCG Divisions and a firm of Consultants.'

'Why not the local management?'

'It was felt by those on high that an impartial view was needed. Anyway, young man, we've got an appraisal to do, so let's get on.'

Stuart cleared his throat. 'Let's start with the self-appraisal that you did as a preliminary to this meeting.' Now, Stuart raised his voice. 'You're supposed to take it fucking seriously!'

Steve was taken aback. 'What do you mean? I thought I did take it seriously.'

'Well, how come you thought that you were either "excellent" or "very good" in all categories?'

'Well, there, you see, I could have given "excellent" in all of them.'

Stuart was getting more and more irritated. 'This is supposed to be 360° feedback. You're meant to take it seriously!'

'What? And criticise myself, instead of letting you do it for me?'

'Well, needless to say – your views differ from those of Debbie and myself.'

'Look. I've achieved all of my objectives. I've had no accidents or near misses on my patch; in fact, as you know I take a proactive approach to health and safety...'

'We'll come to that later,' Stuart said menacingly.

'I've met my budget targets...'

'That's pretty easy, since over 80% of it is salary costs, which you don't control, and a child could manage the rest of it.'

'And... I'm the only Technical Manager here who's met the target of 30% sales from new products that was set in 1999.'

'Are you Prince or something?' Stuart's sardonic response drew a blank look from Debbie. 'You keep harking back to 1999. That was the last millennium. Welcome to the brave new world of lean, efficient BCG.'

Debbie finally intervened. 'Yes, Steve. And you seem to have completely ignored the new spending controls and gone ahead with that last plant trial, against the strong advice of the Engineering department.'

'Those blood suckers!' As we know, there was no love lost between Steve and that particular community. 'I stayed well within budget. The trial was important.'

'Important to get one kilogram of material, when you should have had over a hundred?' Stuart countered. Steve felt that Stuart was playing to his audience, as he knew that Stuart had an equally disparaging view of the Engineers.

'We got enough for major customer sampling.'

'Yes, at the cost of £70K. You know that you're a laughingstock around this site. Which leads me to the Health Day incident.'

It was Debbie's turn to join in on the kicking. 'Yes. Stuart, let me lead on that one. You caused me great embarrassment within the company and outside. Fancy copying the CEO on your email. AND TONY BLAIR! TONY BLAIR, I ask you!!?'

'I thought that some of your managers had missed out on the importance of the event for their peoples' future health and wellbeing. I thought it deserved a wider discussion,' Steve answered reasonably.

'"Wider discussion?" Oh, big words!' Stuart decided to persist with the political theme. 'You're sounding like Loony Benn now.'

Steve felt that he had been let down. 'I thought that you supported me!'

'I supported you for your commitment to Health, Safety and the Environment, not sharking attractive young women.'

'Yes, and I admired the way that you were prepared to walk the walk as well as talk the talk,' Debbie added soothingly.

'But you wouldn't support me in the face of your managers...'

Debbie reddened. 'How could I possibly do that in the face of what you were actually getting up to?'

'Getting up to? What do you mean getting up to?'

'I mean quack, unscientific remedies for non-existent ailments.'

Steve became passionate. 'Well, I'll tell you one existent ailment on this site. That's stress, and it's the elephant in this room!'

'Elephant in the room? Don't you business bullshit me!' Stuart snarled.

Steve swallowed hard, remembering Debbie's own address to his team. 'It's not bullshit. The Stress Survey findings were clear and unequivocal. 80% of the people on this site were suffering from high levels of stress, even before Project Mallard. I've merely tried, in my own way, to alleviate that suffering.'

Stuart prepared to deliver the coup de grace. 'If only that wasn't the only criticism of you.'

'Why? As I've said, I think I've achieved some excellent results.'

'You mean your team did.'

'Led by my good self!'

'Well actually, that's not what they think.'

'What do you mean by that?

'I've been talking to them individually. They think that any success has been achieved despite you more than because of you.'

Steve was getting rattled. 'But I wrote the Technical Plan. I allocated resources, then I let them get on with it.'

'Exactly. You let them get on with it.' Stuart had a way of putting imaginary inverted commas around phrases. 'Where's the leadership in that?'

'Well, once people knew what they had to do, I thought that was the best way, rather than to interfere.'

'You never took a stand against anyone, did you?'

'Why should I want to do that?'

'You've never stamped your authority over them.'

'I'm not Sir Alex Ferguson, you know!' (Too right there, Steve!)

'As I said, I've been making discrete enquiries amongst your staff,' Stuart continued. 'Here's a typical comment...'

Stuart put his reading glasses on, produced a piece of paper and read from it. '"Ha. Ha. Good old Steve, he really doesn't do very much. We just have to get round him as best we can." Or try this one... "He seems half asleep half the time and sound asleep the rest of it."' Stuart was relentless. 'Or this one... "I've never accepted him as a boss. I don't consider him as a leader of men or women."'

Steve was shaken, if not a little stirred. 'I'm not sure that this is important. After all, it's the results that count. And by the way, you should hear the things some of them say about you!'

Debbie intervened. 'Now, don't get personal. I've heard enough. Your team doesn't respect you. Your peer group think you're a Bennite, you've brought your business unit into disrepute and you see any rule as a challenge as to how to circumvent it!'

Steve felt that this intervention was particularly unfair, given the ad hominem nature of Stuart's previous remarks. It was his turn to raise his voice.

'I've introduced profitable new products to the business, I've won prizes...'

Steve waved the trophy in front of them.

Stuart rewarded this gesture with a look of utter disdain. 'So what? Pets win fucking prizes! And, as usual, you forget that it's your team that's won the prize!'

'I've shown innovation skills, I've shown creativity, I've created intellectual property! I've identified stress as the principal health and safety problem confronting this business and tried to do something about it...'

Debbie raised her hand. 'Enough already! Let's cut to the chase. Stuart and I have decided to give you an overall assessment of "reasonable", which we think is generous. We toyed with the idea of giving you "below target", but we've decided that "reasonable – with some development areas" would be the fairest.'

Steve was almost in tears. 'I don't believe this. Everyone knows that that's a crap rating.'

Stuart nodded his head. 'Yes, and almost everyone on this site think that's exactly what you deserve.'

Steve was clutching at straws. 'What about Jim? He likes me!'

Debbie and Jim were hardly a mutual admiration society, despite outward appearances. 'Forget about Jim. Jim is in a world of his own. He's the last of the old school, "the Great and the Good so-called". He's only got a couple of months before his retirement, when no doubt he will get a CBE and a place on one of these new QUANGO boards.'

'You mean Regional Development Agencies,' Steve suggested.

Stuart finally came out with something that Steve could agree with. 'Yeah, a complete waste of space if you ask me. No substitute for the indigenous industries just making things, but the politicians like them. It looks visionary and it doesn't break EU rules, which every other country does, except ours, by the way, so they're seen as the way forward. Exquisite management structures to boot, which should suit a lot of the characters around here.'

Steve nodded his head in agreement.

Debbie then clapped her hands and produced a document. 'Anyway, let's not waste any more time. We would like you to sign this document. We will identify training courses that you can go on to remedy your development areas and you will receive a 2% merit rise plus 1% cost of living increase.'

'That's crap, that's really crap. I'm not sure I can sign this.' Steve pushed the document away.

'If you know what's good for you, you will,' Stuart hissed menacingly.

Steve was shocked by the already-completed document. The training course he had attended had insisted that the final document should be a distillation of an informed discussion between Appraiser and Appraisee. It was time to make a point. 'Oh, and what about the career potential section. We haven't discussed that. I'm supposed to get a rating for that, aren't I?'

Stuart smiled for the first time. 'Oh. Yes. Do you want me to explain the colour scheme to you again?'

'Yes. Go on. I missed the half day course that HR ran on this particular aspect of the appraisal process.'

'OK. So, it's green for career fast track – promote within the next two years, blue for 'career on track', promote as appropriate, yellow for no promotion envisaged, and red for no promotion possible, review within 6 months for overall career viability.' Stuart paused for effect. 'You get a yellow.'

'A yellow! A yellow? That means you think I've got no potential. I've no chance of any further promotion. I'll be left in perpetuity on my current grade.' The awful realisation suddenly hit him. 'I'll never get a company car!!' he screamed.

Stuart sat back. 'Tough! Some say you've already been over-promoted.'

Debbie crossed her arms. 'I think that brings an end to these proceedings. Are you going to sign?'

Steve stormed off towards the door, trophy in hand. 'I'll have to think about it!'

Debbie had the last word. 'Well don't be too long about it. It's a very generous assessment, in my opinion.'

It was a long walk back to his office. He bumped into Paula in the corridor. 'Hi Steve. How did it go?'

'Utterly crap, I'm afraid.' Steve might have been a little more guarded with his reply, had she not caught him in a moment of vulnerability.

'Ah, go on. I'll come with you to your office and make you a nice cup of tea.'

'I'm not sure I'm in the mood for that.' Steve tossed his head back a la Greta Garbo. 'I want to be alone.'

Paula countered with an impersonation of Father Ted's Mrs Doyle. 'Ah go on. Yer will. Yer will. Yer will.'

'Oh, alright, then. I guess I do need a little cheering up.'

They reached his office and sat down at the table. Paula brought Steve a nice cup of tea.

'So what did he say then, yer man?'

'He denigrated my record, then they said I lacked leadership qualities.'

'Who's he to talk? The conceited little eejit. Everyone knows that we succeed in spite of him rather than because of him.'

Steve arched his eyebrows, realising the familiarity of the language. 'Indeed! You know he said that people were saying exactly that about me?'

Paula affected surprise. 'Really? We're all behind you, Stephen. You know that. We know you're misunderstood.'

'Hmm. It's getting to the point where I don't know who to trust.'

'And what did Debbie say in all this?'

'Oh, she's still smarting over the Health Promotion Day.'

'Well, you did copy the CEO and Tony Blair on that email you sent her.'

'Humph. No sense of humour, some people!' Steve grunted as he got up. 'And another thing...' he was about to say, when Margaret entered the room and spied the trophy on Steve's table.

She walked over to Steve and gave him a massive bear hug. 'Congratulations Dr Hemmings. You won it, then?'

Steve tried desperately to disengage. 'Thank you, Margaret. Yes. Well, it was a team effort.'

Margaret would have none of it. 'You know that's not true; you were the brains behind it all.' Margaret hugged him again.

Steve finally broke clear. 'Thanks for your kind thoughts, Margaret,' he mumbled, struggling to catch his breath.

Margaret then unleashed her Exocet. 'Are they finally going to promote you, then?'

Steve was still recovering his breath. 'I don't think so, but thanks for your kind thoughts.'

'Anyway, I see you're in deep discussions with Mrs O'Donnell...'

'Dr O'Donnell, please, Margaret!'

'Alright, Dr O'Donnell, then.' Margaret turned grumpy. 'I see you want Dr Hemmings all to yourself. I'll come back later.'

Margaret left them to it.

'Oh well, it's nice to have one fan anyway,' Steve reflected.

'Stephen, you've got plenty of fans!'

'If only that were true.'

'Now, come on. Don't let them get you down. I've got to go back to the lab now, so drink up your tea and cheer up.'

As Paula left the office, Steve sat at his table staring at his trophy, falling asleep as he did.

* * *

Steve finds himself walking into an operations office in an underground bunker. A map is on the wall with women moving arrows around, reflecting the downwards trend of BCG's share price. Steve is wearing the uniform of a Waffen SS Major with a BCG logo armband. He has a document in his hand. Steve walks up to a desk. In it sits the CEO of BCG. The CEO is surrounded by fawning staff, including Jim, the Technical Director. Steve puts the document in front of the CEO. 'Mein Fuhrer, I bring good news from the North-Eastern Front.'

'Good news from the North-Eastern Front? It's a long time since we received good news from the North-Eastern Front.' The CEO does a little dance of joy before turning to his acolytes. 'See? It can be done. You pessimists! You defeatist dolts!! What is your good news, Herr Sturmbannfuhrer?

'I have singlehandedly von a famous victory in the Tees Valley!'

The CEO shouts at his staff. 'See vot can be done vith ze BCG zeal!' before turning back to Steve. 'Tell me more about your victory.'

'I von an Innovation Award.'

'An Innovation Award. Vos that for our revenge weapons?'

'Sorry, Mein Fuhrer. It vos for the nanoparticles in zer sunburn cream.'

The CEO turns to address his staff once more. 'See, zis young man is already planning for next summer's campaign, ven ve finally take Moscow!!!'

'Not just Moscow, Mein Fuhrer. Zis product has global reach.'

The CEO hammers on the table. 'See, zis vill show the City Boys that you can't write off BCG.'

'No, Mein Fuhrer, ve are not finished yet.'

'Ver you outnumbered?'

'Yes, Mein Fuhrer. 5 to 1.'

'You repelled ze enemy?'

'Yes, Mein Fuhrer.'

'Zat is the best news I've heard since ze American President died.'

At this point, Jim steps in. 'You never did like Leclerc Johnson, did you, Tim?

The CEO smiles. 'No, he vos a defeatist. He opposed my annexation of the new businesses.'

'Hardly new businesses, Mein Fuhrer,' Jim feels compelled to point out. 'Some of them were older than BCG itself.'

'Zey ver verth every Reichsmark.'

'Seven billion pounds,' Jim persists. 'That's a lot of Reichsmarks.'

This causes the CEO to hammer the desk again. 'Zey created new living space for BCG. I had to do it. Zat Leclerc Johnson, he dared to question my decision. He deserved zat heart attack.' The CEO shakes Steve by the hand. 'Vell, young man, you haf served ze Fatherland most admirably.'

'Thank you, Mein Fuhrer.' Steve clicks his heels.

'For zat, you vill receive our highest decoration: ze Titanium Cross.'

'Why, thank you, Mein Fuhrer. This is indeed a great honour.'

'Herr Doktor Von Dickson, please pin ze medal on zis young man's chest.' The CEO was not finished. 'And Herr Doktor Von Dickson, you must promote zis young man. He vill haf his company Volkswagen.'

Jim is reticent. 'Not sure about that, Mein Fuhrer. I haf to organise ze firing squads first, then ve vill see.'

'Ah yes, zer Project Mallard. All weaklings and defeatists to be shot! It vill make BCG stronger.'

The CEO turns back to Steve. 'Now zen, young man, have you any questions for me?'

'Are ve going to vin...?' Steve asks hesitantly.

He is interrupted by the CEO. 'Herr Sturmbannfuhrer, you know the rules! Please refer all questions to my Public Relations Office, in writing, before I vill answer zem! Now good luck on your return to the North Eastern Front. Heil BCG!'

The CEO salutes. Steve salutes him back. 'Heil BCG!'

Steve clicks his heels and turned away.

* * *

Steve woke up. The side of his head was stuck to his desk by the trail of drool that had come out of the side of his mouth. He looked at his watch. It had just turned twelve. Time for lunch.

Steve walked over to the Lakeside Restaurant. The Septics seemed even gloomier than usual. The talk was of Project Mallard, the inconvenient ramifications of the bronze-out and the latest difficulties that the company was having selling off its 'rust belt' assets. A still-defiant Steve plonked his tray down and waited for a gap in the conversation.

'Well, perhaps I can cast my own little ray of sunshine.'

Frank was the first to speak for the collective. 'You're not going on about that fucking Innovation Award again, are you?'

'Well. Yes. BCG won!'

This was greeted with a chorus of 'We've heard!'

'Forget it. It means nothing. We're all going to hell in a handcart,' Don wailed.

'And don't think that you'll necessarily escape the rigours of Project Dead Duck. Remember what I told you about the curse of Manager of the Month,' Frank hastened to add.

'It could be worse, I suppose,' Les mused. 'Does anybody here remember the Safety Awards?'

There was a general shaking of heads.

'Well. If a site went one million hours without a lost time accident, they'd give everyone an award, plus a few hundred quid cash bonus,' Les continued. 'We'd all go to the local rec, have a good piss up, and collect our awards.

'Sounds like a good idea. What's not to like?'

'Because, my young friend, no work got done after about 950,000 hours and the tension would build up like you wouldn't believe it.' Les rolled his eyes. 'Finally, one year, there was a massive explosion after about 990,000 hours. Bad business, two men killed.'

'And what caused that?'

'Oh. There was a warning light kept going off in the plant control room. A valve kept sticking.'

'Why didn't they fix it, then?'

'It meant someone having to shin up a steel ladder. Risky. Danger of falling. Lost time accident. "Let's leave it until we're over the million", they thought, "it's only a few days."'

'Then what happened?'

'There was a build-up of stuff, then the valve suddenly opened. Dumped a whole load of hot styrene into the reactor. Fireball. Half the plant wrecked. Two men killed, six badly injured. After the inquiry, they stopped the scheme.'

Steve ate his lunch as silence descended on the table.

Finally, Don spoke up as everyone was getting up to leave. 'Sorry if we seem negative – and well done on the award – but we've seen it all before. This "Project Mallard" is shaping up to be worse than the previous rounds of bloodletting, so watch your back, my friend.'

Once back in the office, Steve's mobile rang, the sound of *Born on the Bayou* getting ever louder.

It was Geoff.

'Good afternoon. Not interrupting anything, am I?'

'No. I've just got back from lunch,' Steve replied wearily.

'Oh. Congratulations on that award, by the way.'

'Thanks. Er, how do you know about it?'

'Amir said. So...how did it go down at work?'

'It hasn't made much difference, I don't think.' Steve could be the master of understatement.

Geoff chuckled. 'Well, Amir tells me your acceptance speech was just a little bit unconventional, shall we say... Anyway, I won't beat about the bush. Is the minge OK, by the way?'

'Oh, Karen. Yeah, she was fine last time I saw her.'

'Legs apart, I hope.'

'Well, if you must...'

'Anyway, can you come round tonight?'

'I was thinking of going out with Karen.'

'What, on a Friday night? Friday night is tashing night.'

'I thought you were planning a quiet night in.'

'I've had to change my plans. Something's come up.'

'What's come up?'

'I can't talk about it right now. Just come round to my house and we'll talk about it then.'

'I thought it was your turn.'

'No, that was a day job. Don't worry, it'll be my turn next time we go out of a night.'

Steve sighed resignedly. 'OK. What time?'

'Around 7.30. OK? '

'OK. Bye.'

Steve had just got back to his desk when his mobile rang again. It was Karen.

'Hello Steve. How did it go?'

'Oh, awful. They pulled me to pieces.'

'How did they do that?'

'I was subjected to a lot of...' Steve sniffed. 'UNFAIR criticism'!

'What? At an Awards evening?'

'Oh sorry, I'd been meaning to ring you about that. Just had a hectic morning, that's all.'

'So how did you get on with that, then?'

'Oh. We won...'

'But that's fantastic, isn't it?'

'Not really. I made an embarrassing speech, where I imitated a Dalek, then I got this rotten appraisal this morning.'

'Oh, dear. Well, I'm not sure whether to celebrate or commiserate with you, but do you fancy taking me out tonight? My mam's regular bingo partner can't make it, so she can babysit.'

Steve promptly dug a hole for himself. 'I'm sorry. If you'd rung 10 minutes ago. I would have said yes.'

'And...?'

'Geoff rang. He wants me to go round to his.'

'And you're going to put him first, as usual?'

Steve dug himself deeper. 'Look, Karen, if...'

'No, I know the score. I hope there's a good reason.'

And deeper...

'Oh. Yes, a very good reason. There's a crisis in the Outcasts team.'

'Honestly. You men!'

And deeper still...

'It's a very important matter.'

This time, Karen let him off the hook.

'You haven't forgotten Billy Elliott next Wednesday, then?'

'No, I've not forgotten. Look, I'll take you out over the weekend. I do need a shoulder to cry on...'

'Well, OK. Probably, you'll want more than that, knowing you.... I'll see you tomorrow, maybe.'

This meeting had better be important, Steve thought to himself.

Chapter 34: 'It's A Dog's Life'

Steve arrived on time at Geoff's house, a courtesy that was rarely reciprocated.

Geoff sat in a large armchair, watching football on a large TV screen. A Yorkshire terrier ran around the room.

Seconds after ringing the doorbell, Steve was ushered in by Geoff's octogenarian mother, Dorothy.

Geoff remained sitting in the armchair as Steve entered the room. 'Good evening, Colonel! Thanks for coming round.'

Steve sat down on a sofa diagonally opposite Geoff.

'Anything for you, Beloved Chairman.'

'Don't be sarcastic. It doesn't suit you.'

'So, why the summons on a tashing night? I had to work hard to persuade Karen that I couldn't see her. Very disappointed, she was.' Steve looked downwards. 'Not the only one, actually.'

'You know that I wouldn't call you if it wasn't important.'

'What is it, then?'

'Crabtree's got wind that there's something up.'

'What? He knows that I'm standing against him?'

'No. I don't think so, but he knows that there's something up. Amir told me. We will have to gird our loins,' Geoff said, opening up a copy of a contact mag that had been sitting on the small table beside him and passing it to Steve.

For the uninitiated, contact mags were particularly popular in certain circles around the fin de siècle. They offered a mixture of dubious phone numbers, details of clubs for swingers and premium cost phone lines, interspersed with 'jazz mag' type pictures of naked women, lurid letters purporting to be from subscribers and the odd article. For readers who want to find out more, vintage copies are available on eBay and Amazon.

'In every sense of the word,' Steve agreed as he cast his eye over the magazine's contents.

Geoff walked over to illustrate a particularly pneumatic pair of boobs. 'Have you seen these? Not many of those to the pound, are there?'

Steve's eyes nearly popped out of his head. 'They can't be real!'

Steve attempted to pass the magazine back, but Geoff gestured him to carry on looking and continued. 'Which brings me to the other thing I wanted to talk to you about. The article next to the picture was rather interesting. It concerned "Dogeing".'

'What? Being the ruler of a northern Italian State in the middle ages (Except it wasn't called Italy then)?'

'No, look here.' Geoff pointed again.

'Ah, dogging!'

'Ah, that's how it's pronounced. Do you know anything about it? Like, what's it got to do with dogs?'

At this moment, Dorothy, came into the room. 'Anyone want any tea?'

'Yes, mother. Two sugars.'

'Yes, please, Mrs Huckstead.'

Dorothy seized upon this. 'See, Geoffrey! He said please! Costs nothing, you know.' Dorothy spotted the magazine. 'Oh, Geoffrey. What's that magazine you're reading?' She peered at the title. '*New Direction*? What's that about?'

'Oh, it's from the Council. They think that they're going to pull the wool over our eyes with a glossy magazine.'

'Ee, it's a disgrace. You're right – the money they spend! You'll let me have it after you've finished, won't you?' Geoff winked at Steve as she continued. 'I want to read what they have to say about fortnightly bin collections and them re-routing the bus service AND them wheelie bins. Proper bunch of villains, they are.'

'I'll let you have it later, mother dear.'

Dorothy went out to the kitchen to make the tea.

'So, what do you know about dogging?'

'Not much. A couple of the lads were talking about it at work the other day. It seems to be all the rage around here.'

Geoff pointed out a particularly interesting paragraph in the investigative piece. 'It says here that couples go in their cars to regular tashing spots and they let other people come and watch them.'

'That's right. But how do they know that they want them to watch? It could be most embarrassing if there's a misunderstanding.'

How prescient Steve's words were, Dear Reader.

Geoff explained. 'It says here that they flash their lights to get them to come closer.' His eyes widened. 'Oh, and it says here that sometimes they invite the watchers to join in.' Geoff rubbed his hands in glee.

'Oh Yeah.' Steve suddenly remembered more of the overheard conversation. 'I think they wind down the windows and open the doors as a signal.'

'This is very interesting. What else do you know about it?'

'No. Nothing.'

'Didn't those lads say anything else about it?'

'Well, there was just one thing...'

'Go on. I'm all ears.'

'They said that there's a couple of spots locally, where they do it.'

Geoff was all ears. 'Go on. Go on.'

'There's the dunes near Redcar.'

'Ah, "the killing fields", as I call them. I know them well. I took many a bird there for a good snaking. Anywhere nearer here?'

'Let me think... Ah. Yes, a layby off the A66, where that underground reservoir is.'

'Know it well. Let's get down there now. You can almost walk it from here.'

Please remember, Dear Reader, the bit about 'almost walk it'.

'Nah. It's too early for that sort of thing. I thought we were going to the Dog anyway.'

At this moment, Dorothy returned. 'What? You two boys are going to the pub again? When I've made you this lovely cup of tea?'

'Don't worry, mother, we'll drink our tea first.'

'If you are going out, you can give me that council magazine to read, then, can't you?'

'Of course, mother dearest.' Geoff grinned.

Geoff and Steve drank their tea. Eventually Steve put his mug down.

'OK. I'm ready. What about you?'

'Yeah. Time for some grog.'

'Aren't you going to hide that mag from your mother?'

'Oh, yes. I'll just put it under this cushion. She won't notice.'

Geoff hid the magazine. They walked out and drove to the Dog.

Inside the Dog, the twin sisters were serving. The pub was rather busier than had recently been the case.

After the usual niceties. Mary announced on behalf of her sister.

'She's just split up with her latest boyfriend. Neither of you two could lend her a shoulder to cry on, then?'

Steve smugly announced that he was spoken for. Geoff was less convinced about Steve's current state of 'spoken-for-ness'.

'For the moment, he is. Not for long though, I reckon. So be patient. Anyway, we have important matters of state to discuss. Come on, Stephen. Let's go and sit down.'

'Don't forget, we've got karaoke on later,' Mary shouted after them. They had both forgotten.

Once they sat down, Steve had a question. 'I forgot to ask. How did it go with Hattie in Rhyl last weekend?'

Geoff shrugged his shoulders. 'Mission accomplished, I suppose. I got a few shags out of her, but we ended up splitting up.'

'How come?'

Geoff grabbed Steve by the arm. 'Listen, you must never take them on holiday. Never!'

'How come? I thought it'd be a chance to spend some quality time together.'

'Quality time, my arse. It's a great chance to find out what annoys you about the other person, and vice versa!'

'But surely, you can't avoid it in the end.'

'Put off the evil day as long as you can. That's what I say. Especially you! Yours has got a brat.'

'Well, I thought it might be a chance to bond with the child.'

Geoff went purple. 'Bond with the child? Bond with the child?' He gave a characteristic roll of the eyes. 'Remember that you are not their dad and never will be. To them you are an intruder who is taking their beloved mummy away from them. Most of them want their real Dads back an' all.'

'I was thinking of taking Karen away somewhere before the winter...'

'Well, at least make sure that the bairn's off the scene. It's bad enough when there's just two of you...'

'Well, I suppose Karen's mum could look after Charlotte... Anyway, tell me more about you and Hattie.'

'We had an OK time. It rained a lot, but that meant more shagging,' Geoff explained. 'The fish and chips were good. We got to see the Tremeloes play at the Pavilion. They were great.'

It was time for Steve to show his knowledge of 60's pop. 'Original line-up? Brian Poole?'

'No, nowt like that. But they played all the old numbers. *Silence is Golden, Here Comes My Baby*. Oh, and they had Herman's Hermits as support.'

'With Peter Noone?'

'No, not him. Far too good for Rhyl, he is.'

'Hardly Herman's Hermits then, was it?' Steve paused to ask a question. 'Sounds like you had a good time. What went wrong?

'Well on the last morning, just as we were packing, she dropped the bombshell.'

'Go on...'

'She told me that she'd started going to a local salsa class and one of the men in her class had asked her out.'

'And?'

'She then had the cheek to ask ME what she should do!'

'So what, did you tell her?'

'I just chased her on the spot. I said that if it was like that, she could sling her hook. End of... Two hundred quid that trip cost me, all told. Two hundred quid, that's about forty quid per shag!!' Geoff changed the subject. 'Anyway, we're here to talk about cricket.'

'Oh. Yes. So, what's this about Crabtree finding out?'

'I tried to change the date of the AGM to this coming Thursday, when I knew he couldn't make it. I said to the Committee, "Why not kill two birds with one stone? We can have our end of season party and elect officials at the same time."'

'So what's happened?'

'He's got wind of it. That's what's happened. Rang me last night, saying he could come on Thursday, after all...'

'So, we don't go ahead...'

'Of course, we don't go ahead. It'll be obvious we're trying to oust him...'

At that moment, Ron himself appeared at Geoff's shoulder. 'Oust who? What you on abaht?'

Geoff had to think quickly. 'Oh, Dougie at work. You know, my manager.'

'Of course, I know him. Good bloke. Why do they want to get rid of him?'

'Oh, office politics, you know.'

'I think I'd better warn him...'

'Oh. No. Don't do that. I'm not supposed to know.'

'Still, we can't have good blokes being stabbed in the bleeding back, then, can we?' Ron said meaningfully. 'And why is it you didn't ask me along? I only live two hundred yards away!'

Geoff had to think quickly. 'We didn't think you liked karaoke.'

As they spoke, a girl sang *New York, New York* very badly.

Geoff turned to Steve. 'I reckon you could do better than that, Colonel!'

Steve noticed that neither Ron nor Geoff was particularly keen to get up and sing. He was reluctant to make a fool of himself two nights in row. 'No. One of you go ahead. I can't sing very well.'

Ron was all too quick to agree for Steve's liking. 'Nah. You're probably right.'

Geoff had the advantage of having seen Steve in action. 'No. Bet you a pint, he can.'

Ron, who was apt to underestimate Steve, agreed straight away. 'You're on!'

'I've only done this on tour, when I've been too far gone to remember.'

Geoff became animated, now that there was money at stake. 'No. You've got to do it. For the honour of the Outcasts.'

Steve started to fill in a slip of paper to perform something by the Beatles.

'It has to be Elvis,' Geoff snarled.

'OK,' Steve mumbled, surreptitiously filling in a slip of paper with *Love Me Do* on it. He went to hand it in to the DJ.

About twenty minutes later, a young man was just finishing murdering *She's the One* by Robbie Williams.

The DJ then announced. 'OK. We're now going to have some Beatles. Let's hear it for Steve, who is going to perform *Love Me Do*.'

Note to the reader: please do not try doing this song at home, or in public. It's a lot harder than it sounds, with quite a few high notes. It's small wonder that Beatles songs are performed a lot less commonly than you might expect. The only really easy one is *Yellow Submarine*, and remember that that was written with Ringo's vocal range in mind. In any case, far better songs are available. To cut a long story short, Steve's performance did little to challenge the considered view of Beavis and Butthead: that the Beatles were asswipes who had ruined music. Nevertheless, he saw it out to the end.

He received surprisingly warm applause. Well, God loves a trier, doesn't He?

Meanwhile, Geoff got up to get Ron a pint as Steve was returning.

'I wasn't that bad, was I?' Steve asked Ron.

'Well, put it this way. The bladdy Crow just got up to buy me a pint. Didn't even say anything. He just got up. I think that says it all about your performance. Pretty similar to your cricketing efforts, I have to say.'

'But the audience liked it!' Steve protested.

A returning Geoff joined in on the post-mortem as he placed a pint of lager in front of Ron.

'The audience like somebody standing up and making a fool of themselves instead of them.'

'It's a pity we can't give out the potty for bad singing, as well as bad fielding,' Ron observed.

'Disobeying the Chairman's orders always has consequences,' Geoff added menacingly.

'I'm sure I can do better,' Steve protested.

'Well, put it this way, you couldn't do any worse.' Geoff watched Ron take a swig from his ill-gotten pint with some venom. 'I said to do Elvis. You did him brilliantly in Bognor.' Geoff thought for a moment. 'You did an even better Gary Glitter, but he seems to have gone a bit out of fashion these days, so Elvis it has to be.'

Ron looked Geoff in the eye. 'OK, Geoffrey. How's about double or quits?'

Geoff conceded. 'Oh, alright then. It'll keep us entertained. Whatever.'

'I won't let you down,' Steve promised.

'You'd better not. Remember, there may well be consequences.'

Steve scribbled out another slip of paper. There was a long wait while the usual wannabes did their obligatory turns.

Eventually, an insipid couple in hippie dress finished singing *I Got You Babe*.

The DJ announced: 'OK. We've now got young Steve again. Remember how he wowed you with the Beatles. Now he's going to do Elvis. *Heartbreak Hotel*!'

Steve curled his lip and swung his hips and gave a virtuoso performance. The song was much more in line with Steve's rather low vocal range.

Tumultuous applause greeted Steve as he walked off. Ron got up to buy Geoff a pint.

'Let's hear it again for Steve.' The DJ was impressed too.

More applause ensued. Alex rushed over and kissed him full on the lips as he walked towards his table.

'That was mint! Absolutely brilliant!' Geoff stood up to applaud the returning hero.

Steve collapsed in his chair. 'Never again. Never again.'

'What do you mean, never again? You saw the reaction. Alex just threw herself at you as you walked back. No, this needs serious thought.'

Ron returned to the table with two pints. 'Here you are, Geoff, and here's one for you, son. You must be thirsty.'

As Steve and Geoff returned to his house later that night, Geoff's mother came to the door.

'Evening, mother. What are you doing up this late, mother?'

'I've been reading that Council Magazine of yours.'

Geoff looked aghast. 'Really, mother?'

'It didn't have anything about the bins or the buses, but it certainly had some interesting advice on what to do when walking the dog!'

Chapter 35: 'Local Hero'

Steve did get to see Karen that weekend, after a good deal of persuasion on his part. The extra time that the end of the cricket season had afforded him worked to their mutual advantage. Better still, Isa had very kindly taken Charlotte away from them at every opportunity, including a pre-birthday treat in the Mungle Jungle in Redcar.

Their blissful weekend was only spoiled by one thing: Karen's suggestion that he should give up cricket. This idea might have gained traction, just a few days previously. Not now, though. Steve was looking forward to the responsibilities of captaincy. He'd be able to order around first-class cricketers, including internationals. He'd be able to choose where he batted and bowled. Best of all, he would finally be on the Committee. No more potty for him! Steve had merely told Karen that he would think about it. It seemed that Ron Crabtree wasn't going to go down without a fight, in any case.

Meanwhile, there was the Teesside premiere of *Billy Elliott* to look forward to. He could see that Charlotte had been enthused by the prospect of meeting Jamie Bell, who wasn't that much older than her. The film sounded interesting, too.

Come the night, all the local dignitaries were gathered in the Billingham Coliseum.

First, a word about the Coliseum. Thought by locals to be the premier venue in Teesside, this brutalist hunk of concrete had been constructed in the 1960s to entertain and enlighten the local BCG workforce. There was a theatre, a cinema, ten pin bowling, a sports centre, an ice rink (it was host to the Billingham Eagles hockey team, formerly known as the Billingham Bombers), a restaurant and even a night club. None of this, however, stopped it being a very ugly concrete monstrosity.

Steve was also there with Karen and Charlotte, who was wearing a birthday sash and tiara. Steve was sipping from a glass of complimentary white wine, as was Karen. Charlotte was sulkily holding a fizzy soft drink.

'Why can't I have glass of wine?' she demanded noisily.

‘Shhh! You can have one when you’re old enough, my petal!’ Karen cooed.

‘Why don’t they have Children’s Wine? It’s my birthday. I want to get pissed!’

Steve looked heavenwards and muttered to himself. ‘Brat!’ This did not go unnoticed by Karen.

Happily, the nascent argument was interrupted by the evening’s compere tapping his microphone. This turned out to be the ubiquitous Stan.

‘Good evening, ladies and gentlemen. Tonight is a very special night. It’s the local premier preview of Billy Elliott. I’d like to welcome His Worship the Mayor of Billingham and his counterparts from Middlesbrough, Stockton and Hartlepool.’

Charlotte interrupted the polite applause with another question. ‘Where’s the monkey?’

Her mother shushed her as heads turned towards the birthday delegation.

Stan continued. ‘Now, we’re all very proud of local lad Jamie Bell, but unfortunately he couldn’t be here tonight...’ Stan then added an aside. ‘A couple of months down south and he’s already forgotten where his roots are!’

Stan looked behind him as an effigy was being unveiled. ‘So, we’ve got a cardboard cut-out of him instead!’ Stan pointed out the life-size cardboard cut-out of Jamie Bell, playing Billy, to laughter and applause.

The Mayor then took over. ‘Good evening, ladies and gentlemen. I’m very proud to invite you to this special Billingham Premiere of Billy Elliott.’

There was a mutter of ‘Teesside!’ from one of his mayoral contemporaries.

‘I’d like to thank all those council staff who’ve worked so hard to bring this to Billingham ahead of London and New York.’ This was met with subdued laughter. ‘Just one other thing, before I hand back to Stan... Local lad and Boro’ stalwart Willie Maddren died at the end of last month. We will be having a raffle and collection for Motor Neurone Disease in his memory. Please give generously.’ There was polite applause.

Stan took over again. ‘We’ve also invited several local lads, who were extras in the fill-um. Good evening, lads!’ he shouted.

He was cheered loudly by the extras, who had already been availing themselves of the plentiful complimentary booze – and had separated into two distinct groups.

'Yes, we've got a group, who played striking miners.' This brought loud cheers, followed by a chant of 'Here we go! Here we go! Here we go!'

'And a group, who played the return-to-work scabs!' Stan continued to general panto-like jeers from the audience, which were met with defiant gestures from the increasingly inebriated blacklegs.

'Yes! It's dirty work, but I suppose, someone's got to do it,' Stan quipped. 'So, without further ado, I'd like to invite you all to proceed into the auditorium for our very special Teesside premiere of *Billy Elliott*. Please have your tickets ready, ladies and gentlemen.'

Steve, Karen and Charlotte made their way to the front of the queue for admission.

Meanwhile, the 'pickets' and the 'scabs' had started squaring up to each other.

Steve, Karen and Charlotte were blocked by an usher, a young man wearing a smart new uniform.

'I'm sorry.'

'What's the matter? Aren't our tickets valid?'

'There's nothing wrong with your tickets, madam, but did you realize that this is a 15-certificate film?

'So?'

'No under 15-year-olds, I'm afraid. Your child is clearly under 15 years old.'

'But she's under adult supervision.'

'Sorry, that's not the law. The law states no child under 15 is allowed into this fill-um.'

Steve intervened. 'Why's it a certificate 15 anyway? I thought it was about a boy learning to dance.'

'There's some swearing and bad language and that...'

Steve felt that he had a winning argument. 'But surely, Jamie Bell couldn't have gone to see it either?'

The usher was considering this point when Charlotte started screaming. 'Well, you can fuck off and die!!!'

The scream was so earsplittingly loud that the gathered audience, including the local dignitaries, turned round as one to look on in horror, distracting them from the increasingly ugly confrontation between the extras.

The Usher was unmoved. 'I'm sorry, sir and madam. Ah didn't make the rules.'

Charlotte continued with her maximum-decibel diatribe. 'You're a jobsworth cunt, that's what you are!'

The usher turned to Karen. 'I'm sorry, but I'm going to have to ask you and your husband to kindly take this child away.'

This assumption annoyed Karen. 'He's not my husband. You've got it in for single mothers, you have!'

Steve tried to be helpful. 'Now listen, Charlotte here has been looking forward to this ever since she heard about it,' he said before adding. 'It's her birthday, you know.'

It was the usher's turn to get stroppy. 'Well in a few years' time, yous can buy it for her on DVD then, can't you?'

Charlotte screamed again. 'You twatting, pooing, bum-fucking cunt!!!

'Now, I'm going to have to ask you to leave.' The usher started to speak into his walkie talkie. 'Could we have security to the ticket gate, please? Security, please.'

'Your mother is a bitch and your sister is a whore!'

'Now, then. I'd advise you to go quietly.'

Karen was not giving up. 'You've spoiled this little girl's birthday night, don't you know?'

'I'm sorry, madam, but I do need my job.'

A couple of security guards had managed to tear themselves away from the pickets vs scabs confrontation.

Before they could touch her, Charlotte shouted out, 'Leave me alone, you hairy-arsed baboons!'

The first security guard spoke calmly to Steve and Karen. 'Come on now, madam, sir; please go quietly.'

Steve was more easily persuaded than the two women. 'I think we'd better go, Karen.'

Charlotte remained defiant. 'You can't fucking touch me, I'm a child. This is abuse!!!'

Steve attempted to take Charlotte's hand. 'Come on now, Charlotte, let's go to McDonald's.'

Charlotte shook him off. 'Let go of me, you nonce!!!'

Karen intervened, taking Charlotte's hand and leading her out, followed by Steve. There was an embarrassed silence among the audience, who then returned to making polite conversation.

Meanwhile, things got even uglier between the pickets and the scabs. The pickets were singing. 'One Arthur Scargill. One Arthur Scargill. There's only one Arthur Scargill!'

To which the scabs replied. 'You should have had a ballot! You should have had a ballot!'

The pickets continued. 'I'd rather be a picket than a scab! I'd rather be a picket than a scab!'

A melée ensued. The security men diverted (reluctantly) from ushering Steve's party out of the building.

Stan tried in vain to restore order. 'Gentlemen! Gentlemen! Please desist! This isn't the Sealed Knot, you know!'

Steve, Karen and Charlotte exited the building to scenes of drunken chaos.

There was a tense atmosphere in Steve's Ford Mondeo as they drove back to Karen's. It was she who broke the silence. 'Well, you could have stuck up for us a bit more.'

Steve was taken aback. 'But I did...' Steve was not allowed to finish his sentence.

'Ruined this little girl's birthday, they did, and you didn't raise a hand to stop them.'

Charlotte weighed in. 'Yes. Bugger off, MR BUGGER!!!'

Steve was determined to make his point. 'But I did say something!'

'Not enough. And don't think you're staying the night either. I want a proper man!'

This cheered Charlotte up immensely. 'Ha. Ha. No feeling my mummy's boobies tonight...' She paused for a second. 'Or her muff!!'

When Steve pulled up outside Karen's house, he felt the need to make another point. Not the brightest of ideas, as it happened. 'I think you should control your daughter a bit better.'

Any remote chance of a peaceful outcome was lost in that moment. 'Right! Definitely no staying with me tonight. Or any other night, for that matter. Come on, Charlotte!'

Steve was reduced to incoherence once again. 'But...'

'Yeah. Fuck off, you sad bastard!' Charlotte gave Steve a one fingered salute as she got out of the car with Karen.

Steve drove off reluctantly, still hoping that he would get a recall to Karen's bed.

Later that night, he was lying on his couch when his house phone rang. Steve got up immediately, still hoping for the call to action.

'Hello, Karen,' he answered eagerly.

'Sorry to disappoint you old son, but it's me Geoff, your Chairman.'

'Sorry Geoff. I thought it was Karen wanting to make up.'

'Excuse me, but I thought you two were back together again. In fact, I thought you'd probably be on the nest, as we speak. So, what's happened now?'

'We had a row.'

'You had a row? Tell you what, you want to chase her!'

'Looks like she's chased me – again,' Steve answered forlornly.

'Well. Tell me what happened.'

Steve spent the next few minutes explaining, in his own words, the events leading up to the latest falling out. Geoff was a little puzzled as to how things could have possibly gone wrong, when all Steve had had to do was to sit next to Karen and Charlotte in a darkened room. Steve had to explain the complications that had taken place, in particular Charlotte's tantrum.

'That little brat!' Geoff concluded. 'You should never let them bring their kids along. You know what I've told you. At best, it gets in the way of you shagging them, at worst the little bastards will do their best to try and split you up. They should have been strangled at birth!' he exclaimed, before adding thoughtfully, 'Only natural, though...'

'What's only natural? Strangling them at birth?'

'No. The little angels trying to split you up from their mums. As, I've told you before, you're not her dad. Remember that!'

'How can I forget?'

'Anyway, what did you do wrong?'

'Karen said I didn't stand up for her and Charlotte enough. I should have stopped it from happening.'

'It sounds to me like there was nothing you could have done. Women – totally illogical!'

'So, here I am on my own,' Steve concluded.

'Cheer up, then. It's Wednesday night, and you know what tomorrow is?'

'Thursday?' Steve suggested naively.

'Yes, and this Thursday is Awards Night!'

'Of course, I knew that. I'm supposed to be bloody well organizing it, aren't I?'

'Indeed, you are, and what's more – it's my turn to drive.'

'Yes. I do remember.' How could Steve forget?

'Oh, and I may have a little something extra for you.'

'What would that be, now?'

'That would be telling. You organized the karaoke, didn't you?'

'Yes, of course. And a band, which includes Outcast players.'

'Excellent! First a Tees Valley Invention award, then captaincy of the Outcasts, now you're a karaoke superstar. Cheer up! You're on a roll, old son!'

'But no shag tonight.' Steve was still unconvinced of his state of bliss.

'Don't worry about that. You can stay happily married to your right wrist for a little while longer.'

'Thanks.'

'Any time. Any time.'

'Well, I'd better be getting upstairs to make a tent, then.'

'OK. You do that, and good luck tomorrow night. Cheerio.'

Steve muttered a goodbye as he rummaged through his downstairs desk drawer. Eventually, he pulled out a 'gentleman's magazine' and retired upstairs.

Chapter 36: 'A Day In The Life'

The next day dawned bright. A letter had arrived with a House of Commons portcullis emblazoned on the back.

Hi Steve

Sincere congrats on your Tees Valley Innovation Award for 2000. I applaud your dedication to the pursuit of the value proposition. I agree that we are kindred spirits. Thanks also for your kind remarks about driving out the dinosaurs. It was a tough task, and there are still some recidivists around even today. You will note the behaviour of certain trade unions at last week's (New) Labour conference. What must President Mandela think of our petty internal squabbles? We must be ever vigilant, as recent opinion polls have shown, the Tory enemy is never far away.

I can see that you and I are both modernisers, operating in an ever more global environment. I will certainly welcome your thoughts on the way forward for British Industry!

Best regards

Tony

The day at work was productive, aided by the unexplained absence of Stuart and Debbie – except for one rather unsettling conversation.

Steve walked over to the Septics' table and noticed that Frank and Don were the only ones sitting there.

'Afternoon, gentlemen. Where are the others?'

Frank whispered conspiratorially, 'They're on a course.'

'What course?'

Frank continued to whisper. 'I'm not supposed to say!'

Don was more helpful. 'Oh, go on, Frank. Put the poor lad out of his misery.'

'They're on a "How To Make People Redundant" course for Managers Graded 12 and above,' Frank explained.

'Grade 12 and above? That includes you two. Why aren't you on it?'

'I'm retiring anyway...' Don explained.

Frank clammed up again. 'And I can't tell you...'

'Well, either you're getting made redundant yourself, or there's another reason.'

'No, they do send managers who are getting made redundant on it. It would be a bit obvious otherwise, wouldn't it?' Frank laughed cynically.

'Yes, it's a bit like the old army joke. Step forward, all those with mothers who are still alive... get back, Carruthers!' Don added.

'Well, what goes on, on one of these courses?' Steve was intrigued.

'Don knows.'

'They instruct you on how to keep your self-esteem and that of the departing employee.'

Steve was unconvinced. 'Well, that shouldn't take too long. You shouldn't need a day's course for that.'

Frank became more animated. 'No. It's vital to get it right. On the one hand, you can't be critical of them; on the other hand, you can't be too soft.'

'What do you mean, too soft?'

Don stepped in. 'What he means is that the employee needs to be left in no doubt that he or she's being "let go", as our American cousins term it.'

As usual, Frank had an anecdote to illustrate the point. 'Yeah, remember poor old Ted Mitchell? Reported bright and early for duty the next day, and for a month after that, he did. They needed security to escort him off site before he realised the awful truth. Kicking and screaming, he was.'

Don added, 'That's one of the reasons why they do it on a Friday, nowadays. Gives them a weekend to simmer down.'

'I'm surprised that more people don't kick off,' Steve said.

'Nah. Not worth it.' Frank crossed his arms. 'Not when you get six months' paid gardening leave, three months' notice after that, rehabilitation training, plus a lump sum and a good chunk of pension. Anyway, there's always an HR person not far away, in case things get nasty.'

'Well, I'd tell them where to stuff the rehabilitation training if it were me.'

Frank gave Steve a stern look. 'You have to take it. The benefits are conditional on you looking for another job.'

Steve was incredulous. 'And that's going to help? I've been on those sorts of

courses before. What type of person are you? They may as well base it on your star sign!'

Don nodded his head. 'I have to agree with you on that. Load of drivel if you ask me. I'm glad I'm taking early retirement and I'm not having to endure all that anymore.' Don pulled his tray up. 'Anyway, if you excuse me, I've got a meeting with HR. See you later.'

Once Don had gone, Frank grabbed hold of Steve's sleeve and pulled him closer.

'Do you really think you're going to be OK?'

Like an Egyptian crocodile, Steve was still in denial. 'Yeah. Why not? I won the Innovation Prize, didn't I?'

Frank shook his head sadly. 'Steve! How many times have I told you? It doesn't work like that.'

'But it would be totally unfair, wouldn't it? I'd write to the editor of the Gazette. I'd write to the CEO. I'd write to Tony Blair!'

Frank sighed. 'Yes. I believe you're in regular correspondence with those last two gentlemen.'

'Do you know anything?' Steve asked, suddenly anxious.

Frank shook his head again. 'No. Some secrets get kept even from me. It's just that I've seen it all happening to others like you...'

Steve was puzzled. 'What do you mean by that?'

Frank tried to explain. 'Bright young junior manager, idealistic, full of energy – well, maybe that one doesn't apply in your case. Not like the rest. A bit rebellious, even...'

'But I'm not rebellious!' Steve interjected.

'Sorry, but THEY think you are. Look, Steve. I like you, I like your attitude, but THEY don't.'

'Attitude? What attitude?'

'You really want to tell them where to go, don't you?'

'I don't think so.' Steve frowned.

'STEVE. STEVE. STEVE. You have that innate "fuck off defiance". It's a gift. Not many people have that. They hate you for it.'

'But I've tried to obey the rules, do what's best...'

'I'm sure you have, but... no matter how much you try to kowtow to them, they'll still see through you.'

'I don't understand.'

Frank thought for a few seconds then continued. 'Well let me put it this way: if you'd lived in East Germany, you could have informed to the Stasi about a thousand dissidents, and they'd still have come for you. Shot you without a blindfold, if they'd had their chance.'

Steve called to mind his own hero. 'But Tony Blair was never a prefect at school, and look at him now!'

Frank shook his head. 'I knew Tony Blair at Oxford. I had him down as a "God Squad" prick. You're different.'

'So, do you know anything?'

'No, honestly, I don't, but be careful. The mediocre will always proclaim themselves to be excellent. They don't like people like you showing them up.'

Steve was still sceptical. 'Well, thanks for that, Frank. Are you sure you don't know anything?'

'Yes, I'm sure, and as a friend, I wish you all the best, but just remember: you're not one of them, and you never will be. In fact, they think you suck like a hundred thousand blowjobs. Good luck!'

With that, they lifted their trays and went to the self-clearing trolleys and walked out of the restaurant separately.

On the positive side, initial customer reaction to the new product had been positive. Following some successful laboratory experiments, it looked like the filtration problem was nearly solved. Steve had had a positive meeting with the company patent agent, who was convinced that there was plenty of scope for new intellectual property, and Steve's name (rather than Paula's) would be on the key patent.

About three hours later, Steve was all dressed for a night out. He was pacing up and down his front room, looking at his watch. At last, there was a toot outside. Steve walked out to see Geoff waiting in an unfamiliar car – a yellow Skoda Felicia. Steve nonetheless recognised it as Peter's car. Once Steve had got into the car, Geoff explained that his own car was in dock and that he was 'calling in a favour'. 'Peter didn't mind.' He was getting a lift from Pervez with a couple of the younger Outcasts. Geoff then reminded

Steve that they hadn't had the chance to discuss the captaincy as originally planned.

'So, what do we do now?' Steve asked.

'We relax and enjoy our evening and then convene the AGM at a later date – when Crabtree can't make it.'

Steve then turned to see a large carrier bag on the back seat. 'What's in this carrier bag, by the way?'

Geoff assumed an air of mystery. 'Patience, Grasshopper. All will be revealed in the fullness of time.'

When they finally reached O'Brien's bar in Darlington, the Outcasts were already assembled to celebrate the recent season – not that there was much to celebrate.

O'Brien's was a bit of a clapped-out venue near the centre of town. It had had a revamp in the 1990's, when it had changed the lay-out to a speakeasy type format and its name from the Globe Inn (Irish names were all the rage at the time). Trade had flourished briefly but had now declined to the point that it was now heavily dependent on its karaoke facilities to keep going.

Amir was waiting by the bar. 'Ah, beloved Chairman. How good to see you! Can I get you something to drink – and you, Captain-Elect?'

Geoff put a finger over his lips. 'Shh. I'll have a pint of beer shandy, please.'

Steve was unimpressed. 'Beer shandy? Better than hand shandy, I suppose. I'll have a pint of that guest beer.'

Amir counselled caution. 'Oh, dear. That's very strong – 6% alcohol – are you sure that's wise, Captain-Elect?'

Geoff was shushing him again when Ron appeared on the scene. 'What are you cants up to?'

'Oh esteemed Captain, we are merely discussing young Stephen's unwise choice in alcoholic beverages.'

Ron was unconvinced. 'I bet you are! Nothing gets past me, you know,' he warned. 'And why didn't you offer me a lift tonight?'

Geoff was quick with an alibi. 'We may be planning something later. Didn't want to keep you from your Horlicks and slippers.'

'Probably something absolutely disgusting.' Ron was certainly right about that. 'Anyway, when's this evening's entertainment going to start?'

'Well, some of the lads have formed a group and they'll sing a few numbers...' Geoff said.

'I don't think "sing" is the right word,' Steve commented.

Geoff was taken by surprise, expecting some traditional entertainment.

'They're a doom metal group. I did warn you,' Steve explained.

'What's doom metal?'

'It's a sub-genre of underground music, combining elements of heavy metal and goth rock, played loud and extremely slowly,' Steve continued.

Ron was unimpressed. 'Bladdy hell. Sounds like it should stay underground to me, like six feet under. Who's dis-organising this event?'

'Actually, I am,' Steve replied.

'That explains everything.'

'Then, we have a buffet, and then...'

Geoff interrupted Steve's flow. 'The piece de resistance – karaoke – and our newly discovered star is going to sing us a bit of Elvis!'

'Am I?'

'Of course you are. What do you think is in this bag?'

'What, then?'

Geoff pulled out a full Elvis fancy dress kit including an Elvis jump suit, boots, sunglasses, and a wig.

Ron warmed to this latest revelation, knowing Geoff's predilection for setting team members up for ridicule. Who could have forgotten Neil Paterson's tribute night to the lisping superstar Gene Pitney a couple of decades previous? 'Bladdy hell. I'm beginning to look forward to this now,' he said gleefully.

'But I can't do that...' Steve protested.

'I've invested precious club funds in hiring this costume,' Geoff warned.

Ros, Julie and Di walked into the bar. Ros was the first to espy the Elvis regalia. 'Why, that looks canny. Who'll be performin' in that?'

'It looks a bit tight-fitting around the crotch to me. I hope he fills it adequately, like.' Julie added to all round laughter.

Steve dug his heels in. 'It's supposed to be me, but I'm not getting into that.'

Geoff was insistent. 'Come, now. You can't let your audience down now – can he, now, girls?'

Ros agreed. 'Come on, Steve. Ah hear that yer've let down Karen again. Yer divn't want to be letting us down now, do yer?'

'And as our organiser for tonight, I think he needs to show us all that he can carry off a position of responsibility,' Geoff added meaningfully.

'Alright! Alright! I'll do it. For the sake of the club.'

The sounds of discordant tuning-up could be heard on stage.

Amir winced. 'I think you'd better introduce them, Stephen.'

'I just need another pint before I do that. That guest beer's starting to grow on me. Anyone else?' Steve offered to general shaking of heads.

Steve got his drink, then headed for the stage. His greeting of 'Ready lads?' was met by general grunting, which he took to signify assent, so he proceeded to make an announcement.

'Please welcome on stage a band that some of the team members have formed, with a guest appearance from our best newcomer of the season Pervez Rehman on guitar. Let me introduce to you...'

Steve paused.

'BARABBAS PLODENOID!!!'

Steve returned to where Geoff and Ron were standing.

'What kind of a name for a band is that?' Julie asked.

The band start playing dirge-like leaden metal music. The unrest grew.

'This is hardly Slim Whitman!' Geoff commented.

'They won a Battle of the Bands award this year,' Steve explained.

Ron remained unimpressed. 'Where at? The school for the bladdy hard of hearing?'

'No, The Trimdon Recreation Club, as a matter of fact.'

'Darkest County Durham! Funny buggers out that way. You don't want to meet them on a dark night.' Geoff's words would prove to be eerily prophetic. 'Anyway, can I get you another pint, Colonel?'

Steve did not need his arm twisting. 'Oh. Go on. Another pint of the guest, please.'

'Steady on, we don't want you too grogged up. It might affect your vocal cords. There again...'

Geoff went and fetched Steve another pint. The dismal sounds of Barabbas Plodenoid continued to ring out from the stage.

'*Armies fight into the night*

The dead piled up, their bones so white
The atomic curse, the mushroom cloud
The sirens wailing oh so loud...'

Ron turned to Steve. 'This band is pants, son. You've got to do something.'

Ros turned around. 'Me an' Julie were thinking exactly the same. Do something!'

'Oh. OK, then,' Steve agreed reluctantly.

Steve walked to the stage just as the latest dirge came to an end and spoke to the lead singer. 'Can't you play something a bit more popular?'

'We don't want to compromise our integrity, man.'

'Go on. For the club!'

'But I don't play for the club – and we won a battle of the bands playing this stuff.'

'Can't you do the odd cover?'

There followed a brief negotiation where Steve suggested a number of titles including *Sweet Child of Mine* ('everybody does that!') but was spurned.

Finally, lead singer Lee made a constructive suggestion. 'I do know a former Number One we could do.'

Steve enthusiastically nodded his assent. 'OK. Here's a number you all should know. *Bring Your Daughter... to the Slaughter*.'

This brought further looks of consternation from the audience.

The band started to play.

Di, the quiet one, then surprised everyone by announcing that she 'liked this one.' Without further ado, she grabbed hold of Steve and dragged him onto the dancefloor.

'You've upset our Karen again, I hear...'

'Yeah. Don't know why, though!'

'You just don't understand women, you don't.'

'Well, I'm not alone in that.'

'I like you anyway, but don't tell anyone.' Di moved up closer to Steve.

'Thanks. That's nice to hear.'

The band finished their number to muted applause.

Steve got up on stage and announced, 'OK. Thanks. We're having a short break now for some scran, which I know you've all been waiting for. When we get back there'll be Karaoke until late and finally a bit of disco for those of you with stamina.'

Everyone got into the queue for the buffet. Ron was standing next to Steve. 'I'm watching you, son. I know there's something going off. The bladdy Crow isn't covering his tracks as well as you think.'

'I don't know what you mean, Ron.' Steve tried to look innocent.

Meanwhile, the girls were comparing notes. Ros started the interrogation of Di. 'I saw you dancin' with that Steve again. People will talk.'

'Oh. No. He's still not got over Karen,' Di contended.

'Or his other exes. Steer clear of that one, Di. He's trouble!' Julie warned.

'Well, I think he's cute,' Di insisted.

As the interval drew to an end, Geoff summoned Steve to do his duty. 'Time for your costume change, Elvis. I'll get the DJ to set up the Karaoke.'

'No, I've had another idea...' Steve countered.

'I hope you're not showing signs of "artistic temperament", are you?'

'No. No. I'm getting into this costume, aren't I?'

Steve took the bag and headed for the Gents. He had always dreamt of fronting a band. He had never been able to play a musical instrument, not even a recorder. He had always been told that he could not sing either. This had not dimmed his ambitions of glory, formed watching fellow Teessider Paul Rodgers grinding his lower quarters into a microphone stand whilst miming to *Alright Now* on *Top of the Pops*. At last, he had discovered that by impersonating Elvis, he had opened the keys to the door. Now was his chance! He g0t changed into his Elvis costume and tottered out of the Gents. He found the band around the back of the pub. They were 'spliffing it up'. They saw Steve's Elvis and all started giggling uncontrollably.

'Oh, hi everyone. I was wondering if you could do me a favour?'

Lee, the leader, was his usual unhelpful self. 'What's that?'

Pervez looked him up and down. 'You're not after any more of those little blue pills, are you?'

'Erm.' Steve hesitated, then realised that it was now or never. 'You couldn't accompany me, while I sing?'

Lee remained uncooperative. 'Hardly our style, Elvis. Can't you just use the karaoke machine?' he suggested, before dissolving into fits of the giggles.

'I've always wanted to front up a band, and I just wondered if you could back me up while I sing, if you're able to.' Steve laid down the gauntlet.

Lee continued to be unmoved. 'No way, man. This stuff is definitely not our scene.'

Pervez was more helpful. 'Ah, go on, Lee. Let's give it a go.'

'But we don't know what to play.'

'You mean you don't how to play.' Steve continued to challenge the band's mettle.

Lee looked around at the others, who seemed to be wavering.

'Don't worry. I'll keep it simple. I'll just do *Don't Be Cruel*. That's easy.' Steve reassured them.

The bassist had a suggestion. 'Are you gonna get those chicks up on stage?'

'As backing singers? Yeah. Why not? I think they'll be game.' That was certainly true of Ros and Julie. *Not sure about Di*, Steve thought to himself.

Lee finally gave in. 'Oh alright then. Here Steve, to seal the deal, you've got to have a blast of that.' Lee offered Steve the roach. 'Tried this before?'

'Well, I had some space cake in Amsterdam last year with my ex. Oh, and some Red Leb, when I was a student...'

Lee giggled uncontrollably. 'You think that was strong?'

'Yeah, it was.'

'This'll blow your head off, then. Genetically modified to get you high as a fucking kite!'

Steve took a draw on the joint. 'Nah. No effect.' Steve took a few more tokes, but remained unconvinced.

'Just you wait...' Pervez warned.

Steve was already imbued with a newfound confidence. 'OK, you all ready? Let's go kill 'em, boys!'

'Now you remember to invite those chicks on stage,' the bassist reminded Steve.

Steve staggered out towards Ros, Julie and Di. They all giggled at his Elvis get-up. Steve found himself getting into role. 'You girls wanna, uh, join me on that little old stage over there?'

Di was very sceptical. 'Well, I don't think so!'

Julie was more persuadable. 'To do what?'

Steve lowered his voice. 'To sing some backing vocals for the King.'

Ros scrutinised his overly tight jump suit. 'Go on. Put like that, why not? Just hope that you're king-sized!'

They all got on stage. Steve, nearly tripping over everything en route, before announcing, 'Uh. Huh. Good evening, everyone. I'd like to invite you to join me in a little ol' song called *Don't Be Cruel*.'

The impromptu ensemble gave a surprisingly good rendition, with Steve going over to the girls and singing with them. He got more flirty with them as they lurched into *Teddy Bear*.

'*I just wanna be your teddy bear!*' Steve concluded to rapturous applause, led by Geoff. Steve gave Di a big squeeze.

Geoff wanted more. 'Bravo. Encore. Encore. We must have an encore!'

Amir was not so sure. 'Do you think that's wise, Chairman?'

Ron gave the casting vote. 'Yeah, they're only warming up.'

Steve was becoming increasingly under the influence of the wacky baccy.

'Ok. Here's a little number. Huh. I must have written it an hour ago. It's called...

Let Me Shag You Baby.'

Pervez objected. 'But we don't know the tune.'

'It's OK fellahs, just follow me,' Steve reassured the band.

Steve started to sing in a tune vaguely reminiscent of *That's Alright Mama*.

'I'm just a poor boy round this town
I want to pull some knickers down'

The band followed as best they could.

'So let me shag you baby, I'm in misery,
Let me shag you baby, Lord have mercy on me
So let me shag you baby, I've taken my little blue pill.
Let me shag you baby, I'll make you really ill...'

Steve turned to his backing singers.

'OK Girls. Sing along with me – Shag. Shag. Shag. Shag. Shag. Shag.'

The girls sang along.

'Shag. Shag. Shag. Shag. Shag. Shag.'

Steve continued with the next verse.

'*Let me shag you baby, darling if you please*

Steve rolled his eyes before crawling on all fours around the stage.

Let me shag you baby, honey I'm on my knees,

Let me shag you baby, girl don't be a tease'

The girls sang along.

'Shag. Shag. Shag. Shag. Shag. Shag.'

Steve got up to his feet again and winked at his backing singers.

'Ah will respect your informed decision, of course!'

Steve stood silent for a very long two seconds, before turning to his band

'Sorry, fellahs. I can't think of the rest.' He replaced the mic back on its stand and took a bow.

The audience started to applaud hesitantly, with loud cheering from one or two quarters. Would that it had ended there...

Unfortunately, the increasingly stoned Steve suddenly found new inspiration and grabbed the mic back.

'It's time for *Let Me Shag You Baby Part 2*. The punk version!' he added with a grin.

Steve began singing tunelessly at frenetic pace.

'I wanna shag. I wanna shag.

I don't care if you're on the rag!'

The band struggled to follow Steve's lead. Amid increasing looks of consternation from the audience, Geoff and Amir rushed on to the stage to prevent the debacle getting worse.

Geoff grabbed the mic from Steve and announced, 'OK, ladies and gentlemen. That will be all for the live entertainment tonight.'

To groans from the audience, Amir pulled the plug on the band to underline the Chairman's will.

'Of course, there'll be karaoke to follow, and then a disco,' Geoff reassured the audience. 'In the meantime, let's have a big hand for our club vice-captain Doctor Stephen Hemmings... surely, his future lies upon the stage!'

To general applause, Steve staggered off the stage in the direction of Geoff.

'What the hell are you doing? I was just beginning to enjoy myself.'

'You were making an exhibition of yourself. Nobody's going to vote for you, carrying on like that,' he whispered, making sure that Ron could not hear.

Sometime later, the karaoke had given way to disco. Steve was smooching with Di to *Three Times a Lady* by the Commodores.

Unfortunately, there was a problem. *Can't get wood. Can't get wood. SOS. SOS,* Steve thought to himself.

Di did not seem to have noticed. 'That song you sang was a bit rude. I thought you were a bit more refined than that, an educated man like you.'

Steve disagreed. 'I thought it was rather shagtastic, myself...'

'Oh, you like Austin Powers too then, do you?'

'Yeah, groovy, baby.' He did a quick twirl, a little incongruously, given that he was still wearing his Elvis costume.

Di danced ever closer to Steve. 'It seems we have the same sense of humour. They always say that's important.'

It seems I'm having the same problem as poor old Austin vis-a-vis lost mojo, Steve thought to himself as he put his hands round her nicely rounded bottom.

'Absolutely essential. You have to be able to laugh at small things,' he finally whispered into her ear.

'Ay, it's the little things that matter,' Di agreed, squeezing him to herself.

Steve waited in vain for a response from his loins. 'You can say that again.' Steve recalled being a teenager on an exchange trip to France; how he had been embarrassed by his seemingly uncontrollable urge at a Christian youth disco. Chantal had not seemed to mind at all though. She'd even written a *billet doux* to him after he had got back home.

Di was becoming aware of Steve's discomfiture. 'Steve, is there anything wrong?'

'No. No. Nothing at all.'

'I sense you're holding back...'

'No. Not at all, Di.'

It's just not happening, must be the dope. Where are those blue pills when I really need them? Steve thought to himself.

'It's Karen, isn't it? You still have feelings for her, don't you?'

Steve coughed nervously.

'I know it, you can't fool me...'

Steve decided it was time to cut his losses. 'Oh. OK then DI. I like you, but it's too soon...'

'I understand.'

They kissed and went their separate ways.

All this had not escaped the attention of the Chairman as Steve walked back to him. 'Bloody hell. I thought you were in there.'

'Nah. Not my type.' Steve tried to be nonchalant.

'You could always use her for practice, you know?'

'Nah, too late. Too late.'

'Good, the night is young. Let's go and water our horses and then mosey on down the road.'

As they walked past a back alley, the drummer and the bassist were busy shagging Ros and Julie. They reached the yellow Skoda in the nearby car park. Steve saw Di, sitting alone in her car, waiting for her mates to get back. They exchanged glances. Geoff grabbed Steve by the arm.

'Come on, Elvis. No time for second thoughts. I have just the antidote.'

'You mean you've got some Victory Vs?'

'No, the shenanigans up that alley put me in mind of that conversation we had last week.'

Steve looked puzzled.

'Young sir, we are going dogging.'

'Oh no. No. No. Not that.'

'The night is ripe!' Geoff retorted.

'But look! I'm dressed up as Elvis!'

'All the better. They'll spot a fellow exhibitionist when they see one. All the more chance of getting invited in for a dip!'

A quarter of an hour later, Geoff and Steve were driving through roadworks on the A66.

'Not far to go now. I wish that van behind me would back off.' Geoff looked in his mirror once again.

Steve had a suggestion. 'Maybe they're in a hurry to get to the dogging layby and you're holding them up.'

Geoff liked the idea. 'You could be right; they keep flashing their lights at me. Anyway, here it is. Let's pull in. If nothing else, it'll get rid of the fuckers from behind us...'

He indicated to pull into the layby.

Steve looked behind. 'Geoff, they're following us!'

Geoff could not contain his glee. 'Here we go. Game on!'

Geoff pulled up in the lay-by. The van pulled up about 10 yards behind.

'What now?' Steve asked.

They sat in the car. An owl hooted. The van flashed its lights again. Steve and Geoff turned round in their seats.

'Look, it's a man and a woman in the front and they're both wearing cowboy hats. She's quite fit, too.' Steve started to get excited. 'Ha. Ha. Kinky!' Geoff laughed. 'Maybe that's code, regarding what they're going to get up to.'

'You mean what position they're going to do it in?'

'What do you mean by that?' Geoff was surprisingly slow on the uptake.

'Well, cowgirl's woman on top, reverse cowgirl is ...' Steve started to explain, when the van flashed its lights again and beeped its horn.

Geoff rubbed his hands in delight. 'That's it. We're in. You wouldn't think there were such goings-on around Darlington – home of the Quakers – would you?'

Geoff opened the door of the Skoda, undeterred by the increasingly heavy rain. 'Right, out of the car. Let's investigate more closely.'

Our heroes approached the van. As they got closer, the occupants of the front seats wound down the windows.

'There you go, they must like your Elvis costume. I think you might be on for sloppy seconds here.'

Steve hoped it might help get his mojo back. 'You reckon?'

'I'll go to the feller's side. You give the bird a bit of your Elvis sweet talk...'

Steve approached the driver's side unsteadily in his Elvis boots.

The woman wound her window down. So far so good. 'What de ye want?'

'I was just, uh uh, wondering if you were going to be a hound dog tonight?'

'I beg your pardon?'

'I was just wonderin' if you were goin' to be a cowgirl for us good old cowpokes and love me tender tonight, ma'am?'

'Ah think yer some sort of a pervert, like...'

'But you flashed your lights...'

The man wound his window down 'That was to let you know we didn't like yer slow driving. This is our lass's first turn at driving and yer've spoilt her night.'

'Well, who are you, then?' Geoff enquired.

'We're the Tudhoe and District Country and Western club – and there's four guys in the back, who are gannin' crackers with yous two.'

Steve was in fighting mood. 'Well, bring 'em on, then. We thought you were doggers.'

'Yer filthy, you are!' the woman shouted.

'Ye're tertal porvorts,' the man added, before shouting out, 'Lads!'

The four others piled out of the back. The man in the front put his arm round the woman to comfort her. As he did so, she started to dial 999 on her mobile.

In the ensuing melee, Geoff and Steve saw off their attackers, against the odds, mainly down to Steve's narcotic-induced ferocity. The four retreated back to the minibus.

Steve started walking back to the Skoda. 'OK. Let's get in the car and go home.'

Geoff had, however noticed the conversation that the lady was having on her phone. 'Car? What car? No, we've got to scarper. No way can I have my mother finding out about this if we get stopped...'

'But it's five miles from here to your house.'

'I know a short cut across the fields. It'll cut out at least a mile or so.'

'In these shoes? No way, Baby!'

Geoff was having none of it. 'OK. Stay here and let the Bobbies breathalyse you. You'll get done for drunk in charge of a car or worse...'

Flashing blue lights in the distance added weight to his point.

'Alright. I'd better go with you, then.'

They set off into the fields. As Steve tottered off, the cowgirl got out of the van and took a shot of him retreating into the night with her digital camera. It started to rain heavily, as it tended to do that particular autumn.

As our heroes continued to make their way home, the shocked occupants of the minibus were sharing their recollections of the incident with the Durham Constabulary, who then proceeded to inspect the abandoned yellow Skoda.

The unlikely lads slowly made their way back to Geoff's house across already muddy fields in the driving rain. When they finally got home, Dorothy had been waiting up for them. 'Good evening, boys. How was the dogging?' she asked.

Chapter 37: 'The Day After'

Friday, September 29th, 2000, 9.32 am saw Steve somewhat miraculously back in his office and sitting at his desk. He was wearing ill-fitting clothes: trousers that were too big for him, a striped shirt, and an ill-matching striped tie topped by a blue blazer with brass buttons. Steve was listening to a recording of Tony Blair's speech to the Labour Party Conference. 'I am listening... I hear... I will act.' This had been in response to Nelson Mandela's call to the world's affluent people to assume the role of 'keepers' of the poor.

Steve wrote in his journal.

Oh dear, what a night. What I can remember of it!

List of things to do today:

1. Attend monthly communications meeting

2. Carry out lab safety walk

3. Write monthly report

4. Write further letter to Tony Blair about the state of British manufacturing industry

5. Tidy up house and feed the cat in preparation for kids coming this weekend.

Okay, let's start this letter. I've had second thoughts about all this offshoring to China. I think I need to share them...

Steve started to hammer out a letter on his desktop PC. But let us now rewind to see how the day had started.

Steve woke up naked on the sofa at Geoff's around 8am.

'Shit the bed. Where am I?' he asked himself, just as Dorothy entered the room. Steve hastily covered up his embarrassment.

'Good morning. Good morning. Would you like a cup of tea, dear?' Dorothy announced, unperturbed by the presence of a naked man in her front room.

'Oh yes, please, Mrs Huckstead.'

Geoff came in just as his mother went out.

'My. My. My. What have we here? The kraken awakes.'

'Oh, bugger off, Geoff. Ooh, my bloody head,' Steve replied as Dorothy returned with tea in a China cup and saucer. 'Oh, sorry, Mrs Huckstead.'

'There you go, that'll make you feel better,' Dorothy cooed, as she placed the cup and saucer in front of him.

'You'll have to be out of the house in half an hour. Can't leave you alone with my mother,' Geoff announced.

'But I haven't got anything to wear, apart from that!' Steve pointed to the sopping wet Elvis costume plus boots.

'Don't worry, I'll fix you up with something. I'll have you looking smarter than you've ever been before. Your bosses will think you're a completely different person.'

This reminded Steve that he should have been at the Elton Centre by now. 'And another thing. How am I going to get to work this morning?'

'That's a point. Me too.' Geoff mused. 'I'll give Perverse a ring.'

This reminded Steve of the night before. 'Aren't you worried about Peter's car?'

'What's the problem? Nobody stole it. Peter can handle the boys in blue. He's used to facing embarrassing questions in police stations.'

'What do you mean?'

'Put it this way. If you've been caught in a house of ill-repute with your trousers down, this one should be relatively simple to explain.'

'So, you're going to hang him out to dry?'

'Oh, no. You're right, he's a mate. I'd better warn him about this. Don't worry, he'll get his car back.'

'So, you're really not worried, then?'

'Not at all. And as for young Peter, he's got such a thing about women in uniform that it'll be a treat for him. Loves the attention, you know.'

Steve was less optimistic. 'Not sure it'll be as simple as that.'

Geoff broke out into song – 'I said don't worry, be happy' – before going off to find Steve some clothes. Minutes later, Steve had dressed up in Geoff's ill-fitting and old-fashioned salesman clothes and was being inspected by Geoff and Dorothy.

'Go on, give us a twirl. What do you think, mother?'

'I think your friend looks very smart. All he needs now is a decent haircut.'

'Indeed, very debonair.'

Steve glowered at Geoff as a car horn sounded outside. Steve bade his farewell to Dorothy as he struggled to walk out to the taxi.

Once in the taxi, Steve sat glumly in the back, while Geoff, sitting in the front, finished a phone conversation with Peter.

'No. No reason to worry at all. Tell 'em nothing. You know the drill...'

There was a prolonged pause.

'No. No. No. You've done nothing wrong. You just don't know what happened to your car. It must have been stolen while you were out, and you've only just got back. Thanks Mr Plod for finding it for me!'

There was another prolonged pause.

'You don't have to say anything. They'll have to give it back to you. If there's any WPCs, use your charm on them. Appeal to their maternal instincts!'

From the sounds of the animated conversation, it was evident that Peter needed a lot of convincing.

'Well in fact, what crime has been committed, apart from the theft of your car, of course?' Geoff then decided to come clean about the other aspect of the matter. 'There may have been an altercation with the Tudhoe and District Country and Western club.'

His voice gave way to an interruption before continuing. 'Yes. Yes. Yes, there may have been a little misunderstanding concerning the young lady driving the car, but that needn't concern you – or them, for that matter.'

Finally, Geoff was done with the questions. 'Do remember that the honour of the Outcasts Cricket Club is at stake. I take it I can rely on your complete discretion.'

Geoff then concluded the call.

'You've briefed him, then?' Steve asked anxiously.

'Yes. He knows what to do. I'll say it again, where was the offence? The car hadn't been stolen, by us, I was under the legal limit for driving, and there was a misunderstanding with the occupants of the other vehicle. No one got hurt.'

'My feet did,' Steve groaned, before adding, 'I've got a bad gut feeling about this.'

'You and your guts again! That's the guest beer you drank last night speaking. Don't fret. You'll be fine...'

Geoff turned to Pervez. 'Here's where I want to stop.'

The car stopped. Geoff got out without paying.

As the taxi drove away, there was a prolonged silence before Pervez spoke up.

'Man, you look rough. What happened? Sounds like you two got into a bit of bother.'

'You could say that. I wish Geoff had driven home. My feet are killing me, and I'll be lucky if I haven't caught pneumonia.'

'How's your hangover, mate?'

'Not good. In fact, it's about double what it should be...'

'That's probably the Ganja.'

Steve groaned and beat his head. 'Oh no. I'd forgotten about that... I could get in trouble with work for that, you know...'

'Why's that, mate?'

'They've introduced random testing at work. I heard talk about them imposing a "zero tolerance" policy.'

'You mean like "Robocop"?'

'Yeah, like him.'

'Hero among the taxi drivers, he is. They're not happy about all these charges against him.'

'I'm sure he'll get by. But what about me, though? How long does it stay in your system?'

'Up to a month, I've heard, mate.'

'Shit the bed!'

Once inside the Elton Centre, Steve took one look at the lift and decided that he could not face it in the state he was in. He made the fateful decision to hobble up the stairs instead. Nemesis Adele was coming the other way.

'I'm pleased to see that you've remembered to use the stair rail this time, Dr Hemmings.'

Steve's speech was a little slurred. 'Thank you, Adele. I will always remember in the future.'

Adele became suspicious. 'Are you sure you're fit for work? You sound a bit strange!'

'I'm fine.' Steve's tone was defiant.

'I'm not convinced. I think I should get the company doctor to check you out.'

Steve started to sweat profusely. 'No. No. No. I'm fine, perfectly fine.'

Adele adopted a concerned look. 'I'm only concerned for your health and welfare, you know, Stephen.'

'Well, no need.'

'And you seem to be moving very awkwardly, if I may say.'

Steve proceeded to put his foot in it, quite literally.

'Oh. That's because these are borrowed shoes,' he explained.

'Borrowed shoes? You know, if that was company issue gear, you could get sacked for borrowing somebody else's kit.'

'No, they're not company shoes.'

'What are they, then?'

'They're a friend's.'

'They look about two sizes too big for you. That's a clear breach of health and safety guidelines. All items of clothing should be ergonomically appropriate and fit for purpose.'

'I do work in an office, not a lab, you know.'

'Now, don't you get sarcastic with me, young man. I'll have to think about whether to treat this incident as an unsafe act or a near miss.'

Steve bitterly regretted his decision not to use the lift. 'But all I did was walk past you on the stairs – and I was holding on to the handrail this time.'

'As I said, I'll have to think about this.'

'Please yourself!'

This was not the final mishap. Steve staggered on past Stuart's office. Just as he reached the end of the corridor, the door opened.

'Stephen. A word.'

Oh. No. Busted again, Steve thought to himself, before saying aloud, 'Coming, Stuart.'

Stuart was surprisingly welcoming. 'Come in, come in. Bloody hell. What a sight you look. Where did you get those clothes from?'

'Oh. They belong to a friend.'

Stuart arched his eyebrows. 'Oh, well. I won't ask any further, then. You do seem to lead a very interesting life.'

'Yes. Too interesting, at times,' Steve admitted.

'Now you have remembered that this morning we have a comms meeting...'

Steve reassured Stuart that this was the case.

'And you do know that, once again, Debbie will be our guest...'

Steve's heart sank, not least because of the state of his attire. 'Oh. No. I didn't.'

'Yes, she's going to update us on the latest developments on Project Mallard...'

'I thought that she didn't know anything.'

'That's as may be. She'll still be giving an update.'

'OK. Fine. Anything else?'

'Well obviously, there's a lot of concern around Project Mallard. So, I want you to lighten the mood a little with your good news concerning the Innovation Award.'

Steve smiled; the relief was palpable. 'Oh. OK. What do you want me to say?'

'Well, I certainly don't want you to impersonate a Dalek, for a start.'

'OK. I'll think of something. Is that it?'

'Yes. See you at 10.'

Let us return to Steve in his office and the letter.

Dear Tony

I know that you must be busy with the Labour Party Conference just ending, but I feel I need to write to you about the state of British manufacturing. I take back my words about letting the Chinese manufacture most of our stuff. This simply will not do – unless we want to join the world's poor, rather than acting as their guardians. You may not notice this in London, but regions like ours are losing more and more jobs. Superficially, it looks like unemployment is not rising, but something is profoundly wrong. We are sleepwalking to disaster. No amount of money sloshing round the stock market will hide this situation.

Perhaps we should meet up at Trimdon Labour Club some time over a pint, so that I can give you the benefit of my ideas.

Best regards

Your number 1 fan.

Steve

This left just a few moments for Steve to scribble down some notes for the communications meeting (always remember to get your priorities right, eh Steve?). At least he managed to get there on time.

There was a tense atmosphere in the crowded meeting room as Debbie wound up her talk to the troops.

'So, we expect BCG to come out of Project Mallard stronger and better equipped to deal with the challenges of globalisation.'

Stuart led the distinctly lukewarm applause for a talk that had given away precisely nothing about the company's intentions.

'Thank you. Debbie. Thank you. OK. We'll have our customary Q & A. Ask Debbie any question you like,' he said, hoping that no one would.

Paul was quick to put up his hand. 'You mean slimmed down for a sell-off?'

Stuart looked at Paul sternly over his pince-nez spectacles.

'Now then, Paul. That question was in direct contravention of Business Principle Two: that you should always assume that your colleagues' motives are for the best. Next question?'

Another technician put her hand up.

'When are we going to find out?'

'Well, Alison, the task force has promised to report by the end of next month, which will coincide with the announcement of our third quarter results. Everyone should know soon after that.'

Stuart decided it was time to cut the Q&A short. 'OK. Thanks again, Debbie. Just to change the mood a little, I've got Steve here to tell you about the Innovation Award that our team has won.'

Paula dug a snoozing Steve in the ribs to wake him up. Fortunately, he was sitting behind Stuart, and his slumbers had gone unnoticed for a change.

'Uh. Oh.'

There was a long pause while Steve gathered himself and got to his feet, trophy in hand.

'Thanks, everyone. And congratulations to all of you on the winning of this innovation Award.' Steve paused for applause. 'BCG has traditionally been a company that has stood for innovation and skill – and as an exemplary employer.'

This was met by general noises of assent.

'Well... a lot of people may have written BCG off in recent years, but we're still a major player in this region.'

There were more noises of assent.

'I hope that this trophy goes to show that with the right people we can still beat the world. I know that you have all been involved in winning this trophy, in some way, so I won't single anyone out for particular praise...'

Paula looked disappointed at the lack of a special mention for her. A deep frown crossed Debbie's face as she scrutinised an email coming in on her Blackberry. Immediately, she nudged Stuart, sitting next to her, to take a look. Stuart's eyebrows shot up into the air.

Steve continued, oblivious to Debbie and Stuart's hurried discussions. 'I'd just like to say that you've been a magnificent team, and whatever happens, it's been great working with you. Let's hope that we can carry this on into the future!'

At which, the room broke out into spontaneous applause. The ovation was cut short by Stuart standing up and raising a hand.

'Thank you, Steve. Well said, if I may say so. Now, unfortunately, Debbie has some grave stop-press news for us...'

'Yes. Thank you, Stuart. Many of you will know Professor Roddy Bartholomew, who was meant to be speaking to us today. I have to announce that Professor Bartholomew has left the company with immediate effect. This is owing to a disciplinary matter. I'm sorry, as this is now a legal issue, I can't take questions on this one. Stuart...' Debbie said, deftly passing the hot potato.

'Yes, Debbie.' Stuart had to think on his feet. 'I think what I can say is that this reflects the company's more hard-line policy, to those who transgress personal and gender boundaries. Furthermore, in line with the Business Principle that "no company employee should cause harm to a colleague", I have to remind you that there is now a "zero tolerance" policy towards drugs and alcohol abuse.'

Steve started to sweat profusely and loosened his borrowed, stripey tie. He had temporarily forgotten his encounter with Adele earlier that morning; now it all came back to him.

Paul had an alternative interpretation on things. He spoke without bothering to raise his hand. 'Why's that? Are they looking to reduce redundancy payouts by simply sacking people?'

Stuart adopted his most stern countenance. 'Paul. Once again, I'm disappointed by your cynical attitude. Actually, it is to protect the health and safety of your fellow employees. A concept that I'm sure this team will wholeheartedly agree with.'

Stuart's words were met with general murmurs of assent, except from Steve and Paul.

Paul was not to be put off. 'And what do you mean by "zero tolerance"?'

Debbie intervened. 'What it says on the tin, Paul.'

Paul was about to challenge this sphinxian pronouncement, when Stuart drew matters to a close. 'OK. I think that's all for today. Sorry to have ended on such a negative note. I know we always try to finish with something uplifting, so well done again to Steve and all of you for the Innovation Award.'

There was another round of applause. Steve tried to force a smile as the meeting broke up.

Steve's facial expression became more anxious as he walked back into his office and remembered events at the beginning of the working day.

Margaret was waiting. 'Oh, Dr Hemmings. You do look different today.'

'I had to borrow a friend's clothes.' Before the conversation could go any further, Steve enquired after her son Darren's health.

'He's fine, but you don't look too good.'

Steve insisted that it was a long story but declined to go into further details.

'Did I tell you about the latest letter I got off that nice Dr Mowlam...?'

Steve braced himself for a long soliloquy when there was a knock on the door. Steve greeted it with relief, until he saw who it was.

'Excuse me, Dr Hemmings. I'm not interrupting anything, am I?' Adele asked, as Margaret left the office. 'I'm sorry, Dr Hemmings, but I've had to search my conscience...' she continued.

Steve's anxious expression intensified.

'I've had to report you to the site doctor on the grounds of suspected intoxication at work.'

'But I didn't drive in!' Steve protested.

'That's irrelevant. You could be in clear breach of Business Principle One, that "no company employee should cause harm to a colleague".'

'I know the one,' Steve replied sarcastically.

'Now, don't get shirty with me. I'm only doing my duty.'

'But I've only sat at my desk and attended a communications meeting. That's all I've done all morning.'

'Well, now you've got something else to do!' You're expected at the Medical Centre in fifteen minutes.'

Steve looked anxiously at his watch.

'Any delay and they'll assume that you're delaying deliberately to try to cheat the breathalyser!'

'Oh my God! You're having me tested?'

'Yes. I consider it my duty.'

'But how am I going to get down there? It's nearly 2 miles away and I haven't got a car today.'

'You should have thought of that before you turned up for work in such a state. Why not phone a friend?'

Steve pulled a face at Adele's uncharacteristic attempt at humour.

'I'm sure you'll get someone. Good luck. I do hope that the tests prove negative.'

'Tests? Did you say tests?' Steve emphasized the 's' at the end of the word.

'Yes. They'll test you for drugs as well. It's standard procedure now.'

Steve went a deathly white.

'But surely, you'll have nothing to worry about on that score. You don't mess about with drugs, do you? A man of your stature!'

Steve recovered his composure a little. 'No, of course not. I'll be fine.'

'Good, and as I said, good luck; I'm sure you have nothing to worry about.'

Adele bustled out of the office. Steve flicked a V sign at her retreating posterior and re-envisioned her being burned to a crisp inside the 'Dicker Man'. He then picked up the phone and dialled Paula's extension number.

In her considerably smaller office, Paula viewed her dial display as the phone rang.

'Hello, Steve. What are you doing ringing me at this time? I was just going to go and get my lunch.'

'Paula, I'm sorry; something has cropped up. Can you give me a lift to the Medical Centre?'

'Of course. What's wrong?' Paula was concerned that Steve had a genuine medical problem.

'Oh. Nothing, nothing.'

'You know I'll get it out of you on the way down.'

'Maybe, but please come quick.'

Once inside Paula's Toyota Starlet, the interrogation began.

'Come on, then. Spill the beans. What's the matter with you?'

'Nothing. Really nothing.'

'Well, how come you've been summonsed to see Dr Connor, then?'

'Oh. OK. Maybe you can put my mind at rest at the same time.'

'Put your mind at rest? I'm intrigued. What do you mean?'

'You'll have to keep quiet about this. Not a word to anyone, you understand.' Steve put a finger to his lips to emphasise his point.

'Why, sure? You can count on me.'

'I have to take a drink and drugs test.'

'Why in the name of Jasus is that?'

'It's that Adele Hitler. She saw me stumble on the stairs, as I came into work.'

'And she assumed that you were pickled?'

'Not just that, I'm afraid.'

Paula was incredulous.

Steve continued hesitantly. 'You did biochemistry and pharmacology subsidiary courses at Uni, didn't you?'

'Yes. What of it?'

'Do you know how long cannabis stays in the body after you've taken it?'

'STEPHEN!!! You haven't!?'

'Just a few puffs. Erm... it didn't have any effect on me...' Steve said, channelling the outgoing US President.

'What, last night?'

'Yes, last night,' Steve said sheepishly.

'Well, it'll very probably show up as a positive, then,' Paula replied all too matter-of-factly. 'From that point of view, you'd have been much better off taking heroin. Stays in the system a lot shorter time.'

'Shit the bed!'

'Cheer up. You're not a regular user, are you?'

'Certainly not!'

'If you only took a few puffs, you could claim it was a false positive. Demand a re-test. You just might be OK!'

'Thanks for the tip. Knowing my recent luck, I won't be.'

Steve thanked Paula profusely as the car pulled up at the Medical Centre. As he walked into the building, a board on the wall announced that Dr Connor was indeed on duty. Steve sat down on a hardbacked, red-seated chair and waited.

Presently, a silver haired man, well into his 60s, popped his head out of the surgery door.

'Would that be Dr Hemmings come to see me?'

They exchanged pleasantries and shook hands before Steve sat down in the surgery.

'Now, I'm afraid you've been called here in somewhat unfortunate circumstances,' Dr Connor continued.

Steve nodded.

'Now, you know I need to do a breath test for alcohol and a blood test for non-prescription drugs.'

'Yes, I know,' Steve said wearily.

'OK. I'm going to ask you to blow into this device until I say stop.'

Dr Connor handed Steve the breathalyser. Steve started blowing. Dr Connor looked at his watch.

After 5 seconds... 'OK. Keep going. You're nearly there.'

Steve put in one last breath, then handed over the device.

Dr Connor frowned. 'Hmm...'

Steve looked worried. 'Am I OK?'

'W-e-e-l-l-'

'Am I under the limit?'

Dr Connor shook his head. Steve started to feel sick.

'It's open to interpretation. Basically, you're borderline,' Dr Connor went on to reassure Steve. 'It's OK, I'll report it as a negative. You would have been over the limit when you drove in, though.'

'I didn't. I had a lift.'

'Ah, well. I'm glad to hear that. Probably more good luck than good judgement, though, am I right?'

'Yeah. I woke up at a friend's house. I had to get a taxi.'

'Good. Good. Good. Well, I'm sure you will have no worries about this next test, will you?'

Steve blushed bright red and shifted about uncomfortably in his chair.

This did not escape the attention of Dr Connor. 'Well, we can always have a re-test, can't we? Can't have the health and safety zealots winning now, can we?'

Steve was pleasantly surprised at this welcome support. 'Well, thanks Doctor, I thought you'd have been on their side?'

'No, not me. I remember my predecessor Eoin Staunton – always well refreshed, he was. Didn't stop him from being a good doctor. You do know when you're drinking too much, don't you?'

Steve shook his head.

'When you're drinking more than your GP! Ha. Ha. The old ones are the best!'

Steve laughed along with the doctor, before the latter continued.

'Anyway, this place has got so miserable lately. More and more people coming to me with stress-related ailments. It used to be scabies and other social diseases. Times have changed!'

Steve felt that he had found an unexpected ally. 'Well, exactly. That's what I've been campaigning against.'

'Yes, so I hear...' the doctor knew more than Steve gave him credit for. 'I heard about your little injury, too.'

Steve blushed bright red again as Dr Connor took the sample.

'OK, then, Dr Hemmings. You can get on your way now. We'll be in touch if there's any problems.'

They shook hands again.

As Steve returned to the waiting car, he was starting to feel a bit better. He had 'passed' the breathalyser. It looked like Doctor Connor was on his side regarding the dope test. His address to the troops had gone down well, and as for Roddy Bartholomew – he'd had it coming for a long time.

'You were a long time,' Paula said grumpily as he got into the car.

'Oh. Yes. Me and the Doctor got chatting. One of the old school, he is.'

'You mean he's permanently pissed. Anyway, how did the breathalyser go?'

'Oh. I passed it, just. Good thing I didn't drive in, though.'

'Not like my brother Sean. The Guards got him one morning near Christmas in Dublin. Just four pints of Guinness he'd had, or that's what he claims.'

'The doctor also said he'd do a re-test for me on the other test, if it became necessary.'

'Well, that was very generous of him. Why?'

'Old school, as I said, old school. So... I think I'm in the clear.'

'Let's hope so, eh?' Paula smiled.

The sounds of *Born on the Bayou* emanated from Steve's pocket.

'Geoff. What can I do you for?' Steve answered cheerily.

'This is no time for frivolity!' Geoff retorted. Before Steve could ask why, Geoff was already waxing lyrical.

'They kept Peter for three hours – three hours! Only just got away from the Police Station, he has.'

'I thought you'd said he'd be alright.'

'Well, he was, eventually. They couldn't prove anything, but not before they gave him the third degree.'

'Why was that? You said that no crime had been committed, so they couldn't do anything.' Steve tried to whisper, so as not to pique Paula's interest.

'You haven't seen the headlines, have you?'

'Headlines? Where?'

'Both the Evening Gazette and the Northern Echo.'

Geoff then recommended that Steve should buy copies from the Elton Centre shop to see for himself.

'They can't be that bad, can they?'

'I'm afraid they are worse,' Geoff pronounced solemnly.

Steve rang off as hastily as he could to avoid questioning from Paula.

As the car arrived back in the car park, Paula fixed Steve with a quizzical look.

'Now, what was all that about?'

'If I told you, you wouldn't believe me. Thanks for the lift,' was all Steve could mutter as he dashed from the car.

'Any time!' Paula shouted ironically to the departing figure.

Steve rushed Basil Fawlty style to the shop, which was in the corner of the Lakeside restaurant, almost tripping over his ill-fitting shoes on two occasions. On his way, he passed Paul the Cynic.

'Afternoon, Elvis.'

Then Howard, another technician, hove into view. 'Uh. Uh. Uh. Steve.' Howard curled his lip for extra effect.

'Shit the bed!' Steve said to himself.

Steve finally reached the shop and picked up copies of the Northern Echo and the Evening Gazette. Both had a hazy picture of him, in Elvis garb, on the front page.

Steve started with the Northern Echo, which boasted the headline '(I'll Be) Doggone'.

Steve read anxiously:

Members of the Tudhoe and District Country and Western Appreciation Society were shocked by the behaviour of an Elvis impersonator in a layby near Darlington last night. A young woman was allegedly propositioned, and a fight ensued.

'This guy just loomed up at me out of the rain,' said mother of two Cheryl Milburn, 33, from Spennymoor. 'He came over to our van, which we'd had to park because of his friend's bad driving and tried to chat me up. I can't tell you the disgusting things he asked me to do...'

It is thought that the two unnamed individuals had mistakenly believed that the van occupants were 'doggers'. Dogging is the name given to a new craze which has hit the northeast, whereby people come to watch others having sex in their cars in laybys and remote areas.

'Four of our lads got out of the back of the van and saw them off,' continued Ms Milburn. 'The cowards ran off and left their car behind when the police came.'

Police are searching for the occupants of a yellow Skoda Felicia car in connection with this incident.

'Mother of Jesus! Shit the bed!!' Steve said.

The Evening Gazette was, if anything, even worse. It boasted the headline 'Hound Dogging' and offered readers an in-depth exposé by a 'Special Correspondent' of the dogging craze that was scandalising Teesside. This could be found on page 6.

Steve was hastily turning the pages when Les's voice boomed out from the Septics' table.

'Nothing to do with you, I hope, Stephen?'

'Uh. No, of course not.'

'Aren't you coming to join us, then?' The other Septics all tittered.

Steve made his excuses, hastily bought a curled-up sandwich and scurried back to his office.

Steve read the front-page article in the Gazette. It gave him no further cause for comfort.

'They should be castrated, men like that,' continued Ms Milburn. 'If they ever come to Spennymoor or Tudhoe, our lads'll have 'em. I hope that the Bobbies lock 'em up and throw away the key.'

Steve was about to turn to page 6 when he was interrupted by Margaret.

'Oh, you're reading about it. Disgusting, isn't it, Dr Hemmings?

'Yes, terrible. Still, do remember, a man is innocent until proven guilty,' Steve was at pains to point out.

'They should bring back hanging, they should. None of that namby-pamby Tony Blair "tough on crime, tough on the causes of crime" business.'

'Now, I'm sure that your friend Mo Mowlam wouldn't agree with that sentiment.'

'Well, as she had to hobnob with murderers in Northern Ireland, I don't suppose she would. Disgusting, it is...'

Margaret's flow was interrupted by the arrival of Paula. This gave Steve a welcome opportunity to shoo a reluctant Margaret out of his office.

Paula glanced at the Gazette headline, which Steve had failed to clear out of view.

'Ha. Ha. Everyone thinks it could be you.'

'It's not the National Lottery, you know,' Steve retorted, before adding anxiously, 'How come?'

'You know Paul's sister...?'

'Yes, I met her a couple of times.'

'She was on a girls' night out when you appeared in the Dog.'

'So...'

'She said you were very good as Elvis.'

'Well, that was nice of her, but doing a good Elvis impersonation in a karaoke is a long way from this.' Steve pointed at the Evening Gazette front cover for emphasis.

Paula peered at the blurred photo. 'You have to say, that guy does looks a bit like you.'

'How can you tell? He's in fancy dress, and I don't do fancy dress,' Steve protested.

'Anyway, I've come to talk about customer sampling for Kalkos...'

Steve was relieved at the change of subject. Steve and Paula got down to discussing the new product launch. The rest of the afternoon passed off without incident until Steve took a ride home in the back of Pervez's taxi.

'You saw the Gazette headline then, did you?'

'Yes – and the Northern Echo.'

'It wasn't you, was it?'

'What do you think?'

'There's not that many Elvis impersonators out and about on Teesside on a Thursday night, but I'm saying nothing.'

'OK. Well, that woman was lying. It was all a misunderstanding,' Steve explained, just as the sounds of *Born on the Bayou* emanated from his pocket.

'Good afternoon, Geoffrey Huckstead speaking. Where are you?'

'In Pervez's cab.'

'Excellent. Excellent. I think we're in the clear.'

'How come?'

'Well. I've rung round the lads, and they've been sworn to secrecy.'

'What about the people in the pub?'

'We were in a function room, remember? No-one else in there. '

A relieved look started to come across Steve's face. Then...

'What about the landlady? She'll have seen me.'

'Ah, right. Thereby hangs a tale...'

'Don't talk in riddles. What do you mean?'

'Well, Peter had to give an alibi when they had him at the cop shop.'

'So, he said where he was? Couldn't really get out of that one,' Steve concluded.

''Fraid so. They'd already got hold of her before I could ring.'

'And...;'

'She said that they'd been round and told her there'd been complaints.'

'So, she told them about us!'

'Not a bit of it. Stop worrying. She got rather cross with them, she did. "None of my gentlemen would do a thing like that", she said, then asked them to leave the pub. Chased 'em out, she did.'

'Have you really spoken to all of the lads?'

'Well, not Pervez, but you can square him up, can't you?'

'I think I already have.' Steve nodded at Pervez. 'What about Crabtree? When he knows what we're up to, won't he spill the beans?'

'Never! He's from Bermondsey, remember. Never grass up one of your own to the Old Bill. You know the score. The Krays and all that...'

Steve could not help correcting Geoff. 'Well, actually, it was the Richardsons who controlled South London, if you must know...'

'Ah, I see you're recovering your old pedantic self. Just square up Pervez while you're with him.'

Steve had another thought. 'What about my clothes? They're still at the pub. They could do a DNA test.'

'It would only work if you already had a criminal record,' Geoff reminded Steve. 'Can't see the Cleveland Constabulary being that bothered, anyway. Tell you what: I'll send one of the lads round incognito to find them. Bryan works nearby. I'll get him to call round.'

Steve had another thought. 'What about the fancy dress shop? You need to return the Elvis costume. They're bound to say something, especially with the state of it.'

Geoff chuckled. 'I don't suppose you know that Gorgeous Georgia, the proprietor, is an old flame of mine. We're still on good terms. I'll get mother to give the kit a thorough wash first. Don't worry on that score!'

'I think it might be a good idea to put back the election a bit until the dust settles.' Steve remained a little cautious.

'Yeah. You're probably right. Maybe a month or so...'

'OK. I'm feeling a bit calmer now.'

'You've every right to. It's just a storm in a teacup. Not the first time the Outcasts have had bad press...'

Steve had another thought. 'What about the girls? They spragged me over Coffin Dodgers.'

'They wouldn't sprag you. There's a couple of them can hardly speak intelligible English, so I wouldn't worry about them.'

Steve remained troubled. 'What about Karen? She's bound to get to hear of this. Hell hath no fury as a woman scorned and all that...'

'Nah, she won't. Anyway, all you did was not back her up over her brat's bad behaviour. She wasn't even there...'

'But her friend Di was – and I danced with her...'

Geoff's voice took a stern tone. 'Stephen, you're getting paranoid. Di obviously likes you. Talk to her if you must. See if you can get a shag, while you're at it.'

Steve was finally reassured that all angles had been covered. Geoff finished the call by reminding him to speak to Pervez, who conveniently provided him with the cue.

'That was about last night, wasn't it?'

'Yes. I need to tell you something...'

'What's that?'

Steve pondered for a second. The beetle brows of Brian Close on the dashboard brought much-needed inspiration.

'I was just thinking. What would Closey do?'

'Ah, Closey!'

'Remember when he played at Old Trafford in 1976?'

'Yeah, one of his last test innings?'

'He finished up black and blue from West Indian bouncers. One in particular, from Wayne Daniel knocked him to the ground.'

'Yeah, and he wouldn't rub it.'

'What's more, his Somerset protégé Viv Richards was fielding at short leg.'

'Yeah, must have been difficult watching his mentor getting roughed up like that.'

'Yes, exactly. It got too much for him. He went over to the old man and said in a quiet voice, so his teammates couldn't hear: "Are you alright, Skip?"'

'What did Closey say then?'

'What do you think? He told him to fuck off.'

'Ah, Closey. What a hero!'

'Yeah. So, the moral of the story is to keep a stiff upper lip.'

'Ah. You mean I shouldn't say anything to anyone about last night. Why didn't you come out with it straight, rather than talking in riddles? Of course not, you're my mate.'

'Thanks, Pervez.'

'No need. No need for all that Closey stuff, either. He wouldn't have talked in riddles. He'd have just said "Shut up, or I'll belt yer."'

'Yeah, I suppose he would.'

Once back inside his untidy house, Steve attempted to do some much-needed housework.

Steve was finally clearing up some cat poo, but something was on his mind. *Should I ring Karen? Does she know about the Gazette? Does she know about me dancing with Di? Does she know that I couldn't get a hard on? You know how these girls talk...*

At that moment, Steve's land line telephone rang.

Karen (for it was her) was quickly into her stride. 'What have you been up to, then?'

'What do you mean? What have I been up to?'

'You know very well. The girls told me everything. How you got drunk. Sang a disgusting song. Groped Di, and then... and then there's this story in this evening's Gazette.'

'Now then, I never groped Di. Who told you that?'

'Well, that was what Ros and Julie told me.'

'And you believed them? Maybe you should talk to Di.'

'OK. Maybe I will. What about this article in the paper? Everyone's very concerned. They give me pitying looks, like "How could you have had a relationship with such a perv?"'

'That woman was telling lies. All lies.'

'All lies? Like you weren't there and it wasn't Geoff who was with you? And it wasn't a yellow Skoda that Geoff had been driving?'

'Erm, nothing's proven.' Steve recalled the works of Bob Dylan. 'Remember Hurricane Carter!'

'Hurricane who?'

'Middleweight boxing champion, got wrongly convicted of murder, because of a white Dodge Polara...'

Steve was interrupted by Karen.

'Stephen, cut the crap! It's too much of a coincidence!'

It was time to come clean. 'Alright, Karen, it was us. But what that woman said about me suggesting doing disgusting things with her, that's not true. It was all a misunderstanding.'

'Well, what did you say to her?'

'I can't remember.'

'Can't remember? Can't remember!?'

Actually, Steve was telling the truth. 'It's a blur, a complete blur.'

'Well, I'm not surprised about that. The girls said you'd been at that wacky baccy an' all.'

'They shouldn't have told you that.'

'Of course they should have. They're my friends.'

'I thought you once told me they weren't really your friends.'

'Now don't get clever with me. This time, they've been acting as friends should, by telling me the truth.'

'I think you should talk to Di.' Strange how Steve's advice coincided with that of the Chairman, although for very contrasting reasons.

The conversation continued for a couple of minutes until Steve plucked up the courage to ask the burning question.

'Karen...'

'What?'

'You're not going to report me to the police, are you?'

'I don't believe you sometimes!'

'What do you mean by that?'

'Of course not. Me and my family have suffered enough shame and humiliation as it is.'

Steve inwardly heaved a sigh of relief, then remembered Geoff's words of wisdom.

'Karen?'

'Yes, Steve?'

'What are you doing tomorrow night?'

Steve's intentions were all too obvious.

'You really are UNBELIEVABLE!'

Karen slammed the phone down.

'I'll take that as a maybe then,' Steve said to himself as he sat down on the sofa, only for the phone to ring again.

'Karen, not so soon...'

'So sorry to disappoint you; it's your Chairman speaking. Did you speak to TFM, then?'

'What's TFM, apart from Teesside's very own commercial radio station?'

'The Former Minge. So, did you speak to her, then?'

'Yes. Yes. Yes, of course I did.'

'Is she going to sprag on you, then?'

Steve thought not.

'Good. Good. Excellent. What we all want to hear. Any closer to getting a dip again, then?'

'No, don't think so.'

'Good, then you can come to the meeting tonight.'

'What meeting tonight?'

'I've convened a special meeting for some of the more loyal lads from the club to meet in the Dog tonight at 9pm.'

'Tonight? What for?'

'Well, firstly, there's tying up any loose ends from last night's unfortunate disturbances.'

'Loose ends? I thought you said there weren't any?' Steve started sweating.

'Nothing we should worry about, but nonetheless, there is much at stake. Like your personal freedom.'

Steve began to feel sick. 'I thought you said it was all sorted.'

'Of course, it is. Just a couple of loose ends to tie up...'

'But why do we need a meeting?'

'There is one other matter,' Geoff said ominously.

'What's that?'

'Crabtree, of course. He has an informer. We need to get to the bottom of this.'

'But then, why are we meeting in his local, of all places?'

'He's on business "darn the smoke" and the Dog's the most convenient place for everyone.'

'You mean for yourself...' Steve said to himself before acquiescing to Geoff's wish.

'Oh, OK, then. I'll be there.'

'9 o'clock sharp, don't forget.' Geoff signed off with those words.

When Steve arrived at the Dog and Gun at 9.05pm he found the Chairman was at the bar with a group of players, including Peter, Amir, Pervez and Neil. Steve was relieved to note that Bryan was there with a large carrier bag in hand.

'Look lads, it's the late Dr Hemmings,' Geoff pronounced.

Steve was more than a little annoyed, but muttered his apologies, nonetheless.

'Sorry Geoff, but it was all rather short notice.'

'These lads got here on time, alright. I hope you don't continue in this vein, once you're the Outcasts' captain.'

Steve tried to ignore the chairman and ordered himself a drink.

'A pint of Old Knacker, please, Mary.'

'When I say you're late, you're actually just in time!' Geoff corrected himself.

Steve looked puzzled.

'Just in time to get me a pint! Mine's a lager.'

'And a pint of lager, please, Mary.' Steve sighed.

'Actually, while you're at it, I think you owe young Peter at least a pint, after all the trouble he was put to this morning – on your behalf!'

'Another pint of lager, please Mary.' Steve looked heavenwards.

'Oh and Bryan here has retrieved your clothes from O'Brien's. I think he should be compensated. Count yourself lucky he got in before anyone else did.'

Steve made a shushing gesture at Geoff before buying yet another pint.

'In fact, I think you can probably get a full round in, it'll help cement your position as Captain-Elect.'

Steve turned resignedly round to Pervez, Amir, Neil and the others.

'Alright fellas, what do you want?'

To Steve's relief, there was a general shaking of heads.

Amir acted as spokesman. 'I think that we are alright, Dr Hemmings, but thank you so much for your generosity in offering.'

Alex was hovering behind Mary. 'So, why isn't Ron Crabtree here tonight?

'Oh. This doesn't concern him.'

'It wasn't that dogging incident in the layby, was it?'

'Now, why should that be, ladies?'

'Got all the village talking it has – and you've got a reputation for your Elvis impersonation.'

Steve blushed as Geoff intervened. 'How dare you suggest that the fine, upstanding gentlemen of the Outcasts cricket team could be involved in such an unsavoury incident!'

Amir backed the Chairman up, as was his wont. 'Hear, hear, beloved Chairman. We are ambassadors for the beautifullest game in the world.'

'Absolutely right, Dr El-Nile. No, it's merely an administrative matter.'

Alex put her arm round Mary.

'Go on. We'll believe you. Thousands wouldn't!'

Geoff was impatient to get down the meeting started. 'Well, in that spirit, could we please borrow the meeting room upstairs to enact our business?'

'I suppose so. Just make sure that you leave it as you find it.'

The players duly trooped upstairs and sat around some very old and rickety tables.

Geoff stood at the front. 'Right, gentlemen, we have some serious business to discuss.'

Steve looked very nervous.

'Firstly, we have the matter of last night's alleged incident. We need to clear that up.' Steve fidgeted with his pen. 'Secondly, we have the forthcoming election of officials for the Outcasts cricket club. In particular, the captaincy.'

'Oh, yes. Most important,' Amir agreed.

'Thirdly and most seriously, there is the presence of an informer in our midst!'

This was met with gasps from around the room.

'So, to the alleged incident last night.' Geoff paused for effect. 'Firstly, I'd like to thank Peter Kennedy for his noble performance at Darlington Police Station earlier today.'

'Thanks, Mr Chairman.' Peter answered loyally.

'Not since the heyday of Sir Geoffrey Boycott has anyone played with such a straight bat for such a long time.'

'Yes, three hours it was.' Peter shook his head. 'Three hours!'

'And you gave them nothing? Not even a sniff?'

'No, Mr Chairman. In the end they had to let me go.'

'And on the subject of sniffing, were there any decent looking birds there?'

'Well, there was one nice one who brought me a cup of tea.'

'I knew it. I'm surprised if you didn't go and loosen off balls in the massage parlour over the road straight after.'

Peter blushed scarlet red.

Geoff rubbed his hands with glee. 'I knew it. It's the uniforms that do it for you, isn't it?'

'I-I-I didn't, you know,' Peter stammered.

'Your secret's safe with us. Let's have a round of applause for the noble Peter.'

The players applauded Peter.

'Yes. Give him the clap that he so richly deserves.' Geoff smirked to general laughter. 'Now then, just to make sure that we all understand, is there anyone who could still sprag on us?'

'No, I contacted the players that you didn't, Mr Chairman,' Amir volunteered.

'And I talked to the pub landlady. She was very sound,' Geoff continued.

'What about those ladies who came?' Neil asked.

'Well, I wouldn't call them that. Stephen, you squared up TFM, didn't you?'

Steve sighed. 'Yes, Chairman. She won't tell anyone. She says it's too embarrassing for her and I think her mates will stick by her.'

'Excellent. Let's just make sure that the rumourmongers don't get carried away with this one, but I think we're nearly in the clear – or rather, you are, Stephen. I think you can breathe again.'

Steve was beginning to look a little relieved when Amir intervened. 'Well done, Mr Chairman, in your selfless efforts to protect the reputation of the Outcasts Cricket Club. A round of applause please for our beloved Chairman!'

The players applauded.

'And now, for the captaincy of the Outcasts Cricket Club. Some of you know will know of the trail of destruction that our present captain has left in his wake...'

'Please outline, Mr Chairman,' Amir asked.

'A string of humiliating defeats, and worse... cancelled fixtures. This has been the worst year in the Club's history. And I got to thinking, what would Closey do?'

'But didn't the Yorkshire committee sack him when they shouldn't have, Mr Chairman?' Pervez asked.

'You're forgetting the fact that he was the man who sacked the aforementioned Sir Geoffrey Boycott in 1986,' Geoff countered.

'Didn't that cause a civil war within Yorkshire cricket, Mr Chairman?'

'You're getting a bit pernickety tonight, Perverse...'

'I just need to be convinced that we are doing the right thing. I've got on with Ron OK since I joined the club.'

'Believe me, he has left doom and devastation behind him. He has been the bane of poor Neil's life. Hasn't he, Neil?'

'Yeth, Geoffwey,' Neil agreed, seemingly oblivious to the torment that Geoff had inflicted upon him over the years.

'Indeed, it is now our supreme and holy duty to replace Crabtree! Pervez, believe me, there will be no Outcasts Cricket Club for you to play for next season if we don't.'

'And you're sure that it's Steve you want in his in his place?' Pervez remained sceptical.

'Yes, a fine upstanding young man – and Elvis impersonator second to none.'

'OK, I'll vote for Steve, because he's my mate, but you've got to get the club sorted out.'

'Don't worry, we will. Firstly, we need to sort out our AGM.'

'Why not next week, Mr Chairman?' Amir enquired.

'No, Ron's about and it's going to be tight. By the way, Neil, where's the Treasurer tonight?'

'I'm afwaid I didn't ask him. He and Ron go back a long way. Played football together – wemember.'

'Yes, you're right. All the more reason to find a convenient date. Hmm. I suppose we've got until Christmas.'

'Is that it, then, Chairman? Can we go?' Amir seemed anxious for the meeting to end.

'No. No. No. As I said, there is a viper in our bosom – a mole in our midst.'

'Surely not, Mr Chairman?' Amir affected incredulity.

'Yes indeed, there is. Crabtree's been onto this from the beginning.'

'Why do you think that?' Peter spoke up.

'He's already managed to sabotage two attempts to hold the AGM in his absence. I've reassured him that all he has to do is send his apologies for absence and he'll be fine. Re-elected, no worries.'

'And he hasn't bitten?' Peter continued.

'No, because he knows there's something up.'

'Maybe he just doesn't trust you,' Peter suggested.

Amir was outraged. 'That is a most appalling suggestion. How would he not trust a man of the Chairman's integrity?'

Geoff was met with silence as he glared round the room. 'No, gentlemen. Believe me. I am convinced there is an informer in the Club, and unfortunately, they're sitting in this room.'

Steve spoke up. 'But, who would it be? We all want Crabtree out.'

'Indeed we do, Mr Chairman,' Amir agreed.

'You are the only members of the club who know about this. It has got to be somebody here.'

Steve drifted into a *The Good, the Bad and the Ugly* reverie.

***

Steve, wearing a white hat, Crabtree, wearing a black hat, and Amir stand in a triangle in a desert graveyard, ready to shoot. A clock is ticking.

In the middle, there is a potty marked 'Outcasts' Captaincy ('Crock of Shit')'.

The clock ticks. Steve and Crabtree eye each other. Amir can't make his mind up whom to look at.

The clock ticks on.

Finally, Amir reaches for his gun.

Steve immediately shoots Crabtree dead, turns and shoots the gun out of Amir's hand, then rides off into the sunset, holding the pot aloft.

***

Pervez nudges Steve awake.

'Maybe someone told another team member when they were under the influence, and it has leaked out,' Amir suggested.

The Chairman ignored this in a rather blatant attempt to deflect attention. 'Maybe, but whoever it was will face the ultimate punishment. Chairman's special measures!'

Amir became fearful. 'Oh. No, not that, Mr Chairman. That would be too terrible.'

'That man will wish he had never been born!' Geoff declared.

'I know, Mr Chairman; you have a very long memory. I remember the time I ran you out on 99 at Whitby... 18 years later...'

Geoff chuckled. 'Yes. I could teach Tony Soprano a thing or two about vendettas, you know.'

Amir nodded his head sagely. 'Indeed you can, Chairman, indeed you can.'

Geoff surveyed the room. 'Now does anyone want to confess before this goes further?' His question was met with silence.

'I'm prepared to be a lot more lenient if someone owns up to this now...' Again, no one spoke up.

The Chairman turned to Amir. 'Very well then. Dr El-Nile!'

There was a long silence. Amir blanched.

'Dr El-Nile... as President of this club, I am appointing you to be Molefinder General. Are you happy to carry out this task?

Amir heaved a huge sigh of relief. 'Oh. Thank you, Chairman. Thank you. Indeed, it is a great honour.'

'Good. Because whoever it is will wish that they had had their bollocks cut off for preference.'

'I will leave no stone unturned,' Amir assured the Chairman.

'Good, but no own goals. No making Crabtree more suspicious than he already is. Capiche?'

'Understood, Mr Chairman.'

'Right. I think we can now declare this meeting closed. Thanks for coming.'

There was chorus of thanks from the floor before Geoff had the final words. 'And remember, gentlemen, this meeting never took place.'

As the other players dispersed, Steve still had a pint of the undrinkable Old Knacker to finish off. He decided to return to the bar.

Alex kindly agreed to change it for a pint of lager.

She enquired after the state of his relationship with Karen.

After some initial reticence, Steve told her about recent developments and the phone call earlier.

'Her friend Di's right. I think she does still care about you,' Alex concluded.

'But what should I do?' Steve thought about driving over while he was still capable.

'I think you're better at expressing yourself with the written word than the spoken one,' Alex advised. 'Instead of writing endless letters to that useless local MP of ours, why not send one to someone you care about?'

It needs to be pointed out that not everyone had personal computers or email accounts at that time. This included Karen, who had only recently acquired a mobile phone of her own.

'You mean put pen to paper?' Steve hadn't thought of this line of attack.

'Why not?' Alex asked, 'It looks to me like you've got nothing to lose.'

Steve contemplated the suggestion.

'And one more thing...' Alex had one final piece of wise counsel. 'Don't share any of this with your friend Geoff!'

'Why not?'

'He's a bad influence. I'm not sure he's got your best interests at heart.'

'But, he's always had such good advice for me...'

'You sure about that?' Alex arched her eyebrows. 'It strikes me that on the one hand he doesn't want to lose his drinking partner...'

'And on the other?'

'He's jealous. His pulling days are coming to an end. The last thing he wants is to see you establishing a successful long-term relationship with a good-looking and intelligent younger woman.'

'OK. I'll bear it in mind.'

Alex came from behind the bar and gave Steve a big hug before he left the pub.

'Good luck,' she cried out as he walked out of the door. 'And one other thing...'

'What's that?'

'Make sure you send her some nice flowers to go with the letter!'

Once he got home, Steve decided to follow Alex's advice and sat down to write, glass of malt whisky in hand. He also looked up a suitable local florist in the yellow pages.

26 High Street
Rokeby
County Durham

October 6th 2000

Dear Karen

I'm sorry about what happened at the film premiere. My friends say that I did nothing wrong, but I acknowledge that I could have been stronger with the 'Jobsworth Usher', even though there wasn't much that could be done to get Charlotte into the film. She is well under 15, after all!

Anyway, I was hoping that we could see each other again, despite the unfortunate way in which we parted at the end of the night. Your trusted friend Di thinks that I still have strong feelings for you and that we should try to resurrect our relationship if we can. It would be wonderful if we could recreate the intimacy that we felt when we first got together.

I have to admit that I find Charlotte a bit of a handful at times. She is obviously intelligent beyond her years and misses her father very much. I can never be a substitute for him but feel that I can lend a helping hand in educating her about the world – if she'll let me. It would be great if we could all get together (your mum too) and watch *Billy Elliott* once it comes out on DVD.

Finally, I'm very sorry that you feel embarrassed by the 'Elvis incident' that was reported in the local newspaper. I have to say that it was all very out of character and brought on by a state of advanced intoxication. Please rest assured that all evidence has been destroyed and that there is no possibility of you being associated with the perpetrator, whoever it may have been.

I do hope this letter finds you well and that you can consider letting me back into your life.

With all my Love

Steve xx

Chapter 38: 'Who'll Stop The Rain?'

The following Monday, Steve received a letter of his own.

> **Dear Steve**
>
> **Thanks for your compliments regarding Nelson Mandela. I think that I will have to be going a long time before I can aspire to be as a great a statesman as him.**
>
> **I'm not sure that it's appropriate for us to meet face to face. I'm sure that you have erudite opinions on the economy, but believe me, I am not short of advice on that matter, especially from you-know-who.**
>
> **You are, of course, free to join the Labour party, and I would be most happy to see you as a constituency member.**
>
> **Best regards**
>
> **Tony**

Steve frowned at the contents. The Prime Minister did not seem to be taking his views seriously. All in all, however, it had proved to be a good day; Stuart had given permission for a further plant trial on the Costa Brava, despite the dreaded 'bronze-out'. He had shown Alex a photocopy of his letter to Karen, which he had duly posted from the Elton Centre. It had met with approval, although she had questioned the intimacy bit.

'You mean you're desperate for sex, don't you? Intimacy, my arse! Let's hope she doesn't see through that one.'

Steve couldn't help smiling at that perceptive observation.

Indeed, the next day a suitably impressed Karen rang him and invited him around. Just this once, Geoff had not provided a counterattraction, and Steve wisely chose to keep this development from him. Even better, 'intimacy' was swiftly resumed! There was a difference, however. Karen explained beforehand that although she had missed the physical side of their relationship, she was now wary of commitment.

'We could be fuck buddies,' Steve was about to suggest.

Happily, Karen finished his sentence before he could complete it. 'Friends with benefits,' she said, adding that she had read all about this arrangement in an issue of Cosmo that had been lying around in her employer's waiting room. Steve felt like all his Christmases were coming at once!

What else can one say about the rest of October 2000, except that it rained a lot? All the better for indoor pursuits, as Steve and Karen spent more of their time together in bed than out of it.

Towards the end of the month, these proceedings were interrupted by Steve's business trip. He was able to escape the rain for a pleasant week on the Costa Brava. As an added bonus, the BCG-approved hotel had a topless private beach.

Steve did not let this distract him too much; he almost ran up his limit for personal phone calls by phoning Karen each night. This was either after returning from a local seafood restaurant or nightcaps in the hotel bar (which the obliging bar staff wove skilfully into his final bill as 'meals'). There was no word from the Chairman, but no news was good news, Steve reasoned.

Chapter 39: 'Back To Life, Back To Reality'

Finally, on the last day of the month, we find a suntanned Steve back in the office bright and early. He wrote in his journal.

Tuesday, October 31st 2000, 8.25a.m

Well, that trip to Spain (sorry Catalonia) certainly was a success!

Number of nipples seen on hotel private beach: 11 (she had her back turned to me). Number of muffs observed: 2.

Number of acts of self-pollution: 2 (now there's a coincidence).

Number of senoritas shagged: zero (well it was a business trip, and I am supposed to be in a relationship).

Number of hours spent on the phone to Karen: ~3 (just under the BCG limit. Phew!).

Number of 5 course meals out on the company: 6.

Number of bottles of wine consumed: 12 (the 'bronze-out' doesn't seem to have affected my Catalan colleagues).

Number of ciggies smoked: 100 (no longer duty-free, but still much cheaper over there).

Number of kilos of powder produced under my 'supervision': 79.

Overall, not a bad trip at all. I think I was right to award myself a 'duvet day' yesterday to get over my jet lag.

Stress reduction and all that – true leaders have to set an example.

List of things to do today:

1. Hold plant trial de-brief with Paula.

2. Write non-scheduled report on the trial for Stuart and Debbie.

3. Send emails to my hosts Sergei and Olga, thanking them for their continuing hospitality.

4. Write monthly report.

5. Write further letter to Tony Blair about the state of British manufacturing industry. I really was not satisfied with his response to the last one. I will try again.

Oh, and must fix up an 'intimacy session' with Karen sometime soon.

Typically, Steve decided that the letter to the Prime Minister took priority.

Dear Tony

I really think that you need to think again about the plight of British industry. Despite the best efforts of our top scientists, the counsel of despair regarding manufacturing continues. We cannot go on fooling ourselves that this country's economy can be sustained by the banks and the City of London. And why are you helping a bunch of Tories, anyway? Your support lies up here in the Northern heartland. You should remember that.

I remain available to offer you friendly advice at any time.

Regards

Steve

Unfortunately, Steve did not have time to hide his prescient writings before Paula marched into the office.

'Oh, you haven't been writing to that eejit Tony Blair again, have you?'

Steve hastily covered up his screen. At least she hadn't spotted his journal.

'So, how did the trial go, then?'

'Oh... Pretty well. I think we got more than one kilo for you this time.' Steve's smile was not reciprocated. In fact, Paula seemed a little grumpy.

'How was the weather, then?'

'Better than here, I hear. I didn't really have time to notice,' Steve lied.

'What, with getting wined and dined by the hosts every night?'

Steve grinned. 'It's hard work, but someone's got to do it. Oh, by the way, any news of Project Mallard?'

'It's all gone quiet. They're saying it might get shelved until next year.'

'Yeah. Christmas is coming.' Steve broke into song. 'It's now or never...'

'Oh. Have you heard anything more about the Elvis thing...?' Paula gave Steve a searching look.

Steve blushed brightly at this unwelcome reminder of his quasi-fugitive status.

'No. Should I have done?'

Steve was saved from further embarrassment by the sound of *Born on the Bayou* getting ever louder.

'Excuse me, can I just take this?'

Paula agreed to come back in five minutes.

'Hello, Geoff...'

'Ah, hello, stranger. So... the wanderer returns. I've been trying to get hold of you all this past week, don't you know. Where have you been?'

'Well, you know that I've been in Spain on a plant trial...'

'You got back at the weekend, didn't you?'

'Yeah, but I had the kids with me.'

'Oh, the brats. Make sure you get your priorities right!'

'What do you mean by that?' Steve was unimpressed by the Chairman's attempt at irony.

'The Outcasts Cricket Club, that's what. Captaincy thereof...'

'So, when's the AGM then?'

'I've tried to throw Crabtree off the scent, but he's been like a terrier. He knows there's something up. Keeps ringing me up with the same question.'

'So have you got a date?'

'Well... Crabtree takes his footballing lads for training on a Thursday night, so that's the best night. I was hoping to do it this week, but I couldn't get hold of you in time.'

'Well, I did have the small matter of a £100K plant trial to think about.'

'Alright. Alright. Let's go for next Thursday.'

'OK. Where?'

'Let's go for the Dog.' Such was Geoff's confidence that Crabtree would be away training with his team in Fishburn. 'I thought it would suit you, anyway. They say power is an aphrodisiac...' Geoff paused for effect. 'You might be in for a threesome with Mary and Alex before you know it. They'll be all over you, man!'

'OK. The Dog it is,' Steve agreed.

'By the way, any word from "TFM"?'

'Well, she texted me a couple of times while I was away...' Steve lied.

'I hope you didn't answer them. Cost a bomb from abroad, they do. Proving to be a bit of a floater, that one.'

'Floater? What do you mean floater?'

'Like the turd that you just can't flush away!'

'You do have a way with words!' Steve paused, before enquiring nervously: 'What about the Elvis incident, have you heard anything...?'

At that moment, Steve's desk phone rang. Steve could see on the screen that it was the Medical Centre. Steve hastily made his excuses and rang off.

'Hello, Dr Hemmings. This is Nurse Tunstall from the Medical Centre.'

'Y-e-e-s.' Steve answered hesitantly.

'When can you report to the Medical Centre to give a blood sample?'

'I thought I'd already given one.'

'Yes. I'm afraid you'll have to give another one.'

Steve started to panic. 'What? Why?'

'I'm afraid I can't discuss that over the phone. Can you come now?'

Steve agreed that he could be there within ten minutes, put on his jacket, mumbled his apologies to Paula waiting outside and flew down the corridor.

'Now then, slow down, young man. Where are you going in such a hurry?'

Why did he always have to bump into Adele at the most inopportune moments?

'Medical Centre,' he answered curtly.

'Well, I hope it's nothing serious. Don't go breaking your neck on the way.' Adele was being unusually pleasant. 'Good luck,' she added for good measure.

Steve couldn't help muttering underneath his breath. 'If it hadn't been for you, I wouldn't be going there. Fucking zealot.'

Once in the Medical Centre, Steve sat down on an old-fashioned tubular chair and waited.

Nurse Tunstall popped her head round the door. 'Ah. Dr Hemmings. We've been expecting you...' She smiled.

Steve ignored the attempted joke and simply grunted. 'Hello, Nurse.'

'Call me Anne,' Nurse Tunstall continued breezily. 'I suppose you're wondering why I've called you here.'

Steve started to sweat. 'Yes, as a matter of fact, I do.'

'No need to worry...' Nurse Tunstall cooed, before adding the less reassuring, '...too much!'

'What do you mean?' Steve nearly jumped out of his chair.

'OK. Your last test came out slightly positive for cannabinoids.'

'Slightly positive? That sounds like slightly pregnant!'

'Not to worry. Doctor has deemed it low enough to be ambiguous. He's ordered a re-test.'

'Yes, he said.'

'Well... especially given the severe consequences that will follow if you're confirmed to be positive...' Anne's voice took on a sterner tone.

Steve managed to stammer out, 'Well, do thank Dr Connor.'

'Well, we do try to be fair. Now, roll up your sleeve, please...'

Chapter 40: 'Happy Halloween'

That night, Steve was sitting in his untidy house, when there was a knock on the door...

Three innocent-looking children were standing at the doorstep, dressed up in Halloween costumes.

'Trick or treat, Mister,' The first child demanded.

'Wait a minute.' Steve sighed as he emptied his pockets. All he could find was coins from his recent business trip.

'I don't suppose you take pesetas, do you?'

The children shook their heads.

'Doomed currency, anyway.' Steve then remembered last year's goody bags, which remained in his kitchen cupboard. 'Wait a minute.'

Steve brought three bags of one-year-old sweets to the door.

'There you are, boys and girls. Enjoy!' he said, forcing a smile.

The children looked suitably unimpressed with the sticky offerings.

'Thanks, Mister,' the leading child said, with a strong hint of irony.

'De nada.' Steve beamed.

Steve went back to his settee. Just as he was getting back into his TV programme, there was a splatting sound against his window. When Steve opened his curtains, he found the contents of three eggs running down his unwashed windows.

'Little gets!'

Steve hesitated, thinking about cleaning the mess, but sat down again. Just as he was getting back into watching his programme, his house phone rang.

'Shit the bed,' he muttered under his breath as he got up to answer the call.

It was Karen, not in the best of moods, one has to say. 'Hi Steve! Remember me?'

'Oh, hello, Karen. How are you?'

'Well I can't be in the best of mental health, or else I wouldn't be ringing you!'

'Charming. So, to what do I owe the pleasure?'

'I was wondering when you were going to deign to get in contact with me...'

'Oh sorry, I've been busy.'

'Don't you want to speak to me when you have to pay for the calls?'

Before Steve could issue the obligatory denial, Karen's voice was interrupted by repeated banging upon the door.

'What's that noise?'

'Oh. It's kids demanding money with menaces.'

'What do you mean by that?'

'You know – trick or treating. Stupid American idea, if you ask me.'

'Now then, don't be a spoilsport. It's only a bit of fun. Charlotte wanted to go out tonight, but I said she was too young.'

The voice of Charlotte could be heard in the background. 'Yeah. Not fair. Fuck off, mum!'

There was more banging on Steve's door.

'I think I'll have to go and get it.'

'Oh, and not listen to what I have to say?'

There was a splat against Steve's door.

'Oh, go on then. They've egged my door now.'

'Oh dear. They don't do egging around here.'

'What's egging, mummy? Can I do it when I'm older?'

'No, dear. It's very naughty.'

'Bollocks!'

Steve intervened in the mother-daughter dialogue as more eggs splatted against his unwashed windows. 'I bet they don't behave like that in the good ol' US of A. The householders have guns there.'

'Don't be a misery. It's just a minority who spoil it for the others.'

'You reckon? Now, what were you going to tell me?'

'I was thinking, while you were away, and...'

They were interrupted by another furious round of banging on Steve's door.

'Go on. If you're right about this being a minority, they'll let me off this time...'

'Well, as I was saying...' Karen was building up to tell him something important.

'Just a minute, I'd better see to it or else there'll be more eggs.'

'If you must...'

There was more hammering on the door.

'Yes, I think I definitely must.'

'Go on, then...'

Steve went to the front door and opened it just in time to receive volley of eggs.

Splat! Splat! Splatter!

A bunch of hooded youths ran off into the night.

'Shit the bed!'

Steve returned to the phone.

'Now, I heard that. What happened?'

'They egged me this time. I'll need to go off and clean up.'

'Oh, poor you.'

'Well, what was it that you wanted to talk to me about?'

'Well, to cut a long story short, I was thinking that maybe we should start seeing each other on a more serious basis. How do you feel about that?'

'I'd like that very much.' Steve said, scratching his balls.

'Well, I haven't made my mind up yet. I'm still not sure that you don't just want sex.'

'Oh no, not at all, Karen...' Steve crossed the fingers of his free hand behind his back.

'I'm not sure I believe you, but I'll be having a girls' night out with Di tomorrow night. She has offered to help me make a decision.'

'Well, I do hope you make the right one. Listen, I'd better go and clean myself up.' Steve said, continuing to scratch his balls thoughtfully.

They wished each other a good night. Steve put down the phone and went upstairs to clean himself up before slumping on his sofa to resume watching his TV programme with the cat. Within ten minutes, he had drifted off into a reverie.

***

Karen, Di, Ros and Julie are all dressed up as witches and are stirring up a cauldron on a blasted heath. Julie and Ros are wearing particularly low-cut dresses. They try to shove Steve's cat into the cauldron, but it escapes with a loud miaow.

Julie speaks first: 'Hubble, bubble, toilet trouble. We call on the dark powers to find Karen a man.'

'A man with a nine inch cock, forsooth,' Ros adds.

'That's too small, Sister Rosalind,' Julie demurs.

'As you like it!' Ros concludes.

Di steps forward to the cauldron. 'A man who can be relied upon.'

'A man who will be a father to my daughter, exactly like he oughta,' Karen announces her priority.

Julie throws a large pinch of curry powder into the cauldron. There is a flash. Green choking smoke envelops the witches.

Ros: 'A man who looks as fit as hell.'

Karen: 'A knight in shining armour.'

Julie: 'One who doesn't smell.'

Ros: 'One with a massive lance.'

Di (ruefully): 'Made of the hardest steel.'

Julie: 'Indeed, there is Fortune too hard for Nature – with the assistance of a little blue pill!'

Karen: 'Who is this man of whom you speak?

Ros looks into the distance: 'Lo, he rides unto us on his trusty charger.'

Enter Steve in jockey costume, riding a pantomime horse, with a wad of multicoloured, losing betting slips in his top pocket. Cher's *Believe* plays as his entrance theme.

'Good evening, girls. What are you up to?'

'We seek a man for Karen.'

'Well, hey, baby, I'm your man.' Steve smirks.

All the witches join in unison. 'We really don't think you're strong enough!'

'I'm certainly strong in the finish!' Steve leers as he shakes the reins of his imaginary horse.

Julie closes her eyes. 'Wait, an apparition speaks.'

Julie goes into a trance and speaks in a strange, deep voice. Charlotte appears, covered in egg.

Charlotte: 'It is written. Sir Stephen will have his wicked way with the fair maiden Karen. He shall enter into her castle once more and put her to the sword.' The child pulls a face, full of disgust. 'That's my mum, you dirty dog!'

Steve grins. 'That's great, I look forward to that. What about my job?'

'Sir Stuart has a message...' Julie intones.

The severed head of Stuart appears. 'Be bloody and bold. Don't give a fuck. And you may survive Project Dead Duck.'

Steve looks even more pleased. 'Great. Looks like old Stuart might be for the chop. In which case, they'll definitely need me to continue...'

'You have nothing to fear from Sir Stuart or Lady Deborah,' Julie explains.

'Great. While you're on, what about the cricket captaincy?'

'The Son of Pork shall be ennobled, although he will never truly rule the Outlaw Kingdom.'

'Sounds about right.'

An apparition of The Chairman appears with a cricket bat in hand.

That emptied balls and crusty flanges shall meld
Horrible sight! Not to mention smell
For the blood-bolter'd Crabtree smiles upon thee,
And points at them for his.
Be lion-mettled, proud; and take no care
Who chafes, who frets, or where conspirers are:
Sir Stephen shall never vanquish'd be until
The Sherriff of Hutton and the Drake's League's Primrose Hill
Shall come against him.

'Wow, we don't play Sherriff Hutton Bridge until late August next year. I'll take that. Thank you, girls!'

Steve rides off into the distance.

The witches reconvene.

Julie: 'Then when shall we four meet again? In thunder, lightning, fire or rain?'

Ros: 'When the rumpy-pumpy's done, before Sir Steve scores another run.'

Di: 'That will be in the 'Dog and Gun.'

Karen: 'I just wish I could trust this one!'
There is a loud flash. The 'weird sisters' disappear.

***

Steve stirred on his sofa. The cat miaowed and jumped off him, digging his claws in as he went. Steve yelped in pain and got up to go to bed.

Chapter 41: 'Black Coffee'

Wednesday November 1st 2000.

Karen and Di are at the bar of the Dog buying drinks from Mary. *Black Coffee* by All Saints is playing in the background.

'There you are, then – one glass of dry white wine, one half of lager and two alcopops. That'll be £6.50, please.'

Di handed over a tenner and waited for change.

Karen thanked Di and helped her with the drinks. They were interrupted by a quizzical-looking Alex, who had been hovering in the background.

'You're Karen, aren't you?'

'Yes. How come you remembered?'

'I always remember a face, especially an attractive one. You were with Steve for Sunday lunch that time...'

'Yes. You've got a good memory!'

'So, where's the man in question tonight?'

'Oh. He's out with his mate Geoff.'

'Some people never learn, do they?' Alex said conspiratorially.

Di ushered Karen away from the bar to a table, where Ros and Julie were waiting.

'Come on, Karen. Let's go and see how far gone those two are.' Di looked at table where Julie and Ros were already looking very well-oiled.

'What are they doing here in the first place?' Karen asked grumpily.

'Sorry. They overheard my phone conversation with you during the tea break today.'

'Couldn't you have put them off?'

'No. They really fancied a girls' night out, and this pub is on the bus route from Peterlee, so I couldn't get out of it. At least they haven't scrounged a lift off me this time.'

'But we're here to talk about Steve, aren't we? I don't really want to be sharing my intimate secrets with those two around.'

'Oh, there'll be plenty of time, once they've found a couple of local lads.'

As they approached the table, the noise levels reached a crescendo. Ros was regaling Julie with details of her latest sexual misadventure.

'So he says to me as he pulled his flies down, "Can you get hold of it and glide it in for me, please?"'

'He said please! Must have been a real gent.'

'So I said to him, "What have you got, a fucking aeroplane?"' Ros fell about laughing at her own joke. Karen and Di placed the alcopops in front of the others.

Julie opened the discussion. 'Karen, spill the beans! Steve seems a nice enough fellah to me. Why do you keep splitting up with him?'

Ros had a theory. 'Not enough stamina, mebbes?'

Ros nudged Karen. Ros and Julie snorted in harmony.

Karen was not impressed. 'Well, you two might have something to do with it. You couldn't wait to tell me about his trip to Coffin Dodgers and his misbehaviour at that cricket do.'

'Isn't that what friends are for?' Julie asked.

'OK. OK. I just haven't found him the easiest person to have a relationship with.'

'So it is his performance, then?' Ros suggested.

This made Karen even more angry. 'Absolutely not. He's a bit over eager, if anything...'

Di introduced the voice of reason. 'I think you're more concerned about his relationship with your daughter.'

'Yes, that... and the fact that he has been behaving rather strangely lately...'

Ros: 'You mean what happened in that layby. I wouldn't put up with that.'

'He says it's lies, what that woman said,' Karen insisted.

'Well, he was certainly the perfect gentleman towards me, earlier that night,' Di said, looking a little disappointed.

'Yeah, there's that too. He shouldn't be dancing closely with my mates, though, should he?' Karen concluded.

'I think he was just lonely.' Di was quick to stick up for Steve. 'It became clear to me that night that it's you he really wants.'

'Well, I think he's a bit weird, but there's no accounting for taste.' As Julie was saying this, she received a glance from a shaven headed gent with tattoos.

Craig David's *7 Days* was playing in the background.

Julie was quite taken with her new admirer. 'Oh, I like the look of him though, but. Lovely muscle tone.'

'Oh no. Can't be doing with skinheads or tattoos...' Karen said disdainfully.

'You see! Steve's much more your type. Educated man. Good job...' Ros observed.

'Well, that's another thing. I think he's worried that he'll lose it,' Karen mused.

Ros was surprised by this revelation. 'Really? Surely a guy like that can just go and get another one?'

Di was more understanding. 'It's not that easy. Certainly not round here. Just look at how many jobs BCG had in this area ten to fifteen years ago compared to now. My ex worked for them for 18 years. He doesn't anymore.'

'I think he needs the love of a good woman...' Julie grabbed Karen by the knee. 'And you might just be the one to give it to him.'

'Yeah. In more ways than one,' Ros giggled.

'OK. OK. I'll think about it, but I'm not a charity for needy scientists, and I've got Charlotte to think about,' Karen concluded.

'You could do worse, as long as it's brains not brawn that you're after,' Julie said.

'And he's got something big between his legs as well as between his ears,' Ros added.

'I think you should give it a go. I really do. You could be meant for each other,' Di urged Karen.

'I'll think about it. I'm in no hurry.' Karen remained thoughtful.

'Good girl,' Ros agreed. 'It seems to me that his fate lies in the balance. That's the way to keep 'em interested...'

Ros was interrupted by the shaven-headed, tattooed guy sidling up to the girls' table with his similar-looking friend.

'What are you lovely ladies doing in here?'

'Oh, we're just trying to straighten out our friend's love life, like.'

'Why waste time on that when you have your own to think about? Can I get you a drink, mebbes?'

Karen declined the offer. 'Oh. No. Not for me, thank you.'

Di shook her head. 'Not for me, either. I'm driving.'

Julie spoke for the other two lovely ladies. 'Oh, we'll have one thanks. Rude to refuse, eh?'

'Same again, then?'

'Oh. No. I was fancying one of them cocktails they were advertising at the bar.'

'Anything you like, ladies...'

'OK. We'll have a look at what's on offer.'

Julie and Ros got up and went to the bar with their would-be suitors to read the rather tired-looking illustrated list above the bar.

Ros giggled. 'I think I'll have sex on the beach.'

Julie laughed more raucously. 'I think I'll have a long slow screw up against a wall.'

'Our pleasure, girls...'

Meanwhile, at the table, Di had had an idea. 'OK. Finish your drink,' she whispered to Karen.

'Why?' Karen whispered back.

'I'm not waiting around while they let those two scoundrels have their wicked way with them. Let's give 'em the slip and go to the Ship!'

'I thought they were going back on the bus.'

'It takes nearly two hours to get to Peterlee on the bus. They're bound to want a lift.'

Karen nodded her agreement, and the two snuck out of the front door, watched by a smiling Mary and Alex. Eventually, Ros and Julie turned round bearing lurid cocktails with slices of fruit and parasols.

'What the fuck? Where they gone?' Julie exclaimed.

'Well, they could at least have said good night,' Ros said.

The first shaven head patted Julie on the bottom while his mate leered at Ros. 'Never mind, ladies. Now you've got our complete and undivided attention...' The two of them ushered the girls back to the vacant table for further negotiations.

Meanwhile, Di and Karen found their way to the Ship to discuss the vexed issue of Steve. On the one hand, Steve had proved himself to be less than reliable, he hadn't hit it off with Charlotte, he was obsessed with cricket and he was too prone to take advice from his toxic friend Geoff. On the other hand, he was fun, he was intelligent, he was kind, he had a good job and Christmas was coming...

The meeting was inconclusive.

'Why not wait until the festive season is out of the way before making any lasting decisions?' Di suggested.

Karen assured Di that she would not rush into anything and would let Steve know his fate accordingly.

At the same time, Geoff and Steve were holding a contrasting conversation in Yarm. The AGM was fixed for Thursday November 9th in the Dog. No, Amir had not come up with any significant findings in his role as Molefinder, but deemed it safe to go ahead on that date.

Geoff had some kindly advice for Steve. Christmas was coming. Under no circumstances should he get back with Karen. This would prove costly. Not only would he have to buy a present for the girlfriend, but he would also have to suitably convincing gifts for 'The Brat' and her grandmother. What's more...Way! Hay! It was party season! He should think of all the tashing opportunities that were about to come his way. A word of caution was in order though...

'Always avoid girls with seasonal names like Carol, Mary, Holly, Noelle, or Eve.'

'Why is that?' Steve enquired.

The Chairman spoke from bitter experience. He explained that chances were that these ladies would have birthdays around Christmas. Steve would be liable for a double round of present-buying or risk spending Christmas alone with a set of full balls.

Chapter 42: 'The Stolen Election(s)'

At last the day of the election dawned on Thursday, November 9th.

Not the one in America; the important one in Teesside.

The former had been and gone, but it would be weeks before the result was finally resolved.

There had been little to report on the work front. Debbie had organised an internal BCG International Innovation Conference in Middlesbrough that had proved to be something of a Yawn Fest. Steve had been obliged to attend, and was somewhat miffed to discover that he had not even been invited to submit a poster, let alone deliver a keynote lecture – one consolation being that neither had Stuart.

Another consolation was that one of the American delegates was a stunning raven-headed young biochemist called Lesley, who seemed rather smitten with him. Unfortunately, she was constantly surrounded by other hopeful male delegates, who succeeded in cancelling each other and Steve out. Furthermore, he was not a resident delegate, so there was no chance of 'doing a Roddy Bartholomew' after a nightcap, as such activities were already being referred to in company circles. *Maybe just as well,* mused Steve; he was in enough potential trouble as it was. There was still no word from the Medical Centre on the drugs test; he was becoming increasingly nervous about that.

What else did he notice? Paula had blagged an invitation and had been impressing the other delegates with her knowledge of colloidal dispersions. Curiously, she had seemed to be genuinely interested in the seemingly interminable technical lectures. He'd have to watch that girl!

The American delegates seemed to be pretty disgruntled with the provisional outcome of their election. 'How can the winner have one million votes less than their opponent?' they reasoned, in their pointy-headed liberal way. Steve was unsympathetic. He'd had a £10 bet on George W to win and was impatient to collect his winnings. *Suck it up, fellas,* he thought to himself, *there's no real difference between the two candidates anyway...* Steve just wanted his money.

After the Conference finished, it was his own election. Steve felt confident that all was in place for an effortless victory. Steve went home to prepare. This involved repeated visits to the toilet. Steve put this down to nerves, although the consumption of too many rubbery chicken legs at the closing lunch of the conference may have also contributed.

Everything started smoothly enough at the Outcasts' AGM. The Chairman opened proceedings in the upstairs function room in the Dog. The only blemish had been Steve breaking wind on the stairs leading to the room, with the Chairman immediately in tow.

Ten of the Outcasts were now crowded round a table in the upstairs functions room. Crabtree was noticeable by his absence. The Chairman was finishing his speech...

'This has not been a successful season for the Outcasts,' he concluded, peering over his half-moon glasses. 'In fact, it will go down in the annals of our illustrious club as the worst on record. Bad weather, ten lost matches, and worst of all, five cancellations! Gentlemen, we need change. I trust that you will all remember this when we come to the next item on the agenda: Election of Officials.'

Amir intervened. 'With the exception of your post, of course, beloved Chairman.'

'Thank you, Dr El-Nile. Also, with the exception of President.'

Steve sat looking tense. He fidgeted. He was sweating. He snuck a surreptitious sniff of his armpits, hoping that no one would notice.

The Chairman noticed, of course. 'No, Dr Hemmings, you weren't smelling too bad last time I noticed. Just keep your arse to yourself for the remaining duration of this meeting, though, won't you?

'Yes, Mr Chairman.'

'I know all about your vaporous predilections after the last Outcasts tour. Just remember, it's a small room that we're in. Now, I need to vacate the chair temporarily. Dr El-Nile, could you please deputise?'

'OK. Nominations for Chairman, please.' Amir's pronouncement was met with silence. 'OK. I would like to nominate Mr Geoffrey Huckstead to continue as Chairman.'

Steve shot his hand up. 'Seconded.'

'Any other nominations?' The Chairman scanned the room, temporarily forgetting his neutral status.

Nobody put their hand up.

'OK. Show of hands, please.' Amir announced.

The meeting re-elected Geoff unanimously.

'Thank you. It's always very humbling to be reminded of your support,' Geoff said almost sincerely. 'Right. Nominations for President, please.'

Steve's nomination of Amir was seconded by Peter. There were no other nominations.

'I hereby declare that Dr Amir El-Nile is re-elected as President,' Geoff duly announced.

Steve looked anxiously at his watch. Surely, it would be a matter of minutes before he was elected captain of the illustrious Outcasts Cricket Club. Maybe not; there were more posts to fill.

'OK. Nominations for Secretary. Remember, this is a very important role, and includes arranging the fixture list,' the Chairman explained.

Neil Patterson was duly nominated by Amir and seconded by one of the other players. Geoff then asked for further nominations, which Steve felt was unnecessary. He started to fidget.

'Dr Hemmings! What's the matter? Have you got ants in your pants?' Geoff demanded.

Steve blushed. 'No, Mr Chairman.'

'They probably wouldn't want to go inside your Y-fronts!'

Steve pulled a face. 'Boxers, please, Mr Chairman.'

The remark brought laughter from around the table. Steve forced a smile, while noting that the captaincy was next on the agenda...

'Next, we have the position of cap...' Geoff was immediately interrupted by Amir.

'Please – wait a minute, Mr Chairman, have you not forgotten something?'

'What's that?'

'Oh, beloved Chairman, we need a Treasurer.'

'Oh. Yes. So, we do. Please accept my apologies for that omission. Who put out this Agenda?'

Everyone looked at Neil. 'Yeth. Thorry, Mr Chairman. I forgot.'

Geoff shook his head. 'You just can't get the staff these days.'

Barrie Gill was nominated, despite being suspected as a Crabtree loyalist. Another couple of minutes passed while he was seconded and duly elected.

Steve was feeling more and more uncomfortable. To make matters worse, he felt another fart coming on. Surely, he could hang on for another couple of minutes, though, couldn't he?

Finally, Geoff moved on to the next item on the agenda. 'OK. Now for the piece of resistance. Nominations for the captaincy. Please, gentlemen.' The Chairman was interrupted once again by Amir, who had a point of order.

'What is it this time?'

Geoff may have felt exasperated, but this was nothing compared to Steve who muttered audibly, 'Oh, just get on with it.' The pyloric pressure gauge was by now well into the red zone.

'Surely, we should be discussing vice-captain first?' Amir reasoned.

'Why would we want to do that, Mr President?'

'Surely we should build up to this most important position?' Amir continued.

Geoff was unimpressed. 'I think you're making this up as you go along...'

'Surely, it is very important to have cover if Captain is indisposed?'

'We've never bothered electing a vice-captain in the past. Who is the existing vice- captain, by the way?' Geoff temporarily forgot this important fact.

Steve shot his hand up. 'It's me, Mr Chairman.'

'Then I would like to nominate Dr Stephen Hemmings for re-election as vice-captain,' Amir said.

There was an embarrassing pause, as Steve blushed and shifted in his seat. That fart certainly wasn't going away!

Amir's logic was not shared by the Chairman. 'No. No. No, because we need to have a captain first, then he can nominate a vice-captain himself. Now, do we have any nominations for captain?'

Pervez stuck his hand up. 'I'd like to nominate Dr Steve Hemmings for captain.'

At last! Steve smiled. One or two other players shook their heads.

Neil swiftly put his hand up. 'I'd like to second that.'

'OK. Dr Hemmings, are you happy to accept the nomination?

'Yes, thank you, Chairman,' Steve blurted out.

'Any other nominations?'

Steve looked round the room. Nobody else was throwing their hat into the ring.

The Chairman was about to pronounce Steve captain when Ron Crabtree marched into the room.

'What the bladdy hell is going on here, then?' Ron demanded to an embarrassed silence.

'Good evening, Ron. You're just in time for the Captaincy nominations,' Geoff answered phlegmatically to embarrassed laughter around the room.

'Any other nominations, then?' Geoff continued without missing a beat.

One of the other players stuck his hand up. 'I propose Ron Crabtree.'

The nomination was immediately seconded, to Steve's disappointment. It seemed that he wasn't as popular within the club as he thought he was.

'Wait a minute. Wait a minute. Am I right in thinking that I've got an opponent?' Ron demanded.

'You are.' Geoff nodded his head.

'Who is it, then?'

'Dr Hemmings over there.' Geoff pointed to Steve.

Amir looked pleadingly at Ron.

Steve squirmed in his seat. Finally, he could contain himself no longer. He let out a massive, gut wrenching, room-emptying fart.

Pppppwwarrrrppppp

Steve thought to himself, *I hope that doesn't smell too bad. It's usually the silent ones that are deadly.*

Not this time!

Peter, sitting next to Steve, was suitably impressed. 'Bloody hell, Hemmers! Where did you get that one from? I thought I could do a good egger, but I think you've given a new meaning to the name Function Room.'

Geoff held his nose ostentatiously. 'At last, you've found something that you're truly world class at, old son.' The Chairman cleared his throat. 'This would seem like an opportune time to adjourn this meeting, while we wait for the smell to clear. Carried?'

There followed a general hum of approval. The players made for the door as quickly as they could.

The players circulated in the corridor outside the recently evacuated function room. Geoff summoned Amir over.

'Mr President. A word please, while we're outside.'

'Of course, Mr Chairman.'

They walk into an adjacent function room, while the others, including the two captaincy rivals, remained in the corridor outside.

The Chairman closed the door behind him. 'Come on now Amir, what the fuck is going on here?'

'I don't know what you mean, Mr Chairman.'

'I think you do. Out with it!'

'Sorry, Chairman, I can't.'

'Look here. Crabtree has presided over a fucking disaster as captain this season. I try to get him replaced, discreetly, but he seems to know that's something afoot. I'm coming to the conclusion that there's only one person who could have known enough to tip him off.'

'It could have been Neil. You've told him. Or Peter.'

'No, it had to be you. Only you know enough... and then there's the small matter of your behaviour tonight...'

'What do you mean, Mr Chairman?'

'Deliberate delaying tactics, bogus points of order. It seems to me you were trying to defibrillate until Crabtree got here from his football practice. So tell me – WHY?'

'Sorry, Chairman. I just can't tell you.'

'You'll feel all the better for it when you've got it off your chest.'

'No, sorry, Chairman; it's too personal.'

'Alright. I'll call a special motion to have you removed as President.'

'You wouldn't!'

'If it's good enough for the US Supreme Court, it's good enough for the Outcasts cricket club.'

'I still can't tell you.'

'Very well, then. I was thinking of instigating a Chairman's special award – the worst player of the year award.'

The Chairman pulled out the dreaded potty from behind a curtain. 'I've been hiding this specially. I was thinking of giving this to young Steve to bring him down a peg or two, following his intended coronation. I think I've just changed my mind.'

'Oh no, Mr Chairman. Please no.' Amir got down on his knees.

'I know you don't drink alcohol, so I'll spare you that, but I can tell you that Diet Cola doesn't taste too nice out of plastic, especially if we mix it with pineapple juice. Doesn't go down very well either. Lots of burping, lots of spillage. Most undignified, especially with a plastic dog turd floating in it!'

Geoff waved the potty in Amir's face.

'Alright. Alright. Alright. I will tell you. I will tell you. Oh, Mr Chairman, I will tell you...'

Let us leave Amir to his confession and return to the players outside the function room. We find that they had divided into a Steve faction and a Crabtree faction. Steve noted that Crabtree had four players with him. He had only three with him: Peter, Pifco and Pervez. There was a strained silence.

The Good, the Bad and the Ugly played in the background over the pub Tannoy.

Back in the spare room, Geoff was close to a breakthrough as Amir started to open up. 'Alright. Mrs El-Nile and I haven't been enjoying carnal relations lately...'

This did not surprise Geoff. 'Situation normal. I thought she gave you two dips a year. One at Christmas and one on your birthday!'

'I suppose you are right, Mr Chairman, ever since we had our children...'

'That's a long time ago. So what have you been doing for a dip?'

'Must I tell you, Mr Chairman?'

Geoff waved the potty in Amir's face once more. 'Yes, Dr El-Nile, you must.'

'I've been, erm...' Amir hesitated for an appropriate word. '... "seeing" Mrs Patterson, but Neil doesn't know about it.'

'But Crabtree does, eh?' Geoff chuckled.

'Yes, he does, Chairman.'

'How come?' Geoff asked.

Amir explained the incident where Ron had caught them *in flagrante delicto* after the match at Great Naughton.

Geoff laughed again. 'Must have been a bit of a fright – FOR HIM!'

'He didn't say a thing at the time, but he's been reminding me about it recently.' Amir continued.

'How come?'

'He was on to the plot against him from the start. He knew something was up, so he made me tell him.'

'I see.' Geoff looked thoughtful. 'But I get the distinct impression he doesn't know it's Steve Hemmings up against him...'

'Oh, I told him. Indeed, I told him.'

'So?'

'He wouldn't believe me. He thinks that Steve is a joke. "An unworthy opponent", he said. He was sure that you were keeping something up your sleeve. Maybe Peter; maybe Pervez.'

'So, we still have an element of surprise.'

'Yes, Chairman. I think he's still in denial.'

'OK, I'll reconvene the meeting,' Geoff said, lifting the pot. 'I'll just get a little something to fill it with first. I'll get a pint of 'Old Knacker and a pint of diet cola/pineapple mix, depending on how things go...'

'Yes, Chairman. Here, please take the money for it.' Amir proffered a fiver.

'Thanks for the offer, but no thanks. I'll get it out of club funds.'

'Very well, Mr Chairman...'

'Of course, no one must know about you and Mrs Patterson, but you do know what this pot will be filled with if Crabtree wins the election, don't you?'

Geoff waved the potty at Amir once more.

'Yes, Mr Chairman.'

Meanwhile, outside, Steve and Ron were eyeballing each other as *The Good, The Bad And The Ugly* continued to play in the background.

'So, it <u>was</u> you, bladdy hell. The Crow could have come up with something better than you, Hemmers.'

'I have captained cricket sides before, you know.'

'You're kidding.' Ron scoffed.

Steve started to get riled. 'I won a Cup once.'

'Well, I'll go to the foot of our stairs, as they say around here.'

'I've brought along future first class cricketers.' As usual, Steve felt his leadership abilities were being sorely underestimated. 'I'm perfectly capable, you know...'

'Good job it's not going to be put to the test,' Ron said, looking round. 'Because I reckon you're outnumbered.'

Steve still thought Geoff and Amir would tip the balance back in his favour. But then, Amir had been behaving very strangely. It was as if he'd wanted Ron to arrive in time for the election. As for the Chairman, could he really, really trust him to deliver on this, or on anything else for that matter? Meanwhile, the man in question returned with the drinks and a hastily-borrowed clothes peg on his nose. He surreptitiously took the drinks into the spare room, hid them behind the curtain and then came back out to address the troops.

'I'll just go back into the meeting room to see if it's fit for human habitation,' he announced, theatrically removing the clothes peg from his nose.

'I'd give it another five if I were you, Geoffrey.' Ron laughed.

The chairman walked into the room, but quickly backed out again, theatrically reapplying the clothes peg to his nose.

'No, gents. Sadly, the room remains a fall-out zone. As the bar staff inform me that there aren't enough clothes pegs to go round, we're going to have cram into the spare room.'

The players squeezed inside. The chairman brought the meeting to order. 'Let's now vote for who will have the honour of leading the Outcasts next season.'

The players got ready to raise their hands. The chairman paused.

'Now then, I think you'll agree that the Chairman must remain impartial, so I think that in the interests of club unity, it's best that we have a secret ballot. Agreed?'

This proposal met with a general murmur of approval.

The chairman got a copy of the Racing Post out of his pocket and started to tear up slips. He wrote out ten slips with boxes for Hemmings and Crabtree on each of them.

'I'll now hand out the slips. Remember,' he said, looking pointedly at Amir, 'you only get one vote, so make it count.'

Neil was quick to put his hand up. 'Point of order, Mr Chairman. What if it's a tie?'

'Then I will have the casting vote. Now is that understood?'

There was a general murmur of approval.

The chairman handed out the slips to the players, along with bookie pens.

'Please put a cross next to the name of the player who you want to lead the Outcasts out of the darkness.'

'I object to that last remark, Mr Chairman,' Ron shouted, whilst fixing Amir with a telling gaze.

Steve was feeling more nervous than ever.

'OK, lads. Please choose our captain for the 2001 cricket season.'

The players filled in their slips and folded them up, some more neatly than others. Finally, the Chairman went round the table and collected them.

'Bloody hell, Steve, do you want this election to be sorted out this evening?'

The chairman held aloft an exceptionally screwed-up piece of paper, bringing laughter from the players, especially the Crabtree supporters.

'Sorry, Chairman,' Steve mumbled.

The chairman finally opened the slips and starts placing them face down in two separate piles. After nine slips, there were five slips in one pile and four in the other. The chairman frowned and looked at Amir, who was looking very tense. The Chairman unwrapped the last slip and looked at it quizzically.

There was a long silence before the Chairman placed the last slip on the smaller pile.

'Gentlemen, I believe we have a tie,' Geoff announced, to gasps around the room.

Steve and Amir looked relieved. Crabtree looked very angry and shot a murderous stare at Amir.

'As Chairman, I must uphold fair play at all times,' Geoff continued. 'Would the honourable candidates care to inspect the voting slips?'

'Yes, I certainly do!' Crabtree yelled, casting another sidelong glance at Amir.

Steve and Ron then looked at the slips.

'You can't admit this one,' Ron protested. 'It's got black ink over a horse's arse. You can't possibly count it.

Geoff and Steve inspected the slip.

'No. No. No. It's definitely an 'X' against Dr Hemmings' name. You can see the indentation on the reverse side.'

'Well, they're not admitting them in America, you know,' Ron protested. 'Hanging chads is what they're known as.'

The Chairman became impassioned. 'Well, this isn't bloody America. This is the Outcasts Cricket Club, with a proud tradition of fair play! I declare this election a tie!!'

Amir and Steve looked relieved once more.

'So, what happens now, Mister Chairman?' Neil was quick to ask.

'As I told you earlier, the Chairman will exercise his right to make the casting vote,' Geoff replied with a hint of exasperation. 'Honestly!'

Crabtree had a suggestion. 'Surely, common sense must prevail, Geoffrey. That lad,' he said, pointing at Steve, 'looks like a scarecrow, he can hardly hold a bat, and he's just emptied the other room with his stinking arse!'

'Now. Now. Let's put personal attacks to one side. I must do what's right for the club.'

'Hear, hear, Mr Chairman,' Amir agreed.

'I hereby declare that the Captain of the Outcasts Cricket Club for the 2001 season will be...' The Chairman paused for effect.

Amir and Steve looked nervous. Ron sat stern-faced.

'Dr Stephen Hemmings!'

Half the room applauded. Half did not. Steve smiled broadly. A couple of players got up and shook his hand. Amir heaved a sigh of relief. Ron got up to go.

'Wait a minute! Wait a minute!' Geoff raised his hand to stop him. 'We haven't had "Any Other Business" yet.'

'Unless it's a recount, I'm not interested. I've got better bladdy things to do,' Ron said grumpily.

'Stay a minute, Ron. I think you'll enjoy this,' Geoff insisted.

'It better be good.'

'Anyone else got any other business?' Geoff peered around the room to silence. 'Very well, then. I have a very special award.' A general hum of anticipation went around the room.

'You could say it's an award for the Worst Player of the Year,' Geoff said archly, temporarily removing his spectacles.

'Not the potty again!' Steve sensed a sting in the tail.

'Indeed it is, Sir!' Geoff produced the potty out from behind the curtain. 'Now, I've thought long and hard about this – and obviously there are a number of deserving candidates...' Geoff scanned the room, but particularly at Amir. 'I could be awarding this to...'

The chairman went behind curtain again, pulled out the pint of diet cola/pineapple juice mocktail and poured it into the pot. Amir blanched. 'Let me see now...'

Amir started to sweat. The chairman then went back behind the curtain and pulled out the pint of Old Knacker. He poured out the pint. It bubbled up as he did so. 'Oh dear, a bit fizzy, this one. I don't envy whoever's going to drink this...'

The Chairman then carefully placed the plastic dog turd inside the disgusting mixture. 'My special award of a quart of "Chairman's Shandy" goes to ... Dr Steve Hemmings.'

'Shit the bed!' Steve couldn't help shouting out. Elsewhere in the room, there was general laughter, particularly from Ron. Steve reluctantly stood up to take the award. 'You realise that this will probably kill me. Why?' Steve asked Geoff *sotto voce* as he received the poisoned chalice.

'As our new captain, you must lead by example,' Geoff announced, before whispering in Steve's ear, 'I'll explain later.'

Steve tried to drink, but was repeatedly thwarted by the bubbles created by the evil mixture. Much of the contents poured down his front. In the background, there was rhythmic slow-handclapping and laughter. Steve burped violently and looked decidedly green at the gills.

'Come on, Elvis. No Return to Sender, now!' Ron shouted out gleefully.

Steve continued to glug away, finally finishing after about a minute.

'Well done. A bit slow – just like your batting, I'd say,' Geoff concluded.

Steve attempted to make a bow, but the bowing movement provoked another loud and terrible fart.

PPPPPPWWARRRRPPPPP

Steve staggered off to the toilet, emitting another gut-wrenching fart as he did.

'I think that concludes tonight's proceedings. Thank you, gentlemen.'

The players dispersed quickly, which was more than could be said for Steve's latest fart.

About fifteen minutes later, Geoff felt compelled to visit the Gents to see how his friend was getting on. He knocked on the door of Trap 1, from which hellish noises were still emanating.

'Are you alright in there, Skip?'

'What do you fucking well think?'

'Oh dear, you never did have much self-control, did you?'

'I'll be out in a minute, but I'm still not feeling very well.'

Geoff finally felt a twinge of conscience. 'Listen, I'll drive you back to mine. I think you need some supervision. I'll wait by the bar for you, OK?'

Steve grunted agreement from inside the cubicle. At last, a sick-looking Steve finally arrived downstairs. The Chairman was waiting with his coat on, potty in hand.

'Hark, it's the pale rider,' Geoff announced to Mary and Alex behind the bar.

Mary folded her arms. 'Well, he'll get no sympathy from me.'

'Nor me!' Alex pronounced, likewise folding her arms.

'Why ever not?' Steve was not expecting this adverse reaction. Hadn't the Chairman assured him that the girls would be queuing up to get him after his election?

'Because of what you did to poor Ron,' Mary said.

'Yes. What a dirty trick!' Alex added.

'Broken his heart you have, poor lad,' Mary said.

'Honestly. You men, you're just like naughty little boys in the playground,' Alex fumed.

'But it was necessary for the good of the club,' Steve explained.

'For the good of your ego, more like,' Mary shot back.

'Come on, Captain, you won't be getting much in the way of logic around here. Let's go!' Geoff put his arm round a staggering Steve and led him away.

'And don't come back in a hurry. You're both barred!' Mary shouted after them.

'Now bugger off!' Alex agreed.

'I thought you said they'd be attracted to me through my newfound power,' Steve complained to Geoff as they exited the pub.

Geoff shook his head. 'Women. No logic to them. No logic to them,' he pronounced as he ushered Steve into the passenger seat of his car.

Chapter 43: 'It's A Beautiful Day'

For the second time in six weeks, Steve found himself waking up in Geoff's front room.

Geoff's mum, Dorothy, came in while Steve was still sleeping fitfully on the sofa. 'Would you like a cup of tea, dear?'

Steve mumbled his assent, and Mrs Huckstead departed to the kitchen. Geoff entered a few seconds later.

'Good morning, old son. How's your head?'

'Oh, not so good. Could be worse, I suppose.'

'Hmm. Maybe it's your arse you should be worrying about. My God. Have you ever thought about going professional with that thing?'

'I think I'll stick to the day job,' Steve answered wanly.

Geoff agreed this was probably wise as Dorothy returned with a 'nice cup of tea'.

'Now don't you be too long drinking that,' Geoff warned. 'I want you dressed and ready in 10 minutes – that's if you want me to give you a lift back to your house to get your car.'

Geoff was about to throw Steve his clothes when he looked down and pulled a face. He then looked at Steve's shoes and pulled another face.

'Ugh,' said Geoff, screwing his face in disgust.

'What is it?'

'It seems like you've had an accident.'

'What do you mean?' asked a still-groggy Steve.

'Well, put it this way: as a cricketer, it's better to follow on than to follow through.'

Steve was still none the wiser.

'I mean that you've tom-titted yourself, old son.'

'Oh, no. It was that bloody potty. Fair turned my stomach, it did.'

'Now don't you go blaming me for your own lack of powers of self-control!'

Steve wondered what he should do. He didn't really have time to have a shower and a change of clothes, like he should have done.

'Fear not!' Geoff reassured Steve, as he called out, 'Mother, could you get this young man a fresh set of clothes from my wardrobe?'

'Yes, dear.'

'Oh, shoes and all. And while you're up, could you find a black bin liner?

'Why's that?' Dorothy asked.

'I'll explain later.' Geoff decided to spare Steve's blushes.

Mrs H arrived with the same ghastly outfit as last time, except this time with a polka dot tie, plus the black bin liner.

'There you are, dear. Ee, you'll look smart in that. They won't be able to stop themselves from promoting you when they see you in that, will they, Geoffrey?'

'That's right, mother, especially when they learn of his elevation to Outcasts captain.'

'Oh, well done, son.' Dorothy shook Steve by the hand. 'You're going places, you are; I can tell.'

'You can say that again.' Geoff laughed.

Mrs H and Geoff left the room so that Steve could get dressed and put his old, soiled clothes into the bin liner, which was placed on the back seat of Geoff's car.

As Geoff pulled away, Steve had a question. 'So, why did you let me have the potty last night, then?'

'It's perfectly logical, captain.'

'Not to me, it's not.'

'To preserve club unity.'

'How's that going to...' Steve made an inverted commas sign. '...preserve club unity?'

'It was a bit of a sweetener for Ron, to stop him going on about a recount.'

'And you think it worked?'

'Well, it certainly cheered him up, while you were drinking from it.'

'Yes, but you heard Mary and Alex. They said he was devastated.'

'Oh, the mad sisters! I wouldn't take any notice of them!'

'And what about Amir? Why was he behaving so strangely – and why didn't you give it to him?'

Geoff turned mysterious. 'I'll explain later.'

'If I didn't know better, I'd have said it was all for your own amusement!'

'Now then, come on. This isn't the way to start your tenure as Outcasts captain!'

'Well, I'm just beginning to wonder what I've let myself in for.'

'The best job in the world, that's what.' Geoff trotted out his tried and tested sales pitch. 'Twelve international cricketers, we've had, one international footballer, an international rugby union player and the world champion tiddlywinks player!

'Not anymore!'

'Yes, he is! Pat defended his title successfully last month.'

Steve rolled his eyes at the Chairman's obtuseness. 'I meant the Outcasts!'

'So, it's your job to restore us to our former glories.'

'They were over twenty years ago.'

'We will rebuild!' Geoff assured him, before changing the subject. 'Anyway, what sort of day have you got to look forward to at work?'

'Oh, nothing much. Pretty boring, really. Yeah, just a quiet Friday, I suppose.'

They approached Steve's untidy house.

'Fancy a pint at the weekend?' Geoff asked as he pulled up behind the blue Ford Mondeo.

'Yeah, why not? Well, as long as I don't get the call...'

It was Geoff's turn to look heavenward. 'You mean the call of the minge? Snatch mad you are... Anyway, here we are. It looks like Ron's supporters haven't vandalised your car.'

'OK. Thanks for the lift.' Steve got out of the car and started to walk away.

Geoff grabbed the black bag from the back seat and threw it to Steve. 'Here! You forgot this.'

Steve caught the bag. 'See you later.'

'Yes, see you,' Geoff shouted, before adding, 'and I'd put that lot on boil wash, if I were you.'

'Thanks, Geoff,' Steve muttered ironically.

Steve looked at his watch. No time for that. Dalmy was miaowing at him impatiently. Just time to feed him. He opened the door and let the cat in and put some food out for him. On the hallway floor was a letter with a parliamentary crest on it. He picked it up and put it on the passenger seat, along with the black bag. He then drove off.

He got into work reasonably promptly, all things considered. He reached his office without further incident. Curiously, there was no sign of Stuart.

The strains of *Born on the Bayou* came from Steve's phone as he sat at his desk with the black bag perched next to him.

The caller was Karen. 'I've been talking with the other girls. Remember? They seem to think I should give you another chance for a long-term relationship.'

'That would be nice,' Steve said, instinctively scratching his balls.

'Well, I'm thinking about it, OK?'

'OK.'

'But you need to be on your best behaviour from now on...'

'OK.'

'And you're on final, final notice.'

'OK. So, when do I get to see you?'

'I said I'm thinking about it, OK?'

'OK. Bye then.'

'Haven't you more to say to me than that?'

'Well, you said you'd think about it, didn't you?'

'I can tell you've got your mind on other things. I'll call you back later.' Karen could not help adopting an irritated tone.

'OK. Bye then.' Steve adopted a soft tone to try to mollify her.

Steve was at least rewarded with a curt 'Bye' before Karen rang off.

Steve was not given time to reflect on the conversation before Paula entered the office. She spotted the black bag straight away. 'So, what's in that black bag of yours?'

'I'd rather not say. Er, Paula... Am I right in thinking that the lab autoclave can be used to steam clean clothes?'

'What have yer been doing this time? And why are yer wearing funny clothes again?'

'I'll tell you later. But I'm right, aren't I?'

'Yeah. It's against health and safety rules, but sure, why not? The company paid £200K for it to do hydrothermal synthesis experiments and then the project got pulled. So that's what it's ended up being used for.'

Before Steve and Paula could instigate 'Operation Deep Clean', Margaret arrived.

Paula suddenly remembered something else that she really needed to do. 'Ah. Yes. I wanted to ask Stuart a question. He said he'd be in Debbie's office.'

Margaret, proving quicker on her feet than expected, cornered Steve before he could escape.

'Good morning, Dr Hemmings. You seem to be in a hurry this morning.'

'Yes, Margaret; must dash,' Steve said, trying to sidestep Margaret.

'I was going to fill you in on Darren's latest progress at his new school.'

Steve was forced to pause for ten minutes while Margaret regaled him with tales about Darren's new school. Things seemed to be going very well, and he had found a special new friend called Colin. Margaret thanked him profusely for putting her in touch with 'that nice Mrs Mowlem'.

During their conversation, Steve's office phone rang twice. Hopefully, it was not the Medical Centre. He would check once he had returned from dropping off the bag in the lab. Steve acknowledged the thanks and made another move towards the door. However, Margaret was not finished.

'You do look smart today. Any important meetings?'

'No. No. No. Just normal.'

'What are you doing with that black bag, by the way?'

Steve raised his index finger to his lips. 'Oh. Important experiment. I've got to keep it a secret. I'll talk to you later.'

With that, Steve made good his escape down the corridor. He was just approaching the labs when Paula intercepted him.

'Stuart and Debbie say to report to Debbie's office right away.'

'Right this minute?'

'Yes, right this minute! It sounded serious.'

'Shit the bed. It must be that re-test,' Steve blurted out before he could stop himself.

'What re-test?'

'Never mind,' Steve muttered, realising his Freudian slip. 'What do I do with this bag?'

'You'd better take it with you. They said right away!'

Steve set off down the corridor towards Debbie's office, a look of high anxiety etched on his face. Steve rushed downstairs, taking care to grip the handrail as he went – one never knew where the Health and Safety Gauleiter Adele was lurking.

OK. OK. OK. Don't panic, he told himself. *The drugs test is good, don't worry. But, why have they summoned me at such short notice? And I got the message from Paula, such a snake! Come on, maybe it's belated recognition for winning the Tees Valley Innovation Award. No. I don't think so. And why do I still have this bin bag full of soiled clothes from last night with me? I was supposed to have dropped that off in the lab for cleaning.* Steve continued to rush along the corridor. By Christ, it was a long way to Debbie's office. Whoever designed this building should have been shot!

Finally, he arrived at Debbie's door. Despite the sign with the legend 'My door is always open', it was firmly shut.

'Bugger, I'll have to knock.' Steve knocked at the door.

'Come in!' came the command.

Steve pushed at the door. It opened slowly. In the office were Debbie, Stuart and 'Oh Fuck' Michelle from HR.

Above them, the poster of Terry Wogan smiled down benignly upon them.

Shit, thought Steve. *This has to be serious.* Steve walked in and put the black bag down. Stuart, Debbie and Michelle sat stern-faced on the other side of the table.

Debbie opened the batting. 'Sit down, Steve.'

Steve sat down on the chair opposite the firing squad.

'As you can see, we've got Michelle from HR in for this meeting, so you'll realise that this is absolutely non-trivial,' Debbie continued.

Steve turned white.

Michelle interjected. 'Are you alright? You look ill. Would you like some water?' She leaned over to pass him a glass, inadvertently treating him to a full-blown view of her magnificent cleavage. Steve shook his head, suddenly noticing that there was also a box of tissues on the table in front of him.

This time, it was Stuart's turn to speak. 'Let's cut to the chase, shall we?'

Steve could contain himself no more. 'I demand another test. It shouldn't have stayed in my system that long!'

Debbie looked puzzled. 'What do you mean?'

'I'm not a regular user. Stuff your zero-tolerance policy!' He continued to dig himself further into the *merde.*

Stuart broke the silence. 'What are you on about?'

'Every man deserves a second chance. I'll, I'll go into rehab if you like!' Steve volunteered.

Michelle decided it was time to get to the point. 'What are you talking about? We're here to...' A series of beeps, getting ever louder, drowned out Michelle's voice. A disembodied voice came over the Tannoy. 'This is the Elton Centre Fire Alarm test. There is no need for action. Repeat, no need for action.'

Michelle attempted to carry on. 'As I was saying, you'll be anxious to know what all this is about...'

Understatement of the year, Dear Reader!

Unfortunately, Michelle was interrupted again as the series of beeps returned, getting ever louder, drowning out her voice. The disembodied voice repeated. 'This is the Elton Centre Fire Alarm test. There is no need for action. Repeat, no need for action.'

Steve could not contain himself anymore. 'Yes. Are you going to sack me?'

Michelle looked surprised. 'Sack you? We merely wish to inform you...'

The beeps returned, drowning out Michelle's voice once again. The disembodied voice repeated for the second time. 'This is the Elton Centre Fire Alarm test. There is no need for action. Repeat, no need for action.'

'What? What do you wish to inform me?' Steve was able to pose the question before he too was drowned out by the sound of a fire alarm and fire doors slamming around the building. The ringing stopped.

Stuart looked heavenwards. 'Oh bollocks, it's Friday 10am, isn't it?'

Debbie forced a smile. 'OK. Let's put you out of your misery now, then!'

Another series of beeps getting ever louder drowned out Debbie's voice. The disembodied voice returned. 'This has been the Elton Centre Fire Alarm test. If you have noticed any issues arising from this test, please report them to building services on 7777 if you are inside the building or 01642 43777 if you are ringing externally. Thank you!'

Stuart interjected, 'Yes, what we were going to tell you Stephen is this...'

Stuart paused for breath, just in case the Tannoy interrupted him again. Steve felt the palms of his hands getting ever clammier as he clung on to the black bag.

'Under the provisions of the review brought about by Project Mallard, you have been deemed surplus to BCG requirements, and you will subsequently be made...' Stuart hesitated.

Michelle filled the void. 'Be made redundant.'

'What, I haven't been sacked?'

A puzzled Michelle replied. 'No, you haven't been sacked, you are simply being put into transition for the next 6 months...'

Michelle noticed the perplexed look on Steve's face. 'Transition is what we in BCG call redeployment,' she explained kindly, but unnecessarily, leaning over the desk once again.

Steve could not believe his luck. 'So, I've really not been sacked?'

Michelle put him straight once again. 'No, you haven't.'

As Steve made a small celebratory gesture with his fist, Michelle handed over a letter to him.

He opened the letter and read it. As he did so, he began to recover his presence of mind. 'I like the bit about how the company would like to thank me for my contribution over the past eighteen years...'

Michelle tried to soothe his feelings. 'Obviously, this must be very upsetting for you. If you read the letter carefully, it will explain that while you are in transition, you will need to undergo a period of retraining and demonstrate to the company that you are applying for other jobs. You may be offered another post within BCG, when this re-organisation has worked through, but, if not, you will start 3 months' notice on June 1st, 2001.'

All of a sudden, the bitterness started to well up in Steve's soul. 'Fat chance of that. What about my pension?'

Michelle felt somewhat relieved to be asked a matter-of-fact question after Steve's hitherto bizarre ramblings. 'That, I'm afraid, will be commuted, due to your being under 50 years of age.'

Steve was not impressed. 'Buggering hell!' Steve was coming back to his old self. 'They used to protect people my age. Now we get targeted as a nice, big juicy saving!'

Michelle reached for the HR book of platitudes. 'I realise that you're angry...'

Steve felt further emboldened. 'So... What does commuted mean? How much will I get?'

Michelle reached for her reading glasses. 'Slightly less than half of what you might have expected if you'd been fifty. The exact figures are in your letter.' Despite the appalling news, Steve couldn't help thinking how hot she looked when she put on the bifocals.

'Shit the bed! That means I'm probably going to have to work well into my 60s. If I can get another job, that is...'

It was Debbie's turn to try and reassure him. 'I'm sure you will.'

Steve turned on Debbie. 'It's alright for you! You've survived all this. You can go on to a nice gold-plated pension in a few years' time. Join some New Labour sponsored QUANGO, I'll be bound. You were supposed to be a breath of fresh air with your TOGS and your Terry Wogan. You're just the same as the rest of the fossilised, shell-backed antediluvian creatures who have run this company into the ground!'

Michelle leant over the desk, once again showing off her ample cleavage. 'Erm...'

Steve was not to be interrupted. His ire now turned on Stuart. 'And as for you. Your sort will always be alright. Suck up to the management. Blow your own trumpet. You never liked me. I was different...'

Michelle tried once more to mollify Steve. 'Erm. I'll think you'll find...'

Steve continued his diatribe. 'Taking soundings of my staff without consulting me. How was that going to play with them?? Dissing me behind my back to the other managers! Protecting your backside. I suppose you can look forward to a few more years here before <u>you</u> can go off for a cosy retirement!!'

Debbie and Stuart sat impassively.

An increasingly anxious Michelle tried to intervene once more. 'If I could just have a second!!!'

Steve, however, continued in full flow. 'You're all a shower of shit!'

Michelle gave Steve a stern look, which excited him strangely. He placed the bag on his lap to hide his embarrassment.

Michelle raised her voice for the first time. 'Stephen, please!!! Actually, Debbie and Stuart are in the same boat as you. They have also been deemed surplus to requirements by Project Mallard.'

Steve blushed crimson. 'Oh, bugger...'

Stuart broke the ensuing silence. 'Never mind. Never mind. You weren't to know.' He paused. 'I told you to take this restructuring seriously, young man!'

Steve looked round the room. Finally, he blurted out an apology. 'Sorry, Stuart. Sorry, Debbie.'

'Apology accepted.' Debbie sighed. Stuart nodded his agreement.

Michelle smiled brightly. 'Well, I'm glad you've apologised, Steve, because you'll be seeing a lot more of Debbie and Stuart in the near future.'

Steve managed to take his gaze from the top of her dress for all of one second.

'Really?'

'Yes. Debbie will be your new line manager, as the leader of the Transition Team.'

'Yes, I'll be monitoring your job-hunting progress. Hopefully, I can give you a few tips for success on the way,' Debbie explained in that schoolmarmish way of hers.

'Like dressing appropriately for interviews and wearing remotely tasteful ties!' Stuart added snidely as Steve nervously placed the bag back on the desk.

Michelle concluded, 'And you all are required to present yourselves at the ISAL Training Centre in Newcastle on Monday morning for a week of courses.'

Steve gave the three of them a puzzled look. 'What courses?'

Michelle enlightened Steve. 'Firstly, Self-Actualization through Self-Realization, then Understanding Your Character Type and finally "Who Am I and How Did I Get Here?"

'Yes,' Debbie continued. 'We and others in the team will be attending this course and sharing our experiences with people from other organisations, who find themselves in the same situation as us. For instance, I believe that there will be numerous NHS casualties of the Milburn reforms in attendance.'

'But what's the point?' Steve was a hard-bitten veteran of many such courses.

Stuart replied, 'Every point, young man. It will help you to understand yourself and what you want to do in life.'

Debbie was determined to sound positive. 'Yes, you might come up with a whole new direction.'

Michelle smiled that sexy smile. 'Like teaching...'

'Bog off. I'm not doing that!' He conjured up images of a class of rioting pupils, such as the vile trick-or-treaters he had encountered on Halloween.

Debbie tried to mollify Steve. 'Well, maybe something more creative. That's what you like, isn't it?'

'What, around here? I'm not seeing many creative agencies in these parts!'

Stuart chipped in. 'Well, start one then, young man!'

Michelle poured oil over troubled waters. 'Anyway, that's all for Monday to decide. I realise you've got a lot to take in at once, so you are welcome to take the rest of the day off.' Debbie and Stuart nodded their heads.

As she leaned over the desk yet again, Steve could not help fantasising about spending the rest of the day in Michelle's company – and that amazing set of boobs.

Debbie tried to wrap things up. 'Is there anything else?'

Steve thought for a few seconds. 'Yeah! Who's taking over from you, then?'

Debbie tried to explain. 'Well, no one. It's a redundant position.' There followed an awkward silence. However, the company needs a safe pair of hands during this difficult period, so Jim Dickson has agreed to take a caretaker role in managing the R&D teams until he retires next year.'

Steve was livid. 'That wanker! I thought he was on my side. Bloody waste of space. Feathered his nest nicely there. What a nice retirement he's got to look forward to...' Steve's voice almost cracked with anger.

Stuart suppressed a belly laugh. 'Now, then, let's not get personal...'

'And Roy Elliott will be assisting Jim with a view to taking over from him at the end of 2001,' Michelle trilled sweetly.

Steve got to his feet, dropping the bag on the desk. 'That twat! He wouldn't know what innovation was if it came over and hit him over the head!!' he said, recalling Roy's objectionable behaviour at the Health Awareness Day.

Michelle tried to bring matters to a conclusion. 'OK. Any further questions?'

'Why can't you give me something useful to do for the next nine months?'

'It's not company policy.'

It dawned on Steve that this transition thing might not be all bad. Days at the races, afternoons spent in the pub, riotous cricket tours, perhaps the odd afternoon spent in bed with Karen (or a suitable new member of the 'Subs' bench). He'd have more time for his kids, too. All fully paid for.

'OK. Never mind,' he mumbled, although it remained a bitter blow.

Stuart mused, 'And we'll draw a line over all that rehab stuff, shall we?'

Steve nodded, finally finding something to agree with him about. He got up to go.

'Here. You forgot this!' Debbie ran round her desk to throw Steve's bag to the departing soon to be ex-employee. Steve managed to catch it and walked out with all the remaining dignity that he could muster.

'Shit the bed!!!' he cried out loud, once outside.

In his fury, he had not seen that his now ex-colleagues, Paul, Margaret and Paula, had gathered to greet him.

A surprisingly cheerful Paul explained that news of Steve's plight had slipped out when he had been made redundant himself.

Steve asked why he was so happy.

'Result! This is what I've been asking them for, ever since my fiftieth birthday!' Paul did a little jig.

'Well, I'm glad someone's pleased!' Steve replied bitterly.

'Look, I've come to say how sorry I am about what they've done to you. You didn't deserve it,' Paul said calmly and shook his hand.

Paula put out her hand. 'I learned a lot from you.'

Enough to take my job off me, Steve reflected angrily, but decided it was best not to pursue the point. He shook her hand.

Margaret enveloped Steve in a great bear hug and gave him a slobbery kiss full on his lips. Steve wiped his mouth, dropping his black bag in so doing.

Paul was curious. 'By the way, what's in that bag?'

'You really wouldn't want to know,' Steve shouted over his shoulder as he picked the bag up and walked off.

At the end of the long corridor, Les was coming towards him.

'Hello, Steve. I'm glad I caught you. I'm so sorry to hear your news.'

Steve was gobsmacked. 'What, already?

'News travels fast in this place, you should know that.' Les held out his hand.

'We'll all miss you; you were always a bit different.'

Steve grimaced. 'Thanks. I'll try and take that as a compliment.'

Les was emphatic. 'You should!'

My hand's going to drop off if this goes on much longer, Steve thought to himself bitterly.

Les pointed at the black bag. 'They haven't made you empty your office already, have they?'

Steve shook his head. 'No. Not yet.'

Les sensed that Steve was hiding something. 'Well, I won't ask what it is, then.'

'No, best not.' Steve smiled.

Les returned the smile and held out his hand once again. 'Good luck. I'm sure you'll be OK.' They shook hands once again.

On Steve walked. He was finally getting close to the exit.

Out of nowhere, who should pop up but Adele? Steve tried to hurry on, but she blocked his path. 'Dr Hemmings! So sorry to hear about your news.'

Steve was pleasantly surprised. 'Why, thanks, Adele.'

Adele was conciliatory. 'I know we've had our differences, but I admired some of the work you did on Health Awareness.'

I like the shit you did with Rockets, too. That shit was "fat", he couldn't help thinking to himself. That Eminem CD – a Fathers' Day gift from his daughter – had certainly got inside his head.

'It's a pity the management didn't.'

Adele continued to be conciliatory. 'I'm sure someone will.'

'Thanks,' he blurted out. They shook hands.

He walked on.

Adele turned around. 'Wait a minute. What's in that bag? I'm sorry, but I'm going to have to check the contents.'

'You what?' Steve was incredulous.

Adele continued earnestly. 'I'm afraid we've had cases of employees in your circumstances taking their revenge by doing things like ringing the talking clock in Tokyo and leaving the phone off the hook. Not that I'm saying that you would...'

'I haven't had chance to...'

'Then there's people who take away valuable items, like their personal computers. Not that I'm saying that you would...'

'What, in this?' Steve pointed at the inadequately sized bag.

'You could be hiding precious metals or controlled substances. I'm duty-bound to take a look.'

Suddenly, Steve grinned. 'Tell you what? You can have it!' he said, handing over the bag with its fetid contents to Adele.

Steve turned towards the exit, while a perplexed Adele inspected the bag's dark secrets. Finding himself on the outside, Steve flicked a V sign behind him.

'ELVIS HAS LEFT THE BUILDING!' he shouted.

So much for that Macbeth dream I had. Come on, let's take it to the bridge. Steve strode determinedly to his car with a fixed gaze in his eyes.

Chapter 44: 'Bridge Of Sighs'

Steve drove at speed to the edge of the site. *Free Fallin'* by Tom Petty was blasting away on his CD Player.

Apt, Steve thought to himself. He wound the windows down, despite the chilly conditions outside, so that the rest of the site could have the benefit.

His mobile rang as he approached the security gate. No longer caring too much for site regulations, Steve picked up the phone, which had been lying on top of the unopened letter.

It was Karen. He let her know his bad news and the surrounding circumstances. She agreed that it was terrible and tried to console him by assuring him.

'You'll get another job, won't you?'

'Hope so.'

'Are you in the car?'

'Yes, I'm driving off-site. I'm off to the bridge.'

'Steve. It sounds like you're driving far too fast. What do you mean, you're off to the bridge?

'I mean like Thelma and Louise.'

'Oh, don't be so silly, Steve! Listen, I'm at home, me mam's out and Charlotte's at school. I must be mad to say this, but do you fancy coming round?'

He smiled. 'What, to prove that it's not true about unemployed men becoming impotent?'

She laughed. 'Hmm. Something like that.'

'OK, I'm on my way. Just let me read this letter...'

His car pulled up at the exit, still with the phone in his hand.

A security man came out of his booth. 'Excuse me, sir, but you do know that use of a mobile device on this site whilst driving is strictly forbidden.'

'Oh. Sorry. It was an important call.'

'Aren't they all, mate?' the guard commented drily. 'I should report you to the Site Authorities...'

'Don't worry, it won't happen again. They've just fired me.'

The security guard wearily waved him through. 'OK. A lot of it about at the minute. Go on, then.'

Steve pulled into the layby on the other side and opened the letter. Perhaps it would bring good news.

Dear Dr Hemmings
The prime minister has read your letter and its contents have been noted.
He thanks you for your input.
Yours sincerely
Sally Shilling
pp Tony Blair

'They've been taking the piss all along,' Steve hissed to himself.

Karen was still on the other end of the phone. 'Steve? What's that? Who's been taking the piss? Steve, talk to me.' He tried to press the 'off' button but missed and dropped the phone.

He needed a minute to think. He'd been voted captain of the Outcasts, but at what cost? Some might say a poisoned chalice – and not the self-validation he had been hoping for. He'd now learned that he'd lost his job with BCG – forget promotion and fancy company cars. His 'special relationship' with the PM had been an illusion. His world was falling apart. Come to think of it, sex was the last thing he wanted, in that moment.

He switched the CD Player back on and pressed the shuffle button. On came *Stan* by Eminem. This was fate calling him. 'Fuck it, I'm off to the bridge.'

'Well Tony, I hope you get to know about this!' he muttered as he scribbled a note on the back of the letter. He then headed out on to the trunk road, with the steelworks in the background.

Karen's voice could still be heard from the floor of the car as he approached the big roundabout. 'Steve. Steve. Are you still there?'

Now he had the choice. Head left for Nunthorpe or bear right for the bridge. The sliding doors slammed shut. He bore right and headed towards the River Tees.

As he drove along the dual carriage way, interspersed with roundabouts and traffic lights, he thought about his kids. 'I'm still entitled to a death in service payment, that's worth 2.5 times my salary,' he said to himself, realising that he was worth a lot more to them dead than alive. 'Better than being a burden to them. That'll keep them in Play Stations! They'll be alright!'

Finally, he headed 'over the border', ignoring the blandishments of the local working girls.

'Hey Mister. Do you want business?' cried out a French maid as he passed by.

'Not today, love,' he shouted, loosening off his seat belt.

Eminem's deranged fan rant was now reaching a crescendo.

Steve fervently hoped that Blair would similarly wake up screaming when he heard about his demise.

'Steve! What are you doing?' Karen's voice continued to emanate from the depths.

As his car reached the Transporter Bridge, he threw the letter out and drove off the edge.

THE END

Epilogue

By the end of Tony Blair's tenure as PM, most of Steve's colleagues would have joined him on the scrap heap. Some would never work again. Others would soldier on accepting (on average) pay cuts of 30% – when they finally got another job, that is.

For Karen's friends, the outlook was far bleaker. The majority of UK call centre jobs were 'offshored' in the early 2000s, leaving them out of work in areas of already high unemployment, often as the only breadwinner of the family.

During the Blair/Brown years, employment in manufacturing reduced by over 2 million down to 12% of the working population (8% below where Mrs Thatcher had left it). 'New Labour' was, however, upbeat about this, promising a jobs boom in financial services and 'the knowledge-based economy'. Household names in manufacturing, such as GEC, Lucas and chemicals giant ICI, were sacrificed on the altar of City greed. And let's not mention what would happen to the banks not too long afterwards.

Cherie Booth QC rarely accompanied her husband during his 2001 election campaign. She was too busy successfully representing the aforesaid ICI in a court case to ensure workers from one of their former businesses did not get the pensions that they believed were their right.

After stepping down as PM in 2007, Tony devoted his life to travelling the world, joining the super-rich and denying that he ever did anything wrong, especially in Iraq. It is not known how many times he has visited his former Sedgefield constituency, but not that often, we suspect.

Contrast this behaviour to that of Dr. Ashok Kumar (1958-2010), an industrial chemist, like Steve, and MP for Middlesbrough South and East Cleveland (1997 – 2010), who died, while fighting to keep the Redcar steelworks from closure.

About the Author

Doctor Graham Dransfield was born in Stockton-on Tees. He is an Oxford educated industrial chemist and twice divorced father of two, now living in North London. He started writing when he was in Cambridge in 2014 at the behest of his youngest brother Patrick, who collaborated in the writing of this book.

Patrick Dransfield is an English graduate, now based in Abu Dhabi, who has published three books: 'Track of Time, Moments of Transition', and 'The Inner Circle Wu Xing' series Books 1 and 2: 'Duel of the Sorcerers' and 'Sima Qian's Bright Mirror'.